Bel[la ...] unqua[...] yours[...]

She [...] how she had come to lie upon it. Then Louis's weight settled over her and he was kissing her. His kisses went on and on until every breath she took was his. His mouth worked over the gentle slope of her cheek, played about her ear, then lowered. And lifted abruptly away. She heard a low hiss issue from him and could feel the hard scorch of his breath against her throat where the silver of her father's wedding gift glittered.

"Bella, take off the necklace."

"What?" The request was so strange.

He levered up slightly and his golden gaze penetrated deep and druggingly. She could read desire in his eyes, a passion so intense it made her tremble; a need so raw and huge, it humbled her. She couldn't look away and she couldn't deny him. She reached for the thin silver chain and opened the catch. As she held it, he struck her hand and it went flying from her grasp.

With a deep and satisfied sigh, he sank down upon her lips again, drinking from their offering of love. His mouth drew a heated line of kisses from her lips to her chin, then down the concave of her throat, coming to a halt over her pulse point. He nuzzled there, his breath rasping, his lips parting, his hands clasping either side of her head to angle a taut bend. She felt the slow, wet stroke of his tongue.

And his bite.

"Rich ... alluring ... Nancy Gideon weaves a poetic tale replete with hypnotic power and seductive lure!"

Romantic Times

PUT SOME FANTASY IN YOUR LIFE—
FANTASTIC ROMANCES FROM PINNACLE

TIME STORM (728, $4.99)
by Rosalyn Alsobrook
Modern-day Pennsylvanian physician JoAnn Griffin only believed what she could feel with her five senses. But when, during a freak storm, a blinding flash of lightning sent her back in time to 1889, JoAnn realized she had somehow crossed the threshold into another century and was now gazing into the smoldering eyes of a startlingly handsome stranger. JoAnn had stumbled through a rip in time . . . and into a love affair so intense, it carried her to a point of no return!

SEA TREASURE (790, $4.50)
by Johanna Hailey
When Michael, a dashing sea captain, is rescued from drowning by a beautiful sea siren—he does not know yet that she's actually a mermaid. But her breathtaking beauty stirred irresistible yearnings in Michael. And soon fate would drive them across the treacherous Caribbean, tossing them on surging tides of passion that transcended two worlds!

ONCE UPON FOREVER (883, $4.99)
by Becky Lee Weyrich
A moonstone necklace and a mysterious diary written over a century ago were Clair Summerland's only clues to her true identity. Two men loved her—one, a dashing civil war hero . . . the other, a daring jet pilot. Now Clair must risk her past and future for a passion that spans two worlds—and a love that is stronger than time itself.

SHADOWS IN TIME (892, $4.50)
by Cherlyn Jac
Driving through the sultry New Orleans night, one moment Tori's car spins out of control; the next she is in a horse-drawn carriage with the handsomest man she has ever seen—who calls her wife—- but whose eyes blaze with fury. Sent back in time one hundred years, Tori is falling in love with the man she is apparently trying to kill. Now she must race against time to change the tragic past and claim her future with the man she will love through all eternity!

Available wherever paperbacks are sold, or order direct from the Publisher. Send cover price plus 50¢ per copy for mailing and handling to Penguin USA, P.O. Box 999, c/o Dept. 17109, Bergenfield, NJ 07621. Residents of New York and Tennessee must include sales tax. DO NOT SEND CASH.

NANCY GIDEON
MIDNIGHT KISS

PINNACLE BOOKS
WINDSOR PUBLISHING CORP.

PINNACLE BOOKS are published by

Windsor Publishing Corp.
475 Park Avenue South
New York, NY 10016

Copyright © 1994 by Nancy Gideon

All rights reserved. No part of this book may be reproduced in any form or by any means without the prior written consent of the Publisher, excepting brief quotes used in reviews.

If you purchased this book without a cover, you should be aware that this book is stolen property. It was reported as "unsold and destroyed" to the Publisher and neither the Author nor the Publisher has received any payment for this "stripped book."

The P logo Reg U.S. Pat & TM off. Pinnacle is a trademark of Windsor Publishing Corp.

First Printing: May, 1994

Printed in the United States of America

For Elizabeth McKinsey,

*whose enthusiasm helped me
sink my teeth into this project!*

Chapter One

Footsteps.
Light, quick; a definite female pattern of sound. A rhythm slightly louder than that of the rain upon cobbled street.
Fear.
Its scent was on the moisture-laden air, like mist, like night, as subtle in its perfume.
Heartbeats.
Echoing the tempo of the rain, of the footfalls; increasing now; throbbing with life and warmth.
Hunger.
Sharp, pulsing in time to the scents and sounds, yet unlike them, unnatural in origin. It rose without control, as swift and steady as the torrent of the storm, as consuming as the fog rising off the steaming alleyways, akin to the darkness, attuned to the fear. Alive with the lust for blood.

He moved like a shadow through the damp night, though he didn't cast one himself. The icy rain sliced down upon him, but the only chill he felt came from within, from the emptiness there, from the desperate need to know sustaining heat. Burning with a cold desire that brought him out to stalk the slick byways of London's grimy East Side. Drawn by the inexorable craving that both seduced and horrified him. It was strong, that insatiable appetite, stronger than what weak-moraled men felt for drink or gaming or sexual satisfaction. An addictive vice from which there was no relief other than the appeasing taste of the forbidden.

Even as he tried to resist, instinct urged him onward. His senses quivered with anticipation, honed by the rapid pattering panic fed through the veins of his unknowing victim. A taste, no more than a taste, he vowed, as if that would soothe the rage of future conscience. For now, it was enough. Enough to distract him from his noble intents, enough to cloud his mind and allow his thirst to overcome him. Restraint, like remorse, failed to hold back the tide of compulsion. It could not change what he was. And what he was on this dismal night was hungry.

She was a prostitute. Her gaudy clothing claimed her profession, as did the fact that she was out on streets no innocent would tread. She felt danger closing in on her the way she would a chill wind or a bad omen. She shivered and turned to face the fear she couldn't outrun, hoping that by giving it a name, she could escape it. Later, when the Bow Street Runners questioned her, she would recall yellow lights, brilliant, burning, transfixing her, and a voice that came from all around, yet seemed to speak within her mind.

"I will not harm you."

She gave a great sigh of relief as a figure separated

from shadow. A man; a nobleman, from his fineness of dress. A fluttery hand rose to her laboring breast. "Oh, my but you gave us a scare. Be you lookin' for a bit a sport, me lord? For a mere token, I can warm you up right proper on this miserable night."

The gentleman smiled, a flash of stark white upon white. "Yes. Exactly what I had in mind."

His voice flowed like honey, mellifluous and oddly calming. His eyes held an intensity that almost shook her from her notions of business. But she'd been well schooled: get the blunt up front. Moistening her lips with the tempting swipe of her tongue, she named her price and he extended it without a quibble. A real gentleman. She stuffed the money between scented breasts.

"I gots me a place not far—"

"Here will be fine."

She blinked and glanced about the litter-ridden alley. "Wouldn't 'ave pegged you for a queer one, me lord, but 'ere's as good a place as any, if you be in a hurry." She began to ruck up her skirts obligingly, but the touch of his hand stilled her, a surprisingly gentle touch, along one painted cheek. The doxy looked up and was mesmerized by the flare of his gaze. It seemed to draw the soul from her. Or so she would remember. She couldn't look away from those eyes, those glowing amber eyes.

His fingers curved beneath her chin, tilting her face up. His mouth brushed over hers in a whispered kiss.

"Oh . . ."

She was quite taken by that courtly gesture, she who was so unused to tenderness. Her hands opened, releasing her soiled skirts. Her hem dropped to the puddled street as she grasped his forearms and uttered an illicit moan. She leaned into him, mashing her ample breasts to the starched front of his shirt bosom, flinging back her head in wanton encouragement. The power she felt moving beneath the clutch of her fingers startled her. And he was no longer gentle.

His arm curled about her waist, crushing her against him. The hand that so reverently stroked her now became a viselike grip upon her jaw, wrenching her head to an uncomfortable angle. Self-protective terror surged too late to save her.

"Please—" It was a weak beseechment from an already fading will. The need to struggle left her and she was malleable to his purpose.

She never knew why he released her so abruptly and unharmed, aware only that he was gone; and, strengthless without him, she crumpled to the cold, cutting cobbles. She realized after her interview with the police how lucky she was to escape a fate five others had succumbed to. The others were found in hazy daylight, rumpled and weak and marked strangely about the throat. But like them, she had no memory of her attacker. Just the image of yellow lights and the liquid quality of his voice. And the knowledge that she'd barely eluded the clutches of death. A knowledge that would haunt her ceaselessly for nights to come.

What a perfectly beastly night, Arabella Howland thought to herself, as she fought to claim her pelisse from the pull of the wind. Dodging standing pools of water, she managed to gain the front steps of her address without too much damage to her sturdy footgear. The door was instantly opened, offering a dry retreat and the uncompromising scowl of their housekeeper's features.

"Miss Arabella, have you any notion of the hour?"

"No, Mrs. Kampford, but I'm certain you will tell me."

"No need to take that snippety tone with me, Miss," the dour-faced woman warned, as she efficiently stripped her young mistress of her damp outerwear. "A bit of mothering will do you no harm. Heaven knows your errant father has been remiss in his proper duty."

Arabella let that pass without comment, used to the woman's chidings. "Is my father at home?"

"Not yet. He's still at the hospital. 'Tis glad I am to have you here safe and sound, what with the odd doings outside and *him* in the doctor's study."

Arabella was aware of a disconcerting pleasure. "How long has he been waiting?"

"Better than a half-hour, and he's in odd spirits. I don't like him coming to the house and I've told the doctor as much. 'Tisn't seemly with your father so often away. There is something wrong with the man."

"Of course there is, Mrs. Kampford. Why else would he be here for my father's help?"

The elder woman sniffed at that, but cautioned, "Let him wait, Miss. Your father should be home soon."

"Nonsense. I'll not ignore a guest in our house."

"He's not a guest. He's a patient."

"Yes, Mrs. Kampford, he is, but he is a fellow human being deserving of a hot drink on such a night, so please excuse me while I see to his comfort."

The tiny woman frowned and looked as though she meant to block the way until forcibly set aside. Then she sniffed again and carried the sodden wrap down the hall with an indignant air.

Smiling to herself, Arabella paused at the hall mirror, checking the arrangement of her hair. Really, Bessie Kampford was the most possessive creature. One would think she was her child, for all her fussing.

Arabella observed her reflection wryly. Most of the pins had fallen, and what coils of glossy black hair chose to remain in place were hopelessly frizzed by the damp night air. It would have to do. After all, she was no green girl entertaining a prospective beau. Thank heavens those awkward days were years passed! At three and twenty she no longer had to please anyone other than herself. And usually, she didn't make the effort. Except where Louis Radman was concerned.

Something about the man was infinitely intriguing.

Perhaps it was the secrecy. He'd appeared in the midst of the Season to pursue its distractions, but not its more voluptuous delights. More than one comely female was said to have lost her head and heart over the mysterious marquis. Arabella had heard her share of speculation. Some said he was French, some Slavic, but all agreed he was obscenely wealthy and more than slightly eccentric. Though his title and his pocket value opened all the doors of society, he stood cautiously on the outside, content to study the goings-on from its fringe. He accepted few invitations and never issued them in return. He was a paradox of charm and reserve, and Arabella Howland thought him the most exciting man she'd ever known. And she had more of a chance to know him than most. He'd been coming to her father's home office for nearly three weeks for reasons her father refused to divulge. And in all those after-hour visits, she'd managed to secure little more than a polite nod and a softly drawled "Good evening."

Of course, Bella had no reason to think she held the power to charm the likes of Louis Radman. She'd discovered the truth of her appeal most cruelly when she'd come of age. Her comeout in society was classed a disaster even by those inclined to be kind. It wasn't that she lacked for beauty; there was a certain loveliness in all that dark hair and in the strong set of her features. But she had a way of fixing a fellow with her somber gray eyes, a way of molding her lips so they held a hint of inner amusement that was far from flattering. After her first few appearances she was labeled too bold, too high-minded, too large, too opinionated, too everything to be deemed fashionable. And the finishing stroke was that she didn't seem to care what they thought. She took herself off the list of the available without a trace of regret and applied herself to her father's work with a passion she couldn't muster for the social set. For all intents and purposes, life in her father's house suited her just fine. She didn't miss the attentions of men or the complacency of marriage . . . except on the occasions when Louis Radman visited. It was then that her passions betrayed her most annoyingly and she found herself wondering what kind of woman would appeal to the intensely private marquis.

She went to her father's study. Anticipation beat within her breast, but she did her best to quell it. This might be her only chance to converse with the man. Usually the door to the office closed behind him the moment he appeared. She could only hope he didn't find her as unexceptional as the rest of London's elite. Taking a breath to calm her mounting palpitations, she knocked once and entered. The lamplight was dim, casting the large room in shadow. At first, she didn't see him.

"My lord?"

"Where is your father?" Half whisper, half growl, his voice startled her. Her gaze searched the darkness, fixing upon movement there by the damask-covered windows.

"He hasn't come home from the hospital yet. Can I get you—"

"Get him here! I need him here, now!"

The rasp of labored breathing reached her ears, a tortured pull and ebb that dissolved her caution in an instant. He was in pain. Rapidly, she started across the room, careless in her concern. "What is it? Are you all right? Is there something I—"

"Get away! Get away from me!" There was a scraping, a frantic shuffle of furniture being pushed aside as he tried to meld into deeper obscurity. "Come no closer."

Arabella paused. She knew nothing of the condition that had brought him to her father's door. The thought that it might be some sort of contagion held her, but only until the sound of his anguish came again, a low, suffering groan. She went to him without hesitation, then, kneeling beside the chair into which he'd fallen. In the darkness, she was clumsy in her offer of compassion. Questing hands touched the sharp angles of his face. His skin was moist, cold, and rigidly set. He jerked back and half rolled from the chair to awkwardly gain his feet.

"No." It was a moan of sheer torment. He stumbled in haste to put a saving distance between them. By then, he'd reached the room's central pool of light, and Arabella gasped at the sight of him. He was so pale! In the dimness, his flesh seemed almost translucent. Lean features were drawn into taut relief, all highlight and hollow, as if ravaged by a wasting sickness. Wet hair clung sleekly to the contour of his skull. The folds of his greatcoat dragged with the weight of rainwater. Only his eyes burned, a hot, luminescent gold. A trick of the light, surely, for in that moment, she could have sworn they blazed like coals beneath the dark slash of his brows. Then he turned his head away, denying her the sight of his misery.

"Please sit," she coaxed, trying not to betray her alarm. "You're obviously ill. Some fever, perhaps. You must get out of that wet coat. Can I get you some wine or a brandy?" The words rattled out, more like a nervous babble than the professional calm she sought. Her heart was racing with panic and frustration. Raised a physician's daughter, she was not exactly unskilled. If only she knew the source of his malady. Ignorance held her helpless.

"Leave me. Please. I will be fine if you leave me."

As he spoke, he paced. The movements were virile poetry; strong, aggressive strides that devoured the distance from wall to wall across the costly Aubusson and defied the ravages of his expression. He didn't look at her as he stalked side to side with that volatile grace so scarcely contained. At his sides, his hands worked convulsively. He wouldn't be fine; she could tell by watching his agitation. Something was dreadfully wrong and he'd come to her father for help. But Stuart Howland was not at home.

Choosing to disregard his command, Arabella came to him once more. Even without turning, he felt her nearness, for he tensed all over as if with some new and terrible pain.

"Please," she cried out softly. "Please tell me what I can do for you."

For a moment there was silence. Then came the slow, hissing draw of his breath. And he came about to face her. They were quite close. He had no difficulty reaching out to catch her by the upper arms. His long fingers bit into tender flesh, the pressure hurtful. What kind of illness left such strength in a man's hands, she wondered somewhat frantically, but she couldn't move. She couldn't complain. For he was staring down into her eyes and suddenly nothing else existed beyond the pull of his unblinking gaze. An odd lethargy spread through her as she heard him speak, his tone quiet and somehow soothing. It seemed to melt her very bones.

"What can you do for me?" he repeated, as if considering the question. His arms bent until she was compelled forward, until she could feel the force of his rapid breath against her upturned face. There was no warmth to it. Nor was there any sign of weakness or distress in him. Power . . . she sensed power. It engulfed her, swallowing her whole.

"Arabella."

Up until that moment she hadn't been aware he knew her name. But when he spoke it with the intimacy of a caress, everything inside her tingled with shivery sensation. It wasn't exactly pleasure she felt. It was sharper, more starkly defined, almost frighteningly intense. Like his stare. Entrancing yet repelling. The reaction was all wrong, not like her genuine delight at the prospect of seeing him. This . . . this was something almost beyond her control, and with the feeling of powerlessness came the first threads of fear.

His grip was painful. She used that knowledge and the sudden uneasiness to break from whatever thrall he cast over her. Her palms came up to push against the dampness of his coat and she squirmed in protest. For a moment, his grasp tightened. She gave a soft outcry and abruptly the compression eased. Before she could jump away, the hurting squeeze became a sensuous massage.

"I will not harm you."

Her breath was coming in quick snatches. As she looked up into his eyes, self-preserving instinct screamed: *don't believe him!* Stronger than that reasonable panic was the hypnotic hold of his stare. She trembled, yet didn't move to safety.

His hand rose, skimming her cheek with the ridge of his knuckles. "So beautiful," he murmured. "So young and beautiful."

She might have protested that she was neither, but the seduction of his voice made her believe. And with the fear mingled the first stirrings of desire. He thought her beautiful. He was gentle now, and she no longer wished to run. She wanted him to say more, to continue touching her. And he did.

His sensitive fingertips roved the smooth contours of her face, then drifted downward, coming to a light rest along the pulsing artery in her throat, testing her elevated passions, drawn to that rich throb of life. His thumb rubbed over her full lower lip until it was soft and moist. Ripe.

"Yield to me, Arabella." It wasn't a suggestion. It was a velvety command. "You have wanted me. I've felt it from the first."

"My lord . . ."

"Louis."

"Louis . . . yes." She was panting softly, leaning into him, lost to the intoxicating knowledge that this man desired her. But even in her limp state of bliss came the nagging suspicion that something was not right. Though she would try to push away that whisper of unease, it wouldn't leave her.

"I can show you paradise," he crooned, his honeyed accent flowing, enveloping her faint resistance. "I can give you pleasures beyond what you can imagine. I can give eternity with a kiss. Let me drink from your lips. Let me taste of your willingness."

"Yes," came her wavery sigh. Oh, yes. That was exactly what she wanted. She gave herself up to him without a struggle and the first press of his mouth upon hers was, indeed, beyond anything she could have guessed. His lips were still chilled from the night yet were quick to draw warmth as they lingered for a luxurious exploration. Having never experienced a kiss of passion, Arabella was as eager as she was overwhelmed. She gasped in shock and delight as the wet slide of his tongue parted the way for a deeper union. Her fingers sought and clenched in the front of his coat as sensation threatened with swooning waves of surrender. He lifted up slightly, just far enough to captivate her dewy stare.

"Tell me you want me," he whispered with compelling power.

"I want you," she whispered without hesitation, succumbing to his control and to her own desperate longings. As his head dipped down, her eyes closed and her mouth opened, but instead of enjoining his lips with hers, she felt them move with slow, seducing sweeps along the taut curve of her neck. She arched for him, giving him access to that slender column as he gathered her even closer in his arms. She could feel the crashing thunder of his heart, pounding savagely against her tender breast. She was aware of the foreign hardness of his body as he shifted his weight to press more intimately into her receptive femininity. And she wanted him wildly, without restraint, without wisdom. As she had since that first time she'd seen him.

He was nuzzling her throat, sensitizing the soft skin with the stroke of his tongue, making her shiver with erotic yearnings as his kisses evolved into gentle nips of his teeth. She was holding his bent head, drowning in the strange delight of it, her own breathing hurrying to match the harsh rasp of his. A rasp that grew so low and husky it was almost a growl.

"Oh, Louis . . ." She had never imagined this, not

ever. Her eyelids fluttered shut, her head falling back in supplication.

"Miss Arabella?" A firm rapping upon the door echoed like shots. "Would you like me to bring tea?"

With a sound more snarl than groan, the marquis flung her from him. Arabella stumbled and collapsed upon the settee in weak disbelief. What had she done? What had she invited him to do?

He must have been wondering the same, for his features contorted in the worse sort of agony until covered by unsteady hands. "Oh, God, what a monster I've become," he cried hoarsely, as if horrified by his actions. And he reeled away, fleeing her father's office and the house itself, as if all the devils in hell were clutching at his soul.

The streets were stark and deserted. The rain was a ceaseless drizzle, as if the heavens wept over Louis Radman's lost humanity. He wanted to weep. He wanted to wail. But the time for such a display was centuries past and no one in heaven would hear. God had turned from him long ago and he had no right to expect mercy or forgiveness. Nor could he find it within his own wretched spirit.

He'd nearly ruined everything with his damnable lust. The vileness of what he was had almost cost him his last hope. He had weakened to the very cravings he sought to tear from his life. His life. A cruel joke. What kind of life did he have when it was sustained by the blood of others? He fed on their fear. He feasted on their vulnerability. He depended upon their vitality. Like a disgusting parasite. And he killed. Occasionally, he went too far and he took the very essence life he held so precious. The very mortality he longed to embrace. With all his superior strength and his centuries-old wisdom, how could he give way with such feeble stupidity?

It was her. It was Arabella Howland. Thinking of her even now brought back the painful throb of need. It beat through him, that hot, dangerous hunger, driving him further into the darkness of city and soul. He'd wanted her so. He couldn't remember the last time he'd felt such tremendous temptation. The doxy had whet an appetite, but Arabella had him starving.

I want you.

How that made him tremble. Her passion, her strength, her caring nature excited him beyond control. She aroused more than the greedy frenzy for food with that innocent claim. Of course, she had no idea what she was inviting. No woman would want what he was unless she was a prisoner of his hypnotic power. But without will, where was the satisfaction? There was none. There was only emptiness. And he was so weary of that eternal loneliness.

Arabella. Oh, to have a woman like her. To hold her without the fear of instinct overcoming constraint. To love her with the passions of mortal man. Yes, he could give her paradise. Surrender to him would bring a hellish rapture. And eternity, that, too, was within his power. But how could he bring another into the same horror he knew with the setting of the sun? With the rising of the moon came the hunger. Most nights he could control it. Some nights it controlled him. But he never gave in without a fight. Until Arabella offered her white throat and the sweetness of her flesh. For a moment, her kiss had been enough and he'd considered the joys of her female frame with a desire he'd thought lost to him. It had been, what? ... three hundred years since he'd coupled with a mortal woman? Once he'd quenched his thirst at the foul wellspring of his kind, he'd lost his appetite for sex. Blood became the aphrodisiac he'd once found in physical release.

The fact that he'd touched Arabella Howland just for the pleasure of touching, and not as a seductive prelude to opening an artery, surprised him. That he'd responded to the warm press of her with the urgency of a mortal male astounded him. And in that there was confusion and danger. Because she was Stuart Howland's daughter, and the last person alive he could risk with the evil of what he was.

But oh, how he'd wanted her.

He'd gone deep into the dregs of Southwark. He had no fear, but he was not usually so careless with his concentration. The sudden jab of a pistol bore to the kidney took him completely unawares.

"Yer purse, me lord, and be quick about it."

"You're making a mistake," Louis drawled softly.

The muzzle prodded harder. " 'T'would seem you're the one makin' the mistake. Hand over the ready, lest you lose yer spleen."

Hands easy at his sides, Louis turned to face his assailant. The pistol barrel nudged into his midsection with deadly intent. To be fair, he felt obligated to give another warning.

"You don't understand—"

"I understand plenty. Gimme yer valuables. An' I'll start with that there sparkler."

He grabbed for the sapphire Louis wore in his cravat only to find his wrist in a bone-splintering clench. The robber shrieked in astonished agony and fired point-blank into the silken waistcoat.

The shattered hand was released as Louis staggered back several steps, bending double from the shock of impact. Then he straightened. The fabric of his vest front was still smoking, singed black by powder and stained with a meager amount of blood. But there was no gaping wound, a wound that should have been so horrible it would have snatched the life from any mortal man. Instead of falling dead to the street, the marquis gave his would-be killer a sad smile.

"As I said, a mistake. Your last."

Before the fellow could utter a final scream, Louis had him by the throat. A slight twist silenced him forever.

And then Louis Radman fed.

Chapter Two

It was late, Stuart Howland realized, as he slipped inside his town home and out of his wet greatcoat. He hadn't meant for the time to get out of hand, but several students had persisted in their questions after his lecture, and, as always, he'd been caught up in their enthusiasm and admiration. Such a bright bunch, really, so eager to consume knowledge, to apply fees in exchange for that learned skill. In their hungry expressions, in their fevered curiosities, he could well imagine cures in the making for the plagues of mankind. And it flushed him with a sense of importance, the way their reverie did. As if he were some god, some fount of miracles. Untrue, of course, but he didn't discourage that attitude. So he'd lingered longer than he'd meant to and returned later than he ought to and he intuited almost at once that something had happened in his absence. And considering what he'd invited into his house, that filled him with dread.

His daughter met him in a state of ill-concealed agitation. That in itself worried him, for Bella was never discomposed. She had a constitution steadier than most men's, which was why they'd got on so famously since her mother had died and he'd assumed responsibility for her care. It was easy, really, for Bella required none of the usual cosseting one associated with females. She preferred books of anatomy to those of frivolous verse, and table talk centering on erysipelas to erstwhile entertainments of theatre and the social elite. And if there was one thing he loved to the equal of his profession, it was his clear-eyed and calm-headed daughter. Which was why he was so concerned to see her rattled.

"What is it, my dear?" he asked, struggling to make his voice sound normal. "You are particularly pale this evening. Not fretting over my tardiness, were you, poppet?" He pinched her chin as he leaned forward to buss her cheek in a fond display. Her arms went about him, and for a moment, she clung. Stuart began to experience panic.

"It's nothing, Father. Just glad to have you home at last."

"It's *him*," Bessie interrupted, as she took the doctor's coat, ignoring Arabella's glower as she did. Stuart didn't miss the exchange.

"What's this? Has this to do with the marquis?"

Bessie took the opportunity to vent all her anxious objections. " 'Tis unseemly, that's what it is, sir. Leaving the likes of him alone with the young miss. Imagine the scandal of such doings, him already the center of talk, what with his odd habits and—"

"Bessie." The doctor had only to speak her name in that stern tone to silence her tirade. "Is his lordship in my study?"

"No, Father. He left—"

"Like the 'ounds of hell was after him," Bessie interjected with a colorful touch of drama. "I told you, sir, he's a queer one, what with those bright eyes and—"

"Bessie, please." Howland held up his hand, his patience strained. But he was studying his disconcerted daughter. "Bella, did anything—improper occur before his lordship took his leave?" He was going to say unusual, frightening, unholy, but he caught himself. He should have thought of this, knowing what Radman was, knowing the danger. He hadn't considered his own safety, but he should have considered his daughter's. Why hadn't he?

Arabella couldn't bring herself to look into his somber gaze and lie. So she canted her glance away as she murmured, "No, Father." What could she say? That she'd been seconds from rolling around upon the furniture with the man?

"Would you care to explain what happened then?" She could tell by his quiet tone that he didn't believe her . . . and by the unnatural brightness of his gaze that he was more than agitated. He was terrified, and that thought upset her more than any of the night's strange happenings. What was it that she didn't know about the marquis? What was her father hiding from her?

"His lordship was quite distressed to find you not yet home. He became restless and impatient, is all. I fear he was suffering from some physical distress as well. Though I couldn't hazard a guess as to its cause." She did look at him then, straight on and accusingly, as though to say if he'd given her the details of Louis Radman's case, she could have handled things better.

But Stuart Howland was too distracted to notice her chagrin. Now that he was assured of his daughter's safety, other things preyed upon him. He was frowning to himself. "I wonder if I should attempt to find him?"

The thought of him leaving her was too much. For then she'd be alone with the mental images, with the powerful feelings. And she wasn't ready. "Oh, Father, not on this horrid night. You just got in. I daresay, you probably haven't eaten a bite all day, and you're chilled to the bone. Whatever's troubling your patient, I'm sure it can wait until his next visit."

"I wonder," Stuart mused softly. Then he smiled at his daughter. "But you are right. I wouldn't begin to know where to look for him. If he needs me, he can always return."

Bella smiled back, her expression slightly strained as she thought of Louis Radman's return. Then her father surprised her with a warm embrace, drawing her in close and letting his hands remain on her shoulders when he stepped back. And with a casual gesture, his thumbs caught the edge of her standing collar, easing it away so he could quickly scrutinize her flawless and unmarked throat. There was no disguising the relief that loose-limbed his posture and warmed his smile.

"Let's go see what Cook has prepared for dinner, shall we?"

Arm in arm, they went to the table.

Over a bland roast beef and flavorful gravy, Stuart at first saw that his conversation didn't return to

Louis Radman, though thoughts of the mysterious marquis were flitting through his head. Finally, he said, "Bella, Mrs. Kampford isn't entirely wrong, you know."

"About what, Father?"

"About it being—awkward, you entertaining my patients in my absence."

"Oh, Father, really. I must protest."

"You may, but it won't change the fact that you are a young, unmarried female, for all purposes alone in this house. It is not wise to invite gossip or—mischief. In the future, I think it best to have Mrs. Kampford turn away those who come for treatment or counsel while I am out."

Arabella was about to argue when she considered once more what she'd almost allowed to happen in her father's study. She'd almost succumbed to Louis Radman's seduction. "Succumbed" perhaps wasn't the right word; she'd encouraged it. If Bessie hadn't chosen that moment to knock, she might have found herself prostrate upon the sofa beneath the marquis's caresses. And while that notion excited, it also cautioned. Such behavior was beneath her, and it defied the trust her father had always shown her. No gentleman would take advantage of a woman within her father's home without first declaring his intentions. And she knew Lord Radman's intentions were not the kind that he could speak to her father. But it had been wonderful . . . and disturbing.

So she said nothing, and in her silence, agreed to Stuart's conclusion. She would be safe from wicked temptation. And from the illicit charm of the marquis.

Stuart was watching her as he buttered his bread.

He was at a loss with the passion plays flitting across her face. But he knew enough to be wary of them. "Arabella, perhaps it's time we gave thought to your future."

She had taken a swallow of her wine and nearly choked. After a delicate fit of coughing, she wheezed, "My future?"

"My dear, surely you must realize that you are the exception to young ladies your age. While I understand your launch in society was rather disappointing to you, I cannot believe that a woman as intelligent and attractive as yourself hasn't caught the eye of at least a score of gentlemen—or would if you were to give the slightest sign of encouragement."

"Father—"

"Now, hear me out, Bella. You know how much having you involved in my work has meant to me, but you must start considering what you want to make of your life."

"Well, I know I don't want to wed some stuffy aristocrat and end up having vapors and raising a batch of vapid, overweaned children on some moldering country estate."

Stuart betrayed no sign of shock. He was used to her outspoken ways. "Now, Bella, that's not all there is to marriage. Your mother, God rest her soul, was a wonderful woman not given to vapors, and I daresay, you are hardly vapid."

"But you and Mother were different."

"And I want the same for you, child. I want you happy, and I cannot believe that filing my papers and organizing my schedule is a fitting ambition."

"Why not?"

"Because it's lonely business, Bella. I'm not asking that you accept the suit of some prissy nabob. But I am telling you that you'll never find a proper match, locked up in my cluttered office."

She gave him a most annoying smile, like a long-suffering mother to a persistent child. "And where am I to look?"

"For starters, you can accompany me to a small affair given by the Board of Governors at the hospital. The converse will not bore you, and it would do you good to be seen."

"So all those grasping medical students can cozy up to me to get at you?"

"Bella, you are far too cynical for your age." But he was smiling wryly, knowing she spoke the truth. His position on the hospital staff made him someone worth knowing for those up-and-coming in the field of medicine. Careers were made by connections to men in his circle. And he couldn't like the thought of his daughter being a pawn of ambition.

"I will go if it will make you happy," she demurred, with surprisingly little fuss. It would, she suppose, be more fun than the fashionable squeezes she'd endured during her debut. And she wouldn't be among strangers.

"And," her father remarked, "it would be a good chance for you to get to know Wesley Pembrook better."

"Wesley is a parasite, Father. He only pretends to like me because he hopes you'll get him the first available opening on the hospital's junior physician staff."

"I have been very satisfied with Wesley as an apprentice."

"Well, believe me, he has his eyes on higher gain. Such as a partnership in your practice. And what better way to gain it than through matrimony? You know a wife is a necessary piece of equipment for any physician. What female patient would entrust herself to a bachelor? That's all Wesley sees when he looks at me."

"He speaks of you most fondly, child."

"Ummm." She was unconvinced.

"If not Wesley, then some other who strikes your fancy. There must be some male with all the attributes you require in a life's mate."

"That shouldn't be too hard. I require very little, actually. All I ask is that he be cultured, compassionate, articulate, intelligent, broad-minded, self-supporting, exciting, and obsessed with the love of mankind."

"Is that all?" Stuart drawled. " 'Tis no wonder that you're still unattached. I know of no man who is such a paragon. Perhaps you will have to set your sight a tad lower, like down to the level of humanity."

Arabella smiled, but she knew of such a man. She'd described him perfectly.

She'd described Louis Radman.

Roses.

Two dozen on long, graceful stems with pure white blossoms just beginning to unfurl. And a card with one word penned in a bold, ornate script: *Radman*.

Arabella buried her face amongst the snowy blooms and breathed in their delicate fragrance, very aware of Mrs. Kampford's disapproving stare. Aware as well of the warmth flushing her features. He'd chosen white, not red. A gesture of apology, not one of desperate passion. As if he wished to erase the intensity of their embrace with the pristine petals. As if he could.

"Mrs. Kampford, please put these in water for me."

The tiny housekeeper took the armful with obvious distaste. "And where would you like them displayed, Miss?"

"Wherever you think they'd be pleasing to the eye."

That indifferent statement did much to calm the elder lady's suspicions, but she still clucked and shook her head as she carried the flowers away.

Was he sorry? Arabella wondered. Sorry he'd kissed her, or sorry they'd been interrupted? She wasn't certain of her own feelings about what had occurred. She didn't regret the kiss, and she couldn't resist the man. He held her in some dark fascination, and regardless of her sensibilities, she was loath to break it. She should; common sense told as much. A man who was noble in intent wouldn't have risked compromise in such an ardent display of passion. Yet even now she couldn't keep herself from making excuses for his behavior, not when her own had been so far from circumspect. What she had to be was careful, careful she wasn't caught up in anything ill advised. Like letting the moment carry to its carnal end.

She tried to pretend the day was like any other.

She worked about her father's office, organizing his papers, transcribing notes from his dreadful scrawl into her neat script. But all the while she was tending those ordinary tasks, her mind was spinning. Where would he keep his notes on Louis Radman? Somewhere she hadn't discovered them. And what would she find written to describe the case study, if that's what her father was doing? What started as a casual glance about the clutter of heavy furniture became a restless inventory of drawers and files. Once she began, she couldn't seem to stop herself, even though she knew what she was doing was wrong, a betrayal of her father's trust. But if he trusted her, why was he keeping this one secret from her? She used that to justify her invasion of his private papers. But she found nothing except some hastily scribbled receipts of sums paid to a certain Mac Reeves. The name meant nothing to her. And she gained nothing from her covert search except a terrible sense of guilt—guilt that intensified when her father came home for supper and gently kissed her cheek. And he walked her to the dining room with a brief questioning at the roses adorning the sideboard.

"A suitor already, Bella? I'm glad you took me at my word."

"Father, be serious," she scolded, but she was blushing fiercely. Thank goodness he was distracted by the arrival of their meal and thoughts of fostering romance were abandoned for the moment.

As she served them, Bessie Kampford was full of grisly gossip. Did they hear of the body found early that morning? Drained of blood, she'd heard, from the man who delivered fresh vegetables. Had his throat cut ear to ear, the laundress had confided with a gruesome whisper—the third one, if you counted those murdered and not the ones who'd managed to survive. Devil worship, was what she'd heard from a neighboring footman. Vile medical studies was what the letter carrier implied, with a meaningful glance inside the Howland residence.

"And what do you think it all means?" Arabella asked of the nervous housemaid.

"Bella, do not encourage such nonsense," Stuart warned, with a glowering look toward Bessie.

"I think evil's abroad these nights, Miss, and one would be wise to stay within doors," the dour woman confided.

"Bessie, that is quite enough," Stuart snapped, with the authority to send the housekeeper scurrying with a backward glance of care. Then he regarded his daughter with a tolerant smile. "Nonsense, of course—but you would be wise to keep a sensible head about you. One cannot ignore that violence is afoot, and I would like you to promise not to go out unescorted after dusk."

"Oh, Father, I'm not afraid—"

"You should be," came his ominous reply. Then he rose, excusing himself from the table with a brusque, "See that you take care, my dear. You are all that I love in this world, and there are things in it that can hurt you."

Arabella sat for some moments reflecting upon her father's odd caution. She looked up with interest when Bessie returned to clear the table. She watched the woman for a time, then her curiosity could no longer be contained.

"And what kind of bogeyman is it that walks the streets after dark?"

Bessie gave her a scowling glance; then, seeing she wasn't being mocked, she set down her tray and adopted an intimate mood. "Miss, there are strange goings-on all about. Now, I don't myself believe in bogeymen and such, but I know there be men of evil who prey upon the darkness. Bad men who would do anything for coin. Men your father should never have—" Suddenly, as if realizing that what she was about to say could cost her her position, she clamped her jaw tight and began to pick up the tray. Arabella stayed her with a gentle hand upon her sleeve.

"Men like Mac Reeves?" she ventured, knowing she'd struck true when the elder woman paled.

"Where did you hear that name, Miss?"

"It was on some of Father's papers. Who is he, Bessie?"

"He plies the London underworld down in Thieves' Kitchen. He is no one you want to know."

"Then why does my father know him?"

"That, I could not tell you."

Could not or would not. Arabella considered what she'd learned as Bessie hurriedly finished and disappeared into the back of the house. What business could her father, a respected physician, have with an underworld thug? Another secret. Another truth she vowed to learn from him.

It was then that her secret surfaced; her secret passion for Louis Radman. For the moment she heard his after-hours knock, her pulse began a frenzied thrumming and she was up and in the hall to answer it before decorum and common sense could catch her.

At first, she couldn't separate his figure from the enveloping darkness. His stillness was so absolute that when he moved to turn toward her, she was aware of a shock of surprise, for it was as if he'd suddenly appeared on the steps before her. A trick of the poor light, of course, but unnerving nonetheless. His heavy multitiered coat swirled about him like a dark fog, a concealing mist from which his refined features rose in startling contrast. And his eyes burned.

"Good evening, Miss Howland. Is your father at home?"

His voice played along her senses like subtle music, deep and pulsing in its melody. It took a moment for her to react to the question. "Yes. Please, come in and I shall announce you."

He came in from the night, surrendered by shadows into the warmth and life of the Howland home. He moved with a grace that was almost liquid and seemingly weightless, yet the power was there, a deep current of strength beneath that languid glide. And Arabella was remembering the feel of his grip, the intensity of his control, and the helplessness of succumbing to it. And the glory. Her tone was slightly unsteady when she asked him for his coat.

He shed it in a single shrug. He was dressed, as always, with impeccable style. Above the high gloss of his footwear, his trousers clung with an admirable snugness to the swell and sleekness of his thighs. A cutaway coat of dark superfine was tailored to the breadth of his shoulders and sturdy torso, tapering to a lean waist defined by the close fit of his patterned vest. A frill of stark white protruded from the deep vee of his outerwear and culminated at a strong throat with a cravat that was elegance in its simplicity. And Arabella was surprised to note that for all his command of presence, Louis Radman was no giant of proportion. He stood not much taller than she, who was an unfashionable five foot and seven-odd inches in her silk-stockinged feet. It was the sense of power that confused perspective, that overwhelmed mere numbers on a tailor's measure, impressing one with the illusion of greater height and sturdier mass. There was much to Louis Radman that was not quite as it should be.

For example, on this night, the gauntness was absent, as was his terrible pallor. Instead, there was a healthy fullness to his features and a near ruddiness to his skin. And with that smooth, well-fed appearance was an almost unnatural male beauty.

Breeding was obvious in every compelling angle of his face: Old World sophistication with none of the modern-day pasty weakness. Dark auburn hair was cut conservatively close in defiance of the fashionable tumbled waves. Beneath the dark slash of haughty brows that nearly met over a thin aristocratic nose, his eyes were not really gold but a soft hazel-green that appeared molten when the light picked up their deep amber flecks. And set above a determined chin was a wide mouth drawn with sensual arcs and an inviting lower swell ... a mouth intimately acquainted with the shape and softness of her own.

She wasn't sure what she'd expected from this first meeting, but she'd certainly not expected the coolness of his disregard. He was so distant she could almost believe that what had transpired with heavy passion-laden breaths and ardent whispers was no more than a figment of her mind. Surely this was not the man who'd promised her paradise and shredded the fabric of her will. If it was, could he be so unaware of her, so unwilling to spare her the slightest glance as he looked with anticipation toward her father's office?

"I'll tell Father you're here." How much of her pique and injury was reflected in her tone? Not enough to penetrate his distracted mood. Still carrying his greatcoat, Arabella swept toward her father's rooms, managing a regal disdain of posture that was totally lost on him.

Stuart Howland's medical office was in a large room off his study. It was there he met with patients and conducted his research and where Arabella was always free to come and go ... except when the patient was Louis Radman. Then, as usual, Stuart issued the marquis within and the door was firmly closed behind him, barring Arabella from all she was dying to discover.

She lingered in her father's study, hugging the marquis's coat to her. And when she heard voices raise to a heated elevation from behind that forbidding barrier, she hesitated only a second, then leaned in close so she might make out the words.

"... Endangering everything we're trying to do!"

That was her father, and rarely had she heard him in such a fury.

"Do not dictate to me," came the cold cut of Louis Radman's words. "Have you forgotten whence your fortune stems? I pay you well to be here when I need you. What happened was as much your fault as mine."

"Oh, no, dear sir. There you are mistaken. The vileness of your condition is no fault of mine, nor is your weakness. I understood you wanted to change those things. If that's not true, tell me now and I will bid you a good night."

There was silence, long and heavily laced with tension. When Louis spoke again, his tone was low, throbbing with a desperate anxiety. "Please, I need you. Do not abandon me over this—this momentary lapse."

"Lapse? A callous choice of words, my lord."

"You cannot know how I have suffered. You can't imagine the pain, the hunger. It burns until I can't think. Do you believe I enjoy what I must do to survive?" His voice broke, and when he continued, it was with an impassioned plea: "If I did, would I risk so much in trusting you with the truth? Please. Help me. We are close, so close. I can feel it. You are my only hope, my only chance. Do not forsake me because of the wretchedness of what I am." A pause. "Please."

"How long before the—pollutants are gone from your system?"

"A few days."

"We shall continue then."

"And now? What of tonight, and the next, and that after?"

"Your arm."

A soft, "Thank you."

Arabella pressed to the thick wood, listening intently. She caught her breath at the sound of Louis's harsh hiss and trembled to hear the tortured sounds that followed: low, raw, moaning sounds, awful to hear, terrible to imagine.

And then the door was abruptly opened and she nearly tumbled in upon the doctor as he readied to exit. They looked at one another for a long beat, he blocking the room's interior with the position of his body. Then Stuart gripped her none too gently by the upper arm and maneuvered her back so he could shut the door.

"What are you doing, Bella? Listening at keyholes?"

She blushed fiercely in her dismay, but was aggrieved enough to challenge, "If you would not make such a secret of your business with the marquis, I would not be drawn to take such reprehensible measures."

He had a hold of both of her arms to shake her sternly. His expression was immobile. "Louis Radman is none of your concern. He is dangerous and you would do well to remember that. If you force me to it, I will see you locked in your room during his visits."

"I am not a child—"

"Then do not act like one!"

Arabella pulled away from his chastising grasp, and with all the composure she could assemble under such trying circumstances, she turned and stalked from the study, not seeing how her father's features crumpled with worry and distress.

Chapter Three

The rout of Lord and Lady Ainsworthy's had all the dazzle of a society affair. Though the rank-and-file of the medical field wasn't drawn from men of title, the hospital boards were made up of the Polite World whose only claim to eminence was the desire to be linked to a prestigious philanthropic cause. As such, they were wooed by staff physicians and surgeons looking for favor and by the young students seeking an anchoring connection to their future.

Arabella held to her father's arm and watched the scene with a detached interest. What she beheld was a parasitic feeding frenzy, medical professionals latching onto members of the aristocracy to drain them of their resources. Social amenities barely covered their greedy purposes as they circled like birds of prey around influential carrion. Competition lent a sharp edge to civility, and rivalries were as fierce as a gathering of young bucks all eager to gain the attention of some belle flower. She could not recall such blatant attention having been paid to her when she'd made her debut, and perhaps, she thought, that was why she was so caustically aware of the shallow nature of the goings-on.

"Good evening, Doctor Howland, Miss Arabella."

Arabella forced a rigid smile as Wesley Pembrook paid elaborate court over her gloved hand. From his place at her side, she was uncomfortably provoked by her father's approving smile. It wasn't that Wesley was unappealing or a deadly bore. He was an attractive young man with riots of blond curls and a winning smile. He was tall and fit of form from his prowess in athletic pursuits. He belonged to cricket, football, and rowing clubs, hoping to gain the notice of those who frequented the elite events, and avidly participated when not busy as her father's clinical clerk. One could almost believe him sincere in his interest, if not for the calculating gleam in his blue eyes. There was no cheerful animation in his gaze. That stare was as cold of observation as it would be during a lecture on dissection, as if he were studying, weighing, arranging all he beheld in a priority of how things could best serve him. And that was why Arabella could not like him or trust the golden shower of his charm.

"Doctor, would you allow me to escort your daughter for some refreshments?"

"Father—"

But Stuart spoke over her subtle objections, smiling at Wesley, prying her clutching hand from his sleeve to arrange it within the crook of his protégé's arm. And with the doctor's best wishes, Arabella found herself led away from her source of safety into the milling crowd of desperate carnivores.

"You look fetching this evening, Miss Arabella."

His croon was thick as syrup, and her teeth ached in response. His was manipulative flattery, but she knew she did look her best on this special evening. She'd taken extra time to weave her hair up into a sophisticated coil threaded through with pearls. Her gown was of fine muslin, all the style. Its high waist and snug-skirted lines did little to highlight her voluptuous figure, but the amount of generous bosom displayed by the low, square neckline distracted from that fact. And distracted Wesley Pembrook was, to the point of rude ogling. She found it annoying in the extreme. She could imagine him snipping away at the layers of fabric with his gaze the way he would trim bandages back to expose some interesting site of infection.

"We have seen little of you, Mr. Pembrook." It was a statement, not a complaint, but he glowed as if it were. "Your studies must be keeping you very busy."

"I'm readying for my licensing exam. It's been a great privilege serving under your father as houseman. I've learned much from him and value his opinions on the directions I should take to become a fellow consultant here in London. Has he spoken to you of our conversations?"

And then his gaze slanted over to her, a brilliant chill of ambition. Arabella felt an answering plunge in emotional temperature. "No, he hasn't."

"Oh. Perhaps you should take more of an interest, my dear Miss Howland."

"And why is that, sir?" As if she didn't know.

"Because my future plans and yours might be heading in the same direction."

"Really?"

They had reached the refreshment tables, but Wesley pulled her beyond them and out into the wide, empty foyer, where they would not be overheard. And there he began to press his suit. He clasped her gloved hands to his starched shirt front in an amorous pose and whispered fiercely, "Arabella, you cannot be unaware of how I feel for you."

"Oh, I assure you, sir, I am well aware of your motives." She tried to free herself, but his grip tightened, drawing her even closer.

"Then you know we are destined for one another," he breathed in dramatic rapture.

"I know no such thing." She glanced about, uncomfortably aware of their isolation. And of the way he was working himself up to make some grand gesture. Really, she had no patience with him. She adopted her most frigid tone. "Now, please release me. I should like to return to my father."

"Arabella, do not toy with my affections."

"Sir, I assure you, I do not."

"Then if it's a token of my affection that you need, I can happily supply it." And he leaned forward, grabbing for her lips with an arrogant gusto.

Arabella was taken by surprise, yet managed to twist within his grasp so that his kiss fell upon her temple. His mouth was warm and wet and narrow, and a shiver of distaste shook through her . . . along with a tremor of pure anger.

"Let me go!"

"My dear, there's no need to struggle! Your father will have no objections." Laughing softly, as if he couldn't believe she wouldn't welcome his overtures, he tried for her lips again and this time caught the end of her nose. His hands moved, releasing hers to curve about her ribcage in an indecently high position, cupping the weight of her breasts between thumb and forefinger with either span. Then it was alarm as much as fury making her squirm, because he was so strong and so determined.

"Please—"

The rest was smothered beneath the crush of his kiss.

It was finally a sense of revulsion and violation that broke through her shock. But by then, Wesley had one arm securing her to his chest while the other hand made free with her bodice. The sound of conversation in the other room, so terribly close yet far removed, was drowned out by the pounding of her heart. The feel of his fingertips on the soft flesh swelling above her décolletage served to renew her fight. She was growing faint from the lack of air and frantic from the sudden cool of exposure as the scant coverage of muslin was tugged down, baring her boldly for his touch. Good heavens! He couldn't mean to have his way with her, not right here in the hall, where anyone could come upon them and by discovery . . . compromise her, leaving her no choice but to wed to save her family's reputation.

Perhaps that had been his plan all along.

What could she do? Scream? The scandal alone would serve his purpose well. There seemed nothing she could do except endure his crude caress and hate him for the liberties he was taking. And hope her father would be as incensed as she was by his student's unwanted advances.

But what if he wasn't? What if her father was not displeased at all?

"Let her go."

Though softly spoken, it was no less a command.

The instant Wesley's grip slackened in startlement, Arabella jerked back and spun, colliding with a very solid figure. And there she was encircled with a sensation of security as the young medical student seethed at the interruption.

"Just who the bloody hell—"

"Enough."

Again, so quiet, so powerful. A stillness followed, heard even over Arabella's hurried gulps for breath. From the protective cove of Louis Radman's embrace, she risked a backward glance and was stunned by Wesley's expression. It was completely blanked of anger, of will, itself, as if caught in a mesmerist's mental grasp. He was staring fixedly not at her, but into Louis's eyes. She followed that trancelike gaze up to the dark beauty of her rescuer's face.

In anger, he was like a vengeful god. And oh, he was angry. It was manifest not so much by external means, but through a palpable vibration, of fury, of outrage, chafing poorly behind a facade of grace. She could feel it like the prickly concentration of electricity during a lightning storm. Violence charged the air.

"Did he harm you, little one? If so, I will crush him for you. I will grind his bones to powder."

He put out one hand before Wesley's unblinking eyes and curled his fingers into a white-knuckled fist. And in a sudden giddy alarm, Arabella realized that with one word from her, he would snap her assailant's spine as easily as dry tinder. Regardless of

Wesley's superior size, she didn't doubt it for a moment.

She put her hand over that taut fist of retribution, saying hurriedly, "No. It's all right. I was only frightened."

"Reason enough," Louis growled, but his threat relaxed under the insistent entreaty of her hand over his. To Wesley, who seemed powerless to move or think on his own, Louis said with a terse impatience, "Leave us," and without a flicker of objection, the medical student obeyed, as if helpless to do otherwise.

When they were alone, the shock of the encounter shivered through Arabella. She pressed her cheek against the shoulder of black superfine and let distress shake her loosely. She couldn't believe Wesley would be so goaded by ambition as to force his attentions. She felt dirty and defiled and afraid of what had almost happened. Louis simply held her, letting her take from his strength and nearness, letting her recover at her own pace. Her arms were wound about his middle, and slowly awareness of him overcame her horror. Awareness of how firm and warm he was, of the scent of expensive wool and some smoky cologne and the possessive circle of his body around her, protecting her from hurt and shame. And she was aware of her breasts tightening where they brushed, fully exposed, against his broad chest.

"Oh!" It was a squeak of dismay and embarrassment, but when she drew back and tried to cover herself with the modest wrap of her arms, he stilled her with a word.

"Don't."

Arabella froze, the sound of his voice seeping through her, suppressing panic, numbing thought, holding her in a paralysis of mind and body. Even her breathing stopped as the reality of the world fell away. There was nothing beyond the pinpoints of gold in his gaze, the way those dots of light seemed to swirl and seduce until she was overcome with languor. Her arms were heavy at her sides and remained there as his stare slid down from wide, bewildered eyes, to softly parted lips, to the lush perfection of her breasts.

Perhaps only a second had passed, but it could have been longer—minutes, even hours, for all she knew. She lost the sensation of time as he stood there looking his fill. Not with lusting, not with passion or perversion, but rather with the appreciation a master had for a fine piece of work—leisurely, critically, reverently.

And then slowly, gently, his thumbs hooked in that displaced fabric, easing upward, sliding over and around until all that was meant to be concealed was hidden once more. She stood trembling for another long moment, no longer frightened, but frightfully aroused. And confused to think that one man could inspire such loathing with the warmth of his hands upon her, and another such urgent passion. And wondering distractedly why she felt no aversion to Louis Radman's stare.

"Are you sure you are all right?"

His quiet concern woke her completely from the daze he'd cast about her. She blinked and chafed her palms along her arms. An odd feeling burned beneath her skin, a prickly pins-and-needles sensation, as if her limbs had gone to sleep ... indeed, as if her whole body had. To cover her disorientation, Arabella focused on her anger, that powerful emotion returning her sense of self.

"Just feeling very foolish that I should be tricked into such a position. If it had been anyone else but you who'd come upon us ..." She let that trail off, not wanting to think of it. Of being trapped into a pride-saving arrangement with Wesley Pembrook.

"I heard your struggles and could not let them go unanswered."

"You heard—" But how could that be? The foyer had been empty. If someone had entered from the outside, surely she'd have known, would have felt the stir of air, heard the sound of the door, footsteps, something. Her plea for help couldn't possibly have reached into the room beyond.

"You are too trusting, Miss Howland. And things are not always as harmless as they seem, nor are men always able to control the darkness within them when confronted by temptation."

His small smile said he saw her as such, and Arabella's pulse shivered in response. But because she was too sensible to be undone by flattery, she laughed, a bitter sound.

"Oh, I don't believe Mr. Pembrook was overwhelmed by temptation. I believe he was overcome by greed."

Louis frowned. His dark brows met in a heavy vee above the bridge of his nose.

"He would like a place at my father's side," she explained, suddenly aware of how degrading that admission was to her self-esteem. "And one day, he would like all that my father has."

"Including his daughter."

"No, *through* his daughter."

"Then the man is a fool. A dangerous fool. You are too intelligent to be taken in by his deceit and too great a prize to be given away to one so unworthy."

Again he managed to nonplus her with his smooth praise, for she could see no reason to disbelieve he meant what he said, even if she didn't believe it was true. As if he could hear her deprecating thoughts, Louis reached out to lightly stroke his forefinger down her cheek, and again Arabella was consumed by the want to give all to this man who was a stranger and a mystery and more dangerous than Wesley Pembrook had ever thought of being. She'd never had such thoughts about Wesley, or about any other man. Just this one. And she wasn't sure what to do about it.

His hand cupped her elbow gently, as if he thought her made of some fragile porcelain. And for a moment all she wanted to do was step into his embrace, to put back her head and beg for another of his fantastic kisses. But what would he think? After dragging her out of the arms of another man he'd come close to killing for stealing those same liberties ...

"Let me take you back in to your father."

His voice was a caress, as slow and sure as any touch. Arabella shivered again, wondering wildly why she felt so hot, so cold, so tremblingly out of control around him. Her weakness troubled her, but not enough to warn her away. Boldly she put her hand on his sleeve, and tension snapped him taut beneath her touch.

"Please. He would be full of questions about Wesley, and I—I just can't answer them yet."

"Then perhaps you would allow me to escort you in. We shouldn't linger out here alone. I don't like placing you at risk." And he smiled as if he was really talking about her reputation and not about something altogether darker and different.

"I would be honored with your company, my lord."

" 'Tis you who honor me, Miss Howland."

He lifted her gloved fingertips to his lips then, turning her hand over within his, pressed a long, hot kiss to the inside of her wrist. She could feel the heat right through the layer of kid. For a moment his eyes closed and the scorch of his breath intensified until the burning seemed to spread with tongues of fire up through her veins. With an abrupt jerk of his head, he straightened and averted his gaze. She was startled by the rasp of his breathing. Then he was his courtly self again, smiling blandly, waving their way toward the doors and the crowd—and safety. That thought came to her quite unexpectedly. She hadn't felt endangered, but instinctively she sought the press of others. Louis Radman acted strangely upon her sensibilities. She wasn't at all certain she should believe herself protected while in his company.

What was it he'd said?

Things are not always as harmless as they seem.

Once they were within the social crush, the disquieting panic left her. Louis was an exquisite companion, solicitous of her wishes, gracious to all who approached her out of familiarity and him out of curiosity. He seemed well versed about everyone in attendance and about their various fields of study. Strange that she should feel he was somehow restless within the confines of conversation, though he spoke easily enough and was generous with his close-lipped smile. Then she knew, she just realized as if he'd told her aloud, that he wanted to speak to her alone, yet here within the view of others.

"I would enjoy a glass of punch, my lord, and a short respite from all this clever banter."

He bowed to her as if the idea was hers and not somehow planted through his own will. Beyond the refreshment table was a secluded alcove, far enough away from the professional cozes for quiet converse. Louis was careful not to stand too close or to appear in any way improper as he held his glass but didn't drink from it. He was scanning the gathering as he asked, "This Pembrook works with your father?"

"Yes. Father saw great promise in him when he attended his lecture courses. He's managed to ingratiate himself into Father's confidence—and, I fear, into his very practice."

Louis looked slightly alarmed, but his voice never shook from its smooth cadence. "And is he privy to all that your father does?"

"Not all. He clerks for Father at the hospital, but he's not yet managed to worm his way into our house."

"What does he know about me?"

"About as much as I do."

Louis gave her a piercing look. "And what do you know?" A low, vibrating authority took command of his question, and Arabella unconsciously took a step back.

"Nothing. You come, you go. Father has never confided what goes on in his office."

He smiled, suddenly all charm again. His gaze was warm and intimate in its intensity. "And that bothers you, little one?"

How easily he read her moods. Arabella flushed and smiled faintly. "I am not used to being kept in the dark. Father usually values my assistance."

"As he should. You are a most capable woman. It would not be hard to confide in you."

"Will you?" The words slipped out before she could consider them. Then, she wasn't sorry. She stared at him straight on, without a trace of apology for her bluntness, with the indignation of one caught in the chafe of secrets within her own home.

Louis was silent. He studied her intently, and she could feel him weighing her discretion. Apparently he was satisfied, for he chose to reply.

"Your father is treating me for a rare blood disorder I contracted abroad. I sought him out because of a journal article he did on transfusing blood from animal to animal and his work on allergens, a brilliant piece of research. We met and talked, and when we were through, I felt he was the one man who could help me put into application the knowledge I had accumulated over the—years. We have maintained our secrecy for both our sakes. I do not want the particulars of my affliction broadcast through Society, and he does not want it known that he is leaned toward a veiled specialism. It seems his colleagues would see such a move on his part as a threat and would boycott him by refusing to refer their patients and by excluding him from gatherings such as this one. So you see why we had to be cautious."

Of course she did, but that didn't stop her from a certain prickly disdain. "Well," she huffed, "I can hardly be considered a threat. I would never do anything to endanger my father's practice." Then her gaze eased circumvently over the man before her. Or you, she added silently, as she regarded the handsome marquis.

And he smiled at her. "I can see that now. I'm sorry if our exclusion has offended you in any way. It wasn't a matter of trust."

What, then, was it?

She studied him with the learned eye of one who had grown up within a medical household. He seemed fit at the moment, not prone to any wasting malady that she knew of. But she couldn't forget the way he'd appeared that night in her father's study—so gaunt, so obviously ill and suffering. He'd been so desperate during the conversation she'd overheard. And she worried.

"Your condition, is it—is it—" She struggled to find a tactful phrase. He came eloquently to her rescue, his reply a little too blunt for comfort.

"Fatal? No." And with a rueful expression, he added, "Though there are times when I wish it had proved to be."

"Oh, no. Never say that. Nothing can ever be so terrible as to make one wish to surrender life. It is the most precious of all things."

The passionate way that was said made him smile

with an appreciation. "Yes. I believe you are right in that," he said, with a quiet melancholy.

She wanted to reach out to him, to touch his brow, to soothe away the furrow of distress. In fact, she went so far as to take a step closer, when a sudden harsh voice intruded.

"Arabella!"

And she turned to confront her father's furious gaze.

Chapter Four

"Doctor Howland, good evening."

Stuart ignored the marquis's calm drawl. "Bella, get your wrap. It's time we were leaving."

"But, Father—" She let that trail off as she recognized the set of his jaw. There was no point in arguing. That tense clench of his teeth said he would drag her off, if need be. She looked to Louis, trying to keep any overt emotion from her eyes, and she curtsied prettily and murmured, "My lord, a pleasure."

He caught her hand to lift her up from a pool of muslin, holding those gloved fingers for a moment too long before carrying them leisurely to his lips. His gaze never left hers.

"Il piacere e stato mio. The pleasure has been mine, Miss Howland."

And she was falling, drowning in the warm green sea of his gaze as if diving for the gold hidden in the depths of his eyes. Unconsciously she clutched at his hand, shaken by the thought of separation.

"Bella."

The slice of her father's command severed her

fixed concentration. Graciously she drew her hand back and hurried to retrieve her pelisse.

As she moved through the crowd of the medical elite, Arabella was unaware of Wesley Pembrook's sullen stare as it cut from her to the elegant marquis. What had happened, he puzzled. He could fasten upon no logical explanation. He'd been so close to all he desired, then . . . then what? The foreigner had intruded, not only into the scene of his seduction, but into his very brain. He could think of no other way to describe it. His will had been smothered. A strange buzz of distraction still lingered, enough to convince him that he hadn't imagined it. What had the man done to him? Was it some sort of hypnotism? Was that the power he held over Arabella? Who was he, this stranger Arabella Howland would embrace as if he offered a kind of salvation? A man who knew Stuart Howland was a man he should know. Wesley vowed to discover the truth of it and find some way to use the information to his advantage. But not tonight . . . not when his mind was veiled with a dizzy languor. But he would find out all there was to know about Arabella's mysterious knight errant.

With her coat draped over her arm, Arabella approached Louis and his father. They were involved in an intense discussion and didn't notice her as she slipped up behind them. Their words held her, the meaning devastated her, and all the light within her heart dimmed in an instant.

"You will stay away from her."

"I will not harm her."

Stuart snorted at that. "You may not be able to control yourself."

Then came Louis's bewildering reply. "I've had three hundred years to learn control."

"It hasn't served you very well, Radman."

"Besides," the marquis confided with a chilling sobriety, "I would never allow an interest in your daughter to jeopardize our research. That is my main objective, and I'll let nothing distract me from it. Nothing."

Arabella squared her shoulders and interrupted with a cool, "Father, I'm ready to go."

Without sparing the marquis a glance, she handed her pelisse to her father and let him assist her into it. So, his lordship considered her a mild distraction. Well, she wouldn't dream of interfering with his purposes. Let him whisper with her father behind closed doors. It was nothing to her. To prove it to him, she took her father's arm, meaning to leave the gathering without a parting sentiment or look ... until a quiet word insinuated itself within her mind.

Arabella.

She turned in response to find Louis's unblinking gaze upon her. And she could swear—could swear!—that he had spoken her name aloud. Her father didn't react as if he'd heard him. But she'd heard his call to her as clearly as she heard her father's terse command.

"Come, Bella."

So she pulled her gaze from those eyes of mesmerizing hue and hurried to her father's side away from the danger of Louis Radman.

* * *

The dreams began that night, dreams so vivid, so erotic in content that Arabella awoke each morning in a sweat of enraptured panic. They were dreams. They had to be dreams. But they were so real.

In those dreams that were more like memories, she'd hear his voice.

Arabella.

She'd awaken, or dream that she did, and sit up with covers clutched beneath her chin. And across the floor up to the foot of her bed came a stream of silvery moonlight. From that pale, ethereal beam, particles began to shift and swirl, like fanciful motes, collecting, growing denser, taking shape and the form of a figure, of a man. That man was Louis Radman.

There he'd stand, his eyes transfixing her, glowing with a glitter of gold. There was something hypnotic in his total stillness. Then he would say, though his lips would never move with the actual speaking, *Arabella, call to me.* And she would, dropping the sheet from her bosom, stretching her arms outward in invitation.

"Louis."

And he'd come toward her, as silent as a drifting shadow, gliding with no real effort of movement. With the mere gesturing of one hand, the covers stripped from her, fluttering down, as if carried on some mystical breeze, to settle at the end of her bedstead. She couldn't move. She didn't want to.

"Louis, love me."

She'd say those words without reluctance, without restriction, because this was a dream and that's what she'd always wanted to say to him. That's what she'd always wanted from him. And he'd sit on the edge of her bed, though there was never any actual give to the mattress as there'd have been in the acceptance of a man's weight.

Soon, little one. Soon we will be together. But for now, we must be patient.

And she'd lie back into her bank of downy pillows, wanting him to come down to her, encouraging him with the wanton undulations of her body, with the wicked, wanting entreaty of her gaze.

"Touch me, Louis. Kiss me. Make me yours."

How easily those words came, those shameless words, as excitement stirred and simmered deep within her.

Soon . . .

And as if he couldn't bear to leave her in such a desperate state of unfulfilled desire, his hand moved casually, never quite touching her, floating, skimming above the outline of her nightdress. And all along her skin, she felt such a flood of heat, a melting warmth that rippled and teased her to the edge of rapture. He was seducing her with his mind, loving her with his thoughts, and she writhed and arched with the delight of it until all at once a sense of focus returned, a sense of reality. And she would find herself alone in her bedroom, panting, perspiring within the twist of her nightclothes, so sure, so sure that he'd been there, that he'd somehow provoked the illicit magic without ever once putting a hand upon her.

But that, of course, was impossible.

* * *

The announcement that she had a visitor spurred a flurry of anxiousness within Arabella. For five nights, she'd carefully avoided the sight of Louis Radman when he'd come to see her father, and for five nights she'd awakened from those explicit dreams craving him like an dangerous addiction. She went through the days in an edgy exhaustion, often curling up on the sofa in her father's study to catch an hour of undisturbed rest. Her father was concerned about the state of her health. She was concerned about the state of her mind. This unnatural fixation was controlling her life and she didn't know how to break from the enslaving pattern. She was afraid to confront the source, afraid that with one look, Louis would read all within her confused gaze. But hiding from him was building a suspenseful yearning that was almost as bad as the dreams.

And now he'd come to see her. She was fluttery with panic and flushed with anticipation as she swept into the parlor. Early evening lamplight outlined his form against the far window. She paused, breathless with excitement, and then he turned.

"Miss Howland, I've come to offer my apology."

Arabella stared at Wesley with an unconcealed frown, aware of a plummeting disappointment. She didn't want an apology from the man. She didn't want anything at all from him.

"And now you have," she answered coolly. "So, if there's nothing else . . ."

"Arabella, don't be cruel." It was a pretty petition, she'd have to give him that. His expression was suitably contrite, his tone tugged with just the right amount of regret. But she didn't believe any of it and said so.

"I'm sorry, Mr. Pembrook. I cannot find it to forgive you."

"You don't mean that!" But it wasn't shock or disappointment that flared briefly behind his gaze. It was panic. And anger. A fierce irritation that she would complicate his ambitions by what he considered her unreasonableness. He reached out to grasp her forearms, but she wrested away.

"I will thank you to restrain your demonstrations, sir. I do not like to be handled."

"Only by him, is that it?"

"Him?"

"By Radman."

Taken by surprise, Arabella felt a betraying flood of heat suffuse her cheeks, but she held to her aggravation. "The marquis does not maul me in public places against my will, nor does he expose me to the threat of scandal."

"What *does* he do?" Wesley snarled.

"That is none of your concern, Mr. Pembrook!"

"It is. What more must I do to convince you of my intentions?"

"You've done more than enough already."

But he didn't react to her level accusation. Instead, he drew himself up into the picture of wounded male pride and jilted affection to mourn, "Arabella, I have been clumsy in my court. That's not because my suit is insincere. I'm a man of medicine, not a creature of poetic spirit. I am not good at games of romance."

"Then why don't you try honesty?"

He sighed and gave her an intense look. "I care for

you, Arabella, and I want our futures to be one and the same. I will not lie to you and say it is passion that spurs this attraction. Much of it is purely practical. You are from a medical family. Your father is a man I admire. You would understand the stresses and sacrifices a physician must make. You are, in fact, the perfect wife for a man of science. You are the woman I need to fulfill my destiny."

That was honest. Perhaps if he'd spoken this way from the first, she might have considered such a union. She was a practical woman and she valued honesty above all things. But that was before Wesley had forced himself upon her. That was before Louis Radman had bewitched her. There was no future for her with Wesley, and it would be cruel for her to let him believe there ever could be.

And he didn't take the news well.

Wesley had all the earmarks of a truly great physician. He was ambitious, aggressive, self-assured, and independent, and he thought himself infallible. He absolutely could not believe it was some fault within himself that Arabella objected to. So he sought some other means to justify his failure to woo her into a sensible union of matrimony.

"It's Radman."

"This has nothing to do with Louis."

"Louis, is it?"

Realizing she'd spoken unwisely, Arabella pressed her lips together. It was nonetheless too late to take back the intimate use of the marquis's name.

"Who is this man and what is he to you?"

"That is—"

"It is my concern. Something is not—right about

that man. The other night, he mesmerized me. Do not laugh. I am not a man given to fancy. It's true."

She wasn't about to laugh; she knew it was true.

"Arabella, it is dangerous to seek an alliance with such a man, a man whom neither you, nor anyone else, seems to know anything about. I am speaking from my own fondness for you."

Of course, he was. That, and a good smattering of jealous pique.

"Arabella, you have always been such a straight-thinking and pragmatic female."

Yes, she was. Everything about her was dull and staid and predictable, and she didn't like Wesley very much for pointing out those attributes. She took no risks, she indulged in no imaginative flights, and she relied on logic for her every move. Except with Louis. Nothing about her feelings for him was logical, and perhaps that bit of romantic nonsense was the reason for her attraction. He made her feel—alive.

"What has he done to earn such favor with you? Has he charmed you, too? Has he clouded your mind with his own?"

That was much too close to the truth for Arabella to feel comfortable. A man like Wesley would never understand such a human weakness. "Don't be absurd. I am not some weak-willed miss to fall prey to some charlatan's tricks. What would he have to gain by wooing me?"

Indeed. What *would* he have to gain?

Her father's assistance.

That whispered with ugly insinuation through her

heart and soul, and she blocked it with a fierce determination.

"What does a man hope to gain if his intentions are impure?" Wesley argued.

"He was not the one who was trying to unclothe me in the Ainsworthys' foyer," she countered. But much of her ire was driven by fear—a fear that Wesley was right, that Louis was using her, as he himself had tried to use her. Why else would a man of Louis Radman's ilk show preference to a bluestockinged daughter of a mere physician? And what if Louis had some strange power to influence the mind? What if he was planting those salacious dreams into her subconscious? Wasn't that more reprehensible than a straightforward assault? She threw up a defense at Wesley, though in truth, the defense was for the state of her own heart.

"Lord Radman is not my suitor. He has no interest in me at all. He is my father's—" Then she caught herself, realizing in dismay how close she'd come to revealing Louis's secret.

"Your father's what?" Wesley prodded, his attention keen and whetted.

"Benefactor," she supplied. "He is financing some of Father's research."

Wesley's eyes narrowed. "What kind of research?"

Too late to back out of that one. Wesley latched on like a tenacious bulldog. So she tried to look innocent, and that didn't quite work, either.

"I really don't know. He didn't confide the details."

"Arabella, you know everything that goes on in

your father's office. What are he and Radman doing?"

And again she could see that rampant ambition in his gaze; that greed for fame and self-interest. The idea of her father's secret incensed him, too, but in his case, it was with a fever to be included, to suck up his share of whatever reputation-making work Stuart Howland might be doing. And in his lust to excel, he completely forgot his reason for coming to the Howland home, that it was to sway Arabella with his charm. He forgot everything, except the hope that he could be on the edge of sealing his success. His fervor was frightening to behold. It made her more cautious than ever.

"I'm afraid you'll have to ask my father or the marquis, for I truly do not know."

"I don't believe you, Arabella." He'd taken a threatening step toward her when a cool voice sounded from the doorway.

"Ask me what?"

The sight of Louis Radman sent Wesley shrinking back with an unidentifiable fear. He'd felt the man's strange power and had no desire to experience its control again. Purposefully, he avoiding making eye contact as he mumbled to Arabella, "Tell your father I will see him in the morning. Good evening, Miss Howland." And when he slipped by Louis, he boldly lifted his gaze as he sneered, "Radman."

The man just looked at him. That's all he had to do to send a jolt of sensation through Wesley's conscious mind. It was like receiving a pugilist's punch to the head. He staggered slightly as pain lanced through his temples with an almost disabling strength.

And Radman smiled, well aware of what he was doing.

"Mr. Pembrook, again, a pleasure."

Then the crushing ache lifted and Wesley practically fled the room.

There was a moment's silence, then Louis's attention shifted to Arabella. She felt the immediate warmth of his regard. Heat tingled along her nervous system. Was it her reaction to him, she wondered vaguely, or was it something he was doing to her? Whichever, she suddenly felt acutely aware of him; of his body heat, his breathing, his scent, as if the width of the room no longer separated them.

"I trust I was not intruding," came his soft-accented purr.

"No. Your appearance was both timely and welcomed."

And they simply stood for a long beat, absorbing the sight of one another. Irritation and suspicion fell from her mind as Arabella found herself lost in the deep mystery of his gaze. It was dark, she noticed with some surprise. His eyes seemed almost black in the unnatural light, as if the pupils had swelled and swallowed the irises whole.

"I trust you are well, Miss Howland. You look a bit tired, as if you've not been sleeping."

"I've been having strange dreams," she confided, before she realized what she was saying. The content of her dreams was the last thing she wanted to discuss with him, but she seemed powerless to evade his questions.

"And they frighten you?"

"They—disturb me."

"Do you wish them to stop?"

"Yes—no. I—I—don't know." She blinked weakly, then with more concentration, and finally turned her head to the side. Once they no longer shared a gaze, she was able to think more clearly. What on earth were they doing discussing her dreams? It was as if he was well aware of what went on in them. And she experienced a quiver of alarm, as if he'd planted the thoughts and was asking how she liked them. Too well ... she liked them all too well. They were arousing, exciting, dangerous—but no, they didn't frighten her. Nor did Louis frighten her. Even when she glanced up to find him standing at her elbow and was unaware that he'd ever moved in from the hall.

"What were you and Pembrook discussing?" His tone was caressing. His purpose was cold steel.

"He came to apologize for the other night."

"Is that all?"

When she didn't answer right away, his forefinger curved about her jaw, raising her chin so she couldn't look away from him. She could feel the intensity of his stare burning, penetrating, as if he could actually see into her mind. She rebelled against the intrusion.

"Yes," she lied, just to see what he would do. Then she gasped as the pressure of his thoughts seemed to force themselves upon hers, ruthlessly. She tried to pull away in a stifled panic, but his grip tightened, his fingertips indenting flesh and muscle. And though she was afraid of a strength that could pulverize fragile bone, she staunchly refused to yield to his intimidation.

"Please, my lord. You hurt me."

Instantly his grasp relaxed, easing before bruises formed to become a gentle stroke along stubborn jaw and down slender neck. He smiled slowly.

"You are a remarkably strong woman."

"I do not like to be bullied, sir."

"I shall remember that." His fingers were massaging her throat. "There are much more pleasurable means of persuasion."

He took a step closer and her hand rose automatically to hold him at bay. But the moment her palm pushed against his chest, the want to struggle was gone. The feel of him beneath the staid evening wear was too intriguing.

"Your heart beats like a tiny bird's when startled to flight," he observed. "Haven't I promised not to harm you?"

"I'm not afraid," she stated boldly.

"No?" A smile quirked his sensuously shaped lips.

"Nor should you be. I told Wesley nothing."

His smile widened and his eyes heated to a deep golden fire. A responsive warmth started inside her. She felt strangely compelled to seek the firm wall of his chest, wanting to languish there and lift up for his kisses. But instead, she ducked her head and wiggled quickly from his grasp and his control.

"I'll tell my father you are here."

"I thought you were not afraid," he taunted gently, as she hurried to the door.

She paused there and looked back at him, favoring him with a small, provocative smile. "I'm not. But I'm not foolish, either."

The sound of his amused chuckle followed her

down the hall as did his soft call of, "Sleep well, Arabella."

She did sleep well, deeply and dreamlessly and undisturbed. When she woke, it was past dawn, and though wondrously refreshed, she was plagued with a sense of disappointment. How alone she felt, as if Louis had chosen to desert her. But that was silly. How could a dream desert one?

She could have pondered over that until in a fever of distress, so she chose not to. Instead, she dressed and went down to breakfast, greeting her father with a cheery smile, as if he were the only man of note in her life.

"Good morning, Father."

"I have left a mountain of paperwork for you this morning, my dear. Are you certain you don't mind being trapped inside on such a promising day?"

"Oh, not at all. I shall take some time to walk about if my eyes grow weary, but never fear, I shall finish before you arrive home."

Stuart nodded somewhat distractedly. She waited for him to speak, wondering over his hesitance.

"I received a note from Wesley Pembrook, asking me to meet him today. Have you any notion of what that's about?"

"No," she began slowly, not raising her eyes to his probing gaze. "Should I?"

"I was wondering if it had anything to do with the two of you."

Her gaze flew up at that, full of fire and fury. "Father, there is no two of us, and there is not going to be. I can't make myself more clear than that."

"Now, Bella, I'm aware that Wesley overstepped his bounds the other night, but you cannot hold eagerness against a man when he's smitten with a pretty woman."

"He—he told you?"

"He said he was rather forward with his kisses and you resisted, as well you should." He sounded proud of her fortitude, but not distressed by his protégé's aggression. And Arabella was furious.

"Is that how he explained it?"

"I do not care to intrude upon what goes on between you and your suitors, Arabella. I only wish that you would seriously entertain any proposals you might receive."

"Has Wesley said something to you?" she gasped in dismay.

"Not yet. But I feel it is only a matter of time."

"Oh, Father—"

"Now, Bella, do not go missish on me. We can discuss this at another time. I have early rounds to do before my lecture. I'll try not to be too late."

But he was, despite his best-intentioned claim. And it was dark before Arabella happened to glance at the clock in her father's study to see the hour was past seven. She sighed and regarded through weary eyes the stack of transcriptions she'd completed. Enough, she decided, pushing back from her chair meaning to see to her neglected supper when a furtive tap sounded upon the rear door to her father's office.

Wondering who would come calling at such an hour and at the rear entrance, Arabella went to the door and opened it without thinking. There, on the shadowed stoop, stood three men supporting a fourth. It was too dismal to make out their individual faces, but their style of clothing was rough and of lowering class origin.

"I'm sorry, but my father is unable to receive any patients. You'll have to try the hospital."

"Oh, Miss, I think you be mistakin' the reason for us being here," growled the one closest to her. He stepped forward a bit, just far enough for the light from within to highlight his coarse features and a blackened-toothed smile. His accent was of the East End. "I be Mac Reeves, and what I gots for yer dear daddy won't keep long."

Arabella's eyes had adjusted enough to the dimness to make out some details of the others. The men on either end were big, burly brutes with looks that were bovine and cruel. The man in the middle was quite obviously dead.

Chapter Five

"Step on outta the way, there, ye gawky chit," one of the bulky duo called. "I done risked me neck enough fer one night and don't mean to be caught dandling some cove we done stole from the hospital crib."

Arabella gasped in horror. The men were graverobbers, and the corpse they carried had been exhumed from the hospital's burial ground. "You can't bring—that in here!"

"Why the 'ell not? Payin' good money for it, you are."

"Shut yer trap, Ollie," snarled Reeves. "Now, Miss, like I was saying, this here delivery ain't gonna keep long and we ain't gonna dally about. We wants our money and we wants to get. Where's the doc?"

Though she was loath to tell the likes of them that she was alone in the house, she could think of no other way to stall them. "He's on his way and should be here momentarily. If you'll just be kind enough to wait—" She started to shut the door, meaning to bolt it from inside, when Reeves slapped a meaty hand against the wood, levering it open.

"We wants our pay and we wants it now."

"Please—" Arabella cried, truly frightened as the man Ollie grabbed her arm and roughly shoved her aside. She stumbled and would have fallen if strong arms hadn't caught her from behind. She was righted and before she was aware of movement, Louis had crossed in front of her, his hand wedging beneath her assailant's chin, lifting him, all two hundred plus pounds of him, right off his feet. In a matter of seconds, the florid face took on a bluish cast and the man's feral eyes bugged. Louis was choking him.

"My lord, please!" She placed her hands upon his shoulders in a plaintive gesture. She could feel the raw power beneath her palms and the anger surging like an unstoppable tide. Ollie flopped within his crushing grip like a fish on a hook. "Louis, please. Release him," she insisted.

With one disdainful push, Ollie was propelled thirty feet backward, where he came to rest upon the cobbles of the mews. His shaking hands rose to his bruised throat, rubbing anxiously as he struggled for breath. But it was Louis's voice that put terror into him: so low, so certain.

"You touch her again and you will find someone digging you from your eternal rest."

There was an uneasy silence; then Reeves, always the businessman, stepped forward. "We weren't meaning the lady no harm, sir. We jus' be wantin' pay fer our night's work."

"And you will be paid when you return for the—

waste. Now, put that on the table inside, and be quick."

A wheezing Ollie scrambled up and warily helped his mate maneuver the corpse into Howland's office, while a greedy Reeves surveyed the finely dressed gent who shielded the doctor's daughter. My lord, she'd called him. If the bloke was of title, Reeves scented out a possible fortune to be made. He wasn't above blackmail, not at all, and even as his men were draping the lifeless body across the table, his mind was spinning, avidly hatching schemes of profit. When his two underlings scurried out, he made a show of doffing his tattered cap and grinned at the ashen-faced lady.

"Tell the good doctor that it's sorry we are that we missed him, but that we'll be back. He can count on it."

The door was slammed in his grinning face.

Very aware of the fragile figure clutching at his back, Louis turned slowly and let Arabella sag into his embrace. It was dangerous folly for him to hold her. He knew it, yet he couldn't resist. So warm and sweet, so filled with the pulsing of life. She nestled into him like a trusting kitten, shivering weakly, clinging with surprising strength. The thought of the street vermin placing her in jeopardy sent hot rage coursing through him, but the fact that he was the greater threat was slow to surface. Because he wanted her close, he wanted to enjoy the feel of her.

He lowered his face into the untidy spill of her dark hair. Soft, smelling of some crisp spring herb. He nuzzled those glossy tresses, nudging without real purpose until he found himself at her bared throat.

Sleek and fair. Vulnerable. He was drawn to the rapid beat channeling down that slender column and pressed his mouth against it, feeling the beat of life beckoning seductively. His eyes rolled and drifted shut and his hunger rose, cleverly disguised as passion.

A week, a long, torturous week since he'd last drawn nourishment. His insides burned with a glassy fire. So cold, so cruel, that searing heat, gnawing for want of satisfaction. He could feel the doctor's powders working in him. They blunted his perceptions, numbed his senses, reduced his powers. But they did nothing to curb his voracious appetite. The emptiness was like damnation, endless and agonizing. Inescapable. And the cure was here, offered so sweetly.

Wait. Howland is coming. Wait for him. Wait for a chance at life.

But he couldn't heed that internal command. The need was too strong, too immediate. And the monster within roared to life. An exquisite pain shot through his gums, lancing all the way up to his cheekbones, and he moaned softly into the smooth curve of her neck as the changes began that would allow him to sate his hunger. Hunger so fierce it was like madness. There was no hope of halting it until Arabella sighed, blissfully unaware of her precarious situation. Her hand lifted, touching shyly to the back of his head, stroking gently through his hair. And remarkably, inexplicably, the beast in him was tamed in an instant.

"Bella." My God, what had he been about to do?

She stirred in his arms, her face lifting, her gaze

beseeching. What did she see? Surely not the monster, for there was no fear or revulsion in her eyes, no hypnotized daze. Was it the man he'd been? He'd almost forgotten what that man was like, yet Arabella Howland brought memory back with the expectant part of her lips. And that man's desire was as strong as a fiend's hunger.

He cupped her cheek in his palm and felt her shiver at his touch. It was probably chilled, but she didn't withdraw. Instead, she leaned into him, her eyes slipping shut in anticipation of his kiss. Quickly he ran his tongue along the line of his teeth to make sure they were even. Then he lowered his head and took her eager lips with all the urgency of the man who'd walked three centuries before.

He couldn't remember the women of his time being so bold in their pursuit. Yet when Arabella encouraged his kisses most aggressively, he quite liked it. There was such a wellspring of natural passion to her, nothing cunning or calculated. She chased new sensations with a scientist's curiosity and a child's delight. And her enthusiasm carried him away with it.

Her mouth was warm and giving; slanting, tasting, teasing over his, tantalizing his senses to a provoking degree. The tip of her tongue danced along his lower lip before dipping in to tempt his into a fanciful waltz. When he would pull back in a circumspect caution, she caught his face between her palms, holding him still to prolong that thrusting, tangling union. Finally, he cuffed her wrists within his hands and gently, firmly pried her away.

And the sight of her all passion-flushed and panting was worse than the intoxicating taste of her kisses.

"Little one, you play with fire when you play with me," he rumbled. "Push too far and you will get burnt. You don't know what you're asking for."

With her eyelids at a sultry half-mast, she smiled and explained quite calmly, "I like to explore the unknown. The danger only adds to the challenge. I learned that from my father."

"And what I would teach you, your father would not wish you to know."

"Teach me, Louis." She pressed forward against the restraint of his grip, her bosom flattening upon his shirt front, her well-kissed lips moist and ready.

"No, *signorina*. The time is not right. It would be unwise and unsafe."

Her eyes flew open, registering her objections. "But, Louis—"

"Hush, little one." He glanced over his shoulder. "Your father is here."

Arabella heard nothing above the pounding of her own excited pulse, but then the door to her father's office opened and he stood there assessing the scene through eyes that grew outraged when they fixed upon her lightly bruised and swollen mouth.

"What is going on here? Would you please explain—"

Arabella took a quick stride forward, interrupting him with a grand gesture. "No, would you care to explain—this?"

The sight of the cadaver effectively distracted his temper. He crossed to the corpse with a disgraceful eagerness, waving a dismissing hand at his daughter.

"Leave us, Arabella."

She drew a deep breath, readying her protest when Louis lifted her hand in his. That breath stayed suspended as he carried her fingertips up for a light kiss. His eyes, bright and golden, delved into her own.

"Go," was all he said in a soft undertone, and despite her reluctance, she couldn't resist the command. Like the dreams. She was moving away, backing from the enticing sight of him even when she longed to stay. It was as if he was giving her a firm mental push, one she could not disobey.

When the door closed behind her, Stuart turned full attention to the body, well aware of the marquis lingering at his shoulder.

"The fools," he grumbled, as he checked the corpse's extremities. "The hypostasis is complete. See the way the underside of the body is discolored from the settling of blood? This man has been dead for more than eight hours." Then he looked up angrily at Louis. "What were you doing with my daughter?"

"I was kissing her," he revealed blandly.

"How?"

The yellowish eyes narrowed and the marquis's accent thickened as he drawled, "The way a man kisses a woman who wants to be kissed. Not with the sloppy greed of your pupil Pembrook." His features twisted with disgust. "It was of her own will."

"Was it? At least Wesley is human and I needn't fear for her life."

"Just for her virtue. I will be human again, too." And his eyes flared with a determination to match the doctor's. "Now, what must we do?"

Drawn back to the work at hand, Howland observed him carefully. "Your color is good. Have you—abstained?"

"Yes."

Stuart lifted up one of his hands, noting the chill of his unnaturally pale flesh. "How do you feel?"

"Weak."

The doctor glanced up chidingly. "And?"

"Hungry."

No comment. "Keep your hand up and out. I want to try something. Let's see how the serum is working. Quite a residual effect should have built up in your system by now."

Louis stood patiently, palm outstretched, until he saw what the doctor meant to place in it. He jerked back with a savage hiss of breath. "Silver."

"Yes. Now put your hand out."

"No."

"Do it."

Slowly his hand inched out and he held himself rigid while distrustful eyes watched the physician lower the silver-handled letter opener into the exposed well of his palm. Louis gasped when it touched, expecting a sear and sizzle that never came. Perplexed, he prodded the handle with a cautious forefinger, then lifted it with an amused smile.

"It doesn't burn. Normally, this much concentrated silver would have eaten right through my flesh."

"Good. Your resistance is building. And once we

remove the corrupt humors from your body and replenish it with a pure flow—"

"Do it now!"

"I'm afraid not."

"Why?" Louis was animated and wildly hopeful as he passed the bit of silver from hand to hand. He was on the edge of mortality; he could feel it. And he was impatient. "You have what you need. Let's get on with it."

"Radman, you probably know better than I how the blood thickens once the heart no longer circulates it through the body. The blood in those veins could not be transferred into your own."

"Blood is blood. I don't understand."

Howland took the opener from him and used it to make a deep cut in the dead man's wrist. What little fluid leaked from the gash was sluggish and dark. "See? Totally useless for my purposes."

The marquis grew very still. His gaze was riveted to that dark, vital flow. Even his breath stopped as Louis rubbed his fingertips along the table top, smearing them in the puddle of deep crimson. Then he brought them up to his mouth to suck them clean. He made a soft sound in his throat. It was a murmur of rapture. His voice had lowered a rumbling octave when he spoke.

"But not useless for mine."

Stuart Howland was a man of science and logic. Though he'd come to believe the marquis's story of vampirism, a part of him was still unaccepting ... until now. Until before his startled eyes, he saw exactly what a vampire was. As he watched, Louis Radman changed into something totally alien and totally terrifying.

It was the smell of blood. It acted upon Louis like a fever until his brain burned and he was conscious of nothing else. And the taste, the rich texture upon his tongue, goaded him into a frenzy of primal lust. For food. For life. For power. The allure was too great, the instinct too strong.

One puny mortal barring the way with a cry of, "No, you mustn't," had as much effect as a gnat to be swatted away. So, he did and with one casual flick, the good doctor went sailing across the room to crash against his bank of files and slide, dazed, to the floor.

With no more distractions, Louis sank down to savor the feast. He tore into the dead man's arteries, moaning with the ecstasy of it. Though there was no longer warmth, there was a dizzying fulfillment and an almost drunken delight in the act of drawing deep and swallowing. The sense of raging emptiness slowly abated as he went about his grisly meal. And then that insignificant human was back, pulling at him, trying to drag him away.

"Stop. You must stop."

Stuart was met with a growl and a hiss that was low, wet, and animal. The eyes glaring up at him were gold and red and terrible in their fury. Fully distended fangs gleamed sharp and deadly, tinged with the same gore that smeared mouth and chin. This was not Radman, who could be reasoned with. This was a demon. The undead.

Stuart did the only thing he could think of. He swung the letter opener, and as he'd hoped, the creature was quick to intercept it with a movement so liquid and sure, it was a blur to his eyes. Then came an obscene crackling, steaming as the silver lay clenched within Louis's hand. Howling, he released it, but the pain from the mark cut deep into his palm continued to burn. Clutching the afflicted hand to his chest, he staggered back, wailing horribly, features contorting into a nightmare of agony and disbelief. He reeled about in a blind haze, knocking over instrument stands and a fern basket before finally collapsing and curling up into a tight ball of misery.

"What have you done to me?" he cried, panting, thrashing against the throb of anguish that raced through his system like infectious fire.

"It's what you did to yourself," Stuart replied without sympathy, as he wiped away a trickle of blood from where the vampire had struck him. The man's strength—my God, it was incredible. And so was his torment, now. But Stuart was hesitant to approach.

"Are you in control again, my lord?"

"Yes," he hissed through gnashing teeth. And when he looked up, his eyes were hot and molten, but no longer unholy. The awful fangs had receded as well. Still, Stuart was understandably wary.

"If you will allow it, I might be able to help."

"Then help me," he snarled, levering himself up into a seated position. He hugged his hand, rocking over it as the agony swelled in rhythmic waves clouding his mind like a delirium. Then the doctor was bending over him, freeing his injured hand, sprinkling the scorched flesh with the same powder he'd been treated with over the past weeks. Slowly, almost gently, Howland bound his wound with clean linen as he spoke somberly of consequence.

"You understand now, don't you?"

"A rather cruel lesson, Doctor."

"But I made my point. Your recovery is only as certain as your resistance."

"And now that you've seen what I am, you can understand, too. You can see why I am so desperate to escape the hell of my existence. 'It will have blood; they say, blood will have blood'."

"Ah, Shakesphere. Macbeth, isn't it?"

"Clever Will could always turn an amusing phrase."

Stuart stared at him. "You knew—"

"I've known many people," Louis snapped tersely. "I've known kings, queens, poets, and princes. I've seen empires rise and fall. I have seen too much and I am so weary of continual change. I want to live no more than one natural lifetime. I am so tired of watching those I know and love die without me. I want only to sink into that natural sleep when my time comes."

"But it already came once, didn't it? You are—dead, aren't you?"

Louis gave him a wry smile. "Are you arguing philosophy with me, Doctor? 'I think, therefore, I am.' Well, I do and I am and I was cheated from the rest of my years. It was not my choice, this living damnation. Can you return that life which was stolen from me?"

"As I've said, I don't believe in demons."

Louis chuckled softly. How could the man say that with any conviction—now?

"I believe in science and I think what you are suffering from has to do with certain factors in your blood, a mutation, if you will, that acts upon the normal cells and warps them into something—inhuman. It's this alteration that produces your sensitivity to light and extreme allergic reaction to certain chemical properties like those found in silver and garlic. And heightens your dependence upon blood. Drain off the impurities and end the contagion."

"That simple."

"Not simple. But possible. How is your hand?"

Louis seemed surprised by the question. He flexed his fingers slowly and murmured, "Better." But to Howland's discerning eyes he still appeared gaunt and shaken from his usual stoic control. And suffering from the hunger.

There was a rapping on the rear door. "Rest," the doctor instructed, as he stood and went to see to the late-night visitors. Louis laid his head upon uplifted knees and did as he was told. He rested and he listened to Stuart Howland's conversation with Mac Reeves.

"The body you brought me was too old."

"Too old? You didn't go naming any age, now, did you?"

"Not age, you fool. He'd been dead too long. His body was already beginning to decompose. He was useless to me."

"Does that mean you aim to welsh on paying us?"

"I will pay you if you will listen and do as I say. Tomorrow night, bring me a recently deceased."

Tomorrow night. Louis seized upon that with an anxious thrill. Tomorrow night, then perhaps he could walk the daylight hours again. Just one more day of his unliving hell.

"How recently, gov?"

"Thirty minutes, no more."

"Where do you expect—"

"That's not my problem, now, is it? If you can't handle it, I can always call—"

"No, no. If the price be right, I can get you whatever it is you be wanting."

"Fine. Now, take away—that, and dispose of it discreetly. And be quick about it."

"Yessir. You 'eard him, mates. Grab on and let's get a move on."

As the burly twosome removed the corpse, Mac Reeves made careful note of the ragged wounds on the arm and the blood fresh on the face of the aristocrat huddled on the floor. Something foul and fishy was going on within these proper walls and he could just bet it wasn't something either of the gents would be pleased to hear on the morning gossips' tongues. Smiling to himself, he tipped his hat to the doctor and followed his men out. If they hurried, they could still unload the corpse to one of the hospital porters and the poor cove would end up on a surgeon's dissection table in the next day's lecture class.

When they were alone, Louis managed to totter to his feet. He wiped his face with his uninjured palm and refrained from licking his lips. The hunger was quieted by the taste he'd taken, but there was no sense in provoking it.

"Can you get home safely, my lord?"

Louis smiled. "I am immortal. What could happen?"

"Do not get—distracted again."

"I won't. Then tomorrow night, we're going to—"

"See about returning you to the living," Stuart concluded for him.

Chapter Six

Arabella had her questions waiting at the next morning's breakfast table. She still was unsure of how they'd escaped asking the night before. Something to do with Louis; his eyes, his voice. It was blurry in her mind. She must have been more weary than she'd imagined, for the moment she'd left the two of them with their unearthed companion, she'd gone straight to her room to a deep, unshakable slumber. She hadn't known when Louis had left the house or heard any of the commotion Bessie'd muttered about as breakfast was brought in. But she would have her answers now. Stuart, recognizing her expression, sat down warily and waited in silence for Bessie to serve him. Then, as soon as the servant left the room, he readied for the onslaught.

"Why did you have a body, still reeking of the grave, in your office last night?"

"Arabella—"

"I will not be put off like some child, Father. There were bodysnatchers at our door." Her voice had lowered out of respect for the subject matter, but it was no less intense. "I would like to know why you paid resurrectionists to bring the dead to our home."

"If they would change those damned restricting laws, we in the medical field wouldn't be forced to deal with men such as Reeves to see our research done. It's ridiculous to think the community could be served by the corpses of executed criminals when the number of medical students far outnumbers capital convictions."

"We are not arguing ethics here, Father, nor the law as it exists. I want to know what you were doing here in our house with that corpse."

Stuart took a moment to frame his answer as Bessie brought in a refill of coffee. Then he stated coolly, "As I said, research."

"On Louis Radman's blood disorder?"

His startled look said more than vague words.

"He told me," she continued smugly, pretending to know more than she did. But when her father's brow lowered in consternation, she wondered how wise that was.

"What did he tell you?"

Carefully, she sketched out the conversation she'd had with the marquis, and she couldn't miss the relief that colored her father's features. And she realized there was much about this research that she still didn't know. More secrets.

"So, exactly how does the deceased figure into your studies?"

"What do you know of blood transfusions?"

"I know that there have been cases of infusing the blood from one animal into another and that in

France, lamb's blood was successfully transfused into a boy but all that is highly experimental."

Calmly, as he was cutting his breakfast kidney, Stuart told her, "In Radman's case, what's required is a full fluid exchange."

Arabella stared at him, not understanding the connotations, and at the same time, very afraid she did. "You mean transferring the blood—"

"From one man into another. In Radman's case, from a recently deceased."

Arabella struggled to absorb the enormity of this plan. And the consequence. "You'll kill him. Father, you'll kill him." And a terrible panic settled inside her.

But Howland only smiled and chewed. "His lordship's mortality is the least of my worries. That he'll survive is not the problem. That it will be successful is."

"How could you endanger his life with such an untried practice?"

He quieted her outrage with the reassuring wave of his hand. "Radman is in no danger, Bella. Trust me on that. He realizes that this could be the only hope of curing his—condition, and he is prepared to take any chances necessary. And if it is successful, imagine the consequences."

That glaze of hard ambition crept into her father's face, the same look she so despised in Wesley Pembrook. Seeing it there upon his beloved features alarmed and appalled her. Because it told her he valued Louis Radman's life a lot less than the fame he might obtain from his manipulation of it.

"And another thing, my dear." He said that casually, in a manner that automatically alerted her. "I would prefer nothing of this go beyond the two of us. I needn't advise you of the danger should rumor spread that I am attempting such radical experimentation."

"You don't have to worry. I'll say nothing, but you'd be wise to guard yourself around Mr. Pembrook. He smells glory and will not be put off with pat answers."

"Leave Wesley to me." He didn't add that he'd had to put the eager student in his place during their meeting the day before; a meeting that had less to do, as he'd hoped, with his daughter's future than with Pembrook's ambitions.

"And what of Louis—his lordship?"

"What of him?"

"Does he know your plan to use his case in medical journals to further your own fame?"

He frowned at her. "That's a rather cold assessment, Bella."

"Am I wrong? If so, correct me."

He said nothing to alter her assumption. So she went one step further. "I would like to assist you."

"What?"

"I would like to help during the procedure—if his lordship has no objection."

Stuart smiled wryly. "Oh, I think he'll have plenty of objection, but you can help me prepare my office."

She took that small concession eagerly because she needed to be involved, she needed to assure herself that Louis's life was not in grave jeopardy. But she couldn't. Because she was terribly afraid that the untested experiment would end in tragedy, and with it, all her faint hopes of personal happiness.

She was in love with Louis Radman. She had no great experience in the matter, but the symptoms were all there. He was constantly upon her thoughts. She craved the sight of him, the sound of his voice, the touch of his hand. He was everything she'd ever dreamed of ... and more. And if that "more" was slightly scary, she was not discouraged. The attraction overwhelmed the apprehension. She only knew she wanted to be with him and that she wanted that togetherness to extend beyond the kisses they'd exchanged.

Now her father was threatening her dearest expectations, threatening the very man she loved by the greed of his ambition. She was well aware of the value the medical professionals placed on human life. Theirs was an empirical and unemotional view in which the one could be easily sacrificed for the sake of many. That callous attitude had never frightened her more than it did now. Because now, the man she wanted a future with was the source of her father's experimentation, and that placed her future upon very precarious ground. But there was nothing she could do except hold on to what she could and be there in case she could do more.

The condition of her father's office came as a shock. It looked as though a boxing match had been held in its interior. And then there was the table, with its gruesome stain of blood. She didn't want to think about what had gone on there or what would transpire that evening. She concentrated on the work at hand and as she tidied and organized, she grew more intrigued by the medical precedents her father was about to set.

"What's to keep the blood from coagulating before it's absorbed in the recipient's system?" In her curiosity, Arabella found her thoughts taking a clinical turn. That, she'd learned from her father. Professionalism meant a certain degree of distance, and she couldn't speak coherently on the matter if she thought of Louis's involvement.

"That took some trial-and-error, but by coating all the tubes and containers with moisture-resistant wax, I've found the clotting fails to occur if there's no contamination by air."

"And if his system fails to accept the donor's blood?"

"I don't anticipate that happening," came an unusually dry retort.

"If it does, what happens then?"

"In some cases, there's a rapid destruction of red cells which produces haemolytic shock and after extreme allergic manifestation, death." He spoke this matter-of-factly, then fixed his daughter with a piercing gaze. "Bella, what is your interest in this man?"

"I'm—interested, is all," she replied, bending quickly out of his sight to retrieve the physician's tools that had scattered beneath the table.

"And if I was to tell you this interest is very ill advised, would you heed me and stay away from him?"

She straightened and gave him a straight-on look and a painfully straight reply. "No."

Stuart sighed. "I was afraid that was the way of it. Bella, you are a most sensible girl. Surely you've realized that his lordship's condition is a grave one and often manifests aberrant and sometimes even dangerous behavior."

"But you can cure it," she concluded, with a poignant tug of hope.

"I believe so. But until we are certain, I want your promise that you will not spend time alone with him."

"But—"

"It's for your own safety that I make this request—as a doctor, not as an overprotective father. Please say you'll heed me on this."

Very quietly, she said, "I will," because she knew there was something not right with Louis Radman, something volatile and seducingly lethal, though every time she was with him, emotion overruled logic. Better she show some caution than regret impulse. There was no rush. He'd said his condition was not fatal, and her father had assured her he would survive the procedure. There was no reason for her to worry—except when her father brought in a second table and began to set up his experimental device for the pumping, storing, and delivering of blood, and she felt a certain faintness of heart that would not leave her.

By the time Louis arrived, shortly after nightfall, she was raw of nerve and struggling for composure. In a pinched voice, she asked for his coat, and her hands were shaking as she accepted it. She couldn't meet his gaze though she felt it, intense and probing, upon her. Passing the heavy greatcoat to a disapproving Miss Kampford, who carried it away, Arabella murmured, "If you will come with me, my lord, I believe my father is ready."

As she turned from him, blinking back an insistent moisture, his long fingers curled about hers, drawing her up, drawing her close. He said her name in that low, caressing tone, and everything inside her quivered in response. Still she wouldn't look up at him. He cupped her chin in his other palm and slowly raised it, gently forcing a linking eye contact. His fingertips soothed away the reluctant trail of tears.

"What is it, little one?"

Little one. Such an odd endearment, as she was hardly slight, young, or fragile. But he made her feel small and vulnerable with his soothing presence.

"Do you fear for me?"

That was painfully evident, yet still she strove to erect a brave front before his probing gaze. "My father has assured me that you will be fine."

"Believe him."

She nodded jerkily. Her fingers laced tightly through his and she pushed her cheek into the well of his palm, washing his thumb with a series of quick, damp kisses.

"Bella."

It was a quiet rumble. Then his hand speared back, knifing through the careful arrangement of her hair, yanking her forward and wrenching her head up for the sudden hard possession of his mouth. It was a necessarily brief but wild union of thrusting tongues and tortured breaths then he dragged her away.

"When it is done and all is well, I should like very much to pursue this with you."

"Yes," was all she could manage in a weak little voice.

"Your father is waiting."

Sobered by that statement, Arabella scrubbed her cheeks with trembling fingers and nodded. "This way, my lord." And as she led, she was very aware that he continued to hold to her other hand.

Stuart's office was agleam with artificial light, all its surfaces clean and clinical. When Arabella hesitated at the doorway, Louis nudged her forward with a gentle bump.

"Ah, there you are, Radman. Shall we get started? Bella, you may go."

Contrarily, her fingers clenched about the marquis's. In a strong voice, she said, "I should like to stay. I have assisted my father in many studies, and think I could be of help."

She looked to Louis, her features calm and competent, her eyes beseeching. He weighed her request for a long moment, plumbing the depths of her gaze with an intense scrutiny before giving a brisk nod.

"Very well." But as she expelled a breath of relief, he followed it with a soft warning. "Do not be afraid of what you might see."

"Arabella, take the marquis's outerwear, if you please." Once Louis made the decision to allow her to remain, Howland seemed content with it. He knew his daughter was more than capable to assist. However, as she carried Louis's fine jacket and waistcoat away, he touched her arm meaningfully and told her, "Stay, but do not interfere and do not ask questions."

"Yes, Father." She was happy to comply with any terms so long as she could be close.

Stuart dismissed her from his thoughts and busied himself with his radical invention, and odd assemblage of tubing connected to a glass receptacle and a bellowslike hand pump. "My lord, on the table, if you would. How is the hand?"

Louis extended it palm up to show the unscarred flesh. "Nicely healed. At one time, such a wound would have taken years, even decades to repair."

And as she promised, Arabella asked no questions, though they were burning to be spoken.

Once Louis was stretched out upon the lower of the two tables, Stuart lifted a heavy leather strap and draped it across the prone man's ankles before feeding it through a buckle secured on the other side. Louis was immediately wary.

"What is that for?"

"Safety."

He chuckled low and cynically. "Mine or yours, Doctor?"

"Both," came the candid reply. "Once the procedure begins, you must be completely still."

Louis shifted his feet, testing the bonds. His mouth pursed. "Do you think to hold me with such flimsy ties?"

Stuart was busy buckling a second strap across his sturdy thighs. "Indeed." Another pulled across Louis's broad chest and secured his left wrist. His right arm remained free. Then, Stuart placed a heavy crucifix upon the snowy shirt front, and Louis inhaled sharply. The crucifix was made of solid silver.

The sudden display of Louis's distress was almost as peculiar to Arabella as her father's use of the religious symbol. Was there some significance she was missing? A morbid reminder of the last rites that had the marquis so upset?

"Take it off."

Then her father's strange comment. "Does it burn you?"

"No, but I can't breathe." He was taking short, suffocating gasps for air, as if the cross had a mass a thousand times greater and a weight dense enough to crack ribs. "Take it off!"

"I think not, my lord. Relax. Don't fight against it. It's for your own benefit."

He thrashed, contrarily, within the bindings, but the movements were weak and ineffective, as if the cross was exerting a tremendous downward pressure. Finally, Louis surrendered and lay panting shallowly, a gleam of fury glittering in his amber eyes. When Stuart drew near, talonlike fingers shot out to clench the doctor's throat. Stuart showed no sign of alarm even as his daughter gasped. Easily he caught the marquis's wrist and pulled.

"Release me, my lord. We were going to trust one another, remember?"

"This is not a measure of trust, Doctor."

"It is one of caution. Now, let me go, or we will forget the entire matter." Powerful fingers opened and Stuart stepped back to a safe distance. "Arabella, bring me that basin."

When she broke her puzzled trance and did so, Stuart positioned the bowl beneath the dangle of Louis's right arm and pushed up his shirt sleeve.

"What are you going to do?" she asked, ignoring her vow to be silent.

"Bleed him, of course. The foul humors must be removed first." And he tied off Louis's forearm to encourage the swelling of an appropriate vein.

Arabella held to her skepticism. Though bloodletting was an accepted practice, she had never fully supported it. Theories that it restored vessels which had collapsed under the weight of too much blood sounded farfetched to her. There was something amiss when physicians were more concerned with spilling blood than with staunching it. The only advantage she could see was that once a patient was bled white, he was too lethargic to be much trouble and rested because he was too weak to do otherwise.

"Hold the bowl, Bella." With that, Stuart cut open an engorged vein with a quick slash of his lancet. The instant he released the tourniquet, the steady purge of blood began.

"An irony of sorts, wouldn't you agree, Doctor?" Louis smiled wryly and closed his eyes. And the basin grew heavy in Arabella's hands.

After what seemed like an interminable time, when the streaming rush of crimson had slowed to a weak trickle, she risked a glimpse at Louis's calm features and knew a shock of alarm. They were more than pale; they were translucent. Taut skin hugged the bold angles of his bone structure, creating frightening caverns and ridges. His respiration had dwindled until she could detect no movement. Even his lips had taken on a bluish tinge.

"My lord, are you all right? Louis? Father?" She looked about in a panic, but he had left the room. And she was alone with a man she was sure was dying.

Setting down the full basin, she bent near, touching unsteady fingertips to a throat as cold and immobile as marble. Nothing. "Louis? Oh, God, no." As her hand frantically stroked one chill cheek, dark lashes flickered against them and she could hear the faint expulsion of breath. "Louis, can you hear me?"

"C-cold. So cold."

And his eyes opened, eyes that were cold and glazed and streaked with red. They fixed upon her, effecting a sudden paralysis. Moving fast, so fast it was almost impossible to track, his hand flashed out, twisting in her hair, slamming her down across him. Momentarily winded, she couldn't struggle, but gasped a pitiful "No—" as her head was wrenched by the powerful grasp until tendons strained in her neck. She felt his breath—not hot, but icy—upon that bared bend and the brush of his lips, colder still.

"Louis—"

Her heart was hammering wildly as ungoverned terror surged. Such strength he had, such unimaginable strength. And the sound he made, that deep, vibrating sound, no more human than the growl of a wolf or the snarl of a panther.

"The cross—remove the cross," came his harshly grating voice. "Now!"

"No—"

"Take it off, or I will—I will—" He broke off, panting raggedly. Abruptly, his imprisoning hand opened and she was able to bolt back to safety on wobbly legs.

Pinned inexplicably beneath the gleam of silver, Louis twisted and writhed, jerking against the binding straps with restless, helpless movements. One look at him alerted Stuart Howland upon his return from his study with a journal in which he meant to make notes, and he was quick to race to his daughter's side.

"Bella, did he harm you?"

"No," she whispered.

"Charlatan," Louis roared. "Release me."

"I think not, my lord," he murmured grimly, as he hurriedly secured the free arm to the table with another heavy restraint. "Here. Drink this. It will help."

Louis stared at the cup he offered, his gaze black with fear and a frustrated fury. Then he lifted to obediently swallow down the potion, letting his head fall back and his eyes close as he waited for the powders to work. He fell once more into that almost comalike state that so alarmed Arabella.

Seeing his daughter's strained expression, Stuart patted her arm and reminded her, "You asked to be here, my dear. I didn't promise it would be pleasant."

"What's wrong with him?"

"It's nothing that can be explained away with simple science." But the rest of his explanation was halted by a staccato tapping on the rear door. When Stuart went to answer it, the dim light revealed Mac Reeves and his henchmen and the slumped figure of a man, a man whose head was lolling loosely on his shoulders.

"Fresh enough for you, Doc?" the sinister Reeves queried with an awful grin.

Then the man they restrained groaned and one quick jerk wrought a snap and a telling silence.

"Pay up, gov."

"Place him on the table," Stuart said without inflection.

As they did the gruesome deed, one remarked, "Looks like you gots yer corpse already. Whatcha meanin' to do, what with two of 'em?"

"It's none of your concern, now, is it?" Then Stuart flashed the payment and it was snapped up by a greedy Reeves.

"None o' our business a-tall. G'night, Doc, Missy."

As Stuart began to prepare the newly deceased, he was aware of Arabella's horrified stare. He challenged it with a fierce look of his own.

"We've seen murder done," she whispered hoarsely.

Chapter Seven

"Are you here to help or theorize?" Stuart Howland snapped. He waited, his expression hard and unrepentant in that midnight hour. Then he softened just a bit. "Bella, we are not to blame for the activities of men such as Reeves. We can stand here and argue the humanitarian and legal aspects all night, but that will not serve his lordship. I am a scientist, not a theologian, and I refuse to apologize for that. Every minute we wait, the risk triples. Are you going to help, or do you prefer to wait until our donor's blood is the consistency of clotted cream?"

Arabella's gaze lingered on Louis, who looked every bit as deathlike as the graverobber's victim. Then she swallowed convulsively and braced her resolve.

"What would you have me do?"

"Good girl. Come over here and work these bellows when I tell you. Do not stop until I tell you. Keep up a steady rhythm."

She did as told and soon her father had the warm corpse hooked to his transfusing machine and bade her to begin the pumping. Vital fluid trickled into the bottom of the glass catch bottle, tracking it in a slow, vivid circle, then pooled thick with increasing volume. As soon as the level rose to the top, Stuart shoved up the marquis's other sleeve, slit a vein, and inserted the end of a quill he'd attached to the tubing. Then he went to tie off the other arm so they wouldn't lose any of the new flow entering his body.

Haemolytic shock and agonizing death, her father had said. Arabella held her breath and continued to work the bellows. For a time, both donor and recipient were equally still, equally pale. Then a rattly sighing breath shook through Louis and he began to gasp in labored gulps. With his eyes still closed, he tossed his head from side to side, the movement growing more and more violent. His hands began to work at his sides, fingers scrabbling, tearing at the wood like claws. Knees snapped up against the belts and buckles as his body warped frantically atop the table.

"Keep going," Stuart commanded when Arabella's tempo lagged. "You can't stop now."

With anguished tears bright in her eyes, she continued.

Stuart moved to adjust and tighten the strap on Louis's left arm to stop the quill from being pulled loose. He was concentrating on that task and didn't notice when the marquis's eyes opened. But Arabella did, and she screamed an instinctive warning. For the gaze was wild and blood-red and alive with hatred and pain.

With a howling roar, Louis jerked his right arm free, ripping through thick leather like it was paper and the metal fasteners as if they were cheap tin. He grabbed Stuart Howland by the shoulder. Had he caught him by the neck, the doctor would have been killed instantly. As it was, hooked fingers bit right to bone, tearing flesh and muscle until Howland bent across him, maneuvering so that the back of Louis's hand brushed the silver cross. And shrieking, Louis let him go.

Stuart stagged back, clutching at his injured shoulder. "Don't stop," he yelled at Arabella, who seemed ready to fall into shock herself, because she couldn't look away from those red eyes flaring with such fierce and primal fury, eyes that fastened upon hers and burned right to her soul.

She felt his words batter against her conscious mind.

Arabella, the cross. Lift the cross.

She tried to shake her head, but the daze deepened. His voice increased and intensified in its silent demand.

Arabella, take away the cross. Free me.

And she was reaching numbly, dutifully ... until her father slapped her. The sting of it woke her and she blinked at him stupidly, unaware of what she'd been about to do.

"Work the bellows, child," Stuart instructed firmly, and she nodded, close to tears and not certain why.

On the table top, the mad thing lunged from side to side, unable to escape the weight of silver upon his chest. Arabella couldn't think of it as Louis anymore, not after what he'd done to her father. Not the way he—looked. She was no longer afraid that he was dying. Not with that superhuman strength. He was alive and alert and angry and hurting. Unnaturally sharp teeth gnashed and chomped in a wild rage, gashing his lower lip and spraying a cold spittle. In her mind, no single word formed to describe what she was seeing, no name for the creature writhing on the table. Logic couldn't contain it. She was too scared, her arms too tired from plying the bellows up and down, for theory or fantasy to take root. She accepted what she saw and didn't try to make sense of it.

Finally, the reluctant donor was emptied. The last of the lifegiving fluid passed into the demented being half-strapped and totally dangerous on the next table. Stuart, who was all but unconscious from his own injuries, cautiously withdrew the quill shunt and bound the marquis's arm before sinking to the floor in a swoon.

She couldn't be sure how much time passed while she stood in the shivery stupor, unable to act, unable to think rational thoughts. Then, finally, Louis called to her. It was Louis, not that thrashing, snarling, fiendish thing of moments ago. Not the thing with a name she couldn't speak.

"Bella?"

And he sounded so weak, so fragile, she went to him without hesitation, so grateful she was in tears. "Oh, Louis, are you all right?"

"Burning. Burning."

She saw the blistering welt on his hand as she took it up in hers. She remembered seeing his flesh actually smoke when it touched the silver crucifix, another odd occurrence she couldn't begin to explain. "Your poor hand."

"No," he moaned. "The blood—it's burning. Not

so bad now. Not so bad." And his eyes opened, their color a deep green, and his gaze slowly swept the area. "Your father—?"

"Father!"

She knelt down within the tight wrap of her skirt and bent over the doctor's huddled figure. The wound in his shoulder was ghastly, but he was fighting his way back to awareness. And the first thing he thought of was not his health, but his work.

"The transfer—"

"Was a success," she told him. When he struggled to sit up, she tried to restrain him. "No, you must stay still. You must rest."

"No. Help me up, Bella. I must see for myself."

He was too determined to be discouraged by her words or his own discomfort, so reluctantly, Arabella supplied her support, and together they wrestled him to his feet. Steadying himself by gripping the edge of the table, Stuart exchanged a long look with Louis Radman.

"How do you feel, my lord?"

"About as well as you look, Doctor."

With an unsteady hand, Stuart felt the marquis's sweat-dappled brow and lean cheeks, confirming the warmth Louis's ruddy color suggested. He peered into the clear eyes and then strangely lifted his patient's upper lip to check, Arabella supposed, the color of his gums. Or the length of his teeth. That shivered through her, but still her mind fought against it. As Stuart counted pulsebeats, Louis reached up to lift the cross from his chest. He stared at it in his hand, then gave a raspy chuckle as he lifted the crucifix to his lips and let it fall aside.

"Am I cured, then?" he asked the doctor, with a hesitant optimism.

"Time will tell, my lord. Do you feel any different?"

"Weak. I feel weak, and my mind is slow. I'm not sure."

Stuart wanted to be sure. He pressed his fingertips to his own slow-bleeding wound, then touched them to Louis's mouth. The marquis tasted the smear of crimson with the tip of his tongue, then reflexively wiped it away with the back of his hand. And froze as the significance sank deep.

"Bella, fetch his lordship some water." And when she moved out of earshot, Stuart leaned closer. "What is it, Radman? Is the impulse gone?"

He stared hard at the doctor's torn flesh, but nothing other than a mild revulsion and a wince of guilt stirred within him. No frenzy to feed. No hunger. No thirst. And that was unheard of, for he was always hungry. For three hundred years, the sight of blood brought instant, desperate craving, even after he'd taken his fill. But now the ache in his throat itched for thinner substance, like the cool water Arabella tipped up to his lips. He drank slowly, with caution, for his system was unused to accepting anything other than the vile food of his existence. Yet the water slid down easily, quenching his thirst with a satisfaction he'd long forgotten.

And as he lay back, eyes closed, he murmured, "Dear God, can it be true?"

"Perhaps a side effect from the transfusion," Stuart warned. "We must proceed with care, my lord. Do not assume too much just yet. The dawn will tell."

Louis's eyes snapped open. "The time. What time is it?"

Arabella checked the small watch pinned to her bodice. "Shortly after half past four." Already? The night was nearly gone and she was amazed by its rapid passing.

"I must get home." He tugged against the restraints. "Release me."

"You are too weak yet, my lord," Arabella protested, not understanding his urgency. Louis wouldn't listen.

"I must go."

"It's the only way to be sure," Stuart told him.

Louis took a quick, panicked breath. "I'm not ready. If you are wrong—" He yanked at the straps, but there was none of his phenomenal strength left.

It was then Stuart Howland collapsed. Arabella managed to catch him and guide him through the office into the comfort of his study. There, she eased him down onto the couch and quickly applied a pad of gauze to the gaping wound in his shoulder.

"Radman," he was panting faintly. "I must know. Do not release him ... I must know."

"Rest, Father. You've lost much blood and your body is in shock from it. You need medical attention. What do you want me to do?"

"Send for Wesley."

"No." Her every instinct rebelled against it.

"We've no other choice. I cannot handle things here."

"What will you tell him?"

"The truth."

Not knowing the whole truth didn't keep Arabella

from wanting to keep it from ones such as Wesley Pembrook. "No, Father, you can't."

"I need help, with my arm, with Radman. There is much to do, to explain." He was growing weaker by the second. Something had to be done.

But Arabella couldn't cast Louis's fate upon a jackal like Wesley.

"Rest, Father. I will see to everything. I'll send for Wesley. I'll tell him you were attacked by the graverobbers who tried to steal from you. I'll tell him you were experimenting with transfusion. But you mustn't mention his lordship. You must not tell him of your success. Father, do you hear me?"

But Stuart had faded out of consciousness, and worry for him supplanted all else. She raced to the outer door, and when she jerked it open, discovered a very pale Bessie Kampford.

"Miss, be you all right? Those horrid screams and goings-on. What—"

"Mrs. Kampford, listen to me carefully." Arabella's crisp tone steadied the loyal servant. "I want you to send for Mr. Pembrook. There's been an accident. The doctor has been injured." She spoke over the older woman's gasp. "Listen to me. You must be discreet. No word of this can get out. I'll explain all to you later. Order up a hack and have it brought around back immediately. Then I want you to sit with Father until Mr. Pembrook comes."

"You'll not use our own carriage?"

"No."

"But what about you, Miss? And *him?*" She nodded toward the office meaningfully.

"Do not concern yourself over his lordship. As far

as you know, he was never here this evening. Do you understand? He was never here."

Bessie's eyes were round with fright, but a deeper light of protectiveness prevailed. No matter what the trouble was, she would see it spared her beloved employers. "You can count on me, Miss."

"I know I can, Bessie." And she leaned forward to give the tiny woman a hug. "Now, go see to what I told you. Hurry, and be silent."

"Yes, Miss."

As Bessie scurried off to do her bidding, Arabella raked a trembling hand through the disarray of her hair. It was madness, what she was doing. She should do nothing and let Wesley assume control when he arrived. She was in far over her head and flailing. But a deep, driving instinct told her to guard Louis's secret from the world—no matter what it took, no matter how gravely it placed her own life in jeopardy. That's what scientists did. That's what love required.

She found her father lost to consciousness but in no further danger, so she rushed into the office. The room was an incredible shock to the visual senses: the violated corpse, the splatters of blood everywhere, the figure of Louis Radman secured by straps. It was a scene out of Bedlam, but she ignored it all as she went to Louis's side. He turned toward her, the movement an obvious effort. His face was flushed and fever dampened, his respiration fast and light. And he spoke to her with a quiet anxiousness.

"Please, I must go now. I must get home before the dawn. Release me, Bella. Please. I am no danger to you."

Was she crazy to believe that, after what she'd witnessed? Still, she touched his cheek with gentle fingertips. "Trust me, Louis."

He regarded her for a long moment, then nodded. She sensed what a tremendous confidence that was and vowed not to betray it. Quickly, she worked the buckles loose and threw off the straps.

"Are you strong enough to stand?" She could hear the sound of hoofs clattering on cobbles in the mews. Their transportation had arrived.

"Help me."

Common sense told her he shouldn't be moved, but the situation called for expedience. Slipping her arm beneath his shoulders, she lifted. He was weak and very unsure of his footing, but she managed to get him to the door, leaving a scene behind that would plague Wesley with questions. She couldn't care about that just yet, not until she had Louis somewhere safe.

After he mumbled an address to the hired driver, Louis dragged himself up into the body of the rig, and there his strength gave out. Throughout the jostling ride, he lay slumped in Arabella's lap, his head cradled in her arms while awareness drifted. All he recognized was her cool touch and the occasional calming whisper of her words. He surrendered to both, trusting her.

Arabella knew enough about the human condition to know Louis Radman was in desperate straits. She considered taking him to the hospital for the professional care she couldn't provide, but quickly dismissed that notion. The hospital was a place where the unfortunate went to die. And Louis wasn't going to die, not if she could help it.

The neighborhood they traveled to was one of quietly neglected elegance. The homes were large and separate, the addresses not fashionable, but still respectable. Just the place someone of retiring nature would seek to be alone. No one there would take notice of another's comings and goings, so she wasn't concerned with her reputation. Not that she'd worry, anyway. All that concerned her was the figure thrust into her care. And he was all-important.

The rig jerked to a rocking stop in front of a brooding gothic-style manse. A single light shone in the interior in one of the downstairs rooms. It was the only light burning in this cool predawn hour. Someone was up, waiting for Louis to come home. It was then Arabella realized how little she knew of him. She knew only what she'd seen, and even that, on this night of shocks and surprises, she could scarcely credit.

"You be wantin' me to wait, ma'am?" the driver called down, as she pushed open the door.

"Yes, if you please." As curious as she was about Louis's world within, she recalled her promise not to linger in his presence alone. And she was concerned about her father and what conclusions Wesley was coming to. First, she had to see Louis inside, so she shook him gently. "My lord, we are home." She hadn't meant to say it exactly that way, but how nice it sounded, so shared and intimate. And in her lap, Louis stirred with a moan. "You must help me get you inside. Can you stand?"

He attempted it with little success. Where had all that incredible strength gone? He managed to drag himself upright, but slouched there, sagging back against the squabs of the carriage, his expression ghastly in the lamplit interior.

"Louis?" She touched her palm to his cheek. It was hot and fever slicked. "Should I see you to the hospital?"

That brought his eyes open and a weak negating shake of his head. "Help me inside," came his hoarse instruction. "I'll be all right then."

"Are you certain? We have no way of knowing how father's treatment will affect you."

"Inside. Hurry."

Together they navigated what was luckily a short walk to the front door. It opened as they approached. There, instead of the expected stuffy servant, stood a slender boy. His features were Asian, and at the moment, drawn with wariness. Arabella guessed his age at perhaps fourteen. His black-eyed gaze flashed in rapid uncertainty between them. He didn't look inclined to let them inside.

"I am Arabella Howland. His lordship is a patient of my father, Doctor Stuart Howland. Do you understand English?"

The boy stepped back, opening the door wider so she could haul the stumbling Louis over the threshold. Then, without a word to her, he slipped his narrow shoulders beneath Louis's other arm. As he shut the door, the first pale grays of dawn were beginning to highlight the eastern sky.

Arabella had the vague impression of crowding elegance and unused spaciousness as they passed several open rooms. The pervading atmosphere was one of damp mustiness, as if the house had been uninhabited for decades. When they reached a door at the end of the wide hall, the boy stopped, his hand on the knob, as if unsure of whether to go farther. And slowly, Louis withdrew his arm from about Arabella's shoulders.

"Louis—"

"Go home, Arabella."

"I can't just leave you like this. What if you need help? What if you need—me?"

He gave her a small sketch of a smile and let his knuckles trail lightly down one pale cheek. "Return to your home, my love. There is nothing you can do for me now. I will come to you when I can. Go, now."

And he nodded to the boy, who was quick to open the heavy door. She could see stone steps leading downward into impenetrable darkness.

"Louis—"

"Go, Bella."

It was after the door was closed between them that the words he'd used settled deep.

My love.

"Louis!"

She tried the knob, but it wouldn't give. The door was locked from the inside. She leaned against the barring portal and closed her eyes.

My love.

Louis sank down into an unnatural rest—unnatural, because it was no rest at all.

When the sealing darkness closed over him, thought and sensation should have ceased, becoming the faint twilight sleep he was expecting. Instead, he was all too aware of things: of the throbbing wounds in hand and arms where he'd been seared and pierced at the Howlands' home. The burning tingle continued with the pulse of new blood through his body. It was an odd awareness, the feeling of warmth, the threads of pain and weariness. They should have been lost to him with the coming of dawn.

Also new to him, and somewhat frightening, was the sense of aloneness. Adrift in complete blackness, he tried to reach out to make a mental link. Nothing. His calls were unanswered. His thoughts stretched out into emptiness. A seeping panic stole over him as he tried and failed again to make that psychic connection. He could hear his heart beating wildly, pumping new blood, new life, as his shallow breaths filled the confining space with moisture. Where was the deep sense of peace he longed for? Where was the disassociating rest? His mind continued to turn frantically and his awareness steeped with smothering sensation, not of the outside world, but of the world within this small enclosure. Finally, it was his own weakness that dulled his mind and quieted his panic. And he slept.

Even the nature of that sleep disturbed him. He was conscious not of peripheral matters, like the sound of footsteps overheard or of the whir of carriages on the street out front. He was plagued by strange images, and with some surprise, he recognized them as dreams. Dreams! As in mortal sleep.

And when he woke, it wasn't with the abrupt surge of sharp and total control. It was a dragging sort of lassitude, a reluctant arrival at a conscious state. He hurt. His body ached, his head pounded. Muscles felt cramped, skin cold. An odd rumbling stirred through his belly, an emptiness that was hunger, but not compulsion. He didn't understand, and he was afraid. He sent an urgent call, a silent command but it went no farther than the limits of his mind. My God, what was happening?

He pushed up with his palms and his arms actually shook with the effort of lifting the silk-lined lid. In the mellow glow of lantern light, he shoved up his shirt sleeves. Flesh that should have been healed to a smooth, unmarried surface showed sore-looking cuts where Howland had spliced into his veins.

"Takeo?"

His voice echoed in the cavernous underground room, as thin and weak as he felt inside.

He climbed out of his resting place. What was usually accomplished with a lithe hop was managed with much groaning and crawling indignity before an unceremonious tumble to the ground. For a time he stayed on hands and knees, aware of how the cold seeped up from the hard-packed dirt floor, more aware still of how badly his limbs were shaking. What was this terrible frailty? Howland. He had to get to Howland to demand an answer.

Feeling as drained and depleted of energy as one of his victims, Louis stumbled up the stairs. His perceptions were so muted and uncertain, he didn't know what to expect when he opened the door at the top. Certainly not daylight.

With a fearful gasp, he sank back into the shadows. My God, daylight. He'd lived so long within the glow of artificial brilliance he'd forgotten how beautiful it was, how it shimmered and how it warmed.

But he remembered how it burned. He remembered quite vividly the scorch of his flesh and the crisping of tiny white-hot flames when he'd been just a bit too slow in beating the dawn back to his lair. It had taken three decades for those wounds to heal. It wasn't a lesson easily dismissed, so he was understandably cautious when viewing those sunbeams pooling with beckoning innocence in the upper hall.

Why hadn't he known it was still daytime? What was wrong with him?

Then a wondrous revelation struck him.

What if it had worked?

What if he was now mortal?

Howland had said there was one sure way to test that theory to prove success: if he came up and exposed himself to the pristine light of day and wasn't consumed to ashes within seconds—a rather somber test. He hesitated, crouching like a wary animal upon those cold stone steps. None of his usual powers served him. His senses were isolated and frustratingly leashed within normal limits. How was he to know, unless . . .

He crept forward an inch at a time, pushing his outstretched hand along the wool carpet runner to the soft white edge of light, then nudged it further, just a tad. Fingertips dipped into that bright circle. He sucked a startled breath. He felt heat: warm, welcoming heat. No instantaneous combustion of flesh into flames. So he went further, delving into that stream of daylight, trembling with anxiousness, with hope.

Then, with a ragged little laugh, he rolled onto his back, reaching his face up to the midday hour, basking, soaking up the warmth the way a contented housecat might. When he felt wetness upon his cheeks, he realized he was weeping with the sheer wonder of it. How long had it been? Too long. Centuries too long.

He lay there on the runner for leisurely minutes, closing his eyes to the intensity, opening his soul to the heat. Simply absorbing the natural rays.

"Louis?"

The quiet call took him unawares, and his eyes sprang open in alarm. Then the sense of wonder deepened to a dazed amazement.

Nothing had ever looked so breath-stealingly beautiful as the sight of Arabella Howland wreathed in sunlight.

Chapter Eight

"Louis, what are you doing down there? Are you all right?"

He was grinning wide, his face was wet, and he began to laugh with a breathless excitement. "I'm not sure I can get up, so you must come down here to me."

He stretched up his hand and, bemused, Arabella took it, allowing herself to be pulled down to the floor in an awkward twist of her cocoonlike skirt. And with his hands capping her shoulders, he led her over him, down upon his chest, and down upon his eager mouth. Their kiss was long, deep, and sweetened by relief. Louis soaked it up like warm sunshine. Then, finally, he rolled up over her, bridging his forearms on either side of her head so he could look down upon her.

"What are you doing here, Bella?" he asked at last.

"I brought you home. Remember?"

"Vaguely, just vaguely."

"And—and I could not leave until I knew all was well with you. I was waiting for your servant to ask him how you were. I must have fallen asleep in your parlor. I fear our carriage driver will demand a fortune in payment." Then her expression deepened. "I was so worried."

There was no coquettish flicker of lashes, no modest blush. She gazed up at him with an unashamed intensity. With a self-sacrificing love.

He touched her face with the rub of either thumb, sketching over the exquisite lines in a leisurely glide. "That was not a wise thing to do," he told her, lowering as he did so that their breaths mingled and their lips parted with anticipation.

"It didn't matter," she replied with heartshaking candor. "I was not afraid of you, only for you."

His smile was faint, his voice bittersweet. "Bella, you are far too brave for your own good." Then his expression altered and his tone altered, both growing quiet and somewhat awed. "And so beautiful."

She was about to smile and chastise him for his flattery, for she knew it was not true. She'd slept on his sofa. Her hair was a tangle, her eyes puffy from lack of rest and worry. Her gown was crumpled and stained with grim doings in her father's lab. But she couldn't speak or chide him. Because the soft glow in his gaze confirmed his words and the soft pressure of his mouth atop hers sealed them as truth.

Beneath that warm, attentive kiss, it was so easy to dismiss the fact that she was lying under him on the floor of his hall. When his fingers combed through her loosened hair with a gentle tug and a luxurious kneading massage, it was simple to forget her panic of the night before. The things she'd seen, the horrors she'd considered, seemed far removed, indeed. A nightmare compared to this sweet heaven. When she took his warm, lean face between her palms and felt his kiss deepen in response, it seemed the most unlikely madness that she could have thought of him as something unnatural, as something unwholesome. Sheer emotional folly conceived of fright and unusual stresses. That was all. Not real, not like this. Not like the feel of him above her in the clean spill of daylight. Not like the pure and not-so-pure feelings that surged with his meagerest touch. It had been a violent physical reaction to an untested experiment, not a transformation into an unholy monster. And to drive away the guilt for having entertained such insanity as possibility, she spoke out with complete honesty by saying the one thing she was totally sure of.

"I love you, Louis."

Instead of looking pleased or even offended by her forward speech, Louis was guarded and all too somber.

"You do not know me, Arabella."

"I know enough," she argued. And he smiled at her tenacity.

"Not near enough. But you will. We shall discover it together, for I have forgotten much of what I was."

She didn't question his odd statement because he was kissing her again, and when he was kissing her, no rational process could overcome the pleasure. And it was a pleasure, pure and simple, having his weight distributed along her body, having his mouth mold hers into the shape of passion. She'd waited too long to experience this paradise to be shaken from it by doubts or false propriety. This was the man she wanted. The man she'd yearned for all her life within the forum of her maiden's dreams, and if he were not so weak, if they were somewhere other than the hall floor, she'd have stripped off her gown and her governing principles without hesitation to enjoy him to the fullest and most desirable degree.

Then Louis levered up and his smile was wrought with amusement. "We are lying on the floor. Does that not strike you as a trifle odd?"

"No more so than any of the occurrences of the last few nights."

He eased off her and she felt the absence keenly.

"Come. We must seek out your father. I have many questions for him, and I am sure he has them for me. What is the time?"

As they both sat up on the hall runner, Arabella checked her watch. "Eleven."

"Eleven in the morning," he mused, with a wistfulness lost to her. He took a deep, sighing breath and closed his eyes as he expelled it with a savoring leisure.

"Louis? How do you feel?"

His eyes slit open and he smiled at her. "Awful. Wonderful." Then he extended his hands. "Help me up. I must change into something—presentable." Glancing down, he was chagrined by the state of his clothing, for much of the blood dried to brownish blotches was not his own. "Your father will be frantic."

Her father! Yes, she must get home. But still, she knew his condition not to be life threatening, and being here with Louis ...

Arabella assisted him up, and as they stood, toe-to-

toe and nearly eye-to-eye, she was struck by the difference in him. It was more than the way the daylight warmed his features, softening the taut edges given by evening shadow. There was a vulnerability she found most endearing. The incredible aura of power and invincibility was curiously absent, and for the first time, she felt he was approachable. Softer, somehow. An obtainable goal.

And as he lifted one of her hands to his lips for a courtly kiss, her heart was gone.

"I shall be right back."

"Do you—need any help?"

The thought of Arabella's assistance within his dressing room was a tempting one, but alas, for the moment, unwise as well. The need to see the father was greater than the need to bed the daughter. For the time being.

"I can manage, little one."

He did manage, barely. By the time he reached the top of the stairs, his legs were shaking strengthlessly and his lungs burned for lack of air. He was tired. An odd sensation, one scarcely remembered. There'd been a certain weakness when he hadn't fed, but not this dragging exhaustion of body and sluggishness of mind. Mortal weariness. And he smiled into the labored gasps. He would have to get used to these limitations. He would enjoy getting used to them.

As he turned into his rooms, he was warned by the faint shush of steel. Instinctively, his forearm flew up to deflect the arm wielding the dangerous blade. When the sword swung back to ready another cutting arc, Louis tried to call out, but was met with the frustrating block within his own mind. He tried again, aloud.

"Takeo!"

The boy relaxed his defensive stance. In fact, he looked ready to swoon from surprise. He stumbled backward, eyes huge and disbelieving, his mouth working soundlessly.

"It's all right. It's me."

The boy gestured toward the sunlight leaking between the closed draperies, his expression filled with unvoiced confusion.

"Yes, daylight. Isn't it beautiful? I look forward to seeing it each day of my mortal life."

The boy was still uncertain. His brow furrowed and he seemed to be concentrating. Then he touched fingertips to his brow and shook his head in frustration.

"I'm sorry, my friend. We can no longer talk as we used to. That I will regret. Come. Help me change out of these defiled garments."

Takeo approached him cautiously. Finally, Louis extended his hand and the boy reached out to touch it, as wary as a wild dog with a potential threat. Louis's fingers closed warm and reassuring over the slender ones.

"It is me. Reborn. Takeo, I am alive again."

The boy's smile broke small and tremulous, then stretched wide as he moved to swiftly embrace his mortal friend. Then, just as quickly, he moved away and went to draw out proper attire, wiping at his eyes as he did so.

Slowly, feeling the aches and strains of his body as

if it was as new to him as the sunrise, Louis stripped off the offending clothing and cleansed away the traces of what he had been. And when he glanced up from his washbasin, he was greeted with another startling sight. His hand rose unsteadily to touch his face, a face he'd not seen reflected back in centuries. Yet there, in the small shaving mirror, was the man he'd once been, staring back, unchanged by time's passage. He stood for a long while, hand to his cheek, simply lost in the study of that near and familiar stranger.

Then Takeo nudged him, offering up a fresh shirt, and he was pulled away from his fascination. Yet as he dressed, he cast continual glances into that revealing glass, each time surprised and delighted to find his image returned.

Wesley Pembrook tugged impatiently on the locked drawer of Stuart Howland's desk. He scanned the cluttered surface in search of a lever to use in prying it open. But maybe that wouldn't be such a good idea. Too obvious. He was in the Howland home by request. He'd cleaned up the dreadful mess left by whatever Stuart was dabbling in, including the disposal of a bloodless corpse. He'd run twenty-eight stitches through his mentor's shoulder in an attempt to close the horrendous wound. Now the doctor was abed, drifting on the opiate he'd been given, mumbling deliriously about the undead and his daughter's safety. And Wesley was tormented by curiosity and elation. For he was on the inside now, and in a position to demand all. With the duties he'd performed this morning, Howland could refuse him nothing. The good doctor's indiscretion had secured the future Wesley so avidly sought.

The sound of the front door opening distracted him from thoughts of petty burglary. He heard the housekeeper's silly prattle and Arabella's smoother tones. And then an accented drawl most unmistakable. Radman.

The trio confronted him warily. Then he was displeased to note how Arabella tucked familiarly up against the marquis, making no attempt to discourage the possessive placement of Radman's hands upon her shoulders.

"Wesley, how is my father?"

"Mended, and resting quietly. He suffered a great deal of trauma from the attack of whatever it was—madman or beast."

"I must go up to him right away."

"I am surprised that you would leave him at all, considering his condition." Wesley slid an accusing look to Radman and waited to hear her excuse.

Arabella was unshaken. Her chin went up in defiance of his claim of her negligence. Her tone was cold. "Father was insistent that I find his lordship. I knew his wounds were not life endangering and you had already been sent for."

"And him." Wesley jerked his head toward Radman. "What has he to do with this?"

"Why, nothing. He was not here."

"Then why was his the name your father has been crying out in his fever?"

Louis's hands rubbed reassuringly along Arabella's upper arms. His reply was cool and crisply logical. "I am financing the project Howland was working on. Of course, mine would be the name he called. It's work that's very dear to both of us."

"Being—?"

"None of your concern," the marquis concluded.

Wesley gaped at him, then assumed a haughty posture. "None of my concern? I beg to differ. I have spent the sum of this morning removing evidence of some very odd goings-on. I have disposed of a cadaver. I have sponged up signs of bizarre experimentation—involving two parties. I have sewn up a tear in the doctor's muscle tissue that nothing human could have made—and you tell me it is none of my concern."

"You will be rewarded for your efforts."

"'Tis not reward I seek!"

Louis fixed him with a narrow stare. At first, Wesley recoiled from it; then he realized there was no intimidation to his mind, just an arrogant aristocrat's ire. Whatever powers Radman had he wasn't applying. Or couldn't apply. Wesley squared up in challenge.

"I want to be recognized for my involvement in Doctor Howland's work."

"Oh, I can arrange for you to get what you deserve."

That seeping threat brought florid color to Wesley's face and Arabella's timely intervention. Her hand touched to the back of Louis's, and her quiet words served to settle him.

"My lord, Mr. Pembrook has earned our gratitude this day. Who can say what might have happened had he not seen fit to respond to our urgent plea? When

Father is stronger, I'm certain he will want to thank Wesley in a manner more fitting with his generosity."

Wesley simmered smugly at that praise and oozed, "A kind word from you would go far, Miss Arabella."

"Then, of course, you shall have it."

Radman might have snorted at that exchange, but the medical student couldn't be sure. The marquis looked annoyed and impatient. "Where is your father, Bella? I must see him at once."

Rankled by the man's familiar use of her name, Wesley snapped with authority, "As I've said, he's resting. He must not be disturbed."

"He will be more disturbed if he doesn't see me. And his daughter. I believe you know the way out, Pembrook."

Wesley fumed at the casual dismissing and sought out Arabella with his protesting gaze. She only smiled at him in a weary plea for understanding.

"Thank you, Wesley. But please, you must go to the hospital and quiet any undue questions. Only say my father was attacked by some deranged person seeking narcotics. It wouldn't do for suspicions to be aroused."

"No. No, of course not." That would not do at all. At least until he knew everything. Wesley came to boldly bow over Arabella's hand, ignoring Radman's fierce glower. In the daylight, the marquis's manner was not nearly so fearsome. It was easy to slide a glance down his nose at him from his superior height and give him a direct cut. "If you have need of me, Miss Arabella, don't hesitate to call."

She smiled warmly, even fondly. "I shall, Wesley."

When he was gone, Louis was nearly growling his displeasure. "The greedy leech. How could you stoop to placate him?"

"A leech he might be, but he also has the makings of a dangerous enemy. You'd do well to avoid provoking him, considering all he knows and could yet guess."

"What could he do?"

"He could ruin my father's reputation in the medical community, for one. The rest I will leave to your imaginings, my lord."

He pursed his lips and bowed to her superior wisdom.

Bessie, who had been standing off to the side up to this point, stepped in quickly when Arabella put a hand on Louis's arm to lead him toward the stairs. "Here now, Miss, you cannot be taking a gentleman upstairs," she scolded, in a sober undervoice. All the while, she was studying the marquis with a suspicious frown.

"Father will want to see him."

"Your father has been put through quite enough, thanks to him and his funny doings. Please, Miss, have a care for the doctor's health."

"Mrs. Kampford, believe me, Father will be much relieved after our visit." As she spoke, she stripped off her pelisse.

"Not if you mean to go in lookin' like that."

Arabella raised her hand self-consciously to the untidy spill of her hair, then followed the housekeeper's disapproving gaze. Her gown was stained and wrinkled, obviously slept in. She didn't want to imagine how she appeared. And still Louis was looking at her as if she was the loveliest creature alive.

"I will take his lordship up, and if you would be so kind as to prepare my room, I'll refresh myself while they chat."

Partially satisfied that she could separate her young mistress from the saturnine lord, if not the lord from their home, Bessie bobbed into a quick curtsy and hustled up the stairs in front of them.

"Forgive Bessie, my lord. She tends to be overly protective."

"She has every right to be. You shouldn't disregard the counsel of those who care about you."

"And what do you say, my lord? Are you, then, a danger to me?"

He quirked a faint smile. "Would I be wise to tell you if I were?"

She searched his impassive face. "I think so."

His fingertips ran a light trace along her jaw. He didn't answer.

"Well? Are you?" she prompted, with a maddeningly sure composure.

"No, Bella. I would never harm you." And the emotions rumbling through him were so deep they awed him.

For hundreds of years, he'd thought only of himself, of ensuring his safety and his survival. It was foolish to care and mad to trust. And so solitude became a constant companion and thoughts of warmer ties faded with the advance of calendar years. In such a furtive existence, it was impossible to allow anyone near enough to make an impression upon the heart, let alone the soul. He'd numbed himself to feelings of guilt or human morality long ago. Or tried to. It took a tremendous degree of will to go on through the decades, trapped in his half-life, watching the world change again and again while he remained untouched. Immortality bred incredible arrogance. And boredom: with humanity, with existence itself.

What hadn't he seen in three hundred years? He'd been through plagues and wars aplenty. He'd observed the forward thrust of civilization, though he couldn't claim that mankind itself had moved an inch. He'd lived more than a half dozen lifetimes. He'd learned, he'd traveled, he'd studied under poets and prophets and philosophers. And yet the basic thread of his being remained unchanged because he was unchanged. He was alone and so lonely for the touch of newness that Arabella Howland had taken him like a late summer storm, drenching him with wondrous sensations and shaking him with a tempest of anticipation.

If Stuart Howland had restored his humanity, Arabella had awakened his long-slumbering spirit.

And he would cherish her for the rest of his eternities for that simple gift. But he would rather love her for a single lifetime.

"Follow me, my lord."

He watched her climb ahead of him and was mesmerized by the graceful sway of her skirt. It had been—forever, it seemed, since he'd looked at a woman this way. Over the years, they'd become an insignificant clump identified as mortal female, serving one purpose only, that of slaking his thirst. The seduction, the magic, it all went toward that end. It was nothing sensual, nothing sexual. With Arabella, that definition had been refined. Everything she stirred within him was sensual and becoming very sexual.

Perhaps it was Howland's drug that altered his awareness. Maybe it was Arabella. He didn't know. All he knew was that one night he ceased to be the charmer and became the charmed. Then all of his perceptions and preferences changed. He found himself longing to possess her body the way he'd once yearned to taste her blood. Once those emotions chafed to life, a riot of foreign feelings followed suit. The need for physical closeness. The want of spiritual bonding. The lust for basic coupling entwined with tender sentiment. Needing, wanting, lusting for all those things with just one woman—with the strong-willed and passionate Arabella. If this was being mortal, it was escalating to a restless existence.

It was with some surprise that Louis recognized the restoration of his soul. It twisted within him in a nightmare of guilt the moment he saw Stuart Howland so pale and wracked by pain. He lingered at the opening of Howland's bedchamber while Arabella rushed inside to kneel at her father's side. The tender way she touched the older man's face, the tears that trembled upon her cheeks, that sight tore thought Louis with a wretched consequence. How could she say she loved him after he'd brought such misery, such fear into her home? After he'd come so close to slaying her father as the doctor was serving a patient's selfish purposes?

He watched as the physician's eyes flickered open, as they were overcome with emotion at the presence of his daughter. Relief quaver in his weak claim,

"Oh, Bella, my dear. I've been so desperately worried over you."

"I'm fine, Father. How are you?"

"I've too much to do to lie here in this bed," he grumbled with typical impatience. "Radman—"

"Is here with me."

"Are you all right?" His question was sharp, and she was quick to soothe him.

"Yes, as I've told you. His lordship would like to speak to you while I tidy up. Do you feel strong enough for the interview?"

"Where is he?" He was levering up on his elbows anxiously. Arabella calmed him with the press of her hand upon his sound shoulder. But his excited agitation increased. "Radman is here? Now? My God, what this means!"

Arabella looked around and beckoned Louis to come closer. He approached slowly, weighted by conscience, but Stuart seemed to forget the cause of his injury in his rush of elation.

"It worked. By God, it worked!"

Then the true reality hit Louis. All he knew and was had been drastically altered. And he hadn't the slightest idea what he was going to do, now that it had.

Chapter Nine

It was a gloomy, typical London afternoon, with low, scudding clouds and the threat of drizzle keeping most indoors. Louis had the quiet glades of the park almost to himself as he sank down on one of the benches to rest and to think. So much to consider, so little energy with which to see it done.

Even the glare of overcast sky was brilliant to eyes used to darkness and subtle shadow. Louis closed them to ease the ache of brightness, though he hated to surrender up the sights. A world renewed, a life restored. He sat and absorbed the sounds that only came with the light: vendors shouting, children laughing, birds singing. So many sounds, a veritable feast to the senses. Beautiful, poignant, fragile. Like the life he now held to—but for how long, and to what degree?

Howland hadn't been able to answer that. He could give no guarantees. For so long, Louis had dreamed of seeing a sunrise, of feeling the morning dew upon his face. Foolish wants, because now he realized they weren't enough. He wanted more with such a determined greed. He wanted the security of growing old with one woman, with his children, without fear. And he couldn't have it. All he had was the moment, and that's when he learned another important truth: life was precious only when it was endangered. Immortality culled indifference. But what he had now was so frail, so tentative, it woke him to worldly passions he'd forgotten: to live and love and accomplish. To procreate. Things mankind took for granted until too late. He no longer had the luxury of time. He couldn't sit back and ponder for decades when the minute might be all that was left him. He was vulnerable. He could be hurt. He could be felled by influenza. He could be crippled by a runaway carriage. He could suffer death at the hands of thieves or through the careless envy of Wesley Pembrook. So delicate was this thread of human existence, so fleeting, so dear. And though he treasured it, it terrified him.

A chill shook through him. His body was weak and his mind dull. His senses were barely adequate to serve him. How did men go through their days in such helplessness? Suddenly, Louis felt all too exposed where he sat in the park, trying to adjust to the pulse of daily living. He was eager for the familiar, for safety. No longer infatigable, he had to hire a hack to see him home; and by the time he got there, he was almost too tired to stir. Agitated and alarmed, he hurried inside and bolted the door against the world he'd desired. Because it wasn't his world anymore.

* * *

The Asian youth answered Arabella's knock. Recognition shone in his dark eyes, but he displayed no inclination toward opening the door wider.

"Hello. I'm Miss Howland. Remember me from last night? Is his lordship in?"

The boy regarded her inscrutably.

"If he is, might I see him?"

Still, the silent denial.

"Would you be so kind to tell him I am here?"

"Takeo? Is someone there?"

At the sound of the marquis's voice, Arabella rose on tiptoe to peer hopefully over the lad's head. "Louis?"

He appeared from out of the late-day dimness and came up to place a hand upon the boy's shoulder. "It's all right, Takeo. Miss Howland is a friend. She is welcome in my house."

The youth bowed in acquiescence, first to him, then to her, and backed away.

"This is a surprise."

Louis's drawling tones made Arabella aware of what she was doing. She was a single woman visiting a gentleman's residence, unannounced, uninvited, and unescorted. But she'd been desperate to see him and had refused to consider propriety . . . until she looked the slight distance up into his questioning eyes. And her brash courage faltered.

"My father was very concerned about your welfare—for his notes, you understand."

"I understand."

"It's important to keep careful records on cases such as yours, and—"

"And?" he prompted, with a slight lift of one dark brow.

"And I keep his journals for him, so I thought—"

"You thought?"

"I thought I would—" She was looking into his eyes, and suddenly the power of speech failed her. Her mind went a complete blank. She had no talent for tales, and none came to her in that awkward moment.

"Yes?"

Arabella sighed and gave up the pretense. "My father didn't send me."

"No?" His expression took on the illusion of surprise but she could tell he wasn't. Amusement crinkled the corners of his eyes beneath the haughty arch of his brows. She was abruptly irritated with herself for not speaking the truth outright, as she was known to, and she writhed with inner embarrassment as he asked, "Then, why are you here?"

With unprecedented humility, she murmured, "I was worried, and wanted to see how your were."

His graceful gesture encompassed all, from Turkish slippers and some sort of loose-fitting trouser to the wrap of his burgundy-colored silk dressing gown and the bristle of slightly damp hair. He'd obviously come from the bath, and Arabella felt her cheeks darken. "As you can see, I am fine."

"Yes," she stammered, feeling foolish and shamelessly eager for the sight of him. She knew she should go, yet she lingered, searching for something to say, for some reason to stay.

"Would you like to come inside, Miss Howland?"

Her voice was small, her presumptions huge. "If it's no bother."

"As I've said, you are always welcome here. Please."

Then he stepped aside to allow her to pass. As she did, she was tempted by the scents of shaving soap and warm masculine skin. Right then, she should have realized the danger. Her will was in a state of ready collapse and she wasn't of a mind to shore it up. Instead of behaving with prudence and decorum, she smiled as he took her coat.

"How is your father?"

"Resting comfortably. Well, that's not true. He's chafing to get back to work. Mrs. Kampford has threatened to drug him into obedience if he so much as wiggles."

"Does he know you are here?"

She gave him a chiding look. "If he knew, he would not be resting."

Louis's hand brushed alongside of her arm. "I am sorry, Arabella."

Her fingertips fluttered fleetingly over the tops of his. "I know. I don't hold you to blame for it. Things were rather—out of control last night."

Her forgiveness seemed to astound him, as if he, himself, could not have been so generous.

Arabella was acutely aware of him standing close and of her own desire to be closer, remembering that he'd called her his love, and that hours ago, they'd been lying upon the same rug where they now stood while he kissed her and she told him she loved him. A sense of intimacy drew them together, yet an uneasy nervousness would not abate. What was she supposed to do? Throw herself upon him? Wait for him to give some sign that he was ready for them to pursue the attraction? Hadn't he promised that they would once the experiment had proved a success? Had she come to his house to remind him? Or had she hoped she wouldn't have to?

Uncomfortable in his presence and at the same time content, Arabella paused at the arch leading to one of the formal parlors. Her gaze swept over the crowded interior. "You have an amazingly diverse collection, my lord. I remember only a few pieces from when last I was here, but they were exquisite."

"Feel free to explore, if you like. If you can get through, that is. When one travels as extensively as I have, one tends to drag back memories. Unfortunately, those memories get lost in the clutter."

Arabella toured through the tightly packed furnishings. She recognized artifacts from India, Spain, the Netherlands, even China, and remarked upon it all in wonder. "Is there anyplace you haven't been?"

He stood in the doorway, watching her. "I've never been to the New World—America. I should like to, someday, but the long ocean voyage has deterred me. I have no great fondness of water."

She was studying an Egyptian carving. "How did you ever find the time to see so much?"

Louis laughed softly. "Time loses meaning when one has no home."

She looked up at him then. "Where are you from? I've not been able to place your accent."

"I am—" He shrugged, struggling for the word. "International. But originally I was raised in Florence."

He didn't sound Italian. At least, not like any Italian she'd ever encountered, few though they might be. "Do you visit your homeland often?"

"I've not been back—for a long time. Nothing is familiar anymore. It makes me sad to see it. Perhaps now I will journey there. I've loved ones I've not paid respects to for far too long."

"You've no family?"

"No, no one. No family. My ties are buried and nearly forgotten."

And he turned away slightly, his expression so melancholy she wished she hadn't brought up the subject. "Will you stay in London long?"

"It depends—on how long she interests me." And then his eyes caressed her slowly from head to toe and a blush of embarrassed pleasure filled all the areas in between as Arabella took his meaning. Then she frowned to consider the temporary nature of it. Was she to be a passing attraction? How many women had he known and held an interest in during all his travels? How vain of her to think she alone could hold him. And how hurt she was to think his purpose shallow.

"Well, I have taken up enough of your time, my lord. I should be going."

"So soon?" He stepped to unconsciously block her when she turned to the door. "I would be honored if you'd stay to dine with me. Takeo will be laying out the meal shortly, and I have never cared to dine alone." Then his mouth took a small, cynical twist she didn't understand. And in her happiness, she didn't try to.

"I would enjoy that, my lord. If it is no—"

"It is no bother. I'll have him set out another place. Excuse me for a moment."

While he was gone, Arabella looked again about the treasure trove of antiquities. She was no historian, but she could recognize the significance of some of the pieces, and the value was unmistakable. Art such as this, carelessly stacked in corners, was museum quality. The far eastern objects were the rarest she'd seen. He was from Florence, he said. He traveled. What else was Louis Radman, with his hoarded memories and his century-deep sadness?

"You may keep that, if you like."

Arabella started and clutched cautiously at the obelisk she held. It was heavy, of some rich black stone. The strange etchings on it appeared to be in some language but she was unfamiliar with it. "It's beautiful, but no, I cannot."

"You must," he insisted. "It would please me to think of you enjoying it."

She stroked the cool black surface shyly. "Thank you, Louis. I shall treasure it."

Crossing to her, he gestured wide. "I have many such treasures, each special, each unique in its own way, each chosen for its beauty. However," he murmured huskily, "none come close to your beauty." He stopped before her, standing close enough for the hem of her skirt to caress over his toes. And his fingertips moved similarly along her cheek. "I should like to treasure you always, Bella."

Suddenly shy, and uncertain of his meaning, she offered a wistful smile. "I fear you have no room left here in which to keep me."

"I was thinking of keeping you elsewhere." And

he bent a bit, near enough for his lips to trail across her brow. When he straightened, he found her regarding him unblinkingly.

"As what?" she asked, in a thin voice.

Because he couldn't touch her thoughts or interpret her taut expression, he chose to be careful. "Perhaps it is too soon to discuss these things. It isn't wise to rush—"

Her fingers touched to his mouth, silencing him. "Sometimes, it isn't wise to wait." Her hand then slipped around to cup the back of his head, to draw him to meet the part of her lips. It was a sweet, searching kiss, and she broke from it to study him with perplexity.

"What?" he asked. "Is something wrong?"

"Not exactly wrong. Different."

"Different? How?"

"I—I can't explain it." She could, but she was afraid to try. He was different, less intense, less compelling, less powerful, somehow. The other times he'd embraced her, she'd been lost to an odd dreaminess, helpless to resist him, not wanting to. She'd succumbed to his touch as if destined to do so. There'd been a swallowing of her will by his own. And a fierce, almost frightening exhilaration. She felt none of that now. Now she was wide awake and in full control of her faculties. "You are not the same, somehow."

Louis took a step back. He hadn't thought of this. He hadn't considered what it was that made her love him. What if it was the hypnotic vampire magic and not him at all? What if, as a human, he had no charm or means to captivate her heart? Manipulation of the mind and of the passions had been yet another quality he'd surrendered. Supreme confidence gave before a stirring of inadequacy. Had there ever been a real bond between them, or was it something he created within her? He was suddenly very afraid to find out. In this new world, Arabella was his only constant. How would he cope if he lost her?

She was watching him, studying his subtle shifts of expression with that scientific somberness of hers, and part of him quailed beneath it. What if his shrewd and decisive Arabella found him lacking? It would be up to him to prove to her that difference need not lead to disappointment.

"I am not the same," he told her quietly. "I have been given *la vita nuova*—new life. There was nothing I could offer you before."

She was very still. "And now?"

"Things are—different. I can offer you all that I am . . . if it is enough."

"Enough?" She gave a shaky little laugh. "Oh, Louis, you can't imagine."

"No, I cannot. So you must tell me." He stroked her cheek and she pressed into his palm, her eyes closing languidly as he said, "I have no magic with which to woo you, Bella."

From the cradle of his hand, she looked up at him, her gaze sultry and satisfied. "You are wrong about that, my lord." And her smile was all the invitation he needed to seek out the softness of her lips.

It was a gentle duel of tongues, a give-and-take that was intimate initiation, like the whisper of promises. When Louis's hands framed her features, she sighed into his kisses. When that touched shifted lower, easing down supple neck to sloping shoulders, she leaned into him, pliant and eager. He had no means to dominate her will, and knowing her actions to be of her own volition was for him a strange and strong aphrodisiac. He felt the difference, too. His focus was altered from the thrum of her pulse to the varying textures of her desire. Her mouth was warm and pleasing, sometimes sweetly passive, sometimes wickedly assertive. She was touching him shyly, stroking through his hair and along the back of his dressing gown with hesitance, then with mounting confidence. It was a subtle magic, but magic nonetheless. The slow, beckoning arch of her body against his provoked more potent sensations, and though he'd meant to go cautiously to protect them both within this new realm of circumstance, the excitement rose too quickly to contain, too keenly to control.

With an impatient move, he turned her, pressing her back against the paneled wall. The intensity of his kiss escalated, and she responded with like urgency. When he broke from her lips, Arabella was gasping raggedly. He could feel her runaway pulse as his mouth touched briefly upon the smooth curve of her throat. Quickly, almost fearfully, he moved on, easing downward to the delicate junction of neck and shoulders.

His hands had risen to support the agitated heave of her bosom. Remembering the silken contours, Louis was drawn to sample from that soft bounty, sketching the upper swells with the warmth of his breath and the brief trace of his tongue. Arabella shuddered, her eyes squeezing shut; and her breathing grew jerky. She rolled her head against the dark-paneled wood as her fingers meshed restlessly in his yet-damp hair. Encouraged by the upward thrust of her torso, his hands tucked beneath the fit of her bodice, inside where her skin was heated and her heart beat, fast and furious. His name moaned from her, low and luscious sounding, as he lifted her breasts from the confines of fabric and moved to taste those tender tips.

The height of his arousal was unexpected. Suckling at her taut breast was as erotically charged as drawing from an artery, nourishing his senses as the other had fed his body. The quiver of anticipation massed to an ache of need, a hunger as overwhelming as any he'd felt in his former existence. It was a need only this able woman in his arms could meet, and she gave every sign of being willing.

He came up slowly, rubbing his face along the smoothness of her bared skin, lifting up until they were eye-to-eye. Hers were soft and as dreamy as a new dawn. Her lips moistened and parted with a yearning as desperate as his own. He took a moment to satisfy that craving, slanting, sliding, sucking upon her generously offered mouth. And as he did, he readjusted her clothing so that temptation wouldn't carry them away. When he did, he felt her quick gasp of protest.

"Louis—"

He silenced her with another kiss, then lifted from that succulent surrender to whisper, "I love you, Bella."

A tremor raced through her, and he could hear her frantic swallowing. She stared at him, her eyes glistening as he continued in the same emotion-rough voice.

"I want to make love with you. I want to make children with you."

Again, that fitful shiver. Then her hoarse reply.

"It's what I want, too."

Her hands were on his shoulders, their slender fingers kneading the silken material in an expressive demonstration of desire. He was leaning into her, trapping her body against the wall with the press of his own. She was frail for all her courage, slight for all her stature. Mortal. Vulnerable. As was he. And he was struck at once with the precariousness of their situation and with the fleeting nature of their lives. A panicked urgency spread through him, a need for a greedy, immediate gratification. Because he knew now, as he hadn't before, how quickly the moment passed.

"Bella, marry me. Be my wife. Share my days and nights. Let us live out our dreams and our desires as one."

There wasn't the slightest hesitation.

"Yes. Oh, yes, Louis. Yes."

"Soon. As soon as we can."

"Yes."

"If you want a grand wedding with all the pomp and trimmings, we can wait—"

"No," she interrupted hurriedly. "I don't want a big wedding. I want you. I've always wanted you. Always."

He rested his brow against the top of her head and breathed in slow and deep. It was too good, too good to be believed. "Bella, are you sure? There is so much you do not understand."

"I know that I love you. And I know that I'm sure. My heart and mind are not of a fickle nature, sir."

He smiled at her staunch tone. With her chin in the valley of his cupped hands, he raised her face so their gazes could mingle. He looked deep and drank of the strength and sincerity he saw there. "Your father will object, and he has every reason to."

"Let him. I am of an age where I no longer have to listen."

"But you should, Bella, *mia innamorata,* my love. You should listen to everything he has to say. Listen, and weigh this decision carefully. If you've any doubts—"

"I have none."

He smiled again, somewhat cynically. "But you will."

"Then you can conquer them."

Louis found himself as needful of her optimism as he was of her love.

Then she smiled at him with a touch of playfulness. "You promised me eternity and paradise, remember?"

"Alas, eternity is no longer within my grasp, but paradise, that you shall have."

"Then I'll ask no more of you."

He was about to kiss her again to seal that vow upon her lips when he realized Takeo was waiting in the hall, his youthful features carefully guarded.

"Our meal is ready." He straightened into a pose of propriety and offered his arm in escort. She took it with trembling fingers and clutched tight.

* * *

There was little conversation over their candlelit meal. Louis paid a concentrated attention to his plate, and Arabella was too excited for clear thought. She was distracted as the Asian boy leaned over her to pour her wine. When he withdrew as silently as he'd come, she looked to Louis in question.

"He doesn't have much to say, for a servant."

Louis glanced up and gave a bitter sigh. "Because he cannot. Takeo was born without the power of speech."

Her features crowded with compassion. "How sad for him."

"Oh, please, waste no pity on him. He wants none. A more prideful and resourceful child I've yet to meet."

"And where did you meet him?"

"In the Orient. He was in the service of a man who fought children one against the other, like animals, for money. When I—removed the threat of his master, he attached himself to me out of gratitude. Ours has been a beneficial relationship since then. I provide for him and he watches over me. Much like your Mrs. Kampford."

"He is your only servant?"

Louis shrugged. "My needs are few. I have no lust for luxury or pretense. Will that suit you, Bella? Should you need more—"

"No."

What more could there possibly be?

Silence settled again, and the canted looks shuttling between them simmered. Finally, Louis rose and extended his hand.

"You should go now. Speak to your father and heed his words. I shall understand if, after listening to his arguments, you chose not to return."

She smiled faintly. "If I do not return, it's because he's had me committed to Bedlam." She paused in the hall while he retrieved her wrap. When he slipped it around her and used the excuse to pull her close, her expression sobered. "This is not madness, is it, Louis?"

"All love is madness. But I will suffer it gladly."

"As will I."

He kissed her brow, ignoring the way her body melted against his in tempting supplication. "I love you, Bella. Come back to me."

He stood at the door, watching her race the length of the walk to her waiting carriage while a brisk rain pelted down upon her. Then she stepped within, pausing long enough to wave the hand that held the onyx stone before the conveyance carried her into the night.

Returning to the dining room he'd never used before this night, Louis picked up his glass of wine and sipped from it. How curious he found the differing tastes and texture of a human meal! He'd forgotten what it was like to eat from a varied plate.

And so had his system, he discovered quite acutely, as his stomach wrenched in sudden distress. Unused to the process of digestion, it rebelled with violent heaves and spasms until emptied of the foreign sustenance. It took some time for the cramping to ease, but even as he rose weakly from hands and knees, he had no regrets.

For this day, he had his first walk in daylight, his first normal meal, and his first taste of passion in over three hundred years. It was worth the pain of adjustment. It was worth all the risks. He would be a normal man again. And he would have Arabella Howland.

Chapter Ten

The first thing Arabella noticed was Wesley Pembrook's sensible cloak. It was then she heard voices raised in animated discussion. Frowning, she started toward her father's study and was intercepted by Bessie.

"Thank goodness you be home, Miss. Mr. Pembrook has closeted himself with the doctor, and they've been going on like this for some time. I quite fear for the doctor's state of health."

"I'll see to it, Mrs. Kampford." And she strode forward purposefully, intending to dress down Wesley for agitating her father in his precarious condition. Just as she opened the door, she heard the haughty medical student's claim and was astounded by its audacity.

"For my silence, I'll insist upon a partnership and the hand of your daughter."

"I think not!"

Both men turned at her steely words. Her father was half reclined upon his sofa. He was pale and perspiring, obviously failing the strain of the interview.

Wesley, on the other hand, look flushed with power and confidence. And he regarded her with a smug smile. She spared him no quarter.

"Mr. Pembrook, you show a singular lack of intelligence for a man of medicine. My father is in no shape to discuss business arrangements with you. They can wait until he is stronger and you are closer to taking your licensing exam. As for the other, the state of my affections is not something that can be bartered, and I highly resent being plied in such a manner."

"Bella—" Stuart cautioned. He looked unsettled, and had she been less incensed, Arabella might have been warned by his hesitation. But Wesley's manner of condescending address quite sealed her ire.

"My dear Miss Howland, I fear you mistake the matter."

"I mistake nothing, sir. My father needs his rest. He will contact you when he is able to continue talk of your future. As for our future together, let me make this clear: my interests are otherwise engaged. Now, if you would be so kind as to retrieve your cloak, I'll bid you a good night."

Wesley stared at her in a sullen silence; then he turned back to his mentor. "You would do well to inform her of the facts. It is *your* future in the balance, not mine."

And with that he swept out, sketching a bow to Arabella in passing. She stood back to give him plenty of space, then nearly slammed the door behind him. After a sharp, composing breath, she went to her father's side.

"Really, Father, you have little sense entertaining him in your weakened state. You should be abed."

"Where have you been, Bella?"

She rushed on, evading the inevitable. "Let me call Mrs. Kampford, and we can get you up—"

"Arabella! Where have you been?"

"Attending to a personal matter—"

"You've been with Radman, haven't you?"

She lifted her chin. "Yes. I went to see how he fared. I knew you would be concerned."

"And?"

"He is well. Stronger, and coping nicely. He invited me to dine with him—"

"Did he touch you?"

"Father, we had dinner!" But beneath her outraged bluster, her face was fiery.

"And upon what did you dine?"

"I don't know. His servant prepared some Oriental dish with beef and spices. Did you want the recipe?"

"Do not adopt an attitude with me, girl. And Radman, he dined with you?"

"Yes."

"On beef?"

"Yes."

Stuart remained wary. "And about what did you converse?"

"His travels and his homeland, mostly. He gave me this. Isn't it lovely?"

Stuart paid scant attention to the mysterious black stone. "And?"

"He wished me to convey his regards to you and to tell you he was sorry for your discomfort." She was studying the stone with its ancient writings. The color was still high in her cheeks. She was avoiding something, her father knew.

"Bella?"

"He asked me to marry him."

"Wha—"

"And I said yes."

"You said—what?"

"Yes."

If Stuart Howland was pale before, now he was completely void of color. He seemed at a loss of what to say. And to her horror, she saw his eyes well up with anxious tears. "Bella, you cannot. Please. You do not know—"

"I know that I love him. I cannot imagine a future without him. He's told me to listen to you, to heed your advice; and I will do the first, but as to the latter, I will marry him, Father. There is nothing you can say to dissuade me."

He closed his eyes as if in pain and a haggard helplessness had come over him. Setting Louis's gift atop her father's desk, Arabella took up one of his hands and he clutched at it. For a long moment they were silent. Then he looked up at her from a heartbreaking depth of despair.

"I am too weary now for this discussion. I should like to rest. We will talk in the morning, Bella. Until then, I would have you know how much I love you."

"I know. Please don't be upset—"

"We will talk tomorrow."

And that's all he would say. Arabella called to the housekeeper, and between them, they aided the doctor to his bed. It was a long while before Arabella sought sleep. When she did, she dreamed of Louis Radman. And his eyes were red and his teeth long.

A visit from Stuart Howland came as no surprise. Louis greeted him in the rear conservatory. He was stretched out on a chaise, all sleek grace, basking in the sunlight.

"You are looking well, Doctor."

"What are you doing to my daughter, Radman? What kind of tricks are you playing with her?"

"Why, none, sir. That is quite beyond my capabilities now. As for what I am doing to her—nothing."

"That's not what she has said."

"Oh?" An arrogant brow arched. "And what has she said?"

"That she's going to marry you."

There was a subtle relaxation to Radman's pose that the doctor took no comfort in. "She is a woman who knows her own mind."

"I will not brook your interference here. I have plans for Bella. She is to wed Wesley Pembrook."

"Ha! That miserable worm? Never."

"She will and you will not meddle."

"My dear doctor, the choice is hers and the answer freely given."

"If you persist in this—this obscenity, I will—"

"What?" His drawl was low and icily polite. "You will what, Doctor? Do you threaten me? You forget with whom you speak."

"I do not forget to what I speak. The threat is from Pembrook."

"He knows nothing. Arabella will be my wife, and

I will take care of Pembrook and his paltry blackmail." He looked aloof and supreme in his confidence. And Stuart was sorely afraid. He knew his daughter; he knew how determined she was once her mind was set on something. And her mind was set on having Radman. The tragedy and horror of it were staggering. To think he'd been responsible by bringing the marquis to their house, by letting Arabella associate with him. Surely if she knew—

"She doesn't know what you are."

Radman smiled and tented his long-fingered hands upon his taut midriff. "What I am, thanks to you, is a man who can love and care for her—and for her father. Do not forget that I have three centuries of wealth and power at my command. I do not threaten or take threats lightly. I can be generous or I can be cruel. You could do worse than to have your daughter married to a title such as mine, to an influence as far reaching as mine. Think of what I can do for both of you."

And the doctor thought for a moment, but his greed was subdued by his fear. "I am thinking of what you could do to her."

"I will not harm her. I will give her a life of—"

"Uncertainty! That is the best you can promise her."

For an instant, Louis's attitude faltered and shadows crossed the haughty features now cast in golden warmth. Then he answered softly, coolly. "But life is uncertain, Doctor. I will marry Bella and I will have what I've longed for these past centuries: a normal existence. And you will have all the funding you desire for your research. Think of it. Your daughter's happiness, and your own success. What more could you possibly want?"

"I want to know I'm not giving my only child to a monster."

Louis smiled at him grimly. "If I were a monster, would I be sitting here, or closed below, out of daylight's reach? You have given me life, and I will see you well rewarded. Is there anything else, Doctor?"

Stuart hesitated. He would not underestimate this man. Man or beast, he was powerful. As a friend, he could supply unlimited benefits to his field of study. As an enemy ... he didn't want to consider that. "Yes," he said at last. "I would like a sample of your blood for study."

Calmly, Louis extended his arm. He sucked a harsh, surprised breath when Stuart cut him. It still amazed him that such a small thing could hurt him. Patiently, he pumped his fist and watched the vital fluid spill into Howland's jar.

"You've had no ill effects since the transfusion?" Howland was now all clinical in his approach.

"None."

"No reaction to sunlight or silver? No—unnatural appetite?"

"No."

"My daughter said you were taking in food."

"Yes." Louis didn't add he'd yet to keep any of it down. He assumed that would come with time. His body had a lot to adjust to.

"Any changes, and you will come to me immediately."

"Yes, of course. I have more invested in the success of this than you do, Doctor."

"Come dine with us tonight at seven. If you are going to court my daughter, I'd as soon it be done properly."

Louis smiled and gave a slight bow. "As you wish, Doctor. I shall look forward to it."

And at seven, they dined on an excellent meal prepared by the Howlands' kitchen and delivered up by a scowling Mrs. Kampford. Louis provided a bottle of vintage French wine, and over rims of cut crystal, he and Arabella exchanged speaking glances. Table talk was amicable and general—Stuart's work, Louis's ventures. In all, it was a pleasant evening, the type a prospective suitor spent with his intended's family. And when Louis excused himself with a polite murmur, neither father nor daughter guessed that in his brief absence he was on his knees in the shadows, retching up the meal with a convulsive violence.

Mac Reeves sucked down his gin and kept a sharp eye on the smoke-shrouded door that looked out on Tooley Street in Bermondsey. A reeling pattern of seafaring men stumbled in and out and he was looking for one man in particular, one with whom he'd yet to refine the details of their next riverside robbery. As the moon was full, they couldn't slink about in cemeteries to perform their grim work unseen, so he was looking for other means to earn himself enough blunt to get by until his next sack-'em-up job. Though he drank, he wasn't drunk. It paid to keep the wits about at all times. Indulgence was for safe hidey-holes where he'd bed a tart or two and sop up gin until he passed out. This was a night for business, and it paid to keep alert.

Which was why he was so surprised to find a gentleman standing at his elbow. He'd not seen the man approach, and from where he sat with his back to a wall, the gent couldn't have come up behind him. He just appeared, silent, ghostlike, and Reeves didn't like surprises.

"Are you Mac Reeves?" The drawl was low and heavily accented, some foreign flavor that had a ring of the familiar to it.

"Who be askin'?" he growled, scowling at the fellow; a real dandy he was, too. For all his fine clothes, an experienced bloke would know him for a plump pocket, yet none of the nefarious fellows sitting near them paid him any mind. In fact, none seemed to notice him at all. Reeves felt a disquieting shiver as he stared up at the stranger's smooth countenance.

"Someone who could be very grateful for a little information."

"Yeah, well I ain't in the information business, see? So you'd best be takin' yer fancy arse outta here afore you get rolled for your purse."

"I have no fear for my safety and I know your business, Mr. Reeves, which is why we sought you out."

"We?" Hard eyes flashed about, but he could see no other fitting a tie to the dapper foreigner.

"Mr. Reeves, my companion and I would like to ask a few questions of you. We would pay well for your time."

A sudden clatter of gold across the table top jerked Reeves's breath up short. He was quick to rake it in before anyone else saw. A man weren't safe with his own peers—especially with his own peers. As greedy as he was, Reeves had survived too long on caution.

"I don't know you, and I don't talk to strangers 'bout my business."

The man smiled a slow, silky smile, and he shifted slightly so Reeves could see his eyes. Iridescent pale blue eyes, seeming to pulse with an inner brilliance ... odd, so odd, Reeves couldn't look away.

"Ah, but we are old friends, are we not?" the mysterious fellow murmured, and Reeves found himself nodding. His head was buzzing, but it was like no kick of ruin he'd ever experienced. When the gent said, "Come," he could form no objection. He rose up from his chair, leaving the gold on the table, and followed the tall figure to the door and to a secreted coach wreathed in late-night mists. He stepped inside without pause and settled upon the plush seat next to the fine gentleman. Across from them sat a woman—he could tell by her scent; but her face and figure were concealed within the folds of a cloak.

"Mr. Reeves?" Her voice tingled along his nerve endings in a prickly quiver.

"Yes, mum?"

"We will not detain you for long. We've been led to believe that you are the manipulator behind a series of deaths and deliveries of the dead."

"Y—yes," he heard himself say, and he couldn't believe he was damning himself so easily before two strangers.

"I am interested in several recent corpses, bodies

emptied of their blood. Do you know of what I speak?"

"Yes."

"Good. And to whom did you make these deliveries?"

"To a Doctor Howland, at his home."

"Howland?"

"Stuart Howland. Paid me real good and up front for 'em, too."

"Excellent. And what was he doing with these bodies?"

"Can't say, mum. Odd doings." Then he clamped his mouth shut with an effort. Wouldn't do to spill too much and cut himself out of a tidy profit in blackmail.

"Would these doings involve a dangerously handsome man of breeding with an accent like my companion's?"

That's where he'd heard it before, Reeves realized, in a far distant daze. Now he recalled. His greedy mind managed to scrape up enough resistance so he could mutter a rough, "No, I don't—"

Then the man beside him moved. Reeves assumed he did, though he didn't see any actual motion. Suddenly, the manicured hand was at his thick throat and Reeves could feel his windpipe crumpling beneath an amazing strength.

"Think harder, my friend. His name is Luigino, but he could have changed it to—"

"Louis," Reeves gasped. "Louis Radman."

"Louis," the woman purred. "Yes. And where can we find him?"

"Don't know. Truly I don't know. Can't be hard to

track down, him being an aristocrat an' all. A marquis."

"A marquis," the man drawled, sounding impressed and amused. "Gino has done well for himself, hasn't he, *cara*. And you, Mr. Reeves, have been a great help. We need to reward you for your graciousness."

And just as Reeves was beginning to smile craftily, grateful that the encounter was almost over and that it would see him reimbursed, the gentleman shifted toward him on the seat. And in the poorly lit coach interior, the blue eyes glowed with deep blood-red centers.

With a gasp, Reeves grabbed for the door, but the long-fingered hand had him by the neck, crushing the breath and struggle from him, yet careful not to press so hard as to rob him of consciousness. Careful not to deprive him of the horrible sight of the man's face drawing near, of his lips drawing back in a ghastly grin, of his fangs coming down. Reeves tried to scream.

It came out as a gurgle. For the man had torn his throat open with those sharp, unnatural teeth before leaning back to savor the dying terror in Reeves's eyes.

The last thing Mac Reeves heard was the woman's tinkling laughter.

"Really, Gerard, you are making a terrible mess."

"I'm sorry, *mia amate*. You know how I am when I'm made to wait for what I want. But I'm being selfish. Did you wish a taste?"

The woman folded back her hood and as always, Gerardo Pasquale was stunned by her beauty. Her pouty lips curled in distaste. *"Non,* I prefer to dine with a subtle wine, not the unpleasantness of cheap gin. But you go ahead."

He smirked at her. "Such a lady you are, Bianca. Too much above dirtying yourself with the lower class." He laughed and caught her by the front of her cloak, dragging her forward so he could kiss her. And despite her proud disdain, she sucked eagerly at his lips and lapped the smear of blood from his face, then sat back, breathing hard.

"So," she murmured uncaringly, "you prove I am a creature led by my lusts."

"If not, we would not be here. Or do you prefer to call it love? *Mal d'amore.* Love sickness, no?"

She frowned at his dry remark and her haughty beauty sharpened into something not nearly so pleasant. "Take care, Gerard. Do not mock me. You were most willing to come."

"Yes, but not for the same reasons as yours."

"My reasons are my own. Now, I am hungry." She thumped the roof and called up, "To Catherine Street." For a moment, she watched Gerardo feed and fought down her own twist of need. She was more patient than her avaricious friend. She could wait for more tempting fare strolling unsuspectingly at the Drury Lane Theatre. Pushing aside the window drape, she looked out at the sights. "Ah, London. I have not been here since—let me think, since 1680-something."

Gerardo glanced at her and supplied a crimson-stained smile. "Then you'll have plenty of old friends to look up."

Bianca's lovely features hardened as she let the curtain fall. "Just one, Gerardo. Just one."

And she couldn't wait to renew the acquaintance.

Chapter Eleven

Louis stood up slowly and wiped the blood from the corner of his mouth. He felt as if his jaw had been broken as he worked it gingerly. Across from him, Takeo relaxed his offensive pose and bowed slightly.

"Do not gloat, my friend. There was a time when you would not have come within a mile of striking me."

The boy grinned and bounced lightly on his toes, beckoning with his fingers. Louis smiled back wryly and settled into his sparring stance, balance carefully distributed along a natural, flex-kneed position and fists ready to block or punch. He deflected the first few strikes with an instinctive agility, throwing blows aside and dodging kicks. But it wasn't easy, it was work. And it wasn't the type of fighting one would see at Crawley Down or hear discussed at the Daffy Club or Jackson's Rooms on Bond Street. It wasn't bare knuckling in the traditional English sense, but rather a form of defense that spanned back into the religious temples of China, a combination of graceful self-protection and lethal attack. Takeo had taught Louis the forms because the artful moves intrigued him. Now he was more serious in his interest . . . especially when the boy's foot shot through his guard and planted with a cracking force in the center of his chest. The marquis stumbled back and fell, skidding along the tiled floor, where he continued to lie, gasping for breath.

"I think you've broken my ribs," he wheezed, and the lad rushed over to kneel down.

And as soon as he did, Louis had him by the shoulders and flipped him neatly. Before the boy could scramble up, Louis rolled to his feet and came down with one knee on the youngster's sternum. With a guttural cry, he drove the heel of his hand downward with killing force, halting just shy of Takeo's nose. Had contact occurred, the boy would have died instantly with the shattered bridge of his nose piercing his brain.

"I may be slow, but I am still clever."

The lad grinned in appreciation and bounded up the moment he was released. When Louis urged another round, he shook his head and held his hands up in a harmless manner.

"Come on, Takeo. What's wrong? Have I worn you down?" But he knew just the opposite was true. The boy was worried about him. A swelling had started at his cheekbone, and his body ached in a dozen places from Takeo's well-placed abuse. He'd been stripped down to the barest skills and was fearing they would not be enough to serve him. It was a humbling reduction. He'd had the endurance of a bull and the strength of ten. He could shatter walls with his fists and get such elevation on his kicks, he seemed to fly. Now he was winded and hurting from a light workout, and he was scared.

"Again, Takeo."

But the boy shook his head, placing cautioning hands on his shoulders. Louis flung them off angrily.

"No, I don't want to rest. I must get stronger. I am weak. I am powerless. I am like a baby who is helpless to defend himself. I cannot afford it, Takeo. There are too many who now know my name."

He was thinking of the engagement announcements proudly heralded in the *Morning Post,* the *Gazette,* and the *Times.* Howland had wasted no time in proclaiming his daughter's rise in status—and his own. But with it came the kind of publicity Louis shunned out of habit. He was a creature who'd survived long by his own cunning and his care to exist quietly, with no undo attention that might sharpen into suspicion.

Takeo gripped his master's hand and struck his other over his heart in a gesture of loyalty. Louis's features gentled to a smile.

"You have done well, my young friend, and I have trusted you with my care. Perhaps I worry too much. Better that than too little, eh?"

Takeo's concern didn't lift. He brought his hand up and down to his mouth to pantomime eating. Louis grimaced. Even the thought of forcing a meal woke nausea. He'd yet to find anything his system would accept and it was steadily draining his strength. The scent of cooking meat revolted him. While he enjoyed experimenting with the different tastes and textures, the end result was tearing him up inside. He kept telling himself time would solve his troubles, time and determination. He didn't want to go to Howland, not this close to his wedding date, not until Arabella was his. Because if something was wrong, if he was reverting, Howland would lock his love away and an eternity without her would be twice the hell it had been.

Louis sighed. "All right, I will try." And with the utmost reluctance and discouragement, he went into the kitchen, where Takeo had secured a small corner to cook only for himself up until recently.

On the table was a cut of beef still wrapped in butcher paper. In the tray beneath it, juices pooled. Without thinking, Louis dipped his fingers into the meat drippings and sucked the flavor from them. Rich, fresh, and bloody. And before he could stop himself, he'd ripped the paper away and set upon the haunch of beef like a ravenous dog, tearing off and swallowing great chunks until the gnawing burn in his belly eased. Then his frenzy slowed and he took great care in draining the raw juices into a crystal goblet and drinking them down after rolling the taste about his tongue like the finest of wines.

He was washing his face and hands when the first vicious cramp doubled him. He rode it out, breathing hard into the pain and clenching his teeth to forestall the provoking roil of his stomach. Finally, the urge to retch quieted and he applied fresh water to rinse the slick of sweat off his skin. And he smiled with grim satisfaction. He'd eaten. Not the most elegant of meals, but solid in substance. A small step closer. A baby step. But he wouldn't let that matter; it couldn't matter. He would do whatever was necessary to fit into Arabella's world.

One of the most disagreeable tasks was settling his debts and promises. He'd chosen an informal dinner for the hospital's Board of Governors and few select guests to see it done. That list included Stuart Howland, his lovely daughter, and Wesley Pembrook. And before that august company, he bestowed upon Mr. Pembrook an impressive medical practice brought out with his own coin—to thank the young doctor for his kindnesses to the Howland family. And as Wesley beamed and ingratiated himself to the Board, Louis fixed him with a cold warning stare which Wesley was too foolish to heed.

"That should shut him up," Stuart grumbled as Louis came to bow over his daughter's hand. Over the past few days, the doctor had lost much of his liking for his scheming apprentice. He had nothing against ambition—he just didn't care to have his crumpled reputation used as a stepping stone.

Louis gave him an impassive glance. "If not, there are other measures. As I promised, the threat of Mr. Pembrook is gone." He'd not yet released Arabella's hand and used it now to draw her closer. "Good evening, my love. How well you look. Were we not in the center of attention, I would show you how much I've missed you."

Arabella colored prettily, but her eyes were all smoky intensity. "I will hold you to that, my lord, the moment we are alone."

Pretending not to overhear the intimate exchange, Stuart looked instead toward the fawning Wesley.

When their gazes met, Wesley excused himself and sauntered over to greet them. His stare narrowed as Louis squared up at Arabella's side in what could be described as a territorial bristle.

"Doctor, Miss Howland, my lord." He sketched a graceful bow. "I've come to convey my overwhelming thanks for your generosity."

"Even generosity has its limits," Louis told him in a chill voice. "Bother us again and you will find it overtaxed. And we wouldn't want things to get— unpleasant, would we?"

Wesley raised a haughty brow. "Do I take your meaning, sir?"

"You'd be wise to take what you've been given and be grateful. T'would be quite tragic for an old friend of the Howlands to disappear on the crux to his career success, shall we say, without a trace?"

"Like Reeves?" Wesley sneered in a low aside.

"Who?"

"Mac Reeves, the graverobber you employed."

Stuart shot a frantic look about to make sure no one had overheard, but Louis's glare never flickered. "So that was his name. What of him?"

"No one knows. He simply vanished off the streets one night."

"A hazard of his profession, I would guess, but not of my doing."

"So you say."

"I do. And now, you bore me, Pembrook. Please go away, far away, and trouble me no more. You've gotten far better than you deserve."

Wesley looked to Arabella with a surly scowl. His

gaze was covetous. "As have you, my lord." He bowed to the lady and stiffly took his leave.

"That's the last of him," Stuart claimed with a gruff satisfaction.

But holding to his arm, Arabella was not so sure.

The only thing she was sure of was Louis; she had no doubts there. She loved him, he cherished her, and they were going to be wonderfully happy. No one was going to get in their way; not Wesley, not her father, not even the secrets she'd yet to guess about Louis's past condition. She'd waited too long for this perfect love to let anything spoil it.

And as she sat in the small dressing room of the chapel in which they were to be married, Arabella repeated that vow as solemnly as she'd repeat those to seal her wedded state. Louis Radman was going to be her husband, and on this night was going to share her bed.

She smiled up at her father as Stuart Howland came to bring her before the altar. The doctor's face was somber for such an occasion.

"You have rushed to this point, Bella. Are you sure?"

"Oh, yes," she sighed serenely, and he had to believe her. He'd never seen such a radiance about her.

"Then I wish you every good fortune, my dear. Allow me to gift you with a small token of my love."

Arabella smiled as he draped a fragile chain about her neck and let the delicate silver crucifix rest upon her bosom.

"I want your word that you will wear this always

and that you will call upon its power in times of threat or trouble."

Arabella gave him a bewildered look. Her father wasn't a religious man. Like most of the doctors she knew, he likened himself close to a god. So she was as puzzled as she was touched by his present and his insistence. But because she loved him and she was so happy, she made him that promise and he looked tremendously relieved as he bent to kiss her cheek.

"Come now, daughter. His lordship has an impatient look about him, and the service must conclude before noon." And his eyes misted as she stood and he beheld her with a father's love, for she was the image of her mother in her high-waisted gown of white and silver, with the airy scarf of lace pinned to her headdress of white roses and trailing down to wisp about her bare arms. And he was comforted by the gleaming silver cross. Wrapping her gloved fingers within the crook of his arm, he led her out to where Louis was waiting before an elite gathering of their friends.

From the marquis's side, serving as his rather unconventional groomsman, Takeo smiled shyly at Arabella, and she returned the gesture before lifting her gaze to her betrothed. And once their stares met, Arabella was aware of nothing else. Not of the wary look her father gave her husband-to-be as he passed over possession of her hand, not of the words they spoke to one another, not of the ring slipped upon her hand. Nothing made an impression until Louis bent and claimed their first wedded kiss. And it was sweetly satisfying.

Congratulations were issued and the couple was rushed off for an elaborate wedding breakfast hosted by one of the hospital board. Louis kept to his single glass of champagne, politely declining even a taste of the bride's-cake. His eyes were on his new bride, and they were blatantly hungry. As soon as properly possible, he disentangled her from the party and guided her out to their waiting coach. Within, they rode in silence, just their fingertips entwined until they reached Louis's home.

Their home.

Inside, there was a bustle of activity. Hired servants wound in and out of the rooms, readying for the grand reception planned for that evening. Bessie Kampford was there to embrace Arabella with a deluge of tears. She'd come along with the new bride's wardrobe to help her settle in. Louis stood back patiently and waited to receive his wife's attention. She stood in the center of the hall, a look of confusion on her face.

"Louis, where are all your treasures?"

The parlors had been stripped to the most fashionable necessities and seemed very bare indeed.

With a negligent wave of his hand, Louis said, "I was told there was no room amongst them in which to keep my greatest treasure, so I did away with them all."

She cried out in genuine dismay. "Oh, you didn't! All your memories—"

"Mean nothing to me now. I want nothing of the past to hold me. You are my future, Bella. I need nothing more surrounding me."

Just then, Bessie huffed in, toting several cases and

directing a traffic of footmen bearing trunks. "Where be you wanting these?"

"In the big room at the head of the stairs," Louis told her, without taking his gaze from his wife.

Bessie gave him a level look. "But those be your quarters, my lord."

"Just so. Place my wife's belongings there."

Appearing scandalized, Mrs. Kampford turned to a dreamy-eyed Arabella. "But Miss—Ma'am—"

"The room at the head of the stairs, Mrs. Kampford. I shall be up momentarily."

And as her father's clucking housekeeper herded the bearers up in front of her, Arabella gave her husband a shy smile. He responded by opening his arms and she was quick to fill them, hugging fiercely, with a trembling expectation.

"How soon before we can be alone?" she asked, rather breathlessly.

"Not a timid creature, are you, my love? We could be terrible hosts and draw the shades and lock the doors and pretend not to be at home tonight."

She chuckled and snuggled against him contentedly. "No, I can endure it as long as you're nearby. Oh, Louis, I am so happy."

He glanced down at her and his devoted gaze was arrested. "What is that you're wearing?"

She leaned back and fingered the fragile necklace. "My father gave it to me. I was quite surprised. He's never attached much sentiment to God and church."

"You must wear it, then, to honor him." He lifted the small hand that held the cross and pressed his mouth to the back of it. "He thinks only of you, and in that, I cannot fault him. Now, before I am tempted beyond restraint, go see what havoc Mrs. Kampford is wreaking upon my rooms."

"I love you, Louis." She stretched up to affirm those words with a sweet kiss, then rushed off before she, too, was overcome with the need to barricade herself against the world.

As he watched her hurry up his stairs, Louis Radman felt a tug of tenderness before unknown to him and a swell of protective love for his new bride. And deeper still, a stirring eagerness for the time when all their guests would leave and he could make her truly his own in the way of mortal man.

And as the sun set, their house filled up with well-wishers and celebrants. Candlelight created a soft fantasy orchestrated by the mellow sounds of a string ensemble. In fashionable circles, the event would be deemed a crushing success, for so many stood mashed elbow to elbow, it was impossible to move with any degree of comfort. Separated from her husband by the press of humanity, Arabella clung to her patience and smiled with an inbred graciousness at all who came to extend their goodwill, but her eyes kept straying toward the stairs and her thoughts toward the night she and Louis would have together when he would continue the lessons in love she so desired.

Distracted by those heated anticipations, she was quite startled by the abrupt appearance of a woman before her, a woman who was without a doubt the most beautiful female she'd ever seen. Tall and sleek and sharply lovely and dressed to the envy of the court, the blond woman regarded Arabella with a thin smile and the glitter of her black eyes.

"So, he has married you." That quiet purr was decidedly French in flavor. It was impossible not to feel the threat in her gaze as it moved incrementally from toe to top of head. "I'll admit, you are a rather pretty creature."

Fighting to subdue her annoyance at the bold behavior and her sudden alarm as the black eyes fixed upon hers, Arabella forced a smile and extended her hand. "We have not met. I am Arabella How— Radman. Are you a friend of my husband's?"

"You might say so." The icy blonde took her hand. Her grip was surprisingly strong, compressing Arabella's fingers to the point of pain while her thumb stroked leisurely over the pulse point in her wrist. "Luigino and I go back a long way."

"You knew him in Florence?" Arabella kept her tone calm as she tried to gracefully extract her hand. The woman only smiled. Arabella could feel one long fingernail scraping along her inner wrist.

"In Florence, yes. In Rome. In Milan. In Madrid. In Cairo."

Arabella understood. This woman was Louis's past. She was the one who'd traveled with him while he'd gathered all those treasures. It was impossible not to be intimated by a woman of such poise and chill loveliness. Especially when she smiled to revel in that knowledge of past association.

"I know him in ways that you could never know him, *chérie,* and that is why you'll not be able to keep him from me."

Not the words a yet virgin bride wished to hear on

her wedding night. Arabella blushed awkwardly, then flushed with a tart anger. How dared this woman speak to her in such a fashion? In her home! About her husband!

"Louis has discarded all the things of the past. You may have been his lover, but I am now his wife."

The blonde laughed, a high musical sound that was somehow discordant. "Lover? How quaint. Yes, he was my lover once." Her dark eyes slid to a sultry half-mast and the tip of her tongue moistened voluptuous lips. "And he will be again. Because I know him. I know what he needs."

"*I* am what he needs," Arabella countered, with more confidence than she was feeling. "Perhaps you should go—" Then she looked about, confused. For the woman had simply vanished. The sound of her malicious laughter yet lingered, as did the scent of her perfume. And the terrible feeling of threat to her newfound happiness.

"Bella?"

The brush of Louis's fingertips along her shoulders wrought a hard shudder. That didn't escape him, nor did her abrupt pallor. She looked up at him through stricken eyes, with dampness flooding.

"Bella? What's wrong?"

His closeness, his concern both combined to scatter her insecurities. Louis had wed her, he'd made her his wife. He loved her. What did she have to fear? Nothing except looking the fool for allowing an old acquaintance to stir up her jealousies. Had she thought him chaste? Not the way he kissed. And the comely blonde was probably not the only affair from his past. What woman who'd known his attentive touch would not wish to make love with him? She did . . . desperately.

"Nothing's wrong," she vowed with a firm, denying smile. "Only it's such a squeeze, and I've grown tired." Her palm stroked his sleeve. "And anxious."

He smiled, pretending to be calmed by her flirtatious manner. "Then we shall discourage our guests from remaining. I'll pass the word that we've run out of drink. That should chase them home."

But when he moved to leave her, he found her fingers curled tightly in the fabric of his coat.

"Louis, please stay with me."

He could feel her anxiety, but couldn't guess its cause. Something had upset his unflappable bride. He was quick to relent and to tuck her within the curve of his arm, where he pressed a light kiss to her brow, earning a soft sigh of response. And he didn't move from her side as their company began to thin with their slyly issued good nights. As he felt her tension ease, he could almost believe it was the stress of the evening behind her panic, and as the rooms emptied, he allowed himself to think ahead, to the two of them together, alone and entwined. And he was smiling lustily down at his new bride when he felt her rigidity return. Casually, he turned to follow her gaze and thoughts of romance were rent asunder by the appearance of two who had been uninvited.

"Gino, my friend! It has been—how long?"

Louis's hopes jerked to a tragic halt as the tall handsome man drew him up into a warm embrace. Fond kisses were pressed to either cheek then his friend stepped back to regard him with a wide smile.

"You look so surprised! Why is that? Did you think we would not travel far to wish you well on such a night as this? Gino, you are family. We love you and want what's best for you. Isn't that right, Bianca?"

The svelte blonde stepped in close to rub her knuckles down Louis's taut cheek. "That's right. We love you. Did you forget that?"

And her seductive smile tightened a complete terror inside Louis Radman.

"Is this your bride?" the gentleman crooned. "How sweetly lovely. *Un amore di bambino;* a charming child. Introduce us, Gino."

Still slowed by shock, Louis murmured the exchange of names. "Arabella, this is Gerardo Pasquale and Bianca du Maurier."

"Your pretty bride and I have already met," Bianca said with a taunting smile. "I have told her how we are old and dear friends." And she swayed in close to adhere to Louis's other side even as Gerardo slipped an easy arm about Arabella's waist to separate her from her husband. "And what have you told her of us? Nothing? Shame on you."

To an observer, it would seem a scene of cozy reunion. To Louis, it was a nightmare. He had to think, and his mind was strangely paralyzed. Bianca, of course . . . he had forgotten how powerful she was. There was nothing he could do to protect himself and his bride, but then what could these two demons do in the middle of company?

Why, they could do anything they chose. And Bianca's smug smile reminded him.

She was looking into his eyes, into his thoughts, devouring them, and he could sense her puzzlement. He tried to throw up a mental block, to push her out, and for a moment he was successful. But she was so strong. And as she leaned in closer, he could see her delicate nostrils flare as she scented out live blood.

His.

"Louis?"

It was Arabella's faint call of his name that woke him from the spell Bianca was weaving. His mortal wife was looking to him for guidance, and he didn't know what to tell her. He had to find some way to protect her. And then he remembered Stuart Howland's wisdom.

"Bella, show my friend the trinket your father gave to you. He is interested in such things."

Though she was confused, Arabella complied. And the moment she lifted the small crucifix to display it, Gerardo release her and reared back with narrowed eyes.

"Very lovely," he hissed softly. "As you are lovely. Bianca, we overstay our welcome. Can you not see that our friend is eager to get on with the initiation of his bride? *Fare all'amore.*" His sigh was expressive. "I am so envious."

"I wonder," Bianca mused, as her slender fingers stroked over Louis's cheek and down his throat, pausing there for a long moment. "Is that your plan, Luigino? *Non,* it is Louis now. I must remember. Louis." She was studying him, shrewd and made uncertain by what she saw. Her grip on his neck was massaging, unrelenting, and close to suffocating. "Will you make her one of us? Or shall we provide the welcome?"

"No," Louis gritted out with a fierce control. "Leave. We will talk another time. Not here."

"Yes, we will talk. We have much to catch up on. Bring your dainty bride. I'm sure she would find the conversation—illuminating. Until then . . ." She leaned closer. Louis was powerless to move in her iron embrace. Her lips settled over his with an indecent familiarity, gliding slowly, tongue sliding slickly over the narrow press of his mouth. And she laughed softly at his resistance. "Taming you was always my greatest pleasure, Gino," she whispered against that unyielding line. "Oh, but the victory, so sweet. So worth the time and effort."

"Don't waste your time, Bianca," he growled in warning. "You have nothing I want. You never did."

"That's not how I remember it, *cher*. We shall see who has the better recall, eh?" She moved away from him with obvious reluctance and spared a haughty glance at his wife. "Enjoy him while you can, but you will find some ties are not so easily discarded. Come, Gerard."

The dapper Italian gentleman embraced his friend once more, indifferent to Louis's stiff response. And holding the marquis's face between his palms, he kissed him again in fond European fashion and murmured with a sinister affection, "How I have missed you, Gino! My good, dear friend. I have never forgotten the depth of your love for me. Perhaps it is time to see it repaid." And his attention slid to

Arabella for a lengthy appraisal. Smiling, he followed his lovely companion to the door, then bowing once to the newlyweds, he disappeared after her into the night.

Chapter Twelve

A mood of tension was expected between man and wife when the last of the guests were gone and they found themselves alone. And tension was high in the big bedroom. Arabella watched her husband stride across the room to check the window latches and draw the drapes tight. And when he turned to her, it wasn't with a look of anxious passion. He was just plain anxious.

"Louis, who were those people?"

"Devils," he told her simply, and she trembled because she couldn't laugh and disbelieve him.

"What do they want?"

"Me." Again, the terrifying bluntness. His hands scrubbed over his features restlessly. They were shaking. And that scared her more than the aggressive pair below.

"Louis, that woman said you were lovers and that you would be again."

"No. That isn't true."

"You weren't intimate with her? In Florence, in Rome, in Milan, in Madrid, and in Cairo?" That came out with a jealous escalation, and she didn't care that it did. Jealousy was easier to handle than fright. And the odd pair frightened her.

"In Florence. Long ago."

"And the rest?" She wrapped her arms about herself to still the terrible trembling.

"I was not in love with her, Bella. Never. I was very young, and she was so worldly. I didn't understand what she wanted from me."

"And what *did* she want?"

"To possess me."

How much worse that sounded than just to make love to him. So much more complete and permanent. And dangerous. Tears welled up in Arabella's eyes, and a helplessness she hated. Thinking of that dazzling, sophisticated woman—

"Why did you let her kiss you like that?"

He gave a harsh laugh. How to make her believe that Bianca could have broken his neck with a casual twist of her hand? "One doesn't let Bianca do anything. She takes whatever she likes."

And as much as that alarmed her, it angered Arabella more. "Well, she's not going to take you from me!"

He said nothing.

She swallowed her panic. It went down hard. "But she's going to try, isn't she?"

"Yes." He wished there were some comfort he could give her, but there wasn't. She had no idea, none at all, of what they were dealing with. "Arabella, you must promise me that you will not go out alone once the sun sets."

"Why?" she demanded, somewhat hysterically.

"Will she try to make me disappear, as did the most likely late Mr. Reeves?"

"She will try to use you to get to me." He sounded so calm, so matter-of-fact. As if such behavior was inevitable and acceptable. Well, it wasn't to her.

Arabella took a shaky breath. "Who does she think she is? I'll not allow her to interfere this way. I'll not be kept a prisoner—"

Louis grasped her by the arms. His fingers bit deep with a hard desperation. "This is not a game, Bella. These people are fiends. They will hurt you. They will do worse, if they can. Do not be foolish enough to think yourself safe."

"But you can keep us safe, can't you?"

He looked down into her great trusting eyes and wanted to weep and wail from his own weakness. "I don't know, Bella. I don't know." And he held her, wrapping her tightly in his arms, crushing her to the cherishing beat of his heart. What had he done? What dreadful jeopardy had he brought into her life?

"Louis," she whispered against the warmth of his throat. "Louis, make love to me. Give me something that they can never, ever take away."

He held her for a moment, not sure he could manage the degree of attentiveness necessary while all his thoughts were plagued by troubles. But then she shifted within his arms, her body moving against his in a sensual ripple. Hands that had clutched him began to caress, drifting along his shoulders, through his hair, turning his head so she could claim his mouth with her own needy kisses. Passions provoked and pooled hot in an instant. Perhaps it was the underlying panic that fueled the urgency of the moment, the desperation that chafed desire to a burning intensity. Whatever it was, it was irresistible and immediate.

"I love you, Bella," he mouthed into her hurried breaths. And he busied himself, unpinning her headdress, unfastening her bridal gown just as she was pushing at his coat and vest and shirt, baring him to the waist. She drew a wondering sigh and let her palm rub over the strong swells and sleek curves of his upper body. He was powerfully made, and the feel of hard muscle and fit man did much to soothe her fears and flame her needs. For a moment she leaned into him, content to absorb the heat and scent and mystery of him.

"Don't be afraid, my love." He skimmed her down to the wisp of her chemise and her skin glowed warm and beckoning beneath it. With his hands upon either soft thigh, he began to gather the fabric upward with the gradual inch of his fingertips until they rested on supple flesh. Then with bunched hem in hand, he slowly lifted the frail garment over her head and let it settle like a mist to the floor. His breath expelled unevenly. All she wore were clocked stockings and the tiny crucifix.

When he hesitated, she lifted her head to meet his taut and tender gaze. His eyes were a deep green-gold, steeped in a conflict of eager want and judicious care. He was worried about her innocence, and she smiled.

"I am afraid, my lord husband, afraid I have no more patience. Will you take me to our bed, or must I drag you?"

"You need not apply force." And she gasped as he hugged her up and walked with her to the bedstead as her feet dangled off the ground. When he laid her out on the coverlet, she wasn't content to assume a passive role. Her hands framed his face, pulling until he came down to satisfy her needy lips. And when she was quite thoroughly pleased with his kisses, she began an immodest quest to learn him well. Threats of danger and the world itself as existed outside their door no longer mattered.

Louis rolled to his back and let her explore and experiment. He was bemused by her boldness and aroused by her innocent seduction. Her touch adored him, stealing away his breath, his heart, his control, as it rubbed and circled in its inexorable move down to the snug fit of his breeches. He thought her maidenly status would halt her there, but she showed no sign of hesitation as her hand fit to the thick jut of him outlined by the cling of stockinette. His teeth ground as sensation jolted beneath her provoking caress.

"Louis, these must go." Her voice was a husky rumble as she plucked at the band of his breeches. He stared up at her, purely amazed and somewhat shocked, for all his years.

"Madame, are you certain you've not done this before?"

Looking slightly incensed, she replied, "No. Why would you ask?"

"Because a female in your circumstance does not display your uncommon confidence."

"Should I become more missish, then? Would you prefer I succumb to vapors and cringe under the covers? You have the experience, my lord husband. Tell me how it is done." And she crossed her forearms atop his chest and leaned upon them, waiting for his answer.

"I prefer how you are doing it. I was not correcting, only curious."

"Well, sir, I was raised a physician's daughter and taught that one gives careful study to that which arouses the curiosity."

He smiled. "And I arouse you, little one?"

"Indeed, husband. Indeed you do."

"Then far be it from me to stand in the way of science." He lifted his hips and squirmed out of his breeches and drawers, tossing them carelessly off the foot of the bed. "Continue your observation."

Despite her aggressive claims, Arabella was slow in shifting her attention downward. She knew the basics of anatomy, of course, and had wickedly appeased her curiosity on one of her father's figures of dissective study. But that gentleman was far from a responsive state and in no way prepared her for the difference a living, breathing passion could effect in the male physique. And Louis Radman's difference was quite impressive. She touched him, and she heard his breath pull in raggedly. Her own respiration was altered to an extreme. She stroked him, enchanted by the feel of warm satin-sheathed steel pulsing life within the cup of her hand. After several minutes of handling him thusly, his knees began to shift and shake and his toes to curl. Abruptly, she had her wrist taken and pulled away.

"Bella, you must stop."

His voice was so strained she looked up at him in alarm. His eyes were closed in a face hollowed by tension. He was breathing in quick, shallow pants through parted lips. She didn't understand his distress and said so.

"You've not hurt me, little one, just pushed the point of pleasure too close to conclusion."

"Oh. Oh! Yes, of course, we should reserve the spill of fluids for the seeding of life."

His eyes came open then, darkened by a sharp shock of dismay when they met hers, and suddenly swimming in realization and remorse.

"What is it, Louis?"

"I'm sorry, Bella. I—I don't know that I can create life. We should have discussed this before we married, but it truly never occurred to me until just now. We both wanted children, and I never—I never stopped to consider I might not be able to provide them for you."

Arabella tried hard not to betray her anguish. She forced a calm physician's tone. "Did your previous condition render you sterile?"

How to explain, that life hadn't been possible from death? He'd died in the 1500s, and the power of reproduction with him. But hadn't he been reborn? Wasn't new life flowing through him? And with that renewed vitality, wouldn't all be working as it once had? His body was repairing itself with a natural healing. Could he assume it was producing the fertile links to procreation as well?

"I don't know, Bella. And I can see how I've disappointed you. It is your right to expect a child and your right to withdraw from this marriage if I cannot—"

Her hand covered his mouth, halting the grievously given words.

"No," she told him with a strong conviction. "I wed you because I wanted you. If we can grow a child between us, how wonderful that will be. If not, we will still have one another. Louis, I swear to you, that will be enough for me. I swear I will have no regrets."

He searched her expression for the truth of that claim then with a soft cry, pulled her down to his desperately hopeful kisses. With her passionate response to fuel him, Louis rose to reverse their positions, leveling her onto her back as he slid over her. She moaned into his kisses, arching up as they trailed hotly to the sensitive ache of her breasts, crying out his name as his hands skimmed up her inner thighs, parting the way for his intimate possession. She was too desirous to feel afraid as he pushed against the barrier of her innocence. The sudden pain was unexpected, but the swift, sure thrust of paradise that followed eclipsed all else.

And if he ever had any doubts about the quality of his mortal prowess, Arabella erased them with one sighing sound.

"Oh, Louis!"

He was gentle. At first that was a comfort; then it was an unbearable provocation. His kisses mingled hurried breaths and sultry words, foreign love words that excited with their very strangeness and intensity. He teased her with sweeps of his mouth over hers, making her reach out to him for a deeper connection. He tantalized her with the languid rush and ebb of his body over and within her, lingering, withdrawing until she was ever at a restless edge of anticipation. She held to him, running her hands over his heated skin in rough, impatient strokes, wanting the sensation of oneness to penetrate to the soul. He'd said he couldn't give her magic ... oh, how wrong he'd been.

Louis felt the magic, too, sparked by the enticing friction searing him with every move. Even as a vampire, he'd never felt so powerful. Then, his strength had come from psychic control, instead of this exquisite physical communion. It was Arabella's passion that fed him. He'd had heightened senses before, but they were always so concentrated that much of the smaller pleasures escaped him. Like the tiny gasping cries she made at the pinnacle of each thrust. Like the curl of her fingertips digging frantically for purchase below his flexing shoulder blades. Like the way her body rose and fell beneath him, a seething tide at the command of his forceful rhythm. She didn't feel frail to him now. She was strong and hot and vigorous, a supple female coupling with complete abandon; his mate, his wife, pleasing him and taking pleasure from him in the most basic and private human fashion. And it was every bit as intoxicating as taking blood.

Abruptly, the pattern of Arabella's response altered. Her breaths grew broken and needy. Her hands groped for and found his where they were spread wide on either side of her tossing head, fingers lacing through his and gripping tight. The way she said his name, all wild and free and wonderfully keening as satisfaction spasmed through her, was the most profoundly beautiful thing he'd ever heard. And the feel of her, hot, wet and grasping greedily around him, was enough to fracture his own building tension into

The Publishers of Zebra Books Make This Special Offer to Zebra Romance Readers...

AFTER YOU HAVE READ THIS BOOK WE'D LIKE TO SEND YOU **4 MORE FOR *FREE* AN $18.00 VALUE**

NO OBLIGATION!

ONLY ZEBRA HISTORICAL ROMANCES "BURN WITH THE FIRE OF HISTORY" (SEE INSIDE FOR MONEY SAVING DETAILS.)

MORE PASSION AND ADVENTURE AWAIT... YOUR TRIP TO A BIG ADVENTUROUS WORLD BEGINS WHEN YOU ACCEPT YOUR FIRST 4 NOVELS ABSOLUTELY *FREE* (AN $18.00 VALUE)

Accept your Free gift and start to experience more of the passion and adventure you like in a historical romance novel. Each Zebra novel is filled with proud men, spirited women and tempestuous love that you'll remember long after you turn the last page.

Zebra Historical Romances are the finest novels of their kind. They are written by authors who really know how to weave tales of romance and adventure in the historical settings you love. You'll feel like you've actually gone back in time with the thrilling stories that each Zebra novel offers.

Get Your Free Gift With The Start Of Your Home Subscription

Our readers tell us that these books sell out very fast in book stores and often they miss the newest titles. So Zebra has made arrangements for you to receive the four newest novels published each month.

You'll be guaranteed that you'll never miss a title, and home delivery is so convenient. And to show you just how easy it is to get Zebra Historical Romances, we'll send you your first 4 books absolutely FREE! Our gift to you just for trying our home subscription service.

BIG SAVINGS AND FREE HOME DELIVERY

Each month, you'll receive the four newest titles as soon as they are published. You'll probably receive them even before the bookstores do. What's more, you may preview these exciting novels free for 10 days. If you like them as much as we think you will, just pay the low preferred subscriber's price of just $3.75 each. *You'll save $3.00 each month off the publisher's price.* AND, your savings are even greater because there are never any shipping, handling or other hidden charges—FREE Home Delivery. Of course you can return any shipment within 10 days for full credit, no questions asked. There is no minimum number of books you must buy.

4 FREE BOOKS

TO GET YOUR 4 FREE BOOKS WORTH $18.00 — MAIL IN THE FREE BOOK CERTIFICATE TODAY

Fill in the Free Book Certificate below, and we'll send your FREE BOOKS to you as soon as we receive it.

If the certificate is missing below, write to: Zebra Home Subscription Service, Inc., P.O. Box 5214, 120 Brighton Road, Clifton, New Jersey 07015-5214.

FREE BOOK CERTIFICATE

4 FREE BOOKS

ZEBRA HOME SUBSCRIPTION SERVICE, INC.

YES! Please start my subscription to Zebra Historical Romances and send me my first 4 books absolutely FREE. I understand that each month I may preview four new Zebra Historical Romances free for 10 days. If I'm not satisfied with them, I may return the four books within 10 days and owe nothing. Otherwise, I will pay the low preferred subscriber's price of just $3.75 each; a total of $15.00, *a savings off the publisher's price of $3.00*. I may return any shipment and I may cancel this subscription at any time. There is no obligation to buy any shipment and there are no shipping, handling or other hidden charges. Regardless of what I decide, the four free books are mine to keep.

NAME _____

ADDRESS _____ APT _____

CITY _____ STATE _____ ZIP _____

TELEPHONE
( ) _____

SIGNATURE _____
(if under 18, parent or guardian must sign)

Terms, offer and prices subject to change without notice. Subscription subject to acceptance by Zebra Books. Zebra Books reserves the right to reject any order or cancel any subscription.

ZB0594

GET FOUR FREE BOOKS
(AN $18.00 VALUE)

ZEBRA HOME SUBSCRIPTION SERVICE, INC.
120 BRIGHTON ROAD
P.O. Box 5214
CLIFTON, NEW JERSEY 07015-5214

AFFIX STAMP HERE

hard, will-dissolving shudders. As passion erupted into a fierce liquid stream, Louis closed his eyes and offered an awkwardly unfamiliar prayer. *God, restore my humanity to the point where I can provide her with what she deserves.*

Arabella wasn't thinking about seeding babies or fearsome strangers or anything beyond the heavy lethargy encasing her entire being. A wonderful languor stemmed from the heat of her husband above her and yet within her. Wanting to hold to both for as long as she could, she embraced him with a contented sigh and held his damp head to her shoulder.

The feel of his ragged breath against the side of her throat was so incredibly intimate, a warm, forceful stroking that brought a shiver to her already strained senses. She whispered his name as she felt his tongue rasp lightly along salty skin and his lips press hard enough to experience the pleasurable pulse he'd stirred within her. Then, suddenly, he pulled away, lifting up as if alarmed, only to be calmed by the sight of her smile.

"Louis, if I live to the eternity you once promised, nothing will ever be as glorious as this night; and if I die tomorrow, I'll have no regrets."

Her words disturbed him, though she hadn't meant them to. "We'll have many such nights, Bella, and many tomorrows."

"I know. I just wanted you to know how very well loved I feel right now."

His expression grew even more intense. "I do love you, Bella, as I've never loved anyone or anything. You must believe it was never my intention to place you in any peril." He was speaking of the ominous couple again, and that brought another tug of doubt to Arabella's mind.

"And was this night as memorable to you as yours with her?" She spoke it softly, without rampant emotion, without impassioned tears. She simply needed to know.

"I have forgotten how it was with her." A lie, but he could never tell her the truth of it. It wasn't her feelings he thought to spare, but her basic sensibilities. And his shame, the shame that had never dulled in all the centuries past. Nothing he wanted to discuss with his new bride on their wedding night.

"But she hasn't, has she, Louis?"

He didn't answer.

Arabella rubbed over the taut, intriguing planes of his face, thinking again that he was a most amazing-looking man. And an amazing lover. So she said, almost sympathetically, "I can't really say I blame her. But she lost you to me, and I will never give you up to anyone."

A small smile touched his lips, then he moved off her and cuddled her up to his side, aching with the fierceness of his love for her. Terrified that their nights and tomorrows were in limited supply.

He wasn't sure what woke him. It was dark. A fire burned faintly to illuminate the room. The warm figure burrowed against him was his wife, Arabella, sleeping soundly, her breathing a soft, sonorous whisper.

After giving the perimeters of the room another quick scan, Louis turned toward the woman at his side. Her back was to him. He touched her, letting his palm slide on the silky flesh of her thigh. So soft. He leaned to press his lips to one gently curved shoulder. So sweet. He forced his tension down, letting the hot build of desire slip in to take its place.

Then, with a gasp, he came away from her, sitting bolt upright.

It came again. A scratching. Faint, soft scratching at the window's leaded panes. His gaze was drawn there in a dragging horror. What was behind the heavy bunch of drapery? If he went to the window and pulled back the curtains, what would he see? Bianca, floating on a mist of her own making, her face pale, her eyes red and gleaming? Gerardo, hovering on the night air, smiling with an arrogance that displayed his wickedly sharp incisors. Something wanted in, inside, where his new life could to be torn to bloodless ruin. All he had to do was ease out of the bed, cross to the window, open the drapes, open the casements, and say, Yes, come in.

And he found his feet on the chill of the floorboards. The sensation shocked him. He wasn't aware of moving, of responding to the suggestion.

No!

He had rolled back onto the bed in a denying panic, reaching for Arabella and the comfort she'd provide, when the voice stopped him.

Gino.

Bianca.

He crouched upon the covers, panting softly.

Gino, il mio amore.

The voice reached inside, caressing, alive, unholy. It wasn't the compulsive command to one enslaved nor the mental communication between peers. It was a seducing whisper, insinuating, seeping, seeking control. How strong she was. He'd forgotten how strong.

Gino, have you forgotten as well how it once was for us? Have you forgotten how you wanted me? Don't you want me now? Don't you want me in your arms? Don't you want my kisses?

No!

You wanted me, Gino. You want me still.

No ...

Enough to lie for me, to kill for me.

No ...

Remember.

It hit him like a sensual wave, those memories, in a force hard enough to drive him down upon his back where he arched in a helpless frenzy. The power of those sensations, rippling through him, over him, beneath him, a power that was hot and icy and irresistible.

"No."

Yet he gasped into the fitful tremors, eyes closing in a rapture, lips parting as the invitation lingered there, a desperate entreaty, a yearning like no other. Why fight, when the surrender yielded such glorious splendor?

"No."

Gino, you want me. Let me come to you. Let me lie with you. Let me love you. Then softer, more beckoning still, *Louis.*

His legs were shifting, his body trembling and dappled with sweat. Weakness of mind overwhelmed him. The sense of wanting, needing, so compelling, so . . .

Deadly.

God! She was inside him, working her vile control upon his will.

"No!"

"Louis?"

The light touch of fingertips upon his shoulder made him leap with sudden terror.

"No!"

"Louis, it's Arabella!"

He blinked once again, and then her worried features came into focus.

"Bella."

His arms went about her, his clasp tight and urgently shivering. She felt his rough kisses upon her shoulder, against her jaw, her temple, her brow, and finally, hungrily, upon her mouth. Bruising, forceful. Desperately frightened.

"Louis, it's all right."

His hands stroked her face and hair. They were shaking. His words were shaking, too. "Bella, love me. Love me hard and long. Don't let me go. Don't let me go. Make me forget."

Because she was deeply alarmed by his intense agitation and feared with a womanly intuition that his former lover was somehow behind it, Arabella reacted with an instinctive fervor. Her return kisses were possessive and passionate, scattering in a determined rain over the taut angles of his face, sealing his uneven breaths beneath a firm, mastering press.

And because he was vulnerable, she became strong, assuming a superior position as she kissed and caressed him, straddling him with a boldness she couldn't have imagined in her innocent's mind. She surrounded him with her love, with her heat, with her desire, moving recklessly until friction and fullness wrought pleasure chafing on the edge of pain. Until the panic glittering his gaze gave before a darkening of sensual surrender. His hands clasped at her slender waist, complementing, compelling a stronger surging tempo that goaded him to a sudden sharp relief. And even as she rode out the jerk of his completing spasms, he was moving, tumbling her beneath him so that with several more pounding thrusts she reached a similar point of fulfillment.

"I love you, Bella," he sighed wearily, as tension ebbed and exhaustion left him limp. He sank into the comfort of her embrace, head nestling against her shoulder and limbs entwined about her.

And she held him wordlessly until she felt his breathing settle into a slow pattern of slumber. Then she stroked his hair and kissed his brow and whispered fiercely into the night.

"You will not have him!"

Chapter Thirteen

"Louis?"

Arabella knew he was gone even as she opened her eyes and stretched her hand across the cool sheets.

It was morning. Daylight streamed in through the opened draperies gleaming pristine and pure upon the marriage gown her husband had taken off her. It was neatly folded and laid across the back of one of the chamber chairs, her veil and wreath of roses set atop it. Regarding the dress, regarding her ring, Arabella lay back upon the pillows with a wistful smile. She was now a married woman in every sense of the word. But what exactly did a married woman do with her days? Surely she didn't lounge about in the bed while the sun crept high. Or perhaps she did. Well, she determined, this one wouldn't, and she rose, washed, and dressed, eager to seek out her husband.

The sounds of fighting reached her from the foot of the stairs. With an anxious jump of her heart, she raced toward the commotion, never once pausing to consider her own safety. Her fertile imagination pitted her husband against the two menacing strangers from the night before. As she skidded to a halt between double glass doors opening into a cavernous ballroom, relief made her breathless. Within, she could see two circling figures: those of Louis and Takeo, and while they looked serious in their endeavor, she could not believe they meant to do each other harm.

Arabella had seen pugilists buffeting away at each other before—without her father's knowledge or approval, of course. She'd taken a strange and giddy appreciation in that manly contest of brute strengths. But this combat was as different as a peasant dancing to ballet. The moves were all grace and power and control, a visual poetry of sleek muscle and agile balance. Both men were bared to the waist and gleaming with exertion. Arabella's rapt gaze detailed her husband's form, finding it a breathtaking exercise. He was beautiful: all boldly delineated swells and cords of concentrated force, each moving like shifting liquid beneath taut skin. The man who had partnered her in such exquisite lovemaking was this morning one of the most dangerous and exciting things she'd ever seen. And a well of fierce pride and female admiration rose within her. For every lethal and superbly crafted inch of this man was hers.

Unaware of their audience, Louis and Takeo continued to spar, fencing with feet, with hands, wielding balance and timing like finely made weapons. High spinning kicks packing the force to incapacitate an enemy were designed to miss with a hairs-breadth of warning. Explosive punches were pulled just shy of full impact. The boy's superior technique and training were no match for Louis's aggressive attack. For motivating each form, each offensive lunge, was the threat of a far greater foe lying in wait.

While recovering from a sweeping kick, Louis caught sight of Arabella standing at the door, watching him with such a look of awe and ardor, his concentration shattered. He tried to continue the challenge, but sensing his distraction, Takeo took full advantage, taunting him with a series of clever spearing punches and concluding with playful slaps at his head that he wasn't quick enough to dodge. Finally, with a laugh, Louis held up his hands. The boy immediately relaxed into a bow.

Nothing was quite so arousing as seeing his wife's gaze grow all dark-centered with exhilaration when he approached her. He could hear her hurried little gasps for breath as if she, too, had been involved in some strenuous activity. She moistened her lips and allowed her eyes to travel over him hungrily.

"Good morning, my love. I did not mean to keep you waiting."

"I didn't mind." How breathless she sounded.

"I'll have Takeo fix you some breakfast while I change."

"You won't be joining me, my lord?"

"I've—already eaten. But I will sit with you. If you'll excuse me for a moment."

But she was in no hurry to let him pass. Her fingertips touched tremblingly at his midriff and charted up over the ripple of his abdomen to hard pectorals, sliding from there to the impressive span of his shoulders. Everything within him tightened beneath that gliding caress.

"You were quite magnificent, my lord." Then her

stare lifted and he was wildly stimulated by the blaze of desire in those usually cool gray depths.

Taking one slender hand to his lips, he murmured against it, "You are too kind."

"No," she replied huskily. "I am too fortunate."

Curling his fingers beneath her chin, he bent to kiss her with a stirring brevity. "Let me make myself more presentable; then I can greet you properly."

And it took a huge degree of will for him to walk away from the sultry invitation of her mouth.

He took the stairs in multiples, passion growling through him with a strength quite improper for the early hour. What was a man to do with a wife who sparked such greedy desperation with the mere adoration of her glance? He went straight for his washbasin, plunging his face into the refreshing chill in hopes of cooling his ardor. It wasn't cold enough. Arabella had quickened a heated agitation in his blood not easily stilled.

Restlessly he washed the sheen of perspiration from his body, and when he set the sponge aside, he was surprised by the application of soft toweling to his back and shoulders. Followed by a disturbing trail of kisses.

"Might I assist you, husband?"

The towel was abandoned in favor of bedsheets.

There, what began with fevered kisses quickly escalated into frenzied mating ritual, all aggression, no resistance, until Arabella's soft cries of completion were swallowed up in his own. Then, they shared a tender aftermath, tangled together in a cozy intimacy, stroking and kissing one another with a lazy enjoyment.

"You are totally shameless, wife, and I love you madly."

"If you do not wish to encourage my attention, my lord, then be more discreet in how you are displayed before me."

"Should I go about in monk's robes, then?"

She glanced up, a wicked twinkle in her eyes. "I fear that would not help, now that I know what lies beneath them."

Smiling contentedly, he kissed her brow and released a sigh of sheer satisfaction. But that mellowed mood could not survive the seeping worries preying upon their minds.

"Louis?"

"Yes, little one?"

"Promise me I shall have you forever and always."

When she was met with silence, Arabella looked up to him, the somber set of her features demanding a reply.

"Promise me."

He cupped her face with a gentle touch, his gaze delving into hers with a soul-snatching intensity. "I promise I will never leave you unless it's best for you that I be gone."

She didn't like that riddle, nor the quiet torment in which it was said. "It will never be best for me to be without you, Louis. Never. You must trust in that if you trust in me."

"You are my life and my hope, Bella. Never doubt that I love you." And he kissed her with an infinite tenderness before giving her a push away. "Now, get up, wife, before you tax me beyond mortal limits."

"What other limits are there?" she teased, coming

up over him so that her breasts grazed his bare chest with an impudent provocation. "Might we reach for them as well?"

"No." His sharp tone was followed by a soothing drawl, and her momentary alarm was quieted. "What we have is all I want. It is more than any man deserves."

She smiled at that and kissed his chin, the tip of his nose, and either corner of his mouth before settling upon that luxuriant source of delight. And her anticipation grew apace with his arousal. And more minutes passed in disregard as passion had its way with them.

This time, Louis made sure he was decently clad before addressing her. The barrier of clothing was little help when he observed his wife sprawled in naked hedonistic abandon upon his tangled sheets. She looked up at him through eyes languid and supremely sated.

"My lord, what does the wife of a marquis do when not partaking of marital pleasures?"

"Why do I feel as though you would like to make that a full-time occupation?"

"You've yourself to blame for that, husband. You bring out the wanton in me."

Cautiously, he turned from that avenue of converse. "I believe, madame, that the sole purpose of a titled wife is to see how quickly she can flit through her husband's fortune."

"Am I to spend my time buying clothes I do not need? Or do you think my wardrobe inadequate?" She frowned. She was now the wife of a marquis, not the daughter of a physician. Perhaps she should pay closer heed to her appearance, lest she embarrass him.

"My love, I am content to have you garbed thusly, but t'would cause a stir in company, don't you think?" He brought her a dressing gown. "In fact, it is causing a stir now, so please put this on or I shall never escape your charms."

"I don't want you to escape," she purred, as she accepted the silky robe. It was the rich burgundy one he'd worn the day she'd come to visit him, the day he'd proposed.

"Alas, I must, at least for a time. I have business to attend this morning that cannot wait."

Arabella hurried into the concealing folds of silk and went to him, fearing the sober direction of his plans. "Louis, does this concern them?" She didn't need to clarify that.

"You've no cause for worry, Bella."

But she was worried and she was trembling as she put her arms around him. "Louis, please be careful."

"I will, my love. I know exactly what I'm facing. Now, come down with me and see me off. I fear you've put me off to a late start."

He didn't seem to mind the fact that she was adhered to his side like a cocklebur. In fact, the tight wrap of his arm encouraged it. She was too upset to care what Takeo thought of her, clinging to her husband in obvious distress, bundled in his dressing gown with her hair a wild tangle above it. If she appeared a madwoman, the illusion wasn't so far astray. For upset and overactive imagination had her quite crazed.

Louis halted in the foyer and eased her away. After

looking long into her troubled gaze, he shifted his attention to his silent servant.

"Takeo, my wife is my most treasured possession. See to her care as you would my own. Guard her well in my absence, and let no harm befall her. It is a sacred trust I give you. Do not fail me."

The lad bowed deeply, compelled by honor and love. And Louis had no doubt that he would see to Arabella's safety at the risk of his own. Now, to make Arabella understand.

He turned to her, cradling her impetuous face in the spread of his hand. "Bella, listen to me. If you go out, take Takeo with you. No errand is too slight to deserve his protection. If you love me, you will bow to my wishes in this one thing."

"I love you, Louis, and I will." And bravely she held to her tears until after he was gone. Sniffing them back, she turned to the Asian servant and supplied a wry smile. "Well, Takeo, what are your feelings on shopping?"

He regarded her impassively.

"My feelings exactly. We shall get on famously, you and I."

He ventured a small smile.

"Let us think of something we can do to please Louis. Have you any ideas?"

The boy's brow crowded in thought, then cleared with the bestowal of a surprisingly sweet and youthful smile. Nodding, he caught her hand and towed her into Louis's study. She took the volume he hunted up and studied it curiously.

"What is this? I don't understand. It's Italian."

Takeo nodded enthusiastically. Then he put his

hand to his mouth and lifted it upward, stretching his fingers open in a wide release. He repeated the gesture until she gave a gasp of comprehension.

"Oh! Yes, of course. What a wonderful idea. Thank you."

Then Takeo's animation ebbed and he regarded Arabella warily. Knowing what she did about him, she could sympathize with his reluctance to accept her. She made her words gentle yet firm in conviction and authority.

"Takeo, you've been with Louis for a long time and you've been both family and friend to him. It's not my intention to intrude upon that. I love Louis and you must believe I would never do anything to hurt him. I think it would please him for us to be friends, or if not that, at least not enemies. What do you think?"

He considered her through those black inscrutable eyes, then slowly bowed. And Arabella smiled as her first foothold in Louis Radman's life was secured.

For three hundred years, Louis had been the hunted. He knew how to lose himself in a city, how to become virtually invisible within the teaming mass of society. He'd learned how to protect himself when the most vulnerable, during those daylight hours when he'd been powerless. He was skilled at avoiding suspicions and curiosities and in how to surround himself in secrets. He'd relied on a shrewd cunning and intelligence to keep himself safe from those who would destroy him and upon his supernatural talents to evade detection.

Now, as a mortal, he could see what an impossible task it was to track down those who preyed upon the night. Those who were as he had been. He felt stupid and slow of perception, suffering from what Gerardo mockingly called the human condition of mental lassitude. How was he to best two unnatural beings with the faculties at his command? He had none of their power, their strength, or their speed. But he had something they did not: he had the ability to walk in the sunlight. If he could catch them when they were at rest, they would die as easily as a mortal. He had an advantage over the age-old vampire stalkers; he knew his prey. He knew how they thought, where they fed, what they'd look for in a hiding place.

And they knew him.

It would be only a matter of time before they caught and killed him, if that was their intention. Death was not the worst they could do. How well he knew that.

He'd spent a fruitless day in some very unsavory places. He'd uncovered the resting spots of two masters and five fledglings. A mortal man would have reacted in righteous horror and put an end to them while they were at their unholy slumber. Louis was a bit more philosophical. They'd done nothing to him. Who was he to spoil their wretched existence? Perhaps in time, he could even return and offer them a way to escape their undead state, if that was their choice. If Howland's cure withstood the test of time.

If he lived long enough.

He returned home no closer to finding Bianca and Gerardo than when he'd left. And his temperament was as foul as the weather.

Arabella was waiting for him in the hall. He stood for a perplexed moment, staring at her in all her best finery. "Am I missing something?"

"I've planned a surprise for you, Louis. Go upstairs and change, and we can—"

"I'm not in the mood for surprises, Bella. In the future, you would do well to check with me before you schedule my time." With that curt reprisal, he stalked around her and into his study. He didn't want to acknowledge the way her quiet gasp of hurt speared to the heart of him. He was feeling low enough because his failure could well cost him his happiness and her her very life. He poured himself a glass of spirits, thinking the alcohol might calm him, but one taste only frustrated him further and he pitched the glass, contents and all, into the fire grate, where it made a satisfactory crash and flare. Then he dropped into a chair, chewing on his anxiety. It would be dark soon. How was he going to protect his own?

He gave a slight start when Arabella's hand slid across his knees. She'd knelt beside his chair in a pool of sarcenet to rest her head upon his lap. When his surprise faded, a remarkable sense of peace crept in. He let his knuckles rub along her soft cheek, and her sigh was a sweet curative.

"I'm sorry, Bella. I've ruined your evening."

"No such thing," she chided gently. She caught his hand, pressed a quick kiss to it, then continued to hold it tucked beneath her chin. He could feel her pulse throb a lulling rhythm. "It was presumptuous of me. If you are weary and would rather stay in tonight—"

Stay in. Was that what he wanted? Like bait in a trap? Waiting for them to come?

"No," he announced abruptly. Arabella lifted to look up at him in askance. "And spoil the surprise? What have you in mind, little one? I could use the distraction."

"Truly?"

"Yes. I didn't mean to be such an ogre. Forgive me."

"Forgiven." And she was up in a trice, tugging on his hands. "You must hurry then. Put on your evening attire. We must leave posthaste."

Smiling at her enthusiasm, he allowed his humor to be coaxed as she all but dragged him to the stairs. Then she turned to him, planting a firm, will-rattling kiss upon his lips.

"I love you, Louis. Hurry."

The moment the first aria began, Arabella said a private word of thanks to Takeo. Louis relaxed back into his opera box seat and let the beauty of his home language rush over him. His poignant expression was worth every bit of trouble it had taken to secure the coveted spot at the last moment. Catalani's appearances at the King's Theatre always packed the house from the pit to the fifth tier. It was a place the fashionable came to be seen, and as a new countess, Arabella should have basked in the attention. Yet she was grateful for the dimming of the lights so she could share a private moment with the man at her side.

The music was beautiful and stirring, but Arabella

was more entranced by the study of her new husband. Silhouetted against the faint house lights and the deeper shadows of their box, he was chiseled perfection, his profile strong and proud and flawless. Her husband. The idea still flustered her. Hers to reach out and caress, to take home and love, to hold and adore. She supposed the fact that he was wealthy beyond belief should have held some sway, but it didn't figure in the least when he turned toward her, his eyes softened to a warm green-gold glow and steeped in tender affection. Nothing would compare in worth to that brief gaze and the way he carried her hand to his lips for just the featherlight brush of a kiss.

Contentment settled into a dreamy languor. She found herself leaning against him, her head upon his shoulder, her eyes sagging shut as the sights and sounds within the King's Theatre faded from significance. She heard the low accented voice crooning to her.

Arabella. Arabella, come.

She rose up wordlessly and at Louis's questioning gaze, murmured that she'd return in a moment. He nodded, already drawn back into the mesmerizing power of the story staged below.

He wasn't sure how much time had passed, but suddenly Louis knew it had been too long. Concerned but not yet panicked, he readied to stand when fingertips stroked along his shoulders and he felt a kiss touch to his crown. Sighing, he sank back into his seat and enjoyed the firm massage that worked up his neck to his jaw, then paused for a sensuous kneading at his temples. It was bliss, and he shut his eyes to luxuriate in it.

Then the slow, rubbing movements ceased and the pressure increased, steadily drawing his head back over the edge of the seat until his neck curved in a taut bow. Perplexed, he let his eyes flutter open and he looked up at the soulless smile of Bianca du Maurier.

"Enjoying the opera, *il mio amore?*"

The tension she applied was crushing. Held helpless, Louis couldn't even swallow. Not that he could with the way his mouth went dry.

"What have you done with my wife?" His words escaped in a hoarse rattle.

"Done? Why, nothing. Gerardo is keeping her entertained so we might have a little time together. You are so beautiful. I had forgotten that, Luigino. Time can dull even the most precious memories."

"What do you want, Bianca?" He made his tone crisp and annoyed, and he could feel her recoil. Her agonizing press became a lingering caress along the lean angles of his face and down his neck to begin a feline kneading upon his chest.

"Why, Gino, I want what I've always wanted. I want for you to love me. I want for you to adore and worship me. I want you to be my slave."

He caught her hands and plucked them away with a dismissing indifference. "Well, it is not what I want. It wasn't then, it isn't now, *il nemico.*"

He heard the hiss of her breath and felt her draw in close behind him. "Evil one?" His nape tingled and the flesh of his throat grew tight but he refused to act afraid. Even when he felt the chill of her tongue circling his ear. "Gino," she whispered, all wet and silky. "No—Louis. Louis, is there something you are trying to hide from your old friends? Something like the fact that you have somehow become mortal again?"

When he tried to rise, her fingers clenched in his hair, securing him in place with a fierce twist that angled his head sharply to one side. She nuzzled his neck, tasting with her lips, testing the flurry of his pulse with her tongue.

"How sweet and strong," she murmured thickly, her hunger rising. "Imagine the pleasure of bringing you over not once, but twice." Her breathing was erratic now, blasting against his bare skin like the scorch of death, fetid with the stale blood of her last victim. Apparently, she'd recently fed, or she'd have no such control. For instead of sinking her teeth into his throat, she jerked him about to roughly take his mouth with hers. Louis fought against the gagging revulsion—and against the distant part of him that enjoyed the taste if not the act as her sharp incisors cut into his lip.

Abruptly, Louis moaned low in his throat, and his mouth yielded. Tasting his surrender, Bianca released her paralyzing grip to stroke him into a greater passion. And as soon as she did, his arm hooked around her neck and he flung her with all his might over the edge of the third-tier opera box. Her look of surprise seemed frozen in time. Then she disappeared without a sound.

He didn't wait to see what happened to her. He was certain she came nowhere near hitting the gallery below. She was too agile for that, too powerful and quick to recover from a lapse of control. And he knew he didn't want to be there when she regained it.

The lobby of the theatre was empty when he burst out into it, and Louis knew a sudden and soul-deep devastation.

What had Gerardo done with Arabella?

Chapter Fourteen

Arabella found herself standing in the theatre lobby with no idea why she'd come there. She felt light-headed and unsure of her balance. Had she become ill inside? Knowing Louis must be worrying, she circled to return to their box and found herself blocked by an elegantly garbed figure.

"Buona sera, Signora."

Arabella froze. Devils, Louis had said, but in his evening finery, Gerardo Pasquale looked more the angel. He was tall and very dark, with eyes of a piercing blue. About him was that same unnatural shimmer of beauty she'd first seen in Louis. And as much as she was wary of him, she was drawn to that magnetic aura. She found herself powerless as he lifted her hand for a courtly kiss.

"Are you enjoying the opera? *Splendido!* How wonderful it is. Such sounds. Reminds me of home. Gino, too? Or does he try to forget those days?"

There was a wistfulness to his expression that made Arabella want to console him. "He remembers, but sadly, I think. As if he's lost something of value he cannot restore."

Gerardo nodded, his smile pursed and bittersweet. "It is there we lost our innocence and our love for one another. We were inseparable friends in those days, Gino and I."

"What happened to change that?" she heard herself asking. Part of her wanted to know, while another part urged her to flee while she could, that she was in terrible danger. But it was already too late. She understood instinctively. Something about Gerardo compelled her attention. It was impossible to draw away. And she wanted to know his link to her husband.

"What happens?" He shrugged with a liquid grace. "A woman."

"Bianca du Maurier," she supplied, making that triangle without effort.

Gerardo made an acknowledging sound, one of regret, of pain. "She was so beautiful, my Bianca. I lost my heart to her the first time I beheld her. I was so in love, and in love with the very idea of it." He gave a soft laugh, just a touch of cynicism edging into the warm tones. He took Arabella's arm and wound it casually through his so he could lead her in a companionable stroll toward the deeper shadows of the theatre. In the back of her mind, Arabella tried to protest, but she simply could not pull away.

"Bianca, she was so cruel with my heart. It amused her to toy with it. But she did not love me. For her, it was Gino, whom I loved like a brother."

Arabella listened, a great sadness welling up inside

her as if she was experiencing her escort's pain. How sharp and bitter it must have been.

"And then," he continued quietly, "I found the two of them together, as lovers. Gino, he was so distraught. He came to me with tears in his eyes, begging for my forgiveness. I could not give it, even knowing as I do now that the fault was not his. You see, he had betrayed my trust, my love for him, and that wounded more deeply than Bianca's faithlessness. A sad story, no? Perhaps it would make great opera."

They'd come to a secluded corner where the lights and sound fell short, and there was only Gerardo and his sad tale and his soothing manner. Arabella was gazing up into those brilliant eyes, her own filled with empathic dampness. When he touched her face, her mind recoiled, but her body stood still and passively allowed it.

"So, now you know about Gino and me. Oh, how I miss his company. Such times we had. And now I am so alone. But Gino, how lucky for him to have found a woman such as you. He loves you. I can see that. How envious I am."

His caress intensified, stroking her cheek, smoothing over her hair, a gentle touch, a lover's touch. And Arabella was leaning into it, all languid invitation, lost to the dazzle of his gaze.

"T'would be a fitting punishment for him to lose his love to me, don't you think? Kiss me, Arabella."

And she rose up shamelessly for the taste of his mouth. She couldn't stop herself. It was as if mind and body were somehow separated. She could see herself responding with a wanton eagerness, could feel the fright and distress of having him part her lips with the thrust of his tongue, to take deeply from her. And she writhed with the shame of it. But she couldn't stop. She couldn't halt her arms from winding about his neck or hold in the low, guttural sounds of lustful longing that issued from her own throat. Or control the way her body undulated against his. Or the wanting, the incredible, desperate wanting, so wicked and irresistible.

"Bella."

Louis's soft call of her name sent a mild shock through her. And she wanted to cry out, *Louis, thank God! Help me!* But she couldn't.

The terrible part of it was that it wasn't Louis's voice that drew her away, but rather the fact that Gerardo pushed her gently from him. She stood, silent and shivering, part of her craving to return to the arms of the man who was not her husband and part of her horrified of what Louis must think, to come upon her entangled passionately with another man.

But Louis betrayed no sign of anger or hurt. He merely reached out to take her by the elbow.

"Bella, come with me."

And she refused. She actually pulled within his kind yet unyielding grasp. And she didn't know why.

"Bella, come."

He stepped closer, putting his arm around her quivering shoulders, forcefully moving her while his gaze met that of his old friend.

Gerardo smiled, a slow, taunting gesture, and let him take her, let him know it was only through his will that she went peacefully. And his low, cunning laughter followed.

In their coach, Arabella sat stiff and scarcely breathing. There was something wild and perverse inside her that would strike out at her beloved for taking her from the pleasure of another's arms. But deeper was a cringing horror that she'd allowed herself to succumb to another's seduction. And shame, a tremendous weight of shame and confusion.

Louis sat across from her, watching her through expressionless eyes. He displayed no shock, no fury, no distress of a man scorned. He waited. She wasn't sure what he was waiting for until the numbness began to leave her and great tremors of disbelief rattled along her limbs, a shuddering realization of what she'd done. A small sound choked from her, and instantly, his arms were open to receive her.

"Louis ..."

He cradled her to his chest, holding her while she sobbed in a helpless abandon. She huddled on the seat beside him, clutching at his shirt front until the weeping wore down to a pitiful whimpering. By then they'd reached their secluded street where a light burned in welcome. Where Takeo waited at the door to be waved back by Louis's hand as he carried her, weak and trembling, up the stairs.

When he set her down, she still clung to him, hiding her face against his shoulder, not knowing if she could ever look up at him with such guilt savaging her heart. She felt the tenderness of his kiss at her brow, and the shame kept swelling.

"You must hate me."

"No," he soothed, petting her hair, kissing her again.

"Louis ... Louis, I love you."

"I know. I know, Bella. It's all right."

"How can you say that?" she cried out wretchedly. "How can you pretend it doesn't matter?"

"Because it doesn't. Bella, you were not to blame for what happened."

Her fingers curled tighter in his coat. Tears burned. She had to make him understand the vileness of what she'd done. "But he didn't seduce me. He didn't force me. I threw myself at him. I wanted him to—"

"Don't, little one. You are not to blame. He bewitched you."

She glanced up then, hoping there was some truth to what he said, some way to explain away her behavior. Because she couldn't bear to break the trust of this man who'd wed her. Louis rubbed the tears from her cheeks with his thumbs. There was no disgust in his tender look.

"His trickery is powerful. He can convince you that his will is your own. It's deception, wicked, cruel deception. He can pull you in with promises, but he never speaks the entire truth. You mustn't forget that. He will cloud your mind so he can use you. And he will use you to hurt me."

"Because of Bianca."

Louis hesitated but only for a moment. "Yes. Because once, long ago, she confused me the way he did you. And I have never stopped paying for that lapse of will."

"How he must hate you to wish such a terrible revenge."

"Yes. He hates me. For more reasons than you could ever guess. If only there were some way to undo what was done."

That look of melancholy returned, and with it, Arabella's complete devotion. She touched his face, coaxing him forward to kiss her. With that sweet kiss came a renewed sense of disgrace, and Arabella tried to pull back. Knowing she'd been a victim didn't ease the shame as it should. And understanding that, Louis sought another way to show his forgiveness.

With the greatest of care, he removed her evening finery down to the ivory blush of her skin. When she was supine upon their coverlet, he showered her with attentive kisses, with lingering caresses, murmuring of his love for her while displaying it with an unquestionable passion. He ravaged the softness of her mouth, worshipped the heavy fullness of her breasts until their tips were diamond-hard, stroked and stoked a restless, fevered yearning with the purposeful circles of his hand until she burst beyond the constraints of pleasure. Then, after she'd come back down to a plane of replete luxury, he kissed her once, deeply, and told her once, conclusively, "I love you, Arabella."

How could she possibly disbelieve him?

And after they'd made slow, satisfying love to one another, he held her within the protective cove of his arms until she drifted off to sleep. And he lay awake, warily guarding his bride, wondering when his old friend would tire of the games and come for him in earnest.

In the crystal clarity of dawn, the events of the previous night seemed vague as a dream. Looking at the man asleep beside her, Arabella could not believe she'd ever want another. She lay on her side for long minutes, absorbed in the way his dark lashes curved along his cheeks, musing over the generous peaks and swells of his mouth. And she couldn't fathom ever thinking of another man with anything but indifference.

She was pillowed upon his outstretched arm. His other rested palm down upon his abdomen. She was admiring the fine, strong shape of his fingers when she happened to realize how still he was. There was no movement of his chest. She stared with a dread fascination. None at all.

"Louis?"

She touched his hand and drew back in shock. His skin was so cold, so lifeless. A terrible suspicion shook through her and she cried out in despair.

"No! My God! Louis!"

At the sound of her frantic voice and the feel of her rough shaking, Louis opened his eyes, then screwed them shut with a horrible wail.

"The light! Shut the drapes! Bella, shut them!"

Panicked, she ran to do so. When she returned, he'd rolled up onto his knees and had the heels of his hands digging into his eye sockets.

"Burning," he moaned frantically. "They're burning."

"Let me see."

"No!" He tried to wrench away, but she caught his wrists and wrestled his hands down. His eyes were still squeezed tight.

"Let me see," she urged quietly, easing her thumbs

across the fragile lids, feeling the rapid movement beneath them.

Slowly, he squinted up at her, flinching with discomfort. His eyes were pooled in a sea of red, their centers swollen, their color a hot, molten gold. And he made a low, anguished sound.

She reacted quickly, not with a female's hysterics, but with a physician's cool practicality. "Lie back. Lie back, Louis, and close them. That's right."

He felt her move off the bed and cried out sharply. "Bella, don't leave me!"

She caught at one grasping hand and kissed it lightly. "I won't. I just want to get some cold water and a cloth to put over your eyes. All right? I'll be right back."

He let her go and continued to shift restlessly until she returned to wring the wet rag over his eyes, hoping to flush whatever had gotten into them. Then she laid it out in a mask of cool darkness.

"Better? Louis, what is it?"

He didn't answer. He'd fallen into an agitated state, rambling, muttering odd things about his flesh burning and the blood boiling in his veins. Yet his skin was so cool, without a trace of fever. And she was recalled to that night in her father's office with an insightful terror.

Alarmed, Arabella dressed hurriedly and went to the door, finding Takeo there before she even had a chance to call for him. The boy took one look and rushed to his master's bedside to drop down on his knees, his expression warped with anxiousness.

"Takeo, do you know what's wrong with him?"

The boy looked up at her, perplexed. She tried again.

"Have you seen him like this before?"

He nodded and pointed to her, then made a gesture with his hand as if he was holding something. She didn't understand.

"I can't go back. I can't go back," Louis raved weakly, his thrashing growing more pronounced.

Takeo looked from him to Arabella. Again, he pointed at her, then reached for Louis's arm, turning it palm up, poking at the distended veins.

"Me? No, my father. Yes, of course. Takeo, you must go get my father right away."

The boy shook his head, clinging to Louis's arm in his reluctance.

"I'll stay with him. This is very important." She scrambled about to find a piece of paper, then wrote her father a rather incoherent note, stating that Louis was very ill and pleading that he come right away. She folded it and wrote the address of the hospital on the outside. "Take this. You must get it to my father. He'll know what to do." And she pressed several coins upon him. "Go quickly."

Takeo rose and abruptly cast himself upon Louis's chest, hugging tightly, briefly, before fleeing the room. She could hear the patter of his slipper-clad feet as they practically flew down the stairs. Then there was nothing she could do but sit beside the delirious figure and wait. And hope.

"How long has he been like this?"

Stuart Howland set his case on the floor and

went to bend over Louis, immediately checking his pulse.

"Since this morning." Arabella's voice quavered, stresses creeping up, now that her father was there to shoulder the responsibilities.

"And last night?" He expertly felt brow, cheeks, and neck with the back of his hand.

"He was fine. What is it? What's wrong?"

"What has he said to you?" Ignoring Louis's moaning protests, he pried his eyelids apart. And he frowned at what he observed.

"That the light burned his eyes. That his skin is burning. That his blood is boiling. Father, what is it? He's not dying, is he?"

"No," he dismissed curtly. "But it does look as though his body is trying to reject my best efforts."

"What do you mean?"

"Arabella, leave now."

"No."

"Go." Then his voice gentled. "I'll call you if there is a change."

Arabella looked as though she would object; then, with a soft cry, she ran from the room, unable to leave with any degree of grace.

"It's not as though the dead can die twice," he muttered to himself. Then he peered again into the unholy eyes. "Radman, can you hear me?"

"Do something," Louis groaned.

Stuart stirred some of his powders into a glass of water and propped up his patient with a growl of, "Drink." Louis swallowed, and the doctor eased him down. Almost immediately, his body began to convulse in hard, jerking spasms. Holding him down by the shoulders, Stuart ordered, "Easy now. Let it work. Let it work."

Louis fell into a rapid panting, the worst of the struggle over. Soon, he was still and coherent and anxious.

"What's happening, Doctor?"

"You tell me?"

"I'm reverting, aren't I? Aren't I?"

Howland's silence said it all.

"No. No! So close. So close. There must be something we can do. I can't go back to what I was. I can't." And he lay limply, sucking in shallow breaths, trying not to give in to total despair. "Bella. Where's Bella?"

"I'm going to take her home with me."

"What?" He started to sit up but lacked strength. "No, you can't. I haven't harmed her."

"Haven't yet, you mean. Until you are stabilized, it is much too dangerous."

"She will not leave me."

"Then I'll tell her what you are."

"She still will not leave."

And Stuart feared that was true. He gave up for the moment and jumped to another track. "I will be monitoring you closely. The serum seems to retard the degenerative process. I'll keep you on steady doses."

"Until what?"

"Until I can find another donor. We'll have to try another transfusion. Perhaps the effects are only temporary. Perhaps there is some other agent in your body that destroys healthy cells. I don't know. We are guessing, at best. I'll know better after the second procedure. Are you willing?"

"Have I a choice?"

"When are you going to tell Arabella?"

He looked up at the doctor through his sore red eyes and said softly, "When I have to."

Stuart accepted that grim statement for the moment. "How do you feel?"

"Terrible. Better."

"How long have you known it wasn't working?"

He thought about lying. He thought about Howland taking his love away, but he answered with a glum quiet, "All along. It helped, but it wasn't strong enough. I can't eat, nothing—unless it's raw. It makes me ill, but I can keep it down. And now the light. There must be something you can do."

Howland thought and he shrugged philosophically. "There are always options, my lord, as long as you are willing to take the risk."

"I'm willing."

"All right then. You should be fine soon. Try to—eat."

Louis was silent for a moment, then he looked up with a sudden intensity. "Doctor, if this procedure works on me, will it work on others?"

"Others?"

"Like me."

"Are there others?"

"More than you like to think." And he gave a thin smile.

Howland appeared thoughtful. He was considering the incredible opportunity for experimentation in this unknown realm. He never blinked at the danger. "I suppose it would. I don't really know. I would have to see and study one of your—peers. Are you sure they want to be cured?"

And he lay back, eyes closing, conscience aching. "I owe them the chance."

When Louis emerged from the bedroom, Arabella wrapped around him with a fragile cry and a flood of tears. She refused to be pried away even after Louis's crooning assurances that he was all right. She simply could not make herself let him go. So in the end, he indulged her, letting her weep herself dry while he enjoyed the soggy proof of her devotion. Freeing one hand, he placed it upon Takeo's shoulders, for the boy looked perilously close to tears, himself. His voice was gruff with emotion when he addressed them.

"I am fine, thanks to your quick thinking and the doctor's care. Now, no more of this carrying on. Bella, you are drowning me."

Did she apologize? No. She lifted her head and affixed a wildly passionate kiss upon his lips, not caring if her father was looking on in disapproval. That kiss lingered, lavish and lushly expressive, to the extent of her breath, then she stepped back a scant inch or two to regard him with an intensity from the heart.

"You promised you would never leave me, Louis. I hold you to that vow, my lord. If it's death that separates us, I would gladly cross the grave to be with you."

"Arabella—" Her father's tone was shaken.

But Louis looked long and deep into her calm gray eyes and responded with like sobriety.

"It is my greatest hope that you shall never be forced to act upon that vow."

But he feared she would. And sooner than they both would have liked to believe.

For as the day lengthened into late-afternoon shadow, he received a visit from a furtive little man who demanded coin up front. Closing the two of them in his study, Louis counted out the exact amount and extended it in his hand. When the hireling made a grab for it, his fist closed tight.

"What did you learn?"

The investigator studied that tight fist and licked his lips eagerly. "Well, I searched through all the records, just like you told me, until I found a place like you described. Cost me plenty to prime the right palms, it did."

"And what is the address?" When he was met with crafty silence, he jiggled the gold in his hand. "The address."

When he had it, Louis released the money into greedy hands without regret and encouraged the greasy little man to exit by the rear entrance. Now, to act upon what he'd learned.

Louis stood in the door to the library for a long moment, his emotions crowding up into his throat with a painful twist. Arabella was perched on one of the windowseats with a dusty tome upon her knees, curled up like a child, as beautiful as an angel. Takeo was seated cross-legged on the Turkish rug nearby, his expression watchful and infinitely patient. The boy saw him and responded at once to his beckoning gesture. Unaware, Arabella read on.

Takeo looked up in question, then frowned at the intensity in his master's face. That instinctive fear increased when Louis placed a fond hand against the side of his face.

"Takeo, I entrust Arabella to you. Guard her well and against any who threaten—even if it is me. She must be kept safe at all costs. You will do that for me?"

The boy nodded gravely.

"If I am not back before dawn, I want you to take Arabella out of the city. Take her to the country house, but spend no more than a single day there. If I do not join you, leave England."

Takeo gripped his hand, his dark eyes filled with objection.

"Do not argue with me. If I am not there, I will not be coming, but others might, and you will be in great danger. Do you understand?"

Again, the stiff nod.

"Travel by night and be ever alert. If I should come to you and not be as I am now, I want you to put me to rest, as we discussed."

The boy ducked his head and his slight shoulders gave a telltale hitch. Louis touched the bowed head gently.

"Takeo, I count on you to do this for me. I must keep her safe. I ask for your promise out of your love for me. Will you see it done?"

Takeo looked up slowly, his set features streaked with dampness, and he nodded.

Louis expelled a breath of relief. "Good. You've

been a faithful friend to me. Serve your new mistress as well."

Then he crossed the room and stood over his wife, catching her attention with the light brush of his fingertips along the sweet curve of her cheek.

"What are you reading, my love?"

She showed him the weighty title.

"Philosophy? Rather esoteric fare just before dinner, don't you think?"

She smiled. "You have some wonderful books, Louis. I shall enjoy working my way along the shelves."

He smiled back with just a slight bend of sadness to shape his lips as he played with a lock of hair that had strayed from the confines of its unswept style. "I fear you will have to sup alone tonight. I have an important matter to attend, and it may take some time."

She took up his hand quickly, pressing it with concern. "Are you fit enough for such a task?"

"I shall have to be, little one. Much rides on the outcome. I want you to have no worries for me. Takeo will keep you company until I return. I have placed your care in his hands and have given him explicit instructions. I want you to obey them without question. Do you understand?"

"But Louis—"

"Arabella, you must obey him without question. Do you understand?"

"Yes." But she was beginning to frown with suspicion, so he bent and kissed her soundly until all fretting was chased from her mind.

"I love you, Bella."

And she smiled up at him contentedly, her features innocent, her gaze trusting. "Do not be gone long, my lord. Whom do you go to see?"

"An old friend."

Chapter Fifteen

He stood well back in the shadows, waiting, watching as darkness settled with an ominous chill. Close to his chest, cradled in the bend of his arm, he held a large tabby cat. The animal purred with a throaty pleasure as he absently stroked the matted fur. Then he went completely still as a figure emerged from the fashionable townhouse: a woman.

He watched as she paused to test the night air like a hunting hound. He was a good distance away and hoped that the presence of the cat would disguise his scent. If she smelled live blood, it would be a confusion of man and animal in the midst of potent alley refuse, nothing distinct, nothing threatening. Nothing that would appeal to the refined tastes of Bianca du Maurier.

He waited, breath suspended, until she began to walk in the opposite direction. Even hating her, he had to admire the beauty of that walk: supple, smooth, gliding, moving beyond the human state of time and space. Powerful. Alien. And completely deadly.

He put down the cat and stepped over it as it wound about his ankles. It gave a sudden screeching yowl and darted off into the alley. Louis paid it no attention as he started for the street with a somber purpose. The moment he cleared the mouth of the alleyway, he understood the cat's terror. For out of the soupy darkness lumbered the bulk of Mac Reeves. He was wearing the same clothes he'd died in. The stench was terrible—stale blood and week-old decay. His stare was mindless, dead. But he was fast, too fast for Louis, who saw only a blur before that foul, decomposing hand gripped him by the throat and jerked him up off his feet to dangle helplessly. Darkness swelled to swallow up his vision. And with his last full breath before blackness claimed him, he called one name.

"Gerardo!"

With awareness came pain, a dull, raw ache in his throat from the near crushing of his windpipe. Louis opened his eyes slowly, then blinked. He was stretched out on a comfortable overstuffed sofa, and across from him sat a casually garbed Gerardo Pasquale with a smile of tolerance on his face. That smile widened when Louis's first conscious act was to reach for his neck in search of puncture wounds.

"Really, old friend, do you think I would take advantage of you when you were unable to defend yourself?"

"The man I knew would not," Louis rasped, as he dragged himself into a seated position. "Are you still that man, Gerardo?"

"I am more than any man, *mio bello amico*. Coming here was foolish, you know. But as you are not foolish, I am curious. *Perche?* To talk over times past?"

"In a way, yes."

Gerardo chuckled. "Gino, you know I love you, and you know I am going to kill you. So, why? Why hurry the inevitable? You should be home, enjoying your pretty wife while you can."

"I came because of the friendship we had, because I have never forgiven myself for—what happened. I took your life from you and I would restore it."

Gerardo tented his hands. His expression was one of mild interest and amusement. "Would you? And how would you effect this miracle?"

"I've found a cure for our affliction. You can walk again as a man, in the light of day."

"A cure? Bianca told me, but I did not believe it. Is it true, then, that you are mortal?"

"Close. Very close. I no longer rest like the dead or suffer the hunger. I lead a normal existence, can feel the sun on my face, and hope to fill my wife with a child. Things we loved and lost and longed for. Gerardo, I can give back what I took from you."

He appeared to consider it, his posture relaxed, his mood contemplative. "What of your abilities? Your strength? Do you still possess them?"

"No," Louis said without thinking, then immediately realized his mistake when his friend's gaze drooped into a speculative glitter.

"So," he drawled out long and pleasantly. "You are just a mortal, after all."

"I am alive, Gerardo. Think of it. Think of what you might have—"

"Have? Why, dear Gino, I have everything! I have mankind at my feet. I am a god compared to them. You think I would give up immortality to grub about as a puny human?" He laughed, and Louis saw with a fatal vision how warped his friend had become in the clutch of power. "But then you would, the noble Luigino who champions the virtuous and espouses dignity." His suave features twisted savagely. "What dignity was there in what you did to me?"

Gerardo surged up from his chair, the movement so fluid he seemed almost to levitate. He paced for a time, his glances touching on Louis now and again as he mulled over his thoughts. "So you would like forgiveness, and think by reducing me to a sheep for slaughter, I will take you to my bosom and dismiss all ill will." He paused before the sofa, looking down upon his friend with a detached smile. "Give me your hand on it, Gino, so that I might know you to be sincere."

Louis put out his hand and Gerardo's smooth palm slipped over it. His fingers closed, effortlessly snapping and crushing bone until Louis was on his knees.

"You offer me life? What of those I loved? What do you offer them?"

Louis tried to speak, but great dark swells of pain engulfed his words.

"How will you repay me for the evil that you did? You stole my future. You murdered my family!"

"No . . ."

"Yes, you did! When you left me alone to face the hell of my new life, I ran home to take comfort from those dear to me. I didn't know, Gino. I didn't understand what I was. I could not stop myself. I tore out their throats and bathed in their blood. My sisters, my mother and father. Their screams—their horror—how will you take that from me? I don't want to live as a man with those memories! I could not bear it!"

"I didn't know—"

"Did you care?"

"I didn't want you to die!"

They looked at one another for an expressive moment, flickers of long ago feeling tempering the exchange. For an instant, Gerardo's features softened and his fingertips made a sensitive sweep of his friend's uplifted face, a touch that ended at the pulse point of his throat.

"So you condemned me to this—this life. Oh, Gino, you should have let me die."

"Let me help you now. *Per piacere!*"

A slow sneer contoured the poignant expression. "Help me what? Become groveling and weak, like you? Scuttle about like an insect, when I have known such power! You know! You've had it, you've felt it! The strength! The embrace of eternity!"

"The killing!"

"Yessss." It was a slow, wet hiss, and he looked down with his pale, soulless eyes floating in a sea of red, and Louis knew he was about to die.

When Gerardo's hand forked beneath his chin to lift him, Louis exploded upward, driving his elbow into the soft hollow of the fiend's throat with a force that would have popped the head off a normal man. But Gerardo only blinked, looking surprised. Then he smiled. And with calm deliberation delivered a flat-handed blow that shattered Louis's cheek and jaw as it sent him flying against the opposite wall so hard the outline of his body imprinted in the plaster.

Gerardo was on him before his knees had chance to give way. He came with fangs out and snarling. And Louis butted him full in the face with the top of his head. Gerardo staggered back and Louis scrambled for the door, knowing he'd never reach it. So he stopped and whirled to face the demon who was coming at him in a full bore of fury. And he leapt straight up, shooting the side of his foot out like the bolt from a crossbow. The kick took the vampire squarely in the chest, halting him—but not knocking him back. Not stopping him. Not hurting him. Because Gerardo grinned as he smacked the heel of his hand just beneath Louis's breastbone. Ribs caved in like thin kindling, splintering, piercing vital organs and ripping into his lungs. Louis managed a short-lived gasp and dropped.

Gerardo reached down, wrapping his fingers in the short auburn hair, dragging his dying friend up on strengthless legs. His gaze unfocused, his breath gurgling, Louis managed to whisper, "Bella."

Gerardo leaned close, smiling like the devil he was. "Do not worry, Gino. I will comfort your lovely wife." And he sank his teeth to feed.

After the shock of the bite, there was numbness and tingling, hot and shivering. Then, from an impossible distance away, Louis heard a shrieking cry.

"Gerard! What have you done?"

The sharp fangs were ripped away, and without support, Louis collapsed. From where he sat crumpled against the wall, trying to force breath through the ruin of his chest, he could see streaking blurs of motion. Occasionally, they would become Gerardo and Bianca as they struggled. But it was too hard to concentrate, and all began to fade. Then there was Bianca crouching over him, her touch tender against the agony in his misshapen face.

"Oh, Gino, oh, my love, look what he's done to you."

And incredibly, Louis could swear he saw tears in her eyes.

"Oh, my poor darling, how he's hurt you. I will take the pain away and we will be together again. The three of us."

Louis tried to speak. He couldn't move his mouth. Each faint word was a bubbling torment. "Let me die . . . please."

"I can't, my love." And Bianca was stroking his hair. "If you were to die without me, you would become like Reeves, a drooling, mindless hunger. I could not bear to see your beauty rot and fall away. I could not."

Then she kissed his mouth, waking an exquisite pain before she eased over to the ragged side of his throat.

"No." His protest was weak and he was so weary. "Don't take this life from me." But his eyes were already glazing.

"Gino, it is too late. You die within this frail mortal shell. Let me restore you. Rest in my arms, my love. We will be one again."

"No. Bella . . ."

"She is lost to you, Gino. You will be mine," she vowed, licking at the blood, cradling his broken face against her shoulder to hold him still. She began a gentle suction at the tears Gerardo had opened, that pull increasing as her appetite raged. Louis was drifting then, and it was not unpleasant. The searing pain eased, the weak pulse of his failing heart overwhelmed by a stronger cadence as Bianca invaded him. He had no strength to fight, no will to resist. At last, when his limbs hung slack and heavy and the cold of death worked its way through him, she sat back on her heels, her face close to his.

"Come over with me, Gino. Let go of the mortal ties and fly."

And she watched with an avid, greedy satisfaction, having drained not just his blood, but his very soul. She held his head immobile between her hands, savoring the fade of his life force, taking a hideous ecstasy in absorbing it through the glazing portals of his gaze. And because he'd once hovered over the dying to suck the same psychic thrill and he knew well what she was doing, Louis shut his eyes to deny the obscene pleasure.

Suddenly alarmed because she'd lost touch with him, Bianca gashed her own wrist and pressed it against Louis's lips. Her blood filled his mouth and spilled down over chin.

"Open your eyes, Gino. You must fight. You must come over. Let me help you. Let me guide you."

His head rolled loosely.

"No!"

She caught his chin and rubbed her spouting arteries to his slack mouth, screaming, "No, Gino! Swallow! You must take of my blood. I will not lose you! Gino!"

But she knew he was gone. She could feel his fragile mortal life just slip away and out of her control.

"No!"

Bianca threw him aside like a broken toy and surged up, a howling tower of rage. She rounded on Gerardo, who had the good sense to look afraid. She caught him by the shirt front and began to slap him in her maddened fury.

"How could you do such a thing? You knew I wanted him! You knew how much I loved him!"

"Love? You know nothing of love," Gerardo flung back at her, laughing because she couldn't really harm him. "See how long he appeals to you when he is a slobbering *revenant-en-corps* scuffling to do your command, when his flesh begins to peel away and he takes on the mindless stink of death. *Then* see if you'll crave him for your lover!"

Louis heard them talking, yelling, as all that was human lay dead within him. Their voices quivered, quicksilver inside his mind as the taste of Bianca's blood threaded through his veins. A cooling balm glided along bent and tortured limbs that had known such pain. A healing fount became a wellspring eternal to repair the massive internal destruction, soothing ravaged tissues, piecing together that which seemed irreparably fractured. Strength flowed liquid, pulsing. Power. Tremendous power. Sensation intensified, becoming almost too much, too sharp, too vibrant, humming through him in shocking little ripples. Sound, so huge it was hurtful, deafening at first. Scent; blood, heat, bodies close and far, the night, the mist—all delicious fare to inhale and savor. Sight so keen it dazzled. He saw so far, so clear, he couldn't comprehend it all. A moment of panic sank deep to touch upon a soul that was no longer there. And then he knew. He knew what had happened and what he was.

They looked at him with such astonishment, argument falling away before that surprise.

With one back-handed blow, he sent Gerardo crashing through the big bow window and out into the night. His scream sailed after him, trailing down like a faint ribbon into silence.

"Gino!" Bianca was smiling in genuine relief. She made a move toward him, but his arms rose up so that the satiny folds of his cloak fluttered around him, concealing him in blackness. A blackness that abruptly thinned to just a thread of light and slipped like smoke through the crack in the door.

And Bianca was still smiling when Gerardo appeared beside her, brushing shards of glass from out of his coat.

"How strong he is, more so than ever I imagined." Her voice trembled with noticeable thrill. Then she turned on her male companion with a cold slice of fury. "You will leave him to me!"

Gerardo smiled agreeably. "Have him. I have my revenge upon him. Because the first thing he will do is run home to his bride." He laughed low and viciously. "And what a reunion that will be!"

Arabella heard the front door open. With a soft cry of relief, she tossed aside the book she'd been pretending to read for the last two hours and scrambled from the bed. Her thin white nightgown fluttering about her, she ran out into the hall to the top of the stairs.

"Louis!"

The first floor was dark. A strange phosphorescent light spilled in from the open door, and with it, a thick, roiling mist. A wintery chill seeped up through the house until her quick breaths plumed visibly and she hugged herself. A tremor of alarm swept through her along with that prickling cold. She was about to turn and call for Takeo when the mist began to churn and change, yielding up the shape of a man.

"Bella, my love."

His words tingled within her. Truly afraid, yet compelled by his voice to move forward, Arabella eased down two of the steps.

"Louis?"

He was standing at the foot of the stairs, face uplifted. His features were bathed in an odd blue-silver, a light that was not quite moonlight, not quite natural. It etched his cheekbones with bold, sharp strokes and his mouth with delicate sensual lines. And from out of that eerie, ethereal light, his eyes glowed hot and golden.

"Louis, I was so worried . . ." She clung to the railing for balance. Something about his stare dragged down upon her consciousness with a insistent sleepiness. Her limbs were unresponsive, heavy, tired. But beneath that seeping weariness, panic flickered like a resistant flame.

"I told you not to worry, Bella. I told you I would never leave you."

And there was something in the quality of his

voice—it was bigger, echoing, coming from all around and within her.

He started up the stairs, the mist rising with him, cloaking his feet so it seemed that he moved them not at all, but merely rose without effort. Confused by this trick of light, Arabella retreated, backing up the steps to the landing. Her heart was pounding with an unexplained fright. Her eyes told her it was her husband coming up to her, but her senses decried it, warning with every frantic pulse that she was in dreadful danger.

He stood on the landing before her, his stillness mesmerizing. He was so—beautiful. She stared and lost herself in the looking. His magnetism surrounded and seduced her. His eyes were so deep they went on forever. Then he took a step and she took one away, her breath coming in soft little gasps.

"Don't be afraid," came that smooth, glassy voice, and terror surged within her only to be blanketed by his warm, stifling will. She couldn't move, could barely breathe as he closed the distance between them. His hand reached out to her and she shrank back but couldn't avoid it.

His fingers slid caressingly along her cheek and the solidity of that touch broke Arabella's fearful trance. She exhaled in a rush.

"Oh, Louis, it is you!"

His neck was quickly circled by her arms and his curled lightly about her, drawing her up against him. She hugged him while desperate shivers drove out the last of her tension. She stroked her hand through his hair and kissed his neck, his cheek, and finally his mouth with a reassuring urgency. Then she simply clung.

"I did not mean to frighten you," he whispered without inflection.

She gave a nervous little laugh. "It was silly—I don't know what came over me. You seemed so strange, and I—it doesn't matter now. You're here, and that's all that matters. Are you all right?"

"I am full of the night's chill. I need your warmth to sustain me."

She pushed away, all concern and practicality. "Come to bed. I'll just go down and close—the door." But looking down, she saw that the front door was already shut and the thick fog had dissipated. Everything was dark and undisturbed, as it should be. She shook off a moment of mental confusion and hugged to her husband's arm. "Come. Let me warm you properly."

A fire was burning in the grate, infusing the room with heat and gentle light. Arabella had lit a lamp at the bedside while she was reading. In that sudden brightness, she gave a soft gasp.

"Is that blood?" She turned back the collar of his coat to reveal the brownish stains that liberally discolored his shirt. "Oh, Louis, have you hurt yourself?"

"No, little one. I am fine and fit." He shrugged out of his coat and stripped off the soiled shirt, tossing it aside. She could see there were no marks upon him, but all that blood—Then his hand cupped beneath her chin, lifting her head slightly so her gaze was focused upon his own. And he said firmly, "It is nothing, Bella."

She watched the gold of his eyes swirl and strangely flare, and blinking rapidly, she completely lost her train of thought. "What was I saying?"

"You were saying how much you loved me."

That sounded plausible. "Oh, yes." Her hands rode over the virile terrain of his chest. His skin was cool and sleek beneath her palms. She loved experiencing the feel of him, the strength and awesome contour concealed by his sophisticated garb. The world saw the polish, but only she was shown the power. She was zealously possessive of that knowledge. Her breasts flattened against the hard wall of him as she stretched up for his kiss, a kiss that lingered and deepened until she was woozy with delight.

His hands skimmed the nightdress from her shoulders and it filtered down between them, forgotten as his palms curved about the underswell of her bosom. His head lowered and she moaned in quiet rapture as his kiss burned against the soft flesh of her left breast. His lips pressed there unmoving for the longest while. Then he straightened and captured her dreamy gaze within the intensity of his own.

"Do you love me, Bella?"

"Yes," she answered.

"Do you trust me?"

"Yes." No hesitation at all.

"Would you do anything for me?"

"Yes."

"Would you give me anything I needed?"

"Anything." She looked up into his eyes, her gaze offering an unqualified love for his taking.

He made a brief gesture with his hand and the

lamp on the side table sputtered out. Arabella was about to remark upon it, but the words got lost in the wonder of his eyes. She felt the same helpless magic overcome her, her will malleable to his, her life a fragile gift placed in his hands without regret. Hands that could share such tenderness, hands that could rend so ruthlessly.

Hands covered with the souls of centuries.

"I love you, Louis. I am yours."

She was aware of the bedsheet beneath her, but not of how she had come to lie upon it. Then Louis's weight settled over her. Strange how light he seemed. But then he was kissing her and it no longer mattered. His kisses went on and on until every breath she took was his. He said her name and her body rippled in response. His mouth worked over the gentle slope of her cheek, played about her ear, then lowered. And lifted abruptly away. She heard a low hiss issue from him and could feel the hard scorch of his breath against her throat where the silver of her father's wedding gift glittered.

"Louis," she whispered with a husky impatience, coaxing him with the stroking glide of her hands and the arch of her body.

His kiss touched once again on the ripe white curve of her breast, but didn't tarry there. He slid down the willing, naked heat of her, laving a wet trail along quivering abdomen to the moist valley at the base of her restlessly shifting legs. Lowering there, feasting. Wicked, her dazed mind cried, but so luscious in its decadence, so tempting, provoking such glorious passion. She writhed beneath those wet, taunting kisses, growing delirious with need. Hot sensation peaked in a rush and shattered through her. In the throes of pleasure, she scarcely felt a quick piercing pain along her inner thigh.

Instead of coming down from that euphoric plane, Arabella continued to drift, high and heady from the thrill of it, weightless, floating, even soaring. Such freedom was breathtaking, and she longed to hold to it even as a slow downward spiral began.

She felt as though Louis's kiss was breathing life back into her. She could taste the earthy heat of her own body in that kiss and something else lingering rich and thick with the languid thrust of his tongue. He was covering her and she could feel the hard press of him. He'd finished undressing, though she couldn't be certain when he'd done so. Her hands fluttered over the muscular bulge of his upper arms and shoulders, gliding down the slick heat of his back. His skin was no longer cool; it was burning.

He lifted from the eager part of her lips to whisper with that low, sultry accent, "Bella, I want to be one with you."

"Oh, yes," she breathed back into his kiss. She opened herself to him and was bewildered by his delay. "Louis?"

His mouth moved against hers. "Take off the necklace."

The request was so strange, it momentarily disrupted the dream. "What?"

He levered up slightly and his golden gaze penetrated deep and druggingly. She could read desire in his eyes, a passion so intense it made her tremble, a need so raw and huge, it humbled her. She couldn't look away and she couldn't deny him. So when he crooned, all soft and entreating, "Let me claim you for my own," she reached for the thin silver chain and opened the catch. As she held it, he struck her hand and it went flying from her grasp to land on the floorboards far away.

With a deep and satisfied sigh, he sank down upon her lips again, drinking from their offering of love. She gasped as one forceful thrust of his hips joined them, then he moved between the beckoning spread of her thighs to create the binding tension she'd craved. His mouth drew a heated line of kisses from her lips to her chin, then down the concave of her throat, coming to a halt over her pulse point. He nuzzled there, his breath rasping, his lips parting, his hands clasping either side of her head to angle a taut bend. She felt the slow, wet stroke of his tongue.

And his bite.

His teeth went through the tender resistance of her flesh the way they would pierce the soft skin of a succulent peach, and with a pain that was swift and instantly forgotten. Then the deep, sweet draw of warm nectar. The pleasure was volcanic, a hot, vibrating surge through her veins, even as her body throbbed in wonderful release below. That caressing beat of perfection went on and on, swelling, becoming the hard pulse of Louis's heart racing through her in a powerful, seducing rhythm.

Finally, it slowed, growing languid and lush, flowing all around her and within her. Her hands had risen to clutch in Louis's hair, holding him at her throat, but even that became too great an effort. Her fingers loosened, relaxed, grew numb and finally let go. And her hands thumped slackly to the mattress as consciousness was bled dry and reality faded.

Chapter Sixteen

Awareness came to Louis in a tortured rush, lurching through him on the frantic beats of his heart. Pain, terrible and crushing; his face, his chest. The cold panic of death. Power reborn. Hunger. Hunger. A senseless driving thing, that relentless craving. Animal and instinctive, that vile thirst. That hunger to live, to devour life. To feed on the warm, rich pulse of life and feed and feed until the blood intoxicated. Because that was the kind of monster left behind when all that was human was drained away.

What had he done?

His eyes snapped open to the sight of his bed canopy overhead. He lay still, panting softly, clinging with a trembling hope to the wish that it had all been just a dream. That none of it had happened. That the taste in his mouth wasn't the very blood flushing hot through his every fiber. He closed his eyes and forced down the drunken satiation and he breathed deep, dragging up the awful courage to look, to discover if all had been truth or dream.

He opened his eyes and slowly turned his head, bracing for whatever sight would greet him. Then his breath gushed out in wave of relief for Arabella was there beside him, her eyes closed gently in sleep, her features so lovely and serene, and he found he was shaking all over.

"Oh, Bella, my love, I have had the most terrible dream ..."

Then he touched her cheek, refusing to recognize its pallor, and he leaned over to taste her lips, rejecting their unnatural chill and unresponsiveness.

"Bella?"

Her head moved all too easily at the gentle guide of his hand. There was no denying the wounds at her throat or the bloodstains, dark and sinister, upon snow-white sheets. Or the fact that her beautiful bared breasts moved not at all.

"No." He took a tight breath. "No, no ... Bella ..."

He rolled up to his knees and simply rocked back and forth, overwhelmed by the shock of it. From some deep well inside him came a sound that was half laugh, half sob as he thought of the irony—such irony. Remembering Gerardo's crazed grief as he spoke of killing all those he'd loved. The justice of it was too cruel to comprehend.

"What have I done ... oh, Bella, what have I done?"

Carefully, so carefully, he gathered her up in his arms. She was fragile, like a delicate leaf drained to a skeletal framework by some greedy insect. Her arms trailed down like pale silken sashes and her head lolled back, exposing his savage mark. He held her in a cherishing embrace, his head pillowed on her still bosom, awful sounds beginning to wail and whimper from him as he tried to grasp the fact that she was gone.

"Don't leave me, Bella. Don't leave me alone. Forgive me. You must forgive me. I never meant—I never meant to hurt you."

When he was nearly lost to his all-too-human mourning, his sharpened senses began to detect a faint thrumming that was not his own, a stubborn flutter of life struggling beneath the press of his damp cheek within a form that was not yet hollow.

He lifted up slowly, his own breath suspended, almost afraid to hope as unsteady fingertips sought the unmarked side of her throat. And felt an unmistakable stirring.

She was alive.

The breath sobbed from him as he thought frantically of what do. His Arabella was a fighter—a brave, determined female. But was the trickle of life that remained enough to see her through the night and indeed to survival? The alternatives were all too terrifying. He couldn't lose her. He sat for a moment, adoring her beloved features through a mist of anguish. He couldn't let her die.

Howland. He would take her to her father. He would know. He would be able to restore her.

Hard as it was, he released her and was quick to clothe them both. Dressing her was like dressing a cloth doll. He swept to the door, taking no pleasure in the power surging through him, and shouted for Takeo. The sound of his voice swelled mightily through the halls, waking his servant from the deep, unnatural sleep Louis had cast over him. Scrubbing his eyes and looking concerned, the boy rushed on bare feet, then slowed and stopped in dismay. He was quick to recognize the change in his master, and Louis fought not to shrink beneath that knowledge.

"Takeo, harness up the carriage. There's been—an accident."

The inscrutable gaze for once gave all away as the boy tried to look beyond him into the bedroom. His youthful face was etched with stark distress.

"Do it now!"

Takeo flinched and backed a few wary steps before turning to race down the stairs.

Louis went back into the bedroom, pausing briefly as he passed his shaving stand. And he was drawn fatalistically to peer into the small mirror there, to see—nothing. Nothing but the room behind him. And with a wretched cry, he smashed his fist into that damning glass, shattering it as all his dreams had shattered.

It was hard for Stuart Howland to look upon the figure hunched on his sofa with head in hands, unashamedly weeping without seeing a devoted husband suffering from heartache. But it was also impossible for the doctor not to see beyond to what else Louis Radman was: the bloodthirsty fiend who had drained his daughter near to death. He couldn't help but see the demon he'd given his daughter to in marriage.

Louis heard his step and came up in a stiff bolt of

alarm. There was a desperate wildness glazing his eyes, eyes that glittered like wet gold. Dead eyes.

"Does she live?"

It took all Stuart's control to answer in a level voice. "Yes. Barely."

"But you can save her. You can make her strong." These weren't questions, they were demands; and Stuart was in no mood for them. Not now. And he was not afraid of the killer beneath his roof.

"I don't know. Time will tell if she's strong enough to survive."

Louis took a shuddering breath, his eyes closing as fresh grief streaked his face. A face flushed and ruddy with life stolen from an trusting innocent. "She will. She must."

"And if she doesn't," the doctor made himself ask, "what then? What will she be if she dies?"

Louis spoke slowly, with a matter-of-fact flatness of inevitability. As if he'd seen it so many times, it no longer had the power to shock or disturb. "She will rise up as a *revenant-en-corps*. Without the transformation of spirit, she will walk as a revived corpse, a decomposing body stalking the night in search of victims to sate her hunger, an undead horror."

"Like you," Howland said savagely, but Louis shook his head with a grim sadness.

"Not like me. Nothing like me. Not unless I were to initiate her with my blood, to bring her over at the point of death. If I do not and she dies, she will be no more than a purposeless ghoul preying on anything she comes across, without the cunning or skill to survive."

"In other words, your blood would make her into a clever, immoral killer, instead of a simple beast."

Louis didn't answer. He didn't have to. Instead, he said very softly, very gravely, "Should she come closer to death, I will see that she crosses over to share eternity with me."

"No! You will not turn my child into—into a—"

"Vampire," Louis concluded for him. "It was not my intention, but I will not lose her."

Stuart glared at him, growing angrier by the second. "She would not want to exist as such. She loved life too dearly to wish it so perverted. She would rather die with dignity than continue in damnation."

Louis couldn't argue, because he wasn't sure the doctor was not right. Arabella had vowed to follow him across the grave, but she'd had no idea what that would entail and he couldn't bring himself to thrust a corrupted half-life upon her unless he knew for certain that it was her will. Even if it meant giving up his selfish need to have her with him. So he told the doctor in a somber voice, "Then you must be prepared to do what needs to be done to keep her from rising again."

Stuart turned away from the illusion of his humanity. He asked in a choking tone, "What must I do?"

"The kindest, quickest way is during daylight hours, while she sleeps. Sever the head from the body and kill the evil within her by driving a stake through her heart. She should then be burned and her ashes scattered in flowing water so the spirit will be trapped there."

"That is the only way?" His words quavered with horror.

"There is fire or consumption by the light of day, but those are—unpleasant." Enough said about that.

Howland took a ragged breath. He tried not to associate the grimness of their conversation to the child he'd raised. "If she lives, what then?"

"She will be linked to me for as long as I exist."

The doctor's analytical mind was spinning, reaching outside its usual realm to presuppose the supernatural states effecting his daughter. He came to one logical end. "If you die before her, what then?"

"The curse will end with me. But I cannot die; I am immortal."

But not indestructible. Louis could read that whisper as it rode through Howland's mind. It wasn't spoken aloud. He could feel the man's hatred, his fury, his loathing, solidifying in a dangerous direction. And Louis was cautious.

"If you have done all you can for her, I want to take her with me."

"No."

"No?"

"She must not be moved. Her condition is unstable and critical. She needs my care. There are measures I must take soon, or she will die."

Louis nodded. "I want to see her."

"No. That I cannot allow."

Golden eyes glittered. "I am not going to harm her," Louis drawled out fiercely.

"I am hardly convinced of that, my lord. You will not take her. You will not see her. Ever."

Louis absorbed that with gaze narrowed and replied, "She is my wife."

Howland threw out all remnants of civility. "That unwholesome alliance will not stand! I will not have my child in the hands of a demon! I've seen what good your word is, Radman. I let my lust for fame overcome my sensibilities. No more! You came close to killing her, and I'll not believe you can keep it from happening again. You are what you are, a vile, unholy thing. And you will not have Arabella. Leave this house. Leave our lives. If you think for a moment that she will not hate you for what you've done, you are mistaken. Good night, sir. There is nothing for you here."

If you think for a moment that she will not hate you for what you've done ...

Louis hesitated. He need not have listened. He could have easily swept the threat of Stuart Howland aside and taken what he wanted. But he could not bring himself to harm one dear to Arabella. Hadn't he done enough already to prove everything Howland said was true? And because he was so broken by despair, so filled with self-loathing, he allowed himself to be driven off into the night like the curse he was. Away from his love and his last hope.

Nothing had ever seemed so empty as the inside of his house when Louis returned to it. Ghosts were everywhere: Arabella agreeing to marry him beneath his kisses in the parlor, her radiant smile as she spoke of reading through all the books in his library, the timid way she'd devoured him with her gaze that first day she'd stood on his doorstep. Shadows of happiness that would never know substance again. Because he would never have substance again.

Live or die, Arabella was lost to him, and he could think of no reason to continue an eternity without her.

Takeo was following behind him, a silent, worried watchdog of his every mood. For some reason, the mind link between them had not been rejoined when he returned to his supernatural state. Perhaps he had been human, for just a little while. Just long enough to taste the fleeting splendor of that existence and to ruin the life of the woman he loved. But that frail state had faded fast. Whether or not it would have held, he didn't know. Would never know. He'd been regressing even as he went on his fateful, foolish visit to Gerardo, elsewise he wouldn't have sprung up after mortal death like a powerful phoenix reborn. Elsewise, he would have been in a fledgling's thrall to her who had made him, to Bianca, instead of master of his own course. A course more deadly and destructive than even the wicked Bianca could have devised for him.

He'd been a proud fool to think he could escape his destiny. There could be no salvation for him, no redemption of a soul too lost to preternatural sins of arrogance and disdain for mankind. And he had dragged many with him into that hell. Gerardo. The Pasquale family. How many more over the centuries? Even Arabella.

That thought was unconscionable. She who loved life could not be reduced to his dark state. Not unless it was by her choice, and he had yet to hear her speak it. And he would not hear her speak it if she was to die and pass beyond while separate from him. Years and miles would not reduce his hold upon her. Only death could break it.

Hers.

Or his.

What reason did he have to go on? The residue of his mortal conscience could not stand the strain of Arabella's soul upon it. He'd lost his chance to walk with her in her world, and now his own held no appeal. His own, where Bianca and Gerardo crouched like patient spiders, waiting to ensnare him in their age-old web of vengeance. Where he would go on and on at the expense of the innocent—unless he ended it now. Now, while Arabella hovered at the edge of the veil of death, because once that balance teetered, there would be no retrieving her.

And if she lived, how could he bear the knowledge of her turning away from him in horror and hatred? How could he keep himself from seeking her out again, whether it was her will or not? And of course, it wouldn't be her will. It would never be her will again. He'd taken that from her when he'd taken her blood. She would be his servant, his slave, and he couldn't stand the thought of her dependence when it was her self-sufficiency he'd admired most of all.

He'd had it all, his every wish. The sun, human emotion, the love of a woman, the anticipation of a normal death ... why go backward now? He knew what awaited him, the same that had been there for three centuries, and it held no sense of expectation. What was power without the ability to feel compassion? What was eternity without simple intimacy?

What was he without the woman he'd made into his wife? Why go back when nothing of value lay ahead?

He was standing in the vast ballroom. Darkness there seemed centuries deep. A fitting place for what he had in mind. He crossed to the wall and lifted a heavy saber from its display with crested shield. Then he turned to Takeo.

"It is time for you to see to your promise."

Takeo's gaze was confused, but when Louis extended the saber, understanding was quick and terrible. The boy took a step back, refusing the offering.

"Takeo, you must. Free me from this horror that I am. Save Arabella from the same."

The boy's head shook from side to side and his eyes filled with tears. His mouth moved in a frustration of silence, and the need to express himself had never been more important. He pushed up his sleeve and held his wrist up to Louis, patting the bared surface desperately.

"No."

Impatiently, Takeo reached up to catch the back of Louis's head, forcing it down against the frantic pulse, begging him to make the connection by tempting the vampire hunger with the irresistible scent of life throbbing against his lips. Louis's hand came up to support the boy's arm as his thirst roared, crushing reluctance.

With a swift puncture, the link was forged. Louis felt the boy's blood jet to the back of his mouth and he swallowed with a low moan of helpless rapture. There was nothing like that first taste, the warmth, the strength, the fire. It was glorious. Always. Akin to nothing in Louis's experience, except maybe making love to his first woman. The sharp anticipation, the longing, followed by the surprising pleasure of the act itself. The always amazing feel of drinking up the texture of another's mind. A communication likened to no other.

Master ...

Takeo's voice, so sweet upon the ears of the only one who had ever heard it.

Louis drew back, panting hard, commanding the rage of thirst to quiet. He was then aware of how he'd crushed Takeo to him the way a cat subdued his prey until he'd toyed with it to the point of death. He released the boy with a momentary alarm. There was always that guilty fear that he would go too far. But this time, he'd been able to stop himself. This one last time.

Louis reached out with his thoughts. *Takeo, my friend, it is so good to speak with you again.*

Takeo was quick to respond. *Then do not cut our conversation short, I beg of you.*

You ask too much, young friend. It must be done and I would have it done at your hands, at hands that would strike true out of love.

Please, don't order this done.

I do not order it. I ask. If you will not, I will give myself over to the daylight. I don't want to burn. I am very afraid of that fire. But this way, it is nothing. I've seen it done, and I—I will feel nothing. You would be doing me a great kindness. I am determined to see this done, and you will spare me much suffering. Louis paused, letting his anguish swell until he could see it reflected in the boy's teary gaze. *I cannot go on without her, Takeo. And I cannot bring her over to me. I must end it now, while there is a chance for her soul to survive. Please help me. Do this one thing for me.*

But—but what of me? Who will care for me once you are gone?

Louis smiled slightly. Never had he heard Takeo express a selfish wish before, and he read through it easily. *My friend, do not play upon my sympathies. You know it is you who have seen to my care all these years. You will be fine. I have seen to it. I will miss our conversations. But the time grows late. Release me, then, one last favor.* Louis paused, struggling to frame all his passions in one phrase.

What is it, Master?

Go to Arabella, see her if you can, and tell her—tell her how much I truly loved her.

And saying that, Louis extended the saber again, and this time, Takeo took it, bowing solemnly.

"You have been a good friend to me, Takeo. Like a brother, like a son. Strike true, then see to the rest as it must be done."

I will.

He embraced the boy quickly and stepped away before emotion could interfere with the execution of his plan. Execution—an amusing choice of words, he thought wryly, as he went to kneel before a low stool. Taking great calming breaths, he stripped off his coat and tucked his shirt down away from his neck. He'd seen it done that way a multitude of times during the reign of bloody terror in France—now, *there* were thirsty souls worse than any vampire he'd ever met. But from them he'd learned better the blade have no restriction. He'd seen, as well, what a dull cut or a poor aim could do, and he had no desire to meet an ugly death. Quick and sure—as it should have been three centuries ago. Even as it should have been hours ago. He wondered as he positioned his head atop the cushion if he was the only man to know three deaths in one existence.

Then he heard Takeo step into a firm stance and he gripped the legs of the stool, panting hard into the sudden rise of panic. Oh, God . . . he should pray. But a soul as damned as his would have no audience with God. So instead, he composed a quick plea for Arabella's happiness and squeezed his eyes tightly shut.

Takeo's hand touched to the back of his head, gently shifting him so that his chin was off center and the back of his neck was offered up without obstruction. Louis's fright fell away and he drew what would be his last breath and held it. And he waited, listening to the steady rise of the saber, the pause, and the abrupt whistle of descent.

Louis!

Arabella's voice pierced through his mind, alive with desperate fear and need.

Bella!

And he moved.

The saber cleaved through the stool, burying itself deep into the wood floorboards.

And on his knees, Louis cleared his thoughts to receive her inexperienced call. It came to him, a frail, frightened whisper, yet so clear that his heart took wing.

Louis, where are you? I need you.

And he sent her a reassuring message to still the fever of alarm. *I am here, little one. I am with you. I will be there soon.*

Louis, don't leave me!

I have promised to stay with you always, have I not? Rest. Sleep. Get strong and I will come for you soon. I love you, Bella.

Master, you must take care. You must go below. Dawn approaches.

Louis responded to Takeo's concern with a resigned nod. The boy kicked aside the halved stool with a shaky relief and smiled thankfully as he caught Louis by the elbows, lifting him to his feet.

Perhaps it was selfish and wrong, but Louis couldn't forgo the opportunity to see his Arabella again. If just to explain. If just to plead for her forgiveness.

He'd thought that the vile hunger alive inside him was the most powerful urge imaginable. But he was wrong. Love was stronger.

"Louis."

Arabella thrashed weakly upon her bed, unaware of what was going on about her. Unaware of the two men struggling to save her life.

"Now, carefully, Wesley. Just as I showed you."

"But, Doctor, the accepted way would be to bleed her."

"Fool, have you listened to nothing I've said? She suffers from lack of blood already. Hers must be enriched, not depleted. This is a revolutionary opportunity I'm giving you, boy. Do not argue."

"Forgive me, Doctor, for being narrow of mind. Shall we proceed?"

The transfusing began from father to daughter, with Wesley Pembrook regulating the exchange. When color had returned to the near translucent skin and warmth to her body, her arm was bound and the two medical men sat back to observe. She seemed to rest, but it was not a true sleep. She continued to toss and whisper for her husband.

"What kind of spell does he hold over her?" Wesley asked, as he watched her clutch at the covers in the throes of her restless daze.

"He has infected her blood with his. Unless something is done, she is doomed to become as he is." Stuart looked up at his intense protégé. It was not an alliance he would have chosen, but he was quite desperate, and that left little choice. Few would have believed the tale he laid before this young man. But Wesley never questioned. He'd felt Radman's power, and he didn't doubt. "I was hoping you would find the thought of that as objectionable as I do."

"It cannot be allowed, I agree, but what can we do? What kind of authority would even listen to what would sound like mad claims against someone with Radman's title and connections?"

"A higher authority, my friend. We must take it upon ourselves to see she is saved."

"I am with you, Doctor."

"And for your efforts, I shall see you have what you desire."

Wesley looked avidly at the shifting figure upon the bed. "Arabella?"

"Once it's done. Once you've destroyed Radman."

Wesley smiled grimly. "It will be my extreme pleasure."

Chapter Seventeen

It was nearing four in the afternoon when Wesley Pembrook rapped upon the front door. He waited, scrubbing his dampening palms upon his coat and casting furtive glances about, in case any took interest in his presence there upon Louis Radman's doorstep. None did.

An Asian boy opened the door and looked out at him through flat, suspicious eyes.

"Is his lordship at home?" Wesley asked. "It's urgent that I see him."

The boy shook his head and began to close the door. Wesley stopped it with the brace of his hand.

"Please, you don't understand. It has to do with his wife, Arabella."

The Oriental youth paused.

"The doctor, her father, sent me to find the marquis. There's been a serious change in her condition. If he is not here, might I leave him a message?"

The boy inclined his head.

"Have you something I might write upon?"

With a slight bow, the lad turned, and immediately,

Wesley struck. The blow to the back of the boy's head dropped him straightaway to the hall runner, and Wesley kicked his prone body aside so he could step in and shut the door.

Where did one look for a vampire? Howland said to look below, down below the level of the ground, in a subterranean grave, someplace quiet and undisturbed. The cellar.

He marched down the hall, not bothering to move silently. Radman wouldn't hear him. From the folds of his coat he drew the hawthorne stake, which, along with the mallet he'd used to strike Radman's servant down, he'd brought to rid himself of the obstacle to his greatest success.

After several false starts, he found a door that led down into darkness. Lighting a lamp conveniently placed on a nearby table, he began to descend. The chill was slow and seeping. By the time he reached the bottom, his breath was fogging the dank air. There, he came to a chained door: the gate to Radman's tomb.

It took time to break through those thick links, longer than Wesley liked, and then it was a struggle to push the door inward. It dragged on soft earth. Holding the lantern high to illuminate the underground room, he found himself in an antechamber where dusty racks of wine stood untouched for decades. He moved directly toward an opposite arch that opened into a far greater room. The musty cavern was filled with crates of stored goods, collected belongings from Radman's numerous lifetimes, he supposed. Wesley wasn't interested in the treasure the man managed to amass; he was looking for only one thing. And after a lengthy time spent searching, still, he almost missed it.

For wedged in amongst the other boxes, without pomp, without decoration, without any grandeur at all, was Radman's resting place. It was just a crate fashioned inexpensively, like the rest. But this one had the dimensions of a prone body, Radman's coffin.

Wesley approached it with a smug smile, hefting the stake and mallet with a wonderful sense of malice and retribution. He put them both in one hand so he might use the other to lift open the lid. It was then that his confidence faltered.

Radman lay within, stretched out in state upon tufted white silk, not in slumber or in death, but in an unnatural stasis, eyes closed, hands arranged in a relaxed position upon his bosom as if in light sleep. Yet there was no sign of breath. And Wesley stumbled back, totally unnerved, because telling himself he believed wasn't quite as startling as being confronted with the actual fact.

Radman was a vampire.

For several minutes he stood back, taking deep, composing breaths as he studied the supine form. If Radman was aware of him, he didn't or couldn't show it. Howland had said he was vulnerable only in this tranced state, so there was no time to spare in further hesitation. Squaring up his arrogant bravery, Wesley came nearer and finally sneered down upon the undead corpse.

"Make a fool of me, will you? It is I who laugh now, Radman."

He'd leaned down close with a doctor's curiosity

to examine the florid color of the skin when abruptly Radman's gaze snapped open to reveal eyes like glowing coals. The intensity of that gaze staggered him. Wesley yelped in fright, but before he could leap back, his coat lapel was in the demon's grip, a grip like death.

After wriggling in a desperate panic, Wesley managed to free himself and lunge back to what he hoped would prove a safe distance. But instead of flying out of the coffin in search of his jugular, Radman let his hand sink languidly back upon his unmoving shirt front and his awful glaring eyes drifted shut.

A protective reflex, Wesley told himself, fighting down his tremors of terror. If Radman could have gotten out of the box to slay him, he would have.

Angry for the scare he'd been given, Wesley returned to the side of the crude casket and determinedly aligned the point of the stake above Radman's dark heart.

"Time to visit hell, Milord Devil."

And with that oath, Wesley raised the mallet high.

"Louis!"

His daughter's high-pitched scream brought Stuart hurrying to her bedside. She was sitting up, her eyes wide and staring, her respiration laboring with exhaustion and alarm. There was no recognition for him in her panicked gaze. It was fixed on something else, something that wasn't there.

"Louis," she cried again, with a heavy agony that hurt him to hear, and he damned the vile incubus that had seduced his innocent child.

"Arabella, you must lie back and rest," he said gently. Yet when he placed his hands upon her shoulders to ease her down, she resisted with a surprising strength.

"No." Again, that desperate, wailing cry. "I must go to him. He needs me."

"Who needs you, Bella?"

"Louis. Let me go to him."

Stuart pushed more firmly and finally succeeded in pressing her objecting form back upon the bed. "You cannot, Bella. You are very weak."

"But he's in danger. Please. Wesley—Wesley's trying to hurt him."

How could she know? Had she somehow overheard their plot in her dazed sleep? It didn't matter. The deed was being done, and his daughter would be safe from Radman's snare. She was all that mattered. He should have remembered that earlier and spared them both much.

"You were dreaming, Bella. Everything's fine. You must rest now and gain strength."

She took no comfort from his words, continuing to thrash restlessly, moaning Radman's name, weeping inconsolably for him. And while the sight distressed him, he refused to believe he'd done the wrong thing. Arabella would come to understand that in time; that he'd done it for her, because of his love for her. She would forgive him, someday. Perhaps she would even come to care for Wesley with a fondness, if not with the passion she'd had for Radman. And until then, she would live.

A sob constricting her throat, Arabella tossed

weakly on her pillows and called again out of fear and longing.

"Louis."

As he brought the mallet down with the force needed to drive the stake through Radman's body, Wesley was abruptly struck from behind. The impact propelled him forward, sprawling him over the open casket, across Radman, who was suddenly no longer inert. His cry of terror was cut short by the wrap of Radman's fingers about his throat, a grip that held him helpless as the smiling vampire sat up.

"Why, this is a surprise, Mr. Pembrook," he drawled, in that sinister, silky accent. "I don't recall inviting you for a visit. Or had you come hoping to pay your last respects?"

The stake and mallet were tossed disdainfully to the floor. Radman guided Wesley back, then he swung fluidly out of the crate. About then, the demon's attention was drawn to the boy who'd interrupted the killing stroke. The Asian youth was tottering, still slightly dazed by the blow Wesley dealt him. Radman gestured for the boy to come to him, and Wesley saw his own death in the taut angles of Radman's face as he examined the clotted wound. With a considerate hand, he lifted the boy's head so they could commune silently. And while Radman was distracted, Wesley saw his only chance.

With a strength born of desperate fear, Wesley yanked free and raced for the exit, scrambling, stumbling in his panic. He felt a faint rush of air move by him; then, suddenly, Radman was before him, blocking his escape. For all his slighter stature, the marquis seemed to command mammoth proportion, powerful, threatening, deadly. Wesley floundered back in mindless horror as Radman came toward him, all gaunt-cheeked and red-eyed, oozing malevolence.

"So, you would not heed my many warnings." The words were issued with a soft hiss. "You persist in meddling in my affairs. You think you can just injure or steal away what is mine. Think again, you loathsome parasite. I live off others to survive, but you, you suck off them for your own vanity. The time has come to send *you* to hell."

Then Radman's lip curled back to expose his great sharp teeth and Wesley realized his folly.

It was the last thought he ever had.

Thirst. That was what woke her. Horrible, aching thirst. When she tried to force a dry swallow, the muscles of her throat wouldn't work properly. And the pain. She was confused by it, but when she lifted a weak hand to assess the hurt, she found her fingers taken in a gentle clasp. Arabella blinked her eyes open to focus upon the slightly smiling visage of her father.

"W-water, please." Her voice was a frail rasp, but it was enough to gain the desired result. Her head and shoulders were carefully raised and a cup of cool water was touched to her parched lips.

"Slowly, slowly."

The first attempt nearly choked her; then she was able to drink down the rest almost greedily. She sank back unto the bolster of pillows, absurdly weary from the tiny effort.

"Rest, my dear. After a while, I'll have Mrs. Kampford bring up some soup."

"Mrs. Kampford ..."

"Yes. Now, you rest—"

"Where am I?" Though her vision was slightly blurred, she knew at once she wasn't in her bedroom, though Stuart would claim she was. "No." But she was in the bedroom of her father's house, not in the one she shared with her husband. "Why am I here? Where is Louis?"

Speaking his name brought an expectant tingle, warming, caressing through her. The anticipation heightened, becoming almost painfully acute.

"Where's Louis?" she repeated, and her tone reflected the sudden panic of separation. It was a feeling of aloneness like despair, like grief, an anguish she could not suppress.

"Quietly, Bella. He brought you here last night. You'd—fallen suddenly ill. He brought you here so I might care for you."

"I want to go home now." She couldn't bear the thought of being gone from there, of being apart from Louis. And though she had no strength for it, she sat up and started to throw off her coverings.

"No, child, you must rest. Please do not excite yourself. It's not good—"

"I must go to him. I must!"

"Bella, you cannot." And the heaviness of his tone alarmed her all the more. She lay back, panting wildly, her heart beating with a frantic anxiety as she looked up at her father. His expression was set in fatalistic lines.

"Why? What's wrong with me? Have I some sort of contagion?"

Stuart's smile was a tortured curl. "Of a kind. Time is the cure, and rest. So please try to allow both the chance to heal you."

"Louis is all I need."

It was an odd statement even to her own thinking, but Arabella believed it totally. Louis could make everything right with his presence. But where was he? Surely he had to know how much she wanted him here with her. She felt it then, the icy shiver of threat, not to herself, but to him whom she loved. Louis had been in some dreadful danger, but the sensation wasn't as strong as it had been. In her earlier, nearly delirious state, she could almost swear she'd reached out to him. She could feel the texture of his voice, the calming of his presence though distance separated them. She needed that feeling now, that oneness that was so inexplicable, yet so complete. She felt as if she might die of lonely torment if she had no reassurance soon.

So she closed her eyes and she reached out to him, calling his name, not aloud, as before, but silently, with all her senses straining. *Louis.*

I am here.

Her gaze flew open and she saw him, just a faint shadow in the open door, a shadow without enough substance to block the light from beyond. It seemed to spill through him as if his figure was transparent. And a moment of fright was quickly overcome by longing as he took on a comforting solidity. Her will was gone in that instant, her mind smothered by the intensity of his, her heart beating with the power of his as a trancelike stillness overcame her.

"I've come for my wife."

Stuart jumped up and swung to face the intruder. His stricken expression told Louis everything at once. Howland was behind the attempt upon his life.

"You seem surprised, Doctor. Did you doubt that I would return for her?"

To his credit, Howland drew himself together with commendable courage. He faced down his nemesis unblinkingly, without a trace of apology. "I was hoping you would not. For her sake."

Louis bowed slightly. He admired the man's love for his daughter, and he wouldn't blame him for the extremes he'd taken to protect her. But it wouldn't stop him from taking back what was his. "You have underestimated me."

"Apparently so. Pembrook?"

"Sent on that journey you'd planned for me."

Stuart paled slightly, but he didn't back down or relax the barrier of his own body placed between his child and the fiend that would take her. "And would you do the same to me?"

"With no trouble at all, Doctor, except there are two reasons to refrain."

"And they are?"

"You are Arabella's father."

"And?"

"You might yet cure me."

A silence fell between the two men. Louis didn't advance, but his mere presence was intimidation enough. Wesley was dead, killed by this very creature. Arabella had been close to it, and even now was in the unnatural being's thrall. He didn't need to look behind him to know her features would be wrought up in rapt devotion. She would willingly return to the heart of danger. Stuart needed no demonstration to know Radman could slay him in the blink of an eye. Yet he chose restraint, possibly for the reasons he cited. So Stuart became more physician than father for the moment.

"Why come to me for my help when you spurned it to return to what you were?"

"That was not my choice. I went to one of my kind to offer salvation and his gracious refusal brought me back to this state." He put a slender hand to the side of his throat as if even now he could feel wounds upon that smooth surface. He'd been attacked by one of his own.

Stuart believed him. No man would pretend that degree of reserved anguish. It played upon the angles of Louis Radman's face like the etchings of long-suffering and extreme fatigue. A sort of resigned agony one might adopt when hearing they had a terminal disease.

"You can help me, Doctor," he said with a poignant quiet, but Stuart shook his head.

"No. I want no more to do with you, Radman. It is too dangerous."

"To do nothing is too dangerous." And he nodded his head toward Arabella, who had not taken her eyes from him, whose gaze was absorbed with him, alone for him. He let his control over her notch out a little with a soft psychic call to her. She gasped faintly and started to rise up. Howland caught her by the shoulders in an attempt to restrain her. Her struggles were weak at first, then stronger, as if imbued with unnatural energy. A determined energy.

"Let me go," she cried, trying to claw her way out of her father's concerned embrace. "Louis!" The glazed somnambulance of her eyes had become fever-bright with frustration. She was panting with effort, almost snarling with anger at her failure to get free.

"Enough, Radman. Stop it."

And Arabella slumped back against the pillows in a heavy swoon. Stuart quickly checked her pulse, finding it fast but stronger.

"You see, Doctor, we are one, Bella and I. Joined by God and by another unholy union. You cannot keep her from me. She would crawl to answer my call. She would lie to you, deceive you in any way she could, even kill you to get to my side. She would use her last breath to protect me. To help her, you must first help me."

"You are a foul creature, Radman, using her this way when you would claim to love her."

Louis's expressionless facade never altered, but his response was edged with deep emotion. "I am no monster. If I were, you would not be breathing. What I do is as much for her as it is for me."

"Nonsense," the doctor sneered. "What you do is for you. You are a selfish thing, obsessed with continuing beyond your natural lifetime off the blood and lives of others."

"No. No. I want mortality. I want a natural span of years, and I want to live them out in peace with your daughter. Help me. Continue with the treatments.

Start over, if you must. Cure me of this curse so I can be again the man she married. The man she . . . loves."

"If you will let her alone. If you will let her stay here with me."

Louis stiffened at those terms. He knew Howland was only thinking of Arabella's safety, and if the situation had been other than it was, he would have agreed. But he couldn't.

"No. She must be with me. There are other forces at work here. Other dangers. You cannot protect her from their power. Only I can."

Howland went very still and thoughtful. "You speak of those who turned against you."

"An evil you cannot imagine. Let me take her and protect her. I swear to you, she will not be harmed by me."

Stuart hesitated. He could feel Louis's sincerity, but would grand intention overcome the fiend's urge to feed? Finally, reluctantly, he stepped away from his daughter's bedside and watched with a grim displeasure as Radman crossed with his silky stride to assume his place. Arabella rose up with the cry of her husband's name, her arms outstretched to receive him. Nothing less powerful than complete devotion could have wrought such a tender softening upon Radman's features as he gathered her to him and held her tight.

"Bella, *il mia ragazza, il mia amore,* I've come to take you home with me."

And she nodded into the curve of his throat, trustingly, as if he'd never come close to killing her. The feel of her in his arms stirred through him so sweetly, leaving him vulnerable in a way he'd never been before. Arabella, who'd become more precious to him than life, his slave who had in fact enslaved him. He could close his eyes and feel her thoughts, revel in the warmth, the love, as if it was a great blanket of care he could wrap about himself when the chill of the world would intrude. They were one, and he was as much exposed in heart and mind as she. He could control her, yet she ruled him. It was that simple. And so satisfying. He didn't want to let the moment go. He'd been aware of Howland leaving the room and knew now that he'd returned, but the doctor made no attempt to interfere. He stood graciously aside in silence until Louis lifted his dampened face to regard him.

"I will take good care of her."

"I know you will try," Howland allowed. "Take this."

Louis took the pouch with a curious cant of his head.

"The restorative powders," Stuart explained. "The last that I have. Take a small amount and begin to build up your resistance again. I will make some more, and perhaps within the week, we will locate a suitable donor. I haven't been able to find Reeves—"

"Don't bother looking," Louis drawled.

Stuart didn't care to ask. "Some other avenue, then. Come by tomorrow night and we will start again."

Louis looked at him, expression awash with humility, a look so human, so sorrowful, no trace of the haughty aristocrat remained. "Thank you, Doctor. You give me hope."

"You keep your word."

How is she?

Takeo hovered at Louis's elbow as he laid out a limp Arabella upon their bed.

"Weak, but recovering. We must take good care of her. Tomorrow you must see that she rests and takes in plenty of fluids to build back her strength. And you must be ever alert. You must protect her. Use all my power to keep her safe."

Yes, my master.

Louis sensed his hesitancy and looked to him in question. "What is it, Takeo?"

And you—you will keep her safe, too?

An eloquent accusation if ever he'd heard one. Louis smiled ruefully and placed a reassuring hand on the boy's shoulder. "Yes, I will keep her safe."

Takeo regarded him for a long inscrutable moment, then inclined his head briefly.

"Now, young friend, go rest. I will watch over her tonight while the devils are about. Have you—seen to Mr. Pembrook? He is one I should not like to meet as an immortal."

He will not rise up to trouble us again. That was phrased with a fierce intensity. Takeo had been proved fallible by the crafty doctor's tricks, and he chafed with the guilt that it could well have cost his master's life. Reading those thoughts, Louis tapped him gently under the chin.

"We both made mistakes, Takeo, and we survived

them. Do not dwell in the past. It is a lonely and unsatisfying place to be. I know."

The boy nodded, and with one last look at his fragile mistress, he bowed and silently withdrew.

Once he'd assured himself that Arabella was resting comfortably, Louis changed from his restrictive garb into the fluidly styled trousers and tunic the Orientals favored for freedom of movement. As the fabric settled along the surface of his upper body, he enjoyed a languid stretch, letting sensation ripple through him in smooth, supple waves. It was the power Gerardo had spoken of, and he was not immune to its seduction. Some things were impossible not to enjoy, like the heightened sensitivity that came with being a strong and sensual creature of the night.

He hadn't been a particularly vain or manipulative man, but absolute power did tend to corrupt absolutely. He'd not been a saint. He'd caved in to temptation, to the dark wonder of what he was, but never without an underlying sense of guilt. How had he managed to retain that thread of humanity when Gerardo had cast it off with such obvious relish? His existence would have been much easier had he not felt that tug of conscience almost unknown within his kind. It was a simple thing to lose oneself in the throes of power, to be so elevated above the realm of man made for a contemptuous relationship with mere mortal beings. And he was admittedly arrogant. Yet there was something so admirable about the human spirit; he couldn't resist its fascination. Even as they were drawn to the blackness in him, he was pulled toward their light. An odd coexistence. Even as he walked among them by choice, he knew himself to be a danger. Yet he could not remove himself into the company of his own kind. He found them so hard and callous, as transparent as the veil of humanity they hid behind. No mystery at all. Predatory beings, thriving off the hunger and the kill. A basic and ugly existence.

Beauty. Beauty and peace was what he'd found with Arabella. He looked to her, feeling it warm him even now in his cold, dead state. She'd been intrigued by the magic of the beast, but she'd loved the mortality of the man. Which would move her now? As a man, he'd been able to hold and love her without restraint, but he'd failed to keep her safe. There was no strength in humanity, only a pale nobility that protected no one. In his present form, he could indeed gift her with paradise and eternity. He could love her without end, without limitations. He could carry her to planes of sensual awareness far beyond the tender intimacy they'd enjoyed. He could show her the heavens. He could share everything that he was with her. He could open his heart and—and—

What?

What would he do if she couldn't accept him as he was?

Chapter Eighteen

The hours of the night deepened, and with them, Louis's strange melancholy as he watched over his bride.

He'd come to sit beside her on the bed, and his fingers played idly with a strand of her dark hair.

Would she love him now? Would the truth send her shrieking in horror? He was afraid to find out. Not much in this mortal world scared him, but this did. One frail creature's scorn had the power to devastate him. The longer he sat letting insecurity sway him, the more fretful he became. He looked at the powders Howland had given him. The key to his mortality. If a taste would stir the beginnings of rejuvenation, how would the entire amount affect him? He suddenly had no patience with Howland's cautious steps. He wanted to be human when his Arabella awoke and beheld him. Then he could convince her that it all had been a dream and she need never know what he'd done.

But as a human, how could he guard against Bianca and Gerard when they came? And they would come. Because he'd defied and temporarily defeated them. Their vanity could not stand that. He never wanted to feel again as helpless as he'd been at their hands. As a vampire, he was their equal. As a man, he was nothing, a plaything to be crushed upon a whim.

So he tucked away thoughts of Howland's powders at least until he settled upon a way to reduce the threat of his unholy peers. Until then, he would have to be content with his present state and risk Arabella's damning disgust.

He was drawn to sample the velvety curve of her cheek, rubbing his knuckles along that sleek contour until the pain of longing swelled into an intolerable constriction.

"Bella," he called, and her eyes opened in obedience. He could sense her confusion and her uncertain fright, and he quickly overwhelmed it, swamping her with the heavy vampire charm that accompanied the bond he'd made with her. The effect was immediate and selfishly gratifying. Her eyes darkened with a surge of desire and her arms reached out for him.

"Louis."

His conscience scolded that he was warping her tender emotions to suit his frail vanity. He knew he was, but shame couldn't best his need to feel her devotion. It mattered not at all the minute he bent and felt her wrapped around him in frantic need.

"Bella, tell me that you love me." It was a command, an order that she was powerless to resist. So when she urgently whispered "I love you" against his ear, it was as unsatisfying as it was rewarding.

"Show me," came his next demand, and she was

quick to shower his taut face and neck with hurried kisses. Her hands moved upon him with restless anticipation, and beneath that skilled touch he growled to life; the hunger, the passion, the desperation ... He caught her head between his hands, anchoring it still so he could plunder her mouth with deep, plunging overtures, and she responded with an eager passivity. When he stopped, she stopped, her lips parted damply, her eyes half closed and dulled by dreamy coercion.

And suddenly it angered him that she was a puppet within his control. None of the passion was real. He was manipulating it with his mind, with his wants. She would do whatever he asked, whatever he instructed, but she simply would not respond with the spontaneity he desired. Was that how things were to be between them, Arabella mindlessly submissive beneath his rule? At least she was his. He had her firmly at his side, always supportive, always protective, always ready to jump at his slightest command. He need never fear her abandonment or her distaste. She would be his eager servant. Not because she wanted it, but because he ordered it. She could not refuse. And with that power came a sudden wild need to channel it to its fullest degree, to drown in it like a greedy child who needed to feel love and acceptance at any cost.

"You are mine, Arabella. For an eternity you will be mine. And you will never look away in horror. You will never turn from me in loathing. You will love me. You will love me always."

And he poured it on, the magic, the heat, the power, holding her mental faculties until she was gasping, crying out in a delirious frenzy. He continued to clasp her face between his palms, looking deep as he did into her eyes, searching for some recess where genuine feeling might reside. Not finding it.

It wasn't this shallow pretense he wanted from her. He'd valued her love because it had been given so freely. Taking it by unfair force seemed somehow dishonest and sorely disreputable. Not that he was above trickery. He was excellent at games of the mind. But to have the woman he loved clutching at him in a panting urgency without the remotest hint of self-awareness made him turn from her in disgust.

Not understanding his rejection, Arabella began a desperate pleading for his attention. "Louis, love me. Make me yours. I live for you. I would die for you. Let me die for you." And she draped herself upon him, her head thrown back, her throat offered up in pale purity. He could feel the blood surging beneath that fair flesh. He could taste it as his mouth moistened and pain shot through his gums as his teeth altered into an animal's fangs. And he grabbed her by the shoulders, jerking her against him.

"Yes, Louis. Oh, yes!" she was sobbing in mindless rapture.

And the beat of passion and need thundered into a great driving crescendo where madness and ecstasy awaited. His lips burned against the arch of her neck, her body pressed against him, her bosom heaving, her hands imploring. His eyes rolled back in exquisite expectation, lip curling up, mouth widening, breath catching ...

"No!"

He wrenched away, thrusting her back upon the bedsheets, where she was immediately scrambling after his return of affection. She was crying.

"What have I done? How have I displeased you? Louis, don't turn away from me! Please, I cannot bear it! Please, you must love me."

And carefully, cherishingly, he took her up in his arms, suppressing her wanton overtures with the tight clasp of his arms, calming her with the soothing accented cadence of his voice.

"I do love you, Bella. More than you can imagine. And you do please me. Nothing has ever pleased me more."

"Then why won't you take me? Why won't you drink from me? Let me give you life, my love. That's all I want."

"Shhh, little one. You have no idea what you're saying. Rest and recover yourself, and tomorrow we will talk. Tomorrow I will be braver and will not so shamelessly deceive you."

"I love you, Louis," she sighed, as she drifted off into slumber at his command.

"I hope so, Bella. I hope so."

He continued to hold her, suppressing the scent and the sound of the live blood flowing rich within her. And when she was slack and warm in his embrace, he laid her back and covered her securely. Then he took the pouch Howland had given him and dumped the entire contents into a glass at the bedside. He slopped water into it, swished it once, and gulped it down before saner thought could prevent it. The fiend in him had almost escaped control. He couldn't let that happen ever again. No matter what the consequences.

And the consequences were quick and terrible.

Excruciating pain. Everywhere at once. He made a soft sound of surprise and was dropped back onto the bed beside Arabella, powerless against the punishing agony. He could feel it streak through his system the instant it was absorbed into his bloodstream, racing like wild fire, consuming all in its path like liquid flame. He, who had been so fearful of the fires of dawn, incinerating from an internal blaze of his own making. Frantically he tried to signal Takeo, but the heat flooded his brain, scorching conscious thought to a cinder. And with blackness came a sudden welcomed cooling, a chill that turned to numbness and then to nothingness.

Just as an animal can scent a sudden change in weather, Louis had always been able to smell dawn. Even safely sealed within his resting place, he knew the moment the sun lifted to chase shadows from the world. And that was what woke him.

He was still stretched out atop the bedsheets with Arabella snuggled against his side. Her dark head was pillowed upon his shoulder, and her palm rode the sudden jerky agitation of his middle. He was dazed, and for a time, too disoriented to move. Then he found himself watching a thread of increasing brightness seeping around the seams of the closed draperies. And with a tremendous shock, he realized it was daylight and he was totally exposed.

There was no time to dash for his below-stairs

hideaway. He was trapped out in the open with nothing but the curtain fabric between him and the sun's rays.

He shoved Arabella away from him. He'd seen others of his kind go up in a howling burst of scarlet crackling flame as unnatural flesh ignited and burned with roaring intensity right down to fine ash. It had been his one consuming terror, dying like that. For three hundred years, he'd existed under the intimidation of those flames.

"Oh, God, be merciful," he cried out, he who had never heeded pleas for mercy from his victims, and his hands covered his face in desperation.

Heat. Louis felt its flare then an even glow. He didn't dare to breathe, waiting, dreading that first snap of combustion.

Master!

Gingerly, Louis inched his hands down, peering apprehensively between the spread of his shaking fingers. "Takeo, I—I am alive." Such a marveling wonder in that breathless claim.

But the dawn—it's daylight!

"I know."

Are you all right?

"I think so." Louis looked at his hands. His skin was hot and reddened, as if from prolonged exposure to the sun. He was bathed in sweat and a rash of discomfort. Howland's potions were protecting him, but for how long and to what extent, he didn't know.

You should go below, Master, just to be safe.

Louis was about to nod his agreement when he glanced to his side and caught Arabella's fixed stare.

She was wide awake and fully aware. And when she spoke, there was a hush of horror in her tone.

"What are you?"

His first thought was to blank her mind, to absorb the memories and dismiss them, thus protecting himself. He even went so far as to raise his hand. The words *Remember nothing* were at his lips, but he couldn't command them. It was time his wife had an answer to her question.

"Takeo, leave us."

But, Master—

And Arabella heard him and she was speechless.

"Please. Do as I say."

There was a quiet resignation to his voice, a weary inevitability that touched the heart of the boy. He looked to Arabella, concentrating hard. *Remember that he loves you.* Then he bowed properly and withdrew.

"I heard him," Arabella whispered. "I heard him speak. In here." She touched her temple, then focused again on her husband, wondering over his red flush of color and his look of long suffering.

Can you hear me?

Yes ... but how is that possible? What are you?

"What do you think I am?" He posed that casually, as if everything wasn't depending upon it.

"I—I don't know. Louis, tell me."

"Are you afraid of me?"

"Yes—no." He reached out his hand. She shrank back. "Yes!"

He withdrew the gesture, expression saddened. "Do you love me?"

Her answer was faint and painfully candid. "I don't think I should."

Louis smiled slightly. "That was not an answer."

"I would like mine first."

She was huddled against the headboard, covers tucked up defensively beneath her chin, about as well protected as a kitten beneath the talons of a hawk. She regarded him with distrust and wariness, but not yet with terror. And oh, how he loved her for that glorious show of spunk. He allowed a small smile and felt her begin to respond to it with a slight softening. Then the edge of caution returned to her posture. He could delay the worst no longer.

"I am a demon that stalks the night. I am the haunter of graveyards living beyond the boundaries of death. I am the legend whispered of in dread in cultures since time began, the dark god to whom Egyptians, Greeks, and Romans prayed, the fiend spoken of from China to the Carpathians. I am the nightmare that shadows the door of Christendom—"

He broke off because she was struggling not to smile.

"Oh, Louis, how very dramatic." And he could see she wasn't believing a word of it. So he stopped the eloquent rhetoric and cut to the definition.

"Every culture has a name for what I am. I am called *vapir, vepir, veryr, vopyr, upier, wampiti, vampyr*. It all means the same: a blood monster, a vampire."

She was no longer smiling as her hand rose reflexively to the injured side of her neck. He could see the shadows building in her lovely gaze, a fear of realization rising like the dawn. In an unnaturally husky tone, she accused, "You are making this up, Louis. Why? Why are you trying to frighten me? There are no such things—"

"Then how do you explain Bianca and Gerardo?"

She swallowed hard. She'd never been able to explain them within the rational confines of her thoughts. They were vague, menacing beings, but she didn't want to call them vampires. Because that would mean that Louis, too, was—

"But you can't be," she protested with a quavering logic. "It's daylight, and vampires cannot survive the dawn."

"With my help, your father has discovered a remedy for the sun sensitivity, and for the other—more unattractive symptoms of my condition."

"My father knows about this?" Somehow she couldn't picture the sensible, scientific Stuart Howland dabbling in witchcraft and folklore and the like. But she knew that he was, and that everything Louis was telling her was the absolute truth. And tears were standing in her eyes when she asked in a fractured voice, "Then how could you marry me without telling me all this?"

Louis stared at her for a moment, at a loss. That was her only complaint? That he hadn't been truthful?

She went on in that wounded tone. "I told you you could trust me with anything, and you swore that you did. This secret is a little more serious than a habit of deep play at cards or a fondness for creatures of the stage. Louis, why didn't you tell me?"

He looked at her through emotion-clouded eyes. "I did not want to lose you."

She made a choking sound, her hand raising to cover her mouth as if to hold it in.

"Bella—please believe me. I—I—" He broke off, his breathing suddenly labored, his features running wet.

"Louis?"

His eyes had shut, squeezing tight, as if to ward off pain. A faint tremor through his shoulders evolved into a body-wracking shudder.

"Louis, what's wrong?"

"The light . . . is too strong. I must . . . I must get below before I—I—"

When he put his hands down on the sheets to support himself, Arabella watched in horror as the ends of his fingertips seemed to smoke and smolder.

"Oh, my God."

Without thinking, she flung the blanket over the top of him, shielding him from the source of his torment.

"Takeo!"

The boy burst in at her shrill cry.

"Help me! The sunlight—"

Takeo needed no further explanation. Between the two of them, they got Louis on his feet and hurried him, carefully covered, down the stairs. He was staggering, moaning horribly, and Arabella was sobbing, holding him in her arms as Takeo opened the door to the cool cellar. Louis broke free to stumble down into the darkness, falling to hands and knees at the bottom, where blackness embraced him. He was up moving on his own by the time Takeo opened the lower door and lurched across the dirt floor between the stacked crates. Arabella followed with the lamp, shivering in shock as she saw him roll into one of the boxes and stretch out flat upon his back. She approached with reluctance, not sure she was ready for such a sight; of her husband laid out upon burial silk, his vital functions slowing to a minimal whisper, already sinking into his heavy daytime slumber.

Instead of finding a horror, she was arrested by his serene beauty. The burning flush had left his cheeks and his eyes were a deep sultry green as they dragged down in sleep. He looked suddenly so vulnerable as his hands folded gracefully upon his abdomen. She couldn't help but touch the long, cool fingers and didn't withdraw as they curled gently about hers.

Louis was plainly struggling against the pull of lethargy. He was blinking slowly, fighting to speak. His fingers massaged hers restlessly.

"Bella . . . Bella, I love you. Must explain. Don't . . . leave me."

Then his eyes closed and his hands relaxed. And she found she was weeping uncontrollably.

After long minutes passed and the chill of the dank room had her shivering, Takeo touched her shoulder tentatively.

You go upstairs now, Mistress. You need rest. He will sleep until dusk, and so should you.

But when he reached for the lid to close it over Louis, Arabella gasped in protest. "Do you have to—shut it?"

Takeo bowed to her wish and was taking his hands down when she noticed the mark on his wrist. Two discolored puncture wounds. He saw the direction of her stricken stare and made no attempt to cover the bites. His smile was sympathetic.

He has never, in the years I've been with him, tried to hurt me.

"Then how do you explain that?" She gestured to the swollen holes with a sudden anger. How dared Louis take advantage of a child in his protection!

As if he'd heard her disgusted conclusion, Takeo shook his head. *No. This was not for him. It was for me. So I could speak, so we could talk together. It is a link between our minds. I begged him to do it. You have no idea how good it feels to express myself to another after being trapped in silence all my life. To have the words caught inside . . .* He looked down, but not before she saw the frustration etched upon his face. And she could understand.

"And that is how I can hear you? Because Louis has—" She couldn't quite speak it.

Because we are both one with him.

And as much as she didn't want to, Arabella was soothed by that idea. One with Louis. She hadn't thought they could be any closer after making love that first time. But she was wrong. She looked down at the still figure at rest.

"Does he know I'm here?"

Takeo nodded.

She reached out a hand that trembled to lightly touch his face. His beautiful face, so cool and composed. His mouth, so soft and sensuously made. She leaned down to kiss him, just a brief press to assure herself that he was not dead, laid out there in his coffin. His lips were warm and pliant, as they would be in sleep. And she whispered against them, "I do love you," before quickly straightening. She hugged her arms about herself, shivering with the massing need to weep.

Please, Mistress. Come up where it's warm before you fall ill.

Finally, she responded to the logic of Takeo's plea. She was freezing, and still far too weak to support herself for much longer. She allowed him to lead her away from Louis, depending upon his assistance to climb the stairs. She continued up to the room she shared with her husband, and by then the delayed shock of it was shaking through her. As she crossed the floor in a daze, her foot kicked against something shiny. Looking down, she saw the silver cross her father had given her. As she picked it up, she remembered his odd words—not so odd now, considering. And she fastened the slender chain about her injured throat.

Curled beneath the covers, Arabella tried to rest, but she couldn't close out the questions—the questions that wouldn't stop coming. She looked back with a new perspective, trying to be analytical in her thinking as she pieced together the confusion with what she now knew. It made a horrible picture. Louis coming to her father to cure him of a blood disorder . . . she almost laughed at that. Such a wry sense of humor he had. His restraint with her, and the pull neither of them could resist. His insistence that they not give in to it until—until he was cured. She understood that now. He'd been trying to protect her from what he knew himself to be. A—a vampire. Her mind recoiled from it even now.

But the man who'd wed her and had taken her to their marriage bed hadn't been some undead ghoul.

He'd been—alive. He'd been mortal. The transfusion had altered him. So what had happened? What had thrust him back into his nocturnal existence?

Gradually, her body's weakness overcame her, and as she settled into sleep, she was suddenly bemused. Because it never occurred to her, not once, to flee from this house, or from the creature slumbering below.

Louis opened his eyes and instantly vaulted out of his resting place. He could still feel the heat of Arabella's kiss and hear the sweetness of her words, *I do love you*. If that was so, then there was a chance, a chance that she could accept him as he was. It was almost too much to hope for, yet he was trembling with anticipation. If she loved him, if she would listen to him, perhaps she would stay. Perhaps he hadn't lost everything.

Then he emerged from his subterranean vault, and the first thing he saw was Takeo's pinched features. The boy's gaze was swimming in distress. And Louis said nothing for a moment. Instead, he reached out with his sharpened sense, scanning the house, room by room. Finding them empty. Only then did he ask in a strained voice, "Where is she, Takeo?" And he heard the words that destroyed all hope.

Master, she's gone.

Chapter Nineteen

"Gone?" Louis stared at him rather blankly. "What do you mean, gone? Gone where? When?"

I don't know. She was asleep in your room, and when I went up to check on her, she was not there.

"How could you let her slip by you? Takeo, I placed her in your care! How could you be so—" He broke off because the boy had tears welling up in his eyes and looked so miserably close to wailing. Louis took a deep breath to cap his own panic and put his hand atop the dark head. "It's all right, Takeo. We'll find her."

But in the back of his mind was the nagging fear: *she's left me. She's run and she won't return.* That, coupled with the other dangers preying upon the night, created a terror for the woman he loved that was hard to suppress. He couldn't bear to think of her alone and vulnerable out on the streets, streets hunted by his merciless enemies. And it hurt so deep and made him so disconsolate to think that she would desert him without hearing all he had to say.

She would go to Howland, of course. But as fine

a man as her father was, he hadn't the ability to protect her from the likes of Bianca and Gerardo. Whether she liked it or not, Louis meant to bring her back beneath his roof. She could hate him if she wanted to, but she would be alive to do so. He would not allow her to be harmed by him or because of him.

From his position in the center of his entry hall, Louis closed his eyes and reached out to forge a telepathic link with his errant wife. And he was met with a puzzling void. He tried again, focusing his concentration, communicating his will across the distance. Again, a confusing blank. Either Howland's powders had drained his mental powers ... or he was no longer able to enjoin with Arabella's mind. Which would mean she was dead.

That possibility had just begun to sink in cold and clear when the front door opened and Arabella bustled in, weighted down by parcels. She drew up short when she saw him. He wasn't sure what he read in her eyes. Not fear, exactly, but a judicious caution. And he wasn't sure whether he wanted to sweep her up into his arms, or throttle her for the scare he'd suffered.

"My lord," she began with a stiff formality. "I did not mean to be so late. I'm sorry if I distressed you with my absence."

With the same neutrality, he murmured, "You are here now, and that's all that matters." Then he contradicted himself by demanding, "Where have you been?"

"There were some things I wanted to purchase before nightfall, but there was a terrible snarl of conveyances and it took forever to get back." She moved into the parlor, keeping a wary eye on him over her shoulder as he followed. She was setting down her bags and boxes when Louis came a step closer, then reared back with a jerk of his head, as if she'd waved vinegar beneath his nose.

"What have you got there, Bella?"

"A few precautions to keep trouble at bay." And she laid out for him an assortment of silver crosses, ropes of garlic, bunches of the herb wolfsbane, lengths of whitethorn, one of which was whittled to a point, and a decanter of clear water. His smile was small and somewhat tragic.

"Are those to keep us safe from the threat outside our walls, or to keep you safe from the threat within them?"

She regarded him with complete candor, her gray eyes huge within her all-too-pale face. "Perhaps from both."

"How very resourceful of you, my love. And where did you learn of such things?"

"I spent the afternoon in the circulating library, reading through books of folklore." Then her confidence faltered with an endearing touch of innocence. "Do any of these things actually work?" And she looked to Louis for the answer of how to mount an effective defense against him.

His smile took a wry twist. "Oh, most assuredly. Silver is like a corrosive. We cannot touch it. The garlic we find extremely offensive, and the wood—I assume you mean to sharpen all of them—has immediate stopping power when one is impaled upon it." He spread his arms out from his sides and offered gallantly, "Would you care to try out any of them on me? Or do you plan to wait until I am in a more helpless state?"

"You are not amusing, Louis." She snapped that at him as her gaze worriedly assessed the full-length windows.

"I was not trying to be," was his quiet reply. When she turned her attention back to him, he continued, "If you mean to destroy me, do it now. As I've said, I'm not much for surprises."

Arabella pursed her lips and chided, "And you would just stand there and allow it?"

"I would assist you, if that was your wish. Is it, Bella?" He lifted the sharpened stake to place its point to his breast. "It's not hard. We are creatures with incredible strength and power, yet we are amazingly vulnerable to such simple things. You could finish me with one blow." And he pressed the heel of his hand against the blunt end until a dark dot of crimson formed upon his snowy shirt front. The expressionless features never altered. Arabella looked between his calm facade to that well of blood and with a dismayed cry, knocked the stake away.

"No! No, it's not what I want."

She leaned into him, her head bowed, her shoulders trembling, her hands clutching unsteadily at his. Gradually, he freed himself from her grip so that his palms could surround her face, lifting her head so he could kiss her with a slow, sweet fervor. She started to return the pressure, then wrenched away with a moan of confusion.

"Louis, please . . ." She was quick to reassemble her composure, wiping her cheeks with the flutter of her hands while backing away from him. His kiss was so disturbingly—human. She distracted herself from it by gesturing to her purchases. "So, what should I do with these amulets?"

"You can hang the casements with the herbs—you'll forgive me if I don't help. That should keep an intruder out."

"I should have enough for all these lower windows."

"Both floors and the attic."

"Both—"

Because she looked so doubtful, he chose a visual explanation. He put his hands out slightly away from his body, palms up, and lifted them. At the same time, his feet left the floor, clearing the boards by several inches. And there he hovered until she was suitably pale with belief before lowering easily again.

"Both floors," she echoed faintly.

"Takeo will see to it. You and I have things to discuss between us."

Arabella glanced at him in alarm and reluctance, but she agreed with a faint, "Yes, we do."

"Shall we go up—"

"No! Here is fine."

Again, the small, cynical smile. "As you wish. Are you hungry? Would you like Takeo to fix you something?"

"No." Then she gazed at him with a narrow suspicion. "And you, my lord? How is your appetite?"

"Under control. You need not fear I will give way to temptation and dine upon you, little one."

His sarcasm was lost, for she skewered him with a look and drawled, "But you have, haven't you?"

"Yes."

"So I would assume you were not in control, then. You must advise me of the difference between being in control and lacking it so I might know what to watch for."

Humor was good, Louis told himself, even if it did bite like acid. It meant that she was trying to deal with the truth and she was not going to make a cowardly retreat. And the significance of her statement was not unrewarding. It implied she was planning to stay with him long enough to learn the subtleties of his state. Yet it was too soon to be confident. "So, you can have your stake and cross at ready, yes." He sighed. "Bella, I am not a monster."

Again, she pinned him with that unwavering stare. "All I know is the name of what you are and some superstitious folly that's supposed to protect me from you. I do not know what to believe, Louis."

"Believe that I love you, little one."

That took her off guard and it made her angry. Because she did believe that and she was upset by his familiar use of endearments, reminding her of their degree of involvement and intimacy. She had wed and bed a vampire—a monster, no matter what he claimed. She was upset as well with her own lack of resolve. Even as she feared him, she was longing for his embrace. She needed an element of detachment with which to study the situation.

"Are you dead?"

He smiled. "Do I look like a dead man?"

She was quick to counter, "Is this how you really look or what you want me to see?"

"For a man who lived during the Medici rule in Florence, I do not look so bad. I have a marker in my homeland with the dates 1491 to 1515 upon it, so I should be dust, yet here I am. Do I not look real to you?"

The actual dates shook her. It made everything seem more impossible, yet more true. Arabella stared at him, trying to see beyond the handsome facade, the human facade. What was behind there, behind the human illusion? Something monstrous? Something dead? Something she'd let touch and love her? She shuddered involuntarily, and he went very still, as if he felt her revulsion. And there, for just an instant, the image blurred and shimmered, a mirage, a dream she clung to, yet was without substance. But as soon as she began to perceive what was really there, he blocked the truth from her mind. She knew he did. And it infuriated her.

"What are you afraid I'll see, Louis? Something horrible? Something that will send me screaming from you?"

His eyes darkened and canted downward. "Accept what is before you."

"But it's not real."

His smile was sad. "You are not ready for that kind of reality. This is the form you are familiar with. It is me. It is how I looked when I still lived. Nothing has changed, nothing in three centuries."

"What else are you? Show me if you are not afraid. What do you hide behind this pretty picture that's meant to seduce and deceive by its beauty? Are you like a bog that casts the illusion of smooth green grass to conceal the fetid slime below until the unwary falls in and cannot escape its pull?"

"Bella, you don't want to know." He was growing irritated with her insistence. Or was he simply afraid?

"Yes, I do. Show me, Louis. Show me what I've married. Show me what sleeps in a box downstairs and feeds off the blood of the living. Off my blood! Show me!"

"Is *this* what you want to see?"

And the change was so rapid and absolute, she could scarcely comprehend it. And it was horrible. She'd seen a shadow of it at her father's office. The being she beheld was not the beautiful and elegant Louis Radman, but a frightening apparition of gaunt, pallid skin, eyes that gleamed red with a feral brilliance, thin, cold lips that curled back from teeth shaped like an animal's fangs. He gestured to his face. Even his hands were different, pasty looking, with long, transparent nails.

"Is this what you prefer to look upon? Or maybe this?"

And he continued to shift and change, becoming something altogether alien—not human at all—with wolfen features and fur instead of flesh. But the eyes were the same: those red, unholy eyes. Changing still, a collage of impressions, animal, rodent, awful. Then pin dots of light enveloped him, flaring to a hurtful brilliance before fading to a mist that was thick and mobile, a mist that transfixed and surrounded her even as she started to cry out in terror. It felt cool, then burning hot against her skin, brushing like a caress, awaking a startling arousal of sensation from her. The power, the chill of death, the overwhelming helplessness that smothered her will.

Then his voice spoke close to her ear, within her

mind, a cruel and tormented whisper, "This is what I am. Are you satisfied now?"

And Arabella swooned dead away.

She awoke with a groggy dizziness clinging to her senses. She was lying down, and it took only a moment for her to recognize her surroundings as those of her bedroom, and the figure at the foot of her bed as her husband.

It was Louis again, handsome, slightly melancholy of expression, watching her with a wary anguish. With a gasp, she sat up, clutching the covers as if they would afford a barrier against the horrors she'd seen.

"I'm sorry I frightened you." How terribly sad and sincere he sounded. Then he smiled, and that was somehow worse. "But you did say we should have no secrets between us."

"I want to leave. Let me go, Louis." Her voice snagged upon a pent-up sob.

His somber mood deepened. "I'm sorry, little one, but you are safer here—at least for tonight. If you wish to go tomorrow, I cannot keep you."

"Safer?" Her tone edged on the hysterical. "How can you say that?"

"I've promised not to harm you, Bella."

Her hand lifted to the bandage at her throat. "And what do you call this if it's not harm? You—you *bit* me. You drank my blood!"

"But did I harm you, Bella? Did I hurt you? Did I scare you?" He reacted in his own defense, letting his tone grow silky and his eyes take on that sultry green-gold smolder she found so irresistible. "You seemed to enjoy it at the time. All of it. Remember?"

At that quiet provocation, recall flooded back and she inhaled sharply in the possession of those sensually sizzling memories. His touch, his kiss, the pleasure, the desperate need to give him—everything. She was panting slightly, her senses vibrating, alive with—him. Her body responded, tightening, trembling, moistening with a voluptuous dependence, with a yearning that was a needful ache, with a wanting that was painful to endure. Her eyes closed as she surrendered to the magic, but it was the way she moaned his name in breathy desperation that woke her mind to his manipulation. And she fought it.

"Stop," she whispered raggedly, then more strongly, "Louis, stop!"

And the feeling ebbed and evaporated and she wanted to wail in protest at the emptiness that followed. The sense of separating from him was emotionally shattering. But Arabella held firm against the desire to weaken.

"Don't, Louis. Don't play tricks to cover what it is you do. You fed off my blood like some kind of—"

"Animal? Monster? Perhaps. But isn't that the way of humanity, feeding off one another?"

"This isn't a discussion of philosophy."

"Forgive me. No, it is not. We were discussing a demon, were we not? An unholy and unnatural being quite deserving of all your hate and disgust."

He'd withdrawn behind a veil of indifference, his expression shielded and his eyes opaque. So wary. So vulnerable, despite all he would pretend. She could wound him with her words. She knew that. Because no matter what else he was, as much as he was capable of it, he did love her.

"So, let me try to understand," she began with her analytical crispness. "You are dead, but not really dead. You live, but you are not alive. You say you will not harm me, yet you drain me close to death."

He didn't choose to reply.

"How often do you need to—drink?"

"At least once a week," he answered matter-of-factly. "If I don't, I grow weary and lose my abilities."

"Is human blood the only kind that can sustain you?"

"I can take from animals, too, but it isn't—the same. I don't get the psychic stimulation from their blood, and I grow mentally sluggish after a time."

"So you hunt the night and prey upon strangers."

"Not by choice."

She couldn't help but draw the gruesome parallel and morbidly speak it aloud. "Is that why you married me? To lay in food for the winter?"

He was plainly shocked by her conclusion and began to pace in agitation. "Is that what you think? Is it? That I keep you here to feed off you? That was not my plan, Bella. It was never my intention to—touch you that way. I wed you thinking—foolish me—that all would be well, that we could live together in mortal harmony, that you need never know what it was I had been—and am again. I wed you out of extreme selfishness, because I could not bear to be alone, I couldn't stand to think of an existence without you. I married you because I love you—for no other reason. If you cannot believe that, go now. Go home to your father and I will vanish from out of your life as if I had never existed."

When she said nothing, he risked a glance at her. She was regarding him with a pensive study that was not unsympathetic. He didn't want her pity. And he didn't want her observing him as if he was some curious specimen strapped to her father's table. Restlessly, he moved across the room in his smooth, effortless strides . . . until he passed the mirror. Then he stopped. And he lifted an unsteady hand to his face.

The strange sound he made brought Arabella from her defensive huddle to see what had his attention so entranced. She approached him cautiously, coming up behind him to peer over his shoulder. In the small cracked mirror, she saw him and she saw herself right through him. There was no solidity to his reflection. It was like a glass transparency.

"I am there, but not there." His fingertips touched to the fragmented surface, following the ghostly image he cast. "What does a man do with half a soul?"

Just as her hands were about to settle consolingly upon the slump of his shoulders, Louis spun away from the mirror and stalked the room. She watched him, hurting for his troubled mood, no longer afraid of him, but still far from comfortable with what she'd learned.

"Louis, what happened?"

He drew up and gazed at her mournfully. "Could you be a bit more specific, my love? Much has happened. What did you wish to discuss?"

"You were human when we wed, and when we first—when we first made love."

"Yes."

"But not now."

"No."

"Did my father's work fail you?"

"We never had the chance to test it. There were problems, but we were searching for means to cope with them. We had hopes, and I still didn't think you were in any danger from me. I'm sorry, Bella. I should have been more careful. I should have understood my enemy better."

"Your enemy?" A dawning moment. "You went to see him. You went to Gerardo. Why? Because you came between him and that witch Bianca?"

A soft, deprecating laugh. "Oh, little one, that does no justice to the truth of it."

"Then *tell* me the truth of it."

He hesitated. The look of sorrow intensified in his expression, a look so deep and inwardly tormenting, she couldn't help but respond. She came to him, stopping close, but not touching. He'd gone totally still, waiting for her next move. She didn't think he was breathing. Did he need to, or was that an illusion of life, too?

Gradually, she reached out to where his arms hung rather limply at his side. She touched the backs of his hands. They felt warm and familiar, those big, gentle hands. Slowly, one finger at a time, he gathered her much smaller ones into the cup of his palms until her hands were secured within his poignant grip.

"It is a long and complicated story."

"We have until dawn." And she smiled slightly in encouragement. He smiled back, just a sketch of a curve, and lifted her hands up to lightly kiss them both. Then he held them to his face, pressing her palms to his taut features. She didn't resist or recoil, but instead did a tender sweep of his chiseled cheekbones. And she swallowed back a tremendous swell of emotion, wondering how this man could be a demon, this man she loved.

"We should sit down. You are still not too strong. Get under the covers and I will begin."

Though reluctant to release him, Arabella was anxious to hear his tale, so she slipped into their bed, then was bemused when he perched upon the very foot of it, a world away from her. She said nothing because he was already far away from her—centuries away.

"I was born in Firenze, the only son of a Florentine *grandi*. I led an enviable life of plenty, a *ricchi*, a *nobili*. I studied all the noted scholars and artisans of the day and discussed philosophies with Machiavelli. It was a city of such unequaled beauty, a time of grace and elegance and culture, rivaled by no other. I was raised to believe there was no greater challenge in life than how to make an elegant spectacle of oneself without appearing to. One had to sing and play, recite verse, speak foreign languages, and dance with a spirit of *sprezzatura*. Gerardo always said I was too sober for our times. He was the soul of nonchalance. None could strut and swagger as well as he. He was such a joy to me. Were it not for his friendship, I would have most likely ended my days as a pondering recluse, content to argue the liberty and spirit of man with others as withered and inexperienced as I." He drifted off into a reflective silence, looking back upon those times.

"He told me you were great friends."

Louis glanced at her. His eyes were glistening. "Did he? Yes, we were. He was of a lesser family, a *mezzani* of the *popolo minuto;* the common class, not truly suitable for my acquaintance. So greedy for the fine things, Gerardo was; *uno appetito di grandezza*. Perhaps that's why he cared for me and endured my fits of introspection that drove him near to madness. Perhaps he coveted the life I was born to. I was not opposed to sharing it with him. Wealth is not something one enjoys alone. He was neither scholarly nor culturally inclined, but he had a zest for living that I quite envied. And he could always make me laugh. I loved him like a brother . . . right up until the day I killed him."

Chapter Twenty

In an age where beauty and blond hair won praise in verse and song, Bianca du Maurier conquered the romantic hearts of all the young courtiers. She appeared one evening on the arm of a merchant's son and all of Florence was at her feet. She was witty and sensuous and mysterious; no one knew the slightest thing about her. She dressed like a queen and behaved like a clever courtesan. Gerardo Pasquale was in an immediate thrall of passion and it seemed none could resist her ... none except a rather wary Luigino Rodmini. Which, of course, made him stand out within a crowd of many.

"I thought she was a witch," Louis admitted to Arabella with a soft, cynical laugh. "A naive guess, but I knew evil when I felt it. And she was evil. She cast a spell upon her victims, winding it about them like a web of pretty dross, and they did not mind being ensnared, even when she drained them dry like a filthy spider. Like the black widow that devours her devoted mate. There was something unhealthy about the cadre of her followers and the possessive way they danced attendance upon her. Gerardo was anxious to be among them and he would not listen to my cautions. He laughed at me and called me a silly old woman for my worries. And one night, he went off with her and I did not see him again for several weeks."

How to describe to her the terror in his heart, the fear trembling within a superstitious mind in an age of splendor and ignorance? He'd searched the city for his friend and in that quest discovered a string of missing sons and husbands. He thought he was seeing the devil's work but it was the work of just one devil, and he had no idea what he was facing.

He'd found Gerardo in a slovenly artist's garret, half starved and wasting away with some unknown sickness of the body and spirit. He refused to return home. He refused to let Louis bring him aid. Louis insisted upon staying in the rat-infested hole to care for him, getting him decent food and clothing and fretting. Gerardo got stronger, but still he would not listen to reason and leave. He was waiting. He was waiting for the return of Bianca du Maurier.

"The longer she stayed away, the more frantic he became. Bewitchment, I thought. The more I argued, the angrier he became. He would not believe she had cast him off in favor of another, and then she was there and it seemed he was right. Except she displayed no great interest in his devotion."

Arabella understood without words. Bianca had been intrigued by Gerardo's serious-minded and beautiful-featured friend.

"We were an odd and familiar sight about the city, the three of us, each night until the early hours before dawn. Bianca played us like the fools we were. She toyed with Gerardo's affection, letting him stumble over himself to please her while she tried to entice me. I went with them because I was afraid to leave him alone with her. I thought I could protect him from what I was certain would prove a fatal charm. How he grew to hate me; and his jealousy wounded because it was undeserved—at first. He was in such a fever of upset. I didn't know what to do."

"She'd bitten him, hadn't she?"

Louis glanced toward Arabella and nodded. "But then, I didn't know that was what it was. I had no idea such things as Bianca existed. I was a good Catholic. I thought I understood evil through the Church's rigid interpretations. But Bianca defied their description. I was afraid for my friend's life, not knowing it was our souls that were in such terrible danger.

"She had a way of distracting the mind with the beauty of what she was. You found yourself enchanted without wanting to be. I would catch myself watching her, wishing I could possess her, while Gerardo sat between us, hating me. I didn't want to feel such things for the woman he adored, for a woman I felt was a demon incarnate. But I couldn't help myself. And the more I resisted, the more she was amused and the harder she pursued me. She didn't care that she was torturing Gerardo with her faithlessness. She seemed to enjoy his misery and mine. She was a lovely and treacherous fiend. But knowing that didn't stop me from falling prey to her."

Louis was silent for a moment. In his mind, he pictured Bianca's sweet mouth, the way it shifted so subtly from taunting mirth to petulant moue to a siren's bow. He remembered his indignant shock and secret thrill when she'd kiss him playfully in her lover's presence. Like family, she'd chide, when Gerardo would rant and rage at her. Nothing wrong with a few fond kisses. Except that it was more than kisses. She found every excuse to touch him, just flirtatious caresses that made him flush with confusion while she laughed and called him her pretty little cleric. He'd been in such a torment of desire and moral panic, and Bianca loved provoking it.

He'd told Arabella he'd forgotten how it was between him and Bianca. He'd said that because there was no way she'd understand what had happened when the predatory blonde had come to him one night in Gerardo's absence, wearing a fur cloak and nothing else. How she'd let that robe drop from her shoulders and he'd fallen with it right into hell. Her naked arms snaked about him and her kiss sucked away the last of his noble resolve. They'd spent the night on the floor, rolling and writhing together, engaged in a fevered coupling that had nothing to do with passion. He'd been drunk on the violent sensations, reeling from her relentless demands and the carnal wickedness they wallowed in. There was none of the conscious pleasure he'd felt with Arabella, none of the gentleness, the love, the excitement or anticipation. It was raw, hard, and even angry, that fierce union, filled with darkness and depravity. And he'd loved the nastiness of it ... until he'd seen Bianca smiling slyly over his shoulder and had turned to see a stunned Gerardo watching from the doorway.

"She'd called him so he'd find us there together. I'm convinced of it. The way she smiled without a trace of guilt or surprise. I'm sure she planned it for her own amusement. For me, it was like waking from a strange dream to a nightmare. I couldn't believe the things I'd done with her to betray my friend who loved her. But I hadn't been able to stop myself. I tried to tell him that. I tried to tell him it meant nothing, that I hadn't done it to hurt him or have her, but he was beyond reason. He drew his sword and demanded I give him satisfaction.

"I didn't want to fight with him, not over a woman who was controlling us both like puppets. He would not listen. I had no choice but to meet him. He was the superior swordsman, so it never occurred to me that I could actually wound him. Perhaps I was hoping he would kill me to take away the shame of what I'd done. But when it was over, he was dying in my arms from a fatal thrust through his chest; my sword had slipped and plunged into him. It was a mistake, a tragic mistake. I hadn't meant to hurt him. I was only trying to defend against him. But it was done and I was so crazy with grief that when Bianca said she could save him from death, I begged her to do it. The price was my devotion, she told me, and it seemed little enough to pledge. I didn't know what she was or what she meant to do to us. Had I, I would have slain us both while salvation was still in sight."

He paused for a moment, his eyes closing, and in

the lamplight, remorse shimmered wetly upon his cheeks.

"She made him into a vampire," Arabella whispered, with a dreadful hush of insight.

"She tore out his throat and drank down his blood, then had him drink from hers as he breathed his last. She laughed at my horror when I said she'd killed him. She laughed and said that was not true. I had killed him. She gave him immortality, just as I requested.

"The next thing I knew, I was in my own bed at my family's villa. They said I'd been suffering from some sort of fever of the brain, rambling wild things about the murder of my friend. And when I looked up, there he was, smiling at me from the foot of my bed, and beside him was Bianca. But I knew he was dead. No one would believe me, and they just smiled, those two ghouls, and let the world think I was insane. I wish I *had* been crazy. I wish it had been my friend Gerardo and his cunning whore there to visit me. They were so solicitous of me in my confusion, and their promise that they would be back to see me again gave no comfort."

And they had returned, he continued in a quiet tone, with a composure that betrayed none of his remembered terror. He'd awakened the next night to find Bianca lying alongside him in his bed while Gerardo glowered from the foot of the bedstead as the blond vampiress lapped from the punctures in his throat. When Louis spoke of how she'd forced his face into the gushing wound she'd ripped in her own fair breast, his words faltered slightly, but his expression never varied. He'd choked on the taste of her blood and listened to her laughter as she'd told him almost lovingly that now she'd never lose him. He would be hers for an eternity. If he died, he would rise up again. He hadn't understood. He'd swooned, then, from shock and loss of blood, and when he was discovered weak and delirious the next morning, his family assumed he'd suffered a relapse. Fearful for him, his parents were about to have him locked away when Bianca and Gerardo took him, spiriting him from his home in the dead of night to begin traversing the continent, a strange trio of travelers.

Bianca kept him just weak enough to be docile to her will and protected him from a vengeful Gerardo, who wanted nothing more than to drain him to death. During the day, Louis made the necessary arrangements for the three of them like a sleepwalker, and at night he sat, a somnambulant witness, as the lethal pair lured the unsuspecting to their brutal deaths.

"I truly do not know how much time passed. Months, perhaps years. There were times when I'd look about in dull surprise and not know where we were. Nothing seemed real ... the East, with its brilliant dawns and sunsets, the rich tropic vegetation, arid deserts, dark mosques and temples, the sights and smells and sound of the crowded bazaars packed along narrow streets of Damascus and Egypt, where Bianca spoiled me with expensive gifts and Gerardo would sometimes be of good cheer and make me laugh almost like the old days ... almost ..." And the ache of melancholy was painful to hear.

"I do not know why she didn't kill me. Perhaps it amused her to watch me fret over my mortal soul.

Boredom is such a terrible state when you've existed for centuries. Perhaps she liked taunting Gerardo by keeping me beside her as her slave where she could kiss me and pet me and drink from me at will. She would let me grow strong enough to resist her, then would take an unholy pleasure in draining that spirit away. And when I was weak, she would hold me in her lap, saying she loved me, and plead with me to join them, to come over to their world of my own choice, tempting me with the promise of eternity, with freedom from the darkness in which I lingered, and I was so tired and so faded, at times I wanted to say, yes, do it, take me, release me—but I couldn't. Her pious little cleric, she'd say, then she would kiss me and let me fall to the floor like I was nothing to her, and she and Gerardo would be off into the night.

"And then, one day while they slept, I somehow found the strength to escape them. I was ill much of the time by then, weakened by the traveling, by the constant demands Bianca made upon my blood. I was convinced I was going to die and go to hell." He laughed softly. "I didn't know I was already there. Bianca had no patience with my prayers and terrors, and she left me alone just long enough for my thoughts to become my own again. I was obsessed with seeing my family again and begging their forgiveness. I had been planning it for some time in the fever of my mind, stashing away coins and memorizing travel routes, trying to stay alert while pretending to be passive. I suspect Gerardo knew, but he said nothing. I think he was hoping Bianca would be so angry that I ran, she'd agree to let him hunt me down and kill me.

"When that day came, I stepped out, taking nothing, and placed a princely sum in the hands of men paid to see me home to Florence. I arrived there sick and failing, but I was able to see my homeland and my mother and father before I died within a few days of returning to their door. They laid me to rest in our family plot, never guessing I would rise up again the next night and every night thereafter for three hundred years. But it was never my choice."

He looked to Arabella then, his expression intense and somewhat fearful as he waited for her judgment. A look so lost and so very human that she came to him with the soft cry of his name.

"Oh, Louis."

And her arms were about his neck, her cheek wet and warm against his. And he hugged her up tight, knowing this was as close to heaven as he was ever going to get. He gathered strength from her, not a physical one, as he would from drinking, but a spiritual power absorbed from the love she'd yet to claim. He wanted her so deeply, so selfishly, he thought of ending his story there, with him the sad and sympathetic victim of a cruel and overwhelming evil. Then she would continue to hold him and love him because he'd been wronged and had suffered so greatly for the sake of his friend Gerardo. But the span of his human life was short, making up just a trickle of the time he'd prowled the earth. He knew it would be unfair of him to let her believe he'd gone on as the same self-sacrificing man, tormented by the same moralistic battles. If she was to choose, she had to know all.

"There is more."

The way he said it made her stiffen in his embrace. She pulled back so she could look into his eyes. He tried to block the emotion in his gaze, but it was an impossible feat. How to pretend his precarious soul was not trembling before her will? Then she surprised and amazed him. She touched his face, letting her fingertips explore it as if she had never seen him before, letting that light touch roam the upward jut of his cheekbones and gently sweep along the arch beneath his brows. He closed his eyes and immense feeling rose within him—powerful, poignant stirrings that made him want to weep. And when she saw the dampness standing in his eyes, pooling there with a fragile shimmer, she leaned forward to very softly, very sweetly, kiss him on the brow. A sound of confusion and tender yearning escaped him as he turned his head away. She should not show him such compassion. She didn't know him. She didn't know all that he was and what he'd done.

"I told you I was no monster, Bella, but perhaps that is not entirely true. I did not want to be a monster, but that did not stop the beast within me. To live as long as I have, to exist as I do, there must be a certain willingness to survive at any cost. And to survive, I must—" He paused unhappily, not ready to destroy the care in her expression.

But she finished for him.

"Kill." She said it simply, as a basic statement of fact, and that was indeed what it was.

"Yes. Now, I have learned to be discriminating. I choose carefully, and I try not to take life. But I was not always that way. Control took decades, and many, many fell before me in the night."

Arabella didn't look away from him or that truth he was telling. She'd paled a bit, but her courage was unfaltering. And oh, how he loved her for it.

"When I first awoke, there was no one to guide me, to tell me what I was to make of my new life. Life, such as it was. I was afraid and I was confused. I didn't know how to adapt the mortal change to my moral views. I fought the hunger, and you cannot know what that is like, the agony of it. I could not hunt nor kill until the drive was so great it overcame me. And the horror of it, the vile splendor of it, had me close to crazy. I went mad for a time, stalking the streets, killing carelessly, clumsily, then weeping with the remorse of it and praying and hoping I would die. I was so vulnerable it is a wonder I survived at all. I didn't know how to protect myself, how to make myself invisible to the eyes of men. All I knew was the hunger, the thirst, and they ruled me completely.

"And then one night, when I was crouched over my fresh kill, tearing into it in a reckless frenzy, I felt a hand upon my shoulder and heard a voice—a voice like I shall never forget, all low and silvery, saying, 'No, not that way, my son. Let me show you how it is done.'"

"Another vampire," Arabella gasped. She was totally absorbed in the tale and the teller, entranced by the darkness of it, forgetting all else, all judgments, all disgust, to hear more of the mesmerizing story. She was sitting close to Louis now, fear gone, her hand resting with a absent familiarity upon his chest. He took up that hand, carrying it up to his lips, then encasing it with his own long fingers to nestle it against the curve of his throat, his chin resting atop it. She could feel the vibration of his speech and the fluid roll of his slow swallowing.

"Yes, another vampire. An old one, as old as Bianca, who had seen the Crusades. He lifted me up from the stones and wiped the blood off my face, scolding as he did, 'No need to be an animal about it. There is a certain delicacy to such things. You must not forget that or what you are. You are an elegant creature. Behave as such.' And I was so ashamed and humbled by the grace and beauty of him that I began to weep and to beg him to teach me, because I had no one to show me. He asked who had made me and why I had no master to help me find my way, and when I told him Bianca's name, he seemed distracted and said, 'Yes, I know that one,' and he said that though I was not his fledgling, he would educate me in the ways of our world. He said his name was Eduard D'Arcy.

"I was his companion for five decades. I was not always the best pupil. I was young and too eager to learn all. But he was patient with me and tolerant of my faults. Beside him, I felt stupid and rude, for he had such an air of refinement in all he did, such an aura of peace. He was a truly beautiful creature, not vile and corrupt, like Bianca and Gerardo, and it was a joy to be his student. From him I learned the craft of survival, how to disguise what I was and what I did, to accept with a certain dignity what I'd become. We spoke philosophy and theology. He was very learned and had in mortal life been in the Church. He taught me a reverence for humankind, as if we needed to protect it even as we preyed upon it, as if we, like gods, should be guardians over them. I do not pretend to understand all he spoke of. I was ignorant, for all my background noblesse. His was the wisdom of centuries."

"What happened to him?"

Louis shrugged slightly. "I do not know. I woke one night to find he'd taken all his belongings from our lodging place. He told me I was ready to assume the role of master of my own fate and that he must leave. I was shocked and afraid. I didn't want to be alone. He would not listen to my pleadings or my fears. He said to me, 'Louis,'—it was he who gave me that name, though he spoke it as the French do—he said, 'Louis, you no longer need me,' and he said I needed to find my own way. I was as hurt as a lover would be, for the two of us, we shared much—history. I behaved badly, demanding to know what I'd done to drive him away, what I could do to make him stay with me, and he but laughed in that indulgent way of his and said I should see our parting as something good, not bad, because he was giving me freedom to explore. Of course, I did not want to believe this, and I grew angry because he had hurt me. When he said we should meet again, I told him that was not my wish, that once he was gone, I never wanted to see him again. And I never have."

And a look of sadness overcame Louis as he rubbed his cheek against Arabella's hand, his eyes half-closed and lost to these reflections.

"Does he still exist?" she asked.

"I think so. I would have heard. Ours is a widespread yet small community, and word of our members is quick to travel through it."

"And Bianca and Gerardo, did they never try to find you before this?"

"I think Bianca's vanity prevented it. Or perhaps they'd heard I was with Eduard; I don't know. I heard of them, of course, of how they staked out a territory in Paris and lived and fed well. I grew strong and skilled, and maybe that's what kept them away, the fear that I would choose some sort of revenge. I had come to terms with my immortality and those thoughts never occurred to me."

His gaze had uplifted, his eyes glowing with that soft green-gold mystery as he studied her pensive expression. He moved his lips across her knuckles. She didn't pull away and he was encouraged to explore her fingers and palm with gentle sweeps of intensifying intimacy.

Arabella was far from immune to his tenderness. This *was* her husband, after all, the man who had initiated her in the ways of love. He was different, yet he was too much the same for her to feel the revulsion she should have when he pressed his kisses upon her. He was a demon who admitted to thousands of relentless killings and at the same time, a soul helpless with fear of her disdain. She couldn't hate him, no matter what he was, no matter what he confessed to.

"Why, then, if you were resigned to your fate, did you seek out my father?"

He was silent for a time, thinking of his answer before speaking it. "Eduard left me with a respect for humankind that I've not been able to dismiss. We are governed by laws beyond your world with heightened senses and unnatural power. We are detached from moral life and because of how we must survive, we harden ourselves to that which we once were, pretending we prefer a world that is cold and dark and lonely and the fact that we are being punished for our defiance of natural codes. There are some of my kind who delight in games of hunter and victim. We gloat about our superiority, when in truth we are lower beings who justify our existence with sins of ego and arrogance.

"I have never killed for the excitement of it. I have never stalked for the power it gives. I feed because I must to go on, and one day I wondered why it was so important that I go on. Who was I that my continuance might be worth the lives of so many? I am no sage, no fount of wisdom, no mind of circumstance or artist of note. I am nothing but a vain noble who feared death more than a dignified departure for myself and my friend. I bartered my soul for an abnormal life, and having it brought no satisfaction.

"When I heard of your father's work, I became obsessed with the idea of returning to that which I was. I had studied much toward this end in the meantime, had gathered much knowledge, but lacked the means of organizing and understanding it. I was not a man of medical science. I needed your father to show me how to make use of what I'd learned. I understood only the philosophical things; it is not the length but the quality of life that brings satisfaction. We learn of that too late, if at all. I had a chance to enjoy that quality again, and

I do not regret the risk, only the loss. There was such sweetness in knowing a human life again. Such a fragile beauty. I was a fool to think Gerardo would hold the same appreciation. I owed him the chance because I, a long time ago, took his life through my own weakness. He was not interested in saving his mortal soul, but only in crushing mine. All that happened once before, happened again, and all that I'd gained, I lost."

He fell silent again. His gaze had lowered and she felt him studying the pattern of veins along her slender wrist. And the idea that he was, stirred a strange thrill within her. And an impulse to press her wrist up to his mouth and bid him drink. Would he resist that dark drive if she did?

"What have you lost, Louis? Retrace the steps that brought you mortality."

He looked up then. "I fear I have already lost you. Have I, Bella? Do you see me now as something too loathsome for you to love?"

"You've not lost me, Louis."

His smile was small and cynical. "No?" And purposefully, he raised her arm, fitting his mouth against the inside of her wrist, letting his eyes flutter shut as he drew against her skin with a soft suction. Arabella gasped as a prickly sensation shot through her. She felt the stroke of his tongue along that sensitive flesh, then the sudden hardness of his teeth. And with a cry of fright, she jerked away and rubbed absently at that spot where the moisture of his breath lingered. He smiled again and it was such a defeated gesture. She understood then.

"You will never again trust me, Bella. You will

never allow my touch without fearing its intent. I cannot imagine a loss as keen as that."

And she sat staring at him through her tears, wondering how she could ever prove him wrong.

Chapter Twenty-One

Arabella left him then, left him sitting on the edge of their bed with his mournful eyes and fatalistic smile. She went downstairs, treading quickly and cautiously down the steps, wondering at the same time if she would ever feel safe after sunset again.

Takeo had taken the bunches of herbs from the parlor to drape them at the windows. The bottle of fluid remained, along with the crosses and lengths of whitethorn. She picked up the vial, a cross, and the sharpened stake, and carried them back upstairs, listening as she hurried for the sound of unnatural footsteps behind her, foolish in her fear because she would never have heard Bianca or Gerardo if they were there.

Louis still sat where she had left him, looking abandoned and abject in his despair. His gaze touched upon those things in her hands and he said, in a heavy, inanimate voice, "You're going to kill me."

Arabella didn't answer because she was distracted

by purpose. She saw him stiffen when she unstopped the bottle.

"Holy water."

He said it as if he feared she would throw it upon him.

"Is it true that those of your kind cannot cross its circle?"

"That or flowing water."

And as he watched, curious now, as she began to pour, leaving a thin channel upon the floorboards that began at the head of their bed, circled about its foot, then continued around the other side. Louis came up on his knees. He was panting slightly with agitation, the way an animal does when it sees a trap closing about it. There was an edge of wariness to him that came with the bane of his existence, and he followed her moves, suspicious of them and of her. Because he couldn't believe she could be accepting of the thing that he was.

Arabella lifted the lamp from the far table and carried it toward the bed. She was startled by Louis's reaction, by the way he scuttled back against the headboard, his features a complete void. His voice was a taut whisper.

"Don't burn me."

It took a moment for her to overcome her shock; then she set the lamp atop the night stand, which had been her intention all along.

"It is you who do not trust me now, my lord. I have no plan to harm you."

His eyes narrowed to a golden glitter. "Then why the unbroken circle?"

She smiled with supreme logic. "Why, Louis," she

explained, as if to a simple child, "that is not to keep you in, but rather to keep them out."

His jaw slackened and she could see she'd surprised him. Taking advantage of it, she knelt on the bed beside him and leaned close to kiss him. As she lifted away, she could feel his breath racing lightly.

"What does this mean?" he asked, as if not daring to draw his own conclusions.

"It means I love you. I've loved you almost from the moment that I met you. I've loved you in both your worlds, but I am confused."

"About what?"

"About where you stand now."

"Somewhere in between, I would guess." Then he told her what he'd done, about drinking down all the powders at once, omitting his reason for it. "I am like that shadow in the mirror. I don't fully exist in either realm."

"For how long?"

"I do not know. My abilities have dulled but have not disappeared. The daylight—I was able to tolerate it for a short time. There is a thread of humanity within me, but how secure, how strong, I cannot say."

"Then we shall have to learn to trust in fate, and in each other."

"Does this mean you wish to stay with me?" He sounded as if he couldn't believe it.

"Yes."

The doubt was back, a faint narrowing along his generous mouth. "Is it my dark kiss that holds you to me?"

"No. It's something stronger. This." She took his hand and pressed his palm above her heart so he could feel its eager beat. And then she asked, "Do you want me to stay?"

In answer, he kissed her, and it was not soft nor sweet and it didn't end until she was gasping for air and composure. He came away slightly so that their lips were still enjoined with just a whisperlike touch and his eyes opened to delve deep into hers.

I love you, Bella.

She more than heard the words. She felt them caress along her skin like a warm breeze, seeping inside her to course along the pulse of her blood like a snapping current. And as her body woke to sensation, she was thinking of how it had been when he'd last made love to her, when he drank from her and introduced a spectacular new plane of paradise.

"Louis," she murmured, with a scintillating stir of her mouth against his, "make love with me."

He drew back slightly, just enough for her to sense his alarm, his uncertainty. "I—"

"You can, can't you? I mean, you did. Don't your kind—ummm, I mean, haven't you—"

He smiled because her blush touched him so sweetly. "No, little one. Not since I was mortal. Not until you. I don't know if it's because we cannot, or because we don't have the desire to."

"Do you now? Have the desire?" And slowly her palm moved over his chest, shifting crisp fabric over firm muscle. She felt his breathing alter, deepening, roughening, as her hand slid lower, pausing when she reached his lap, then stroking with an awed appreciation. "A most impressive answer, my lord." Her voice rumbled with expectant passion.

"I cannot promise you that this is not due to your

father's powders and that the ability might wane with their effect."

Her other hand was busy with his shirt studs. "Then let us not waste the ability while you have it."

Sound reasoning, he agreed.

Soon they were down upon the sheets together, her body carrying him easily, eagerly wrapping him up in the tangle of her embrace, with the sharing of their breath. As his kisses grew more and more fevered, she said into them, "Louis, use your magic. Bring back the dream you used to entice me before we were wed."

He hesitated and almost refused. Wasn't what they'd already experienced enough for her? Didn't she understand how dangerous it was, courting those dark emotions? How easy it was to slip from temptation out of control?

But then he lost himself looking down into her fervid gaze and saw that she was not discontent with what they had, but rather caught up in how much more there might be. His only wish was to please her, to dazzle her with what he was, to give her all she dreamed of ... and more.

Hold my eyes with yours. Do not look away. Can you hear me?

Her lips parted in wonder.

Then answer me.

Yes. Yes, Louis. I hear you.

Reach out to me, Bella, and feel my thoughts even as you hear my words. That's it. Embrace them with your mind. Hold them tight. Feel the texture of my emotions. Let them mingle with yours. Can you feel my heart beating close to yours?

Yes ... oh, I can!

It's a rhythm that will always beat as one; your heart and mine. Always. And you will always be able to reach out to me this way. To touch me this way. Let me have your thoughts, my love. Let me feel as you feel. Let there be no limits this time when we are one.

He filled her with one sure stroke and what was felt by one was shared by the other. Heat, friction, fullness, pushing, giving way. The mutual intensity made all sharp and searing and startling beyond belief. It took Louis a long minute to move because he'd been so shaken.

"So this is what it's like for you. I'd wondered ..."

"Magic," she whispered back in a tight little voice. And her eyes closed as sensation swelled. She opened all her senses to receive the surge of him within and the surge of experiences all around, the two combining with a truly marvelous harmony. She could hear the ragged pull of his breathing as if it issued from her own lips, could feel the urgent rip of his emotions and the answering ebb of her own. Sensual harmony, so exquisitely in tune. A flow as strong as the sea, a pulse like none other she'd known. Forceful cause tantalized by stirring effect.

It wasn't just the carnal excitement; it was so much more than that. Her mind ran loose through his, picking up traces of his thought patterns, of his memories, so clear and bright, like the spin of a kaleidoscope. Breathtaking, soul-shaking feelings. His love for her, as strong as the beat of his heart. The sensation of her body hugging to his; wet heat and chafing urgency. Then she gasped as she snagged upon the razor edge of his hunger, sharing for a moment that consuming lust to bite and feed, recognizing the struggle to abstain when every instinct pressured fiercely. The scent of blood, pungent, rich, hot. Hers. She could feel his need, and she wanted to appease it. Had to ease it.

Her hand rose to clutch at the cross and with a jerk, snapped the silver chain. Her other hand clasped the back of his head, thrusting his face against the beckoning arch of her throat. She cried out as she shared the sharp mental spike of his thirst, the hypnotic draw of her heart beating fast in time with his. She experienced his moan of resistance down to the very depths of her soul and the roar of his weakness even as his mouth touched hot to her neck.

"Louis . . . please!" She was confused and dazed and wildly invigorated, sensations crashing and cresting over one another. She wasn't sure what she was begging for, only that she needed it from him and needed it now.

He'd started to open his mouth, filled with driving instinct of his kind. Then Louis gasped in surprise as passion rushed and burst, wiping away all hints of hunger as it shot through him like lightning and rolled through her like thunder, a blinding, cataclysmic force. A perfect complement that clashed with splendid violence and merged in a culmination of pleasures. So intensely satisfying, the link between them was momentarily severed, leaving them to individually grapple with their disoriented bliss.

It was silent for a time, that sweet serenity after the devastation of a storm, with only the hurry of their breathing to mark the power of its passing.

"Louis, I will never, ever leave you, not as long as I live." Arabella made that firm vow as his head rested heavy against her shoulder. There was such power and convincing sincerity in that oath that his gaze was swimming with amazement when he lifted up to look at her.

"Bella, you don't know what it is you're promising."

"Yes, I do."

"I cannot promise to keep you safe, from them or from myself. I cannot guarantee you a tomorrow."

"I'm not asking for one."

"But Arabella, you deserve so much better than that."

"There is nothing better, Louis, than what you've shared with me. It's you who don't understand. I have lived my life in safety and mundane habit. I've been the plain and practical daughter of an ambitious man. I didn't know life could be as filled with passion and pleasure as it's been since I met you. You shook me from my dull platitudes like a shock of dangerous excitement, and nothing, Louis, nothing could ever happen that would make me regret my choice to be with you. So no matter what happens, don't you dare feel a moment of guilt or remorse, because this is where I want to be. With you. And I have never been happier."

She could see he was shaken to speechlessness. So she kissed him tenderly to conclude the conversation. And she tightened the circle of her arms to coax him back down to her, where he lay all sleek and warm and hers.

After a time, he said, "I'll get you a stronger chain."

For the first time, Arabella was aware of the crucifix biting into her palm. She weighed it thoughtfully, then asked, "Would it harm me if you were to—drink from me again?"

His reply was very soft. "Not if I was careful."

"Will you?"

"Be careful?"

"Drink."

"Oh. I—" He broke off, not knowing how to answer her.

"Will the bond between us stay this strong if you don't?"

"It loses its intensity, but it will always be there between us."

"Is it—pleasurable for you?"

"Yes." Roughly said.

"Like making love?"

"Yes." Even gruffer.

"Then we shall try it again as soon as I'm stronger. I'm not afraid, Louis, and I want so much to please you."

She heard his sharp intake of breath. "Bella, I don't expect you to—"

"I know."

"I will not make a slave of you."

"I shouldn't think that would be so bad, being your slave." And her fingertips teased down his chest as she said that. He shifted the angle of his head so he could look up at her, to catch the simmer of her smile. And he returned it.

"I like your stubbornness too much to humble you."

"Then stubborn I shall be. And your lover I shall be. And I shall share with you all that I am, all that you need me to be."

Louis took an unsteady breath. What she was offering humbled him and at the same time made his bloodlust rumble. Imagining how could it be sent a tremor of anticipation growling through him. Arabella: his love, his wife, his slave. Tending his needs for companionship, for shared affection, for sensual gratification, tending to the hunger. Kissing her, caressing her, loving her, drinking from her, all part of one exquisite ritual of desire. The taste of her passion on his lips, gliding hot and renewing down his throat. Her love sustaining him. He couldn't envision anything so perfect as that.

Unless he was careless. Unless the intensity of the moment carried him away and her to an uneasy grave.

"I need to go see your father. He means to start the treatments again. Perhaps this time the success will take."

Arabella said nothing. She was shamed by her want to tell him that if mortality meant losing the beauty they'd just experienced, she preferred him as he was. But that was such a selfish want, she didn't speak it.

"I should go now."

But the moment he made to rise, Arabella clung to him, her words filled with urgent inflection. "Louis, stay with me. Don't go. Stay this night with me, just you and me, together. I—I need you so."

"Bella, my love—"

"Louis, please? I want this night with you to be without fear. Hold me. I want to fall asleep with your arms around me, knowing you'll be safe when I awake. Please. Go see my father tomorrow. Let the devils wait out there. You're mine tonight. Let nothing interfere."

Silence, then a quiet, "All right."

"I love you, Louis."

"Go to sleep. I'll watch over you."

And he held her and guarded her. And later, he woke her and loved her sweetly, with all the tender passion in his heart. And when she drifted off to sleep a second time, so did he, carelessly entwined upon the big bed in mortal sleep where dawn could find him.

"Bella, the circle! You must break the circle!"

Arabella woke with a sense of confused urgency. "Louis? What is it?"

"It's dawn. Break the circle. The daylight must not find me!"

But even as she sat up, she saw that it was too late. There was a part to the drapes, and through it streamed a broad ribbon of morning, flowing like an invisible barrier across the width of the bedroom, a barrier Louis could not pass even if he could escape the consecrated circle she'd drawn around their bed the night before.

"Close your eyes. Don't look at it." And as he obeyed, she pulled the covers up over him even as she grabbed for his silk robe. Belting it about her,

Arabella took a cloth from the washstand and began vigorously to scrub away the sacred line that trapped him as dawn brightened the room about them. Then she ran to draw the heavy drapes tightly together, sealing in a semigloom. She could hear the rasp of his breathing as she returned to the bed. "Louis, are you all right?"

"Hand me my clothes." His voice was unnaturally hoarse as she did as he commanded. He stayed under the sheet, wrestling into the tunic and trousers. "Bella, stay back from me. I don't want you hurt if—"

"If what?"

"If I should go up in flame."

"Up in—" Distress and denial held her fast; then she disregarded caution as he slid out from under the covers.

"Bella, no!"

She took up his hands and tucked them within the folds of the robe. She was remembering the way his fingertips had smoldered. "We must keep the light off exposed skin."

He was trying to pull back. "Bella, you're risking—"

"Hush! We discussed this last night, Louis. I will not lose you, and I'm not afraid to do whatever must be done to see you safe. Remember, you said you liked my stubbornness. And," she concluded with an iron-laced quiet, "if you go, I go. But I would prefer to get us both safely below. Come, my lord, hide your pretty face, lest it be scorched."

For a moment, almost a moment too long, he stared up at her, his eyes huge and luminous. Then he ducked his head and allowed her to draw his face up against the concealing warmth of her bosom. Not an unpleasant hiding place, by any means. They moved slowly together across the room, not pausing even when he gave a sudden gasp as bare feet they'd forgotten stepped through the beam of sunlight.

In the darkness of the hall, he straightened. She could see the effort of composure lining his face. He looked gaunt and worn beneath a sheen of perspiration and was frowning at the sight of yellow light pooling in the lower foyer from the uncovered transom and sidelights on the door.

"Louis, what shall we—"

But before she could finish with her concern, he vaulted lightly over the stair rail and jumped with an almost weightless floating to the shadowed hall below. She stared after him, shaken by his demonstration of mastery of space and suspension. He looked up, his eyes glowing golden in the dimness.

"Bella, come down."

Judiciously, she took the steps.

In the dark inner corridors of the house, Louis was able to move freely, just as he would during the night. He spent some minutes observing his translucent reflection in a small mirror in the dining room until Arabella slipped her arms about him from behind and pillowed her head against the tense line of his shoulders.

"As long as a part of me remains there in the glass, a part of me remains here with you in this world." He gathered up her hands in his and clutched them tight.

Part of you will always remain with me, Louis.

The feel of her love weaving about his conscious

mind with the internal whisper of those words pleased him. And suddenly he wasn't sorry he'd initiated her with his kiss. The closeness, the kinship, were satisfyingly intimate. He relaxed and let her home in on his emotions, let her attach her fledgling sensitivity to the tenderness within him. And he heard and felt her sigh of contentment. Could she be happy with him? He wondered and he hoped and he wished it could be so. Because he had never felt as satisfied with his life as he did now.

Mistress Arabella, might I fix you some breakfast?

She looked to Takeo with a smile upon her face. Such a soft, gentle voice he had; like the voice one would give an angel. "Thank you, Takeo. I believe I would. My lord, will you sit with me awhile, or do you need to go below?"

"I will sit with you. I am not uncomfortable."

"Louis—"

"Well, it is a tolerable discomfort. I will endure it to spend time with you."

As he walked with her to the head of the table, she noticed his uneven gait and glanced down. She gasped. "Louis, your feet!"

"It's nothing. They will heal."

Nothing, he said. She couldn't believe that. "Sit down and let me look at them."

He was smiling patiently as she pushed him into a chair and knelt to draw one foot upon her lap.

"Oh, Louis."

The top of his foot was a mass of blistered flesh and the bottom cooked nearly raw. But he was studying her face with an odd bemusement, as if he felt nothing beyond a curious gratitude for her care.

"Takeo, bring me some cool water and some clean linen."

"Bella, it will be fine. The burns will be gone by the time I rise up again."

"But they must hurt you, and if poisoning sets in—"

"My love, you forget, I am immortal. Such things are only a temporary annoyance."

Despite that claim, his heel gave a hearty jump atop her knee when she applied a cool wrap to it. He sat stoically and let her tend him.

"All this from the brush of the sun. Louis, you must be careful. Do not flirt with the danger of it. It would quite destroy me to see you reduced to the consistency of fireplace ash."

"Delicately put, little one, and it would not please me, either. Stop fussing, *cara*. There is nothing more you can do for me. It is unnatural flesh. It doesn't respond in the way of mortal tissue."

She was massaging the taut calf of his leg with worried strokes. "Is there nothing I can do to ease the hurt?"

"The powders." He was thinking of the way in which Howland cured the silver burn in his palm and he spoke aloud without realizing.

"What powders? Those my father mixed for you?"

"They counteract the toxic effect of sun and silver on me. They alone are what keep me here with you in the light of day. Elsewise," and he smiled somewhat grimly, "I would be fireplace ash. But I have no more, and he was going to prepare some. I will have him look at the burns tonight."

"I'll get some from him while you rest."

"Bella," he began, in a cautioning tone.

"I need to speak with him, Louis. To explain certain things."

"I do not wish you to go out alone. Danger walks in many forms."

"Then let's go. Let's leave this place and the danger behind. While you sleep, I will pack up all we own and we can be gone before they know where to look. Maybe to America. You said you would like to see it. With Takeo and me to watch over you, the trip would not be perilous to you. And we—"

"Could be safe? Not forever, Bella. As I said, it is a small community through which word travels fast. They would find us again. Gerardo will not stop until he has destroyed me."

"Then destroy him first!"

His answer to her appeal was candid. "I don't know if I have enough strength."

"Then run with me."

"I have run for three hundred years, Bella. Now I have reason to stay. If I leave, I will never have a chance to walk as a man again."

"I don't care."

"Bella—"

"I don't, Louis. I don't care if you lie with me in our bed at night, or sleep alone in a box by day. I will not lose you. Who's to say another transfusion will work any better than the last? That it would not prove fatal this time? I would rather have you as you are than not have you at all. I'm sorry if that is selfish. I have waited too long to know a love such as yours. I value it above all things. All things, Louis. Please come with me. Live out my life with me."

"Bella, I will not grow old. You are asking me to watch you die while I stay forever young."

She hadn't thought of that. And thinking of it brought up the obvious alternative. "Or I could stay unchanged with you."

He drew a pained breath. "Bella, you would share damnation with me? Please, my love, think on that very carefully before you consider a road to darkness."

Because she could see it upset him, she let it drop for the moment, glad Takeo had arrived with her meal. As she ate, she watched Louis begin to weave in his chair as his senses eased into their natural daytime dormancy. He was blinking slowly, clearly struggling to stay alert.

"Louis, lie down. Refresh yourself while I go to my father. I'll ask him to make up an abundance of the powder, enough to last you a journey and beyond, if we're forced to take one. Then we'll talk and decide what is best to do."

"Takeo, go with her."

Master, my place is with you!

"Your place is where you are best served. None can get to me when I'm at rest, yet once Arabella leaves the protection of this house, she is at the mercy of many things. Go with her. See she is safe."

And as he settled back into the familiar folds of his below-ground bed, feeling the soft press of his wife's kiss even as his eyes closed, he remembered what he needed to tell her: that Bianca and Gerardo could still work their evil during the day through the hands of their servants. That she must beware. But his eyes were heavy and his heartbeat was slowing and speech was beyond him.

And he slept with the warning unspoken.

Chapter Twenty-Two

"I was worried." Stuart Howland followed up that claim with a crushing embrace. "Are you all right, Bella?"

"Yes, of course." But her reassurance didn't keep him from examining either side of her throat. Her voice was gently chiding. "Father, that isn't necessary."

"You wouldn't say so if you knew—"

"I *do* know."

Howland stepped back, his features blanked with surprise. "He told you."

"Everything."

"And you're leaving him?" That hope quavered.

"No." Aware of Bessie Kampford's curious hovering and Takeo's silent shadow, Arabella took her father's elbow. "Can we discuss this in your study?"

"Can I bring you anything, Miss—Madame?"

Arabella smiled at Bessie's eagerness. "I've already breakfasted, but some hot tea would be nice. Thank you, Mrs. Kampford." Then she was tugging on the doctor's arm.

Once the solid doors were closed with Louis's servant standing guard outside them, Stuart turned to her in a severe mood. "You know what he is and you choose to stay with him."

"You knew what he was when you allowed me to marry him." When he flinched at that curtly spoken truth, she softened her tone. "He is my husband. My place is with him."

"Bella, he is—"

"The man I love!"

"The man he was died three hundred years ago."

"You brought him back to life," was her calm argument. "You brought him back to me. I will not let him go again."

He regarded her in disbelief. "How can you say that, knowing what you do—"

She stared back at him without a flicker of regret.

"Bella, Wesley's dead."

She blinked at that.

"I see he did not tell you everything. Radman killed him."

Louis killed him.

Arabella reeled in a moment of realization. Listening to a tragic story centuries old had a romantic appeal, but hearing the grim fact of the death of someone she knew at the hands of the man she loved ... She was tortured by a brief vision of Wesley Pembrook struggling in Louis's grip. She could imagine his terror at the sight of the fangs, at the feel of the bite, as the blood was being drained from his body. And Louis, the man who'd kissed her and loved her, emptying another human being of life so his could continue. Drinking blood. Swallowing another man's soul. Her fingertips pressed to her lips as a queasy sickness swelled within her on the tide of a cold despair. She shuddered helplessly. Louis Radman was not human. He was not a being through whom natural life flowed. He was a killer, a killer of innocent people.

But Wesley hadn't been innocent.

She clung to that with a saving desperation, able to face her father with crisp fact. "Wesley was trying to destroy him."

"To save you."

"From Louis? Louis loves me. He would never consciously hurt me."

"You wouldn't say that if you'd seen how you looked when he brought you here, pale as a ghost and nearly dead."

"But he brought me here, didn't he? Father, it wasn't his fault."

"Bella, I'm not talking fault. I'm talking fact. Perhaps he killed Wesley to save himself. Perhaps it was some regrettable accident that had you close to death. But those things don't excuse what he is. What he is is a vampire. And what he does is kill. Relentlessly. Week after week, year after year, decade after decade. He is not a man. He has no soul or conscience."

"Yes, he does!"

"Bella, he murders and he drinks the blood of his victims. And you are going to live with him, knowing that? Letting him come home to you after he's been out on the street, hunting and killing his prey? You're going to accept that he's coming to you with another's blood on his hands and in his veins?"

Her jaw firmed and her eyes narrowed. "I don't care."

And her father took a step back, aghast. "How hard he's made you already. Or is that Radman talking through you? I don't like to believe my daughter could throw off her concern for human life."

Arabella had to turn away as her eyes welled up with anguished tears. Because she did care. She could try to pretend she didn't, but it was a lie. She could accept what Louis was, but she didn't know deep down if she could handle what it was he did. She didn't know if she could let him come into her arms warmed by the stolen life of another, without thinking of whom he'd taken into his fatal embrace: a young man with his future before him, a woman with children at home, a father providing for his family? And she knew right then she could never join Louis in his nocturnal existence. She could never develop the indifference or the desperation to do what must be done for her to survive.

She looked back at her father, her stricken expression saying it all. Wordlessly, he hugged her up to him and let her sob against his shoulder. "I love him, Father. I love him so. Please help him. Please find some way to cure him!"

And his tone was all tender assurance. "I will do my best, child. I will do my best."

She was under control again by the time Bessie brought in the tray with its fragrant hot tea, and she sipped from her delicate cup while it trembled in her hand. Takeo had slipped into the room and stood well back behind her chair and as incongruous as possible. She looked back at him and smiled, gesturing to the pot of tea. He shook his head, his black eyes fixed on her father.

"Who is the boy?"

"He's Louis's." She said only that, not knowing what else to add to explain Takeo.

Stuart rose up and went to circle the Asian youth. Takeo stood placidly, but Arabella felt his inner tension and defensiveness, especially when Howland took up his wrist. He jerked his arm back violently.

"It's all right, Takeo," Arabella soothed. "Let him look."

The boy offered up his marked wrist with a prideful disdain. Stuart examined the wounds and let the boy's arm drop.

"Louis's," he drawled out with a mild contempt. "As you are Louis's."

Arabella's chin rose a notch, her pose an echo of Takeo's. "Yes. Louis's. And that will never change, as long as he is what he is. Unless you can change him."

Howland said nothing as he studied his daughter's defiant features. Then he sighed. "I must change to go to the hospital. I won't be long. Would you wait here until I return, Bella? I would like to talk some more on this."

"I won't change my mind," she warned, with a tenacious smile that he couldn't help but respond to.

"That would be too much of a miracle to hope for. And how is Radman today?"

"I need some more of the powders."

"More? I gave him enough to last over a week."

When she explained that he'd taken them all at

once, he appeared thoughtful and demanded to know the effects.

"He can tolerate diffuse daylight for a time, and in other ways, he is quite—human." She looked down, her cheeks staining a modest crimson.

"You are lying with him."

He sounded so astonished, Arabella was moved to retort, "He is my husband!"

"He is unnatural! Have you thought—but no."

"Thought what?"

He was looking at her with that keen, probing interest, the way he observed something that puzzled him. "Of the possibility of a child."

She blushed hotter and muttered, "Louis doesn't think that likely."

"Let's hope not."

She gasped at his cruelty.

"Bella, we don't know what causes his condition. If it's some element in his blood, it could well be passed along to any child you make between you."

That settled like cold panic within her heart. "Or it could be human," she protested forcefully.

"Or both," he amended. "I don't know, Bella. Much of what Radman is is a mystery and an impossibility. If a child is seeded, there are ways to terminate the problem that would not endanger you. You must promise to advise me right away if you conceive."

"Yes, of course," she mumbled. But her eyes canted downward and her expression was numb.

"I must go now. You will wait here for me. I have more of his powders ready to mix. I'll bring them home with me. Until then, stay so that I know you are safe."

"All right."

And she turned a cool cheek up for his kiss and sat in silence long after he'd gone. Finally, she felt the light touch of Takeo's hand upon her shoulder and glanced up at him. His features were unreadable. His eyes were alive with torment. Gently, she pressed her fingers over his.

"Takeo, I would never do anything to harm a child of Louis's. I would love it as I love him, regardless of the consequences. As we both love you."

That satisfied him, for he bowed slightly and his face was suspiciously pinked with a flush of embarrassed pleasure. And he was content to stand sentinel behind her chair as the day progressed from morning to afternoon.

But Arabella was far from the serene picture she presented. Her thoughts were careening. A vampire husband . . . a vampire child.

Strange, how simple and soothing it was to fall back into the pattern of years. Arabella found herself drawn to her father's cluttered desk and the papers strewn across it. He wasn't keeping up with his work, she thought with a fond smile. She started sorting through the sheafs and soon was seated, transcribing his nearly illegible scrawl into the journal he kept. It was calming, that busy work, that plunge into the familiar. It was almost like settling back into those pleasant and uneventful days, sitting in his study, waiting for his return. It was a comforting illusion in her agitated state. Only Takeo was there to remind her of the difference. Takeo, and his link to the being laid out in a basement box, deep in unnatural slumber.

Arabella touched the black obelisk with all its foreign writings. She'd left it anchoring a stack of her father's loose papers. Would Louis go out in search of sustenance tonight? She wondered and it upset her. How many days had it been? She assumed if he'd killed Wesley, he'd also fed upon him. She closed her mind to further thoughts of that. If he went out in search of victims, what, then, made him different from his past companions? Was he any less damned, any less the predator? She had to come to terms with these things within her own mind before Louis rose at sunset. He would sense her confusion and it would wound him. She'd spoken so boldly to him about devotion and loyalty. How frail his promise was becoming. Would her courage fail her and in doing so, cause her to fail him? The first splotch of dampness on the papers below her startled her, but other tears were quick to follow. She was wiping them away when Takeo knelt beside her, his youthful features all matured concern and sympathy.

"What am I to do, Takeo? How can I love him so completely, yet loathe that which he is? He will despise me for my weakness."

No. You are most admirable. He does not expect you to love what cannot be loved, that which he loathes about himself. He has been in pain for centuries, and you are the first relief he's known. The truth cannot hurt him. It's not weakness to cry for the loss of innocence. It's that touch of humanity he loves about you.

"You are very wise for one so young." And she smiled through her dull misery.

I have seen much. I have known evil in men that makes my master a saint in comparison. Sometimes it isn't action, but intention that separates the two. He doesn't kill for pleasure. In fact, he rarely kills at all. He takes only enough to sustain himself, and he leaves those he uses with no memory of pain or fright. Do not judge him too harshly—or yourself. Don't push yourself into making hasty promises. The fact that you are there when he awakes is all he needs from you.

"Then I will always be there when he awakes."

They were sharing a look of mutual conviction when the sound of a knock upon the front door and Mrs. Kampford's voice reached them.

"I'm sorry. The doctor is not at home. Here, now! You can't just push your way in! Wait just a—" There was a low groan and a soft thump.

Takeo jerked Arabella from the chair and thrust her behind him. But there was little he could do when the doors to Stuart Howland's study burst open and several burly brutes confronted them with pistols drawn.

"So we meets again, Missy," growled one of the men. Arabella recognized him as Mac Reeves's accomplice, Ollie. "Only this time, your pretty feller ain't gonna be tossing me around." He chuckled, low and gritty. "Gettin' late, and we gots some anxious friends jus' dyin' to see you."

Stay behind me, Miss Arabella. Don't move. I won't let them take you.

"You be comin' along real quiet-like. I'd hate to do any shooting."

While he stood guard at the door, the other two flanked the desk as Takeo urged Arabella around it. He struck out so quickly, the one on the right side never saw the blur of his foot as it numbed his arm and sent the gun spinning. Arabella dropped the villain to the floor with the crack of Louis's black stone against the side of the fellow's temple. Takeo was across the polished surface in a roll, scattering papers and journals, and Arabella scrambled beneath it, dodging out the other side as Takeo engaged the second graverobber with a series of skull-rattling kicks. Before she could get halfway across the room, Reeves's companion caught her by the hair and yanked her up, screaming with fright and pain and fury. She delivered a few good slaps of her own before his settled in solidly against her cheek and the room went whirling.

"Hold up there, boy, lest you want me to go breakin' up her pretty little face."

Takeo came to an immediate standstill. His eyes were quick to assess the impossibility of an attack with Arabella so vulnerable.

I'm sorry, Missus.

It's all right, Takeo. Her thoughts came with a calm she was far from feeling because the danger was not hers. It was Louis they were after. There was no mistaking that when Ollie turned his head and she saw the irrefutable marks upon his throat. These men were Bianca's henchmen. And if they took her to Bianca and Gerardo, Louis was sure to follow—to his doom. And that she could not allow.

When Louis arrives, don't let him come after me. They're using me to get to him. Don't let him follow.

Tell him—I'm dead. Tell him they killed me, and get him as far away as you can. Don't let him come after me. They'll destroy him. Takeo, promise me!

The boy stood stiff and silent. Before he could give her a reply, the first man he'd struck dealt him a leveling blow with the barrel of his pistol.

"No!" Arabella shrieked and writhed in Ollie's grip. "He's just a boy! Let him alone!"

"He don't fight like no boy," the second man growled, delivering a punishing kick at the immobile figure.

"Let 'im be. Don't matter none. He'll be taken care of when the welcomin' party gets here to wait for the doc."

That brought a renewed sense of panic and struggle to Arabella. Her father!

"C'mon, Missy. Walk nice, lest you want me to scatter the lad's brains, now."

And still dazed, Arabella did as she was told, casting a last look back at the fallen boy, praying Louis would come in time to save him, Mrs. Kampford, and her father from whatever horror his two long-dead friends had in mind, and that Takeo would do as she told him.

Danger and death. Those things scented the air like a strong stale perfume.

Louis blended with the shadows outside the Howland house. He stood with an uncanny stillness, listening, letting his acute senses probe the house. He could feel the presence of two mortals, but there was more, just outside the reach of his newly limited abilities. For the first time, he cursed that thread of humanity running through him like a thin vein of precious ore through rock because it made him weaker than those he had to face.

Having concluded his study of the exterior of the house, Louis chose the best route in. With a subtle movement, he lifted his arms and simply rose up to Arabella's second-story window as if making a gentle leap up a single stair step. Finding the latch undone, he muttered a soft oath at Howland's stupidity as he slipped in through the open casement. For a man of wisdom and science, Howland had damn little common sense.

Arabella's room was dark and deserted, but for a brief overpowering instant, Louis was lost to the aura of her within it. His eyes closed as he drank in the essence of her: the fragrance of her powders and perfumes, the lingering warmth of her upon the sheets and within the clothing yet lining her closets. He could feel her in the bath soaps, in the reflecting glass, in the brush still twined with strands of her long dark hair. A wave of desperate despair rose up in him. If they had harmed her . . .

Then his eyes opened, a glitter of hot gold in the dimness, filled with a deadly purpose that knew no fear. He would not allow her to come to any harm. And he went to the stairs to confront whatever veiled evil waited below.

He made no sound in passing. The carpet remained uncrushed as he slid over it without touching the fibers. He was getting strong impressions now, evidence of struggle and terror. And blood. His nostrils flared and hunger had him moistening his lips. The kill was fresh and close by. The heart had only recently surrendered its fight. Louis's breath was coming faster, excited by the rich scent that distracted and lured him. He crossed the foyer cautiously, wondering if the corpse had been left to draw him into a skillful trap. But his suspecting that still couldn't overcome his compelling need to continue toward the source of temptation.

He saw the soles of the victim's feet protruding from the dining room arch. He approached more slowly, working harder to control the roar of appetite burning within him. He was breathing in short little hisses between clenched teeth as his stare followed a thin trail of blood splotching the hall runner, thickening as it neared the still body.

Howland.

One glimpse told all. He lay face up, eyes sightlessly fixed at some unseen horror on the ceiling. His throat had been savagely torn out. Louis observed the scene dispassionately; he'd long since lost his squeamishness around such things. He could imagine Howland coming home from the hospital. He still had on his doctoring smock and carried the perfumed handkerchief he'd held over his nose while visiting the fetid wards. He'd entered his own home unaware that death awaited and had walked foolishly right into its cold and merciless embrace. There was no sign of resistance. The initial attack had completely drained him.

Louis knelt down at the dead man's shoulder. He felt a disassociated pain of loss because this mortal had been Arabella's father, but no real sorrow touched his heart. That disturbed him. It was the callousness of his breed. He reached out to ease the lids down over the glazed eyes. Had Arabella been here to witness this murder? Had she seen through her own eyes what those of his kind did to serve their hunger? If so, how could she ever look at him in the same way or forgive him for having brought this disaster into her life?

Now she had no one to care for her. No one except him.

"I will care for her, Doctor. I will keep my word to you, I promise."

Without any real awareness of it, he lifted bloodstained fingers to his lips to sample the taste upon them, shuddering slightly with an anticipated pleasure. It was then Louis noticed a fine powdery substance scattered about the body and the ripped pouch the doctor had clenched in one stiff hand. And the significance sank deep and desolate. His future lay scattered upon that floor, tiny granules of hope carelessly dispersed in one wantonly violent act. A terrible fury got hold of him, shaking through him in a great dark surge. They had crushed his dreams of mortality. Now Howland would never bring him back to the world of the living. They'd sentenced him to an eternity of the damned.

With a low snarl, he rose up. Vengeance beat hot and fierce and senseless. He would kill them both. He would rip them apart and scatter their unnatural pieces to the night. How dare they steal his one chance at salvation! They would pay, and pay dearly. The fools had no idea what they had awakened with their petty revenge.

He stalked through the house like an ill wind toward the doctor's office where he felt the two mortal beings—Takeo and a woman. Bella? He wasn't sure. He reached out with his mind, but couldn't touch either of them. Something else was in there with them.

It was dark in the big room, with only a dim light burning. His eyes were quick to adjust. He saw Bessie Kampford huddled near it with a limp Takeo clutched up to her bosom. They both looked mussed and worse for wear. Victims of foul play? The housekeeper's eyes were huge and nearly black with fear as they fixed upon him. Her lips moved soundlessly, as if trying to convey some message that terror had frozen up in her throat.

"Where is Bella?" he demanded.

"Look out, my lord!" The warning rasped from the housekeeper.

But not in time to save him from a sudden slashing agony.

Chapter Twenty-Three

The unexpected brutality of the attack stunned Louis. Pain lanced through his shoulder, spearing to the bone as the horrid odor of decay overwhelmed him. He staggered and the demon latching onto him bore him down to his knees. The fetid breath, the piercing burn of the fangs into his flesh; Louis reeled from it all. His hand flailed and caught upon a wet and moldering coat. The fabric gave way. He grappled again and caught a handful of matted hair. It came out in a great tuft. With blackness swelling up over his consciousness, he tried once more, his palm levering beneath what was left of the *revenant*'s nose to strike upward, the blow allowing him to loosen himself from the creature's bite. He rolled free to one side and came up on wobbly legs. And the beast was on him at once.

Reeves, or what was left of him, had no intelligence to drive him, only a basic hunger. And Louis would serve it as well as any mortal. With his unnatural quickness, he snatched out, his long, dirty nails hooking on the side of Louis's face, tearing downward from cheek to neck to chest in jagged furrows, finally clasping in his shirt front to keep his prey from lunging away. And he bared his great bloodied fangs to strike like a deadly snake for the vulnerable arteries.

Louis drove up with his forearm. There was a satisfactory clack as Reeves's jaw snapped together from the impact beneath his chin. But still he came on, snarling and spraying a loathsome spittle. His free hand grabbed for Louis's hair, wrenching his head at a taut angle. Louis gave with the pull, dropping fast to offset Reeves's balance. The ghoul was clumsy and unable to right himself as the sleek vampire slid out of his grasp, ducked beneath his arms, and pivoted to safety.

Louis was panting heavily as Reeves lumbered upright to regard him through dead, thirsty eyes. Roaring, the mindless thing charged him. Louis's kick struck the shaggy head, his foot flashing back and forth two, three, four times, but the force barely stunned the slobbering creature. Reeves grabbed his foot and twisted hard. Using that momentum, Louis swung his other foot up and over, his heel catching the dead thing in the eye. With a howl of distress, Reeves let him go and clutched at his putrefied face as Louis dropped, then bounded back up at a wavering *en garde*.

It took only a second for the hulking thing to rejoin the attack. It hadn't the capacity for pain or fear or caution, only that relentless urge to kill and feed. Thinking wildly of how he might stop this unstoppable fiend, Louis dealt out several more chopping blows to the monstrous head, then his wrist was circled in an ironlike grip. And when he swung with the other, it, too, was nabbed. With a strength that nearly tore his arms from their sockets, Reeves jerked Louis up to the stench of his coat, wrapping him in a crushing hug to exert a spine-snapping pressure.

Then a blow fell upon Reeves from behind and Louis was able to drag in a quick breath as he stared in some amazement at Bessie Kampford's determined face. The tiny woman held the black stone in her hands and was using it to crack down on Reeves's bovine skull. He heard the sound of shattering bone and the squeezing tension was gone from about his ribs. Louis stumbled back as Reeves went to his hands and knees.

When Bessie hesitated, Louis took the stone from her hand and finished the gruesome task, smashing the creature's head, then scattering the bits of bone so it could not reassemble and rise up again. Then he remained on hands and knees, his senses clouded by the stale scent of old blood and weakness ... until he smelled something else; something infinitely more frightening.

In the struggle, the slow-burning lamp had been upset and tiny flames whooshed up with eager tongues to consume the draperies. In the beat of a second the entire wall was a sheet of fire.

"We must get out," Louis heard the housekeeper saying, but his head was pounding and his heart was hammering and pain was throbbing through every pore. And he heard her say, "The boy—help me with the boy, my lord."

Takeo. The fire. He pulled his disjointed thoughts together to assemble a degree of strength. He and

Bessie Kampford hauled the limp figure through the pyre the office had become, pouring out into the cooler recesses of the hall along with the dark roil of smoke. The woman gave a slight gasp at the sight of Stuart Howland and came to a halt.

"He's dead," Louis told her with necessary bluntness. And though her face was wet with tears, Bessie moved past the body of her employer to aid their escape from the burning house. Through the throbbing in his temples, Louis heard her explain the sketchy details of what had happened.

"Took me unawares, they did, and by the time I got my senses back together, it was dark and I found the boy on the office floor. Thought it was them coming back, at first, so I hid us, but it must have been the good doctor. And then that thing—that horrid thing—it meant to kill us, like it killed Doctor Howland."

The night was a blissful chill, and Louis eased Takeo down to the cobbled mews and sank down beside him, succumbing to a swimming haze. He was dimly aware of fire-alarm bells clamoring in the distance and of Takeo stirring slightly, moaning his way back to consciousness.

"We must get away from here, my lord. You rest a moment and let me hail a carriage."

He couldn't respond to Mrs. Kampford's brusque words, only too grateful for her control of the situation. He put a shaky hand to Takeo's neck, feeling the rapid patter of his pulse. A huge contusion had formed where he'd been cruelly struck beneath his jaw. One more score to settle, Louis thought, a cold inner rage momentarily besting his own pain.

Then there was confusion of sound, horses, men, the crackle of flames bursting out windows and racing up the sides of the house. And Bessie Kampford's calm commands.

"Get up, my lord. Help me get the boy into the carriage. We must be away before any start to question."

He staggered up to his feet, dragging Takeo with him. He remembered the cushiony feel of the carriage squabs behind his head, then nothing, until a cool dampness on his face woke him. He gave a start of surprise and found himself looking up into Takeo's worried gaze. He was stretched out on his parlor sofa, the thrum of pain threatening to pull him under again as soon as he moved.

Master, you must wake up. Miss Arabella—

"Bella," he groaned, using her name as a focus to cling to his fragile control. Bessie was bending over him, cleaning the gore from his face and neck with a wet towel. There was a glaze of shock to her features, but a deeper deliberation in her eyes. She was angry as much as she was afraid.

"My lord, they've taken Miss Arabella—my girl—my—" Her words broke off into a sob. "With her father gone, you are all she has. Please, my lord. You must go after her."

He tried to sit up, but the effort was too great. Takeo had to help him. He was weak, too weak. The hunger was hurting him. The wounds were a constant torment.

Bella . . .

Then he felt the warm beat of life against his lips and he opened his eyes again, stirred by the sensation. Takeo had pressed his unscarred wrist to his mouth and was offering, *Drink, Master. Regain your strength.*

And he was clutching at the boy's arm even as he shook his head. "No, Takeo. You are weak, too. I would not harm you. I cannot take your blood, even to save your mistress." But he didn't let go. His thumbs rubbed back and forth over the lines of life, mesmerized by the pulse within them. And his need burned.

"Take mine."

Louis looked up in astonishment at a sober Bessie Kampford. "What?"

"Take mine, if it's what you need to bring Miss Arabella home safely."

"Do you know what I am?" He asked it softly, transfixing her gaze with the intensity of his, but she didn't falter. If anything, she looked more set and stubborn. A household trait, he was beginning to understand.

"I don't care what you are, my lord. Those people killed the good doctor, and I cannot let them do the same to my—" She caught back her cry behind trembling fingers. When she recovered, she put that hand over the back of his. "Miss Arabella is the closest thing I have to a daughter, and I love her as if she'd been my own. She is a most sensible female, and she placed her trust in you. If she could, so can I. I watched you weep over her when she was ill, and I know that you love her, too. Do what you will, my lord—I'll ask no questions, but bring her back to me."

With the utmost respect, Louis lifted the woman's

hand to his lips, pressing a grateful kiss upon the roughened knuckles. He retained her hand as he coaxed low and soothingly, "Sit here beside me."

She obeyed, seemingly fascinated by his eyes. She never blinked as he unfastened the first few buttons of her staid collar.

"I will not harm you."

And his hand cupped behind her head, angling it slightly as he bent near. He felt her sudden recoil at the touch of his breath against her skin, and his fingers tightened to hold her still as he bit down and felt that hot rush over his lips. She was motionless after that, and he drank deeply, sucking the warmth, the life, the strength from her with each convulsive swallow.

He lost himself in the luxury of his feast, entranced by the sound of her heart pounding in time with his, with the way heat tingled down the corded veins and plumped gaunt flesh, easing the gnawing edge of distress with each draining second. His senses began to buzz, and a sated lethargy weighed down on him as he continued to drink, all too vaguely aware of Takeo's urgent signals.

Master, enough. Stop. You are taking too much from her. You must stop!

But he was drawn into that dark whirlpool of pleasure and relief, sinking, floating on a warm lifegiving tide. So much so that when he was pulled from it, he responded with an inhuman growl and a threatening flash of his teeth. And he would have returned to feed some more if Takeo's words hadn't reach through to him.

She will die if you take any more. You don't want her to die, do you, Louis?

No, no, of course not, his dazed mind relayed to him. And in some far-off bemusement, he realized Takeo had called him by name. He'd never done that before. Dizzy and slightly drunk on the blood, he lay back against the arm of the sofa, his head lolling, his chest laboring while Bessie Kampford slid into a swoon.

Such strength came with each beat of his heart. He could feel it pumping through him, just as he could watch the color flood back into his hands and sense it warming his face. The pain that had so debilitated him was lifting, the terrible wounds closing, healing, and within minutes, he was able to rise up, renewed.

He touched the back of his hand to Bessie's face, glad to feel its heat. It would have sorrowed him to have taken such a valiant life.

"See to her, Takeo. I am going for Arabella."

Arabella was trying to act unafraid.

It was no easy task in the same room with two smugly smiling ghouls.

"Call to him," Bianca cooed softly.

And again Arabella answered with a firm, "No."

They were in an abandoned dockside warehouse where Ollie and his men had brought her to await nightfall and the two vampires that rose with it. They had disappeared nervously as soon as the sleek pair of killers arrived. She could smell the dank water and hear it pulse against the pylons. And she could sense the unnatural duo's hunger. She was far from safe, and only the fact that they wanted Louis was keeping her alive. She sat atop a tarp-wrapped bale, watching the lovely vampiress pace before her. Gerardo sat back from the two of them, only his eyes gleaming luminescent from the deeper shadows.

"Why do you refuse to do this one small thing for us? We mean him no harm. He is one of us. Like family. One of our own kind."

"He is nothing like you," Arabella corrected, with a flare of temper. "And he wants nothing to do with you. I will not bring him here so you can destroy him."

Bianca's laugh was a crystal tinkling, so high and pure it hurt the ears to hear it. "Destroy him? Oh, no such thing! Why would I want to lose that which I've always craved?"

"Can your companion say the same?" Arabella countered.

Looking sharply at the languid gentleman vampire, Bianca frowned. "What he says isn't important. I made your Louis, and I mean to keep him with me for an eternity."

"Haven't you done enough? Hasn't he suffered enough for your vanity and greed?"

The black eyes narrowed and Bianca smiled. "Careful, little mortal, lest you annoy me beyond my tolerance. Gerardo has quite an impatient appetite, and he would like nothing more than to dine upon your warm blood."

Arabella contained her shudder with difficulty. She tore her gaze from the motionless Gerardo to concentrate on Bianca. Her dislike and distrust of the lovely demon fueled her courage. "You mean to kill me anyway. Rather I die alone than bring Louis to you."

"How very sweet. How very—*human*. I'm sure Louis would appreciate the sacrifice. Until he forgets all about you in a decade or so and replaces your memory with someone young and fresh and vital."

Arabella stiffened. And seeing it, Bianca let her chill smile grow wider.

"Oh yes, he will, because when you live as long as we do, attachments are soon dismissed. I am the only one he will have forever and ever at his side. I am the only one who can love him."

Now Arabella laughed, and it was a harsh laughter, without fear. "Love him? How can you even pretend to believe that? You don't torture the one you love. You don't hurt and humiliate them. You don't force them to return affection with threats and lies."

She heard a low hiss and realized she may have gone too far in her goading. It was Gerardo who interrupted to defuse Bianca's fury.

"Bianca, *innamorata,* you are positively gaunt. It's making you ill-tempered and quite unattractive. Go out and sink your teeth into some unsuspecting fool until your youth returns. You wouldn't want Gino to see you looking like a hag."

Bianca scowled, but her hand rose self-consciously to her smooth white cheek. "Perhaps I should take some nourishment before I am tempted to feed upon this one. Watch her, Gerardo, and do not be tempted to any foolishness."

His smile was wide and harmless, totally false.

And with a movement too fast for mortal eyes to follow, Bianca was gone from the cavernous room.

Gerardo came down from the ledge he was perched upon, as fluid as a cat, as swift as a cobra. He was wearing a strange-looking ensemble: a long, loose-fitting shirt of some velvety fabric over snug tights that accentuated long, well-made legs. He looked like a Shakesperean troubadour—or a sixteenth-century Florentine. He approached with that silky unnatural glide, a smile upon his handsome face that lent no warmth to his expression. And Arabella was more afraid of him than of Bianca, because this one meant Louis serious harm.

"Let me go."

He paused and tilted his head in amazement. "Let you go? Why should I do that?"

"You don't want to share your eternity with Bianca with Louis, do you?"

"I don't plan to, *signora.*"

"She won't let you kill him."

"She does not rule me!"

Arabella let her silence convey her answering doubt, and Gerardo was displeased. He began an impassioned pacing—for effect, she was sure. He was glorious and quite gorgeous in his rage.

"She does not love him!"

"But she thinks she does, and as long as she has him, she'll use him to provoke you. You know she will. Do you want to go through the centuries as a pawn in her game? Hasn't she had a long enough laugh over your broken loyalty to one another? He was your friend."

Gerardo stopped and seemed to shimmer; then, in a breath, he was right in front of her, his gaze locked into hers. His pale blue eyes flared and glittered.

"What do you know about it?" he demanded in a quiet snarl.

"I know what Louis told me."

"Oh, and I'm sure it was a wonderful tale as seen through his guileless eyes. Fool. Gino was always a fool!"

"Yes, he was. He was a fool to come to you, to offer you back the life he thinks he took from you at the cost of his own. He came to you out of love and loyalty, and how did you receive him? With treachery!"

Gerardo gave her a mocking smile. "What did you expect? A kiss and a fond 'All is forgiven'?" He puckered up and made an insolent smooching sound. Then his expression hardened. "I think not."

"He did nothing to hurt you! He loved you. And that love still torments him."

"Does it? Good! Poor, pious Gino! Gino, who had everything! All my life, I possessed only one precious thing, and what did he do but steal it from me! Hurt me? Oh, he did worse than hurt me." Behind his remote and mocking facade, true emotion flickered. And it wasn't pleasant. Arabella was fast losing her argument. And her chance to escape the three-hundred-year-old avenger alive. Could she apply to human sensibilities long numbed by hatred and vain excess?

"Not by his choice. Surely you understand that now. You know it was Bianca manipulating both of you. You have to know that." Could one argue logic with an undead fiend? Arabella didn't now, but for Louis's sake, she would try.

He smiled again, and he was so—beautiful. Dark,

sleek, sensuous. She pulled her gaze away, fearing the charm of that illusion.

"Of course, I know. But that doesn't keep me from hating him. What else have I had to sustain me all these years? If it wasn't for that hate, I would have faded to dust a century ago. My love for him, my hate of him, both passions have sustained me."

"And if you destroy him, what will you have?"

"Peace."

He said that so softly, so serenely it made her tremble.

"You see, *signora*, I did love him. Gino, he was a treasured friend. He shared all he had and all he was with me, and it was my greed, my vanity, that repaid him with disaster. I hated him for his unrelenting kindness because I was so unworthy of it. I saw us both damned, and I would release us both. I mean to hold him in my arms and beg him to forgive me when we face the dawn together."

"You can't!" she cried, with a dull sort of shock. In her dazed mind, she could think of only one excuse. "He's afraid of the fire."

"But nothing else can cleanse away sins such as ours. I cannot bear for him to suffer the existence I brought him to through my weakness. To see him in such agony of spirit, it breaks my heart. I had one once, you know."

"Then let me go. Let us go. Give us the chance to be happy together. Prove you cared for him by letting him return to mortality with my father's help."

"Oh, *signora, mi dispiace*. It is too late for that. It is too late for us."

And he reached out his smooth hand to palm the

side of her face. It was a light touch; she felt such sadness in him, she allowed it without recoil. His caress was cool, his gaze was hot blue fire.

"Gino, he chose well. Your Louis was lucky to have you for a time."

He lowered to one knee before her and his mood grew shadowed with longing and a sinister complexity. His fingers vee'd gently beneath her chin, holding her fast while his mouth slid upon hers in a slow exploration. He never closed his eyes. She could feel his bright stare burning through her sealed lids.

"Bella," he drawled, in a sultry accent so similar to Louis's, it gave her a momentary start. Her eyes flashed open and she could see his face so close to hers. What beautiful skin he had, like flawless white marble. "Could you love me?"

"Release us, Gerardo. Please."

And he kissed her again with what could have almost passed for tender passion. Then he murmured, "If I promise to let him escape me, would you stay with me and love me as you have loved him?"

"If you would spare him, I would stay with you, but I could not love you."

His fingers tightened, bruising her jaw. "Why? Why not? What is there about Gino that you don't find in me? Am I not handsome? Do I not have considerable charm? I have wealth. I can give you anything you desire."

"Can you love me in return?"

He hesitated, contemplating the question. His answer was as Louis had warned, a promise wrapped around a lie. "I could make you feel loved."

"But that's not the same thing, is it?"

378

He stared at her, slipping into his thoughts as though she was no longer there before him. Confused and puzzled.

She reached out and placed her hand lightly upon his shoulder. "Gerardo—"

"Gerard, what are you doing with her?"

The sharp snap of Bianca's voice rocked him back on his heels and returned him to his mocking pose. "Why, *il mia amore,* we were discussing human emotion. I don't suppose you can remember a time when your heart was not dark, so I don't think you would have found it to your interest." He stood and regarded her with a cynical smile. "Your rosy color becomes you. Too bad it is the only thing about you that is ever truly warm."

"You are a fool, Gerardo."

He laughed at her. "Ah, and it is that sweet disposition that will win Gino over when he comes. After all, why would he prefer this fragile mortal being to a goddess such as you?" He circled behind Arabella and dropped down so his arms draped casually about her. He nudged her cheek with his own as he looked up at the blond fury with a taunting grin. "Why would he want something so fresh and warm, when he could have a lifeless eternity in your arms?"

"Take her, if you want her, but leave enough life in her to draw Gino here to us."

Arabella caught her breath up in a fearful gasp as the vampire's lips stroked down her neck. He was going to kill her; she knew it, but she refused to plead for a nonexistent mercy. She could hear the eager rumble of hunger in his quiet moan as he bent over her like a praying mantis, graceful and deadly. Then, abruptly, he stood and sauntered away from her.

"Bianca, I grow impatient with this. Let Gino alone. Let him have his *bella moglie* and let them make one another unhappy. Let him play the mooning swain, if it amuses him, but we both know the attraction will age and he will not."

Arabella followed his lithe figure with disbelieving eyes. Had he a heart, after all? Was he going to let them go? She couldn't pretend to understand the workings of Gerardo Pasquale's three-centuries-old mind, but she'd never expected to find compassion there.

"Come," he coaxed his companion with a sudden gaiety. His pale features lit with a certain animation, and Arabella could see what a magnetic man he must have been in life. "Let us enjoy the night. Let us leave this cursed damp place and seek the warm seas of my homeland. Here the mortals taste of wet overcoat. I would feast off ones who were ripe from the sun. Forget Gino as he has forgotten us."

"I forget nothing! And I, too, grow impatient."

Bianca seized Arabella by the throat, her long fingers, obscenely hot with stolen blood, choking off a cry of fright. She was jerked up to face the seething blonde, those black eyes boring into her mind like a piercing fever.

"Call him now. Call him!"

"No." It was a hoarse whisper of defiance.

But the dark eyes intruded, seeping in to numb her will, and even as Arabella fought to clench her teeth and still her throat, she heard herself sending a mental plea.

Louis!
I am here.
And her eyes rolled frantically toward him as he separated from shadow. She could see thin weals upon his lean face and neck as if furrows had been torn in the skin but were nearly healed. And though his coat and shirt were ripped and stained with blood, he showed no sign of injury as he came forward in his strong stride to make a cold announcement.

"I've come for my wife."

Chapter Twenty-Four

"And I've come for you, just as you knew I would," purred Bianca.

Louis's gaze slid over Arabella, assessing her state, pausing at the bruise on her face and darkening with a lethal fury. Then he glanced coldly toward Gerardo, measuring the distance between them before looking back to the lovely demon. "As I've told you, a waste of time."

"I have nothing but time, Gino. May I call you Gino? It brings back such wonderful memories."

"To you, maybe. Call me what you like as you say *arrivederci.*"

"Goodbye? There is no such thing as goodbye to our kind."

Bianca shifted so she was standing behind Arabella. Her long white hands were playing through the wavy dark hair, arranging it up off her neck, twisting it into various rolls, almost as if they were female friends before a vanity mirror. Arabella sat still as stone, her eyes on her husband, her expression carefully masked.

"Gerardo and I want you back with us. Keep this woman, if you like, but be one with us again." Her hands stroked Arabella's throat. "In fact, I would enjoy the company of another woman after all these years with only Gerard's arrogance to keep me amused. Shall I make her one of us?"

A laugh from Gerardo broke the moment of tension. "Bianca, think of it. Another beautiful creature to steal away your light. Would you create your own rival? Now, that might be amusing."

She shot him a venomous look, but was considering his words. "Ah, but you know me well. No, I would not share either of you with another. I must kill her." And her fingers clenched in the glossy hair to wrench Arabella's head to one side, causing her to cry out in pain and terror.

"No!"

Louis took one stride forward and found Gerardo blocking his way. His friend's hands settled firm and strong upon his shoulders, holding him in restraint.

"It is better this way, Gino, *il mio amico*. You can find no happiness with her. You cannot go back. We've closed that door. Your hope is dead, just as the doctor is dead."

Louis looked past him to Arabella and saw understanding blank her features with pain. Her small voice rent his anguished heart.

"Is that true, Louis? Is my father dead? Have they killed him?"

His stoic silence was her answer.

With three such powerful beings in one room, none expected a violent display from the lone mortal woman. Arabella wrenched out of Bianca's grasp, surging up to plant her closed fist in the other woman's face as hard as she could. Bianca stumbled back, not hurt, but stunned enough by the attack to let Arabella escape her. Gerardo was shoved aside so Louis could take up his wife in his arms. Hers went tight about his neck and she clung to him, trembling with loss and rage.

"I'm sorry, Bella. I'm sorry. I never meant for such things to happen," he whispered roughly into the tangle of her hair, while his hard gaze leveled on the other two to keep them at bay. His expression said in no uncertain terms that he would not be as easy to bully as this fragile human, and they were understandably cautious.

She drew back her head to regard him. Her touch moved in gentle absolution against his cheek. "It's not your fault, Louis. And I'm sorry, too. You may have lost your chance to be mortal, but don't give up your humanity to become like them. I love you, Louis."

And she kissed him, hard and firm on the mouth; and he returned it with like passion while never taking his eyes off his centuries-old companions. He didn't trust them to remain patient for the emotional reunion. Though Bianca made no challenging move, her glare was sparking with jealous displeasure. Finally, he murmured into his love's fervid kisses, "Bella, release me. We can finish this later. Now, I have business to attend." He took her by the forearms and moved her safely behind him. Then, to the others, he said again, "I've come to take my wife home."

"Take her," Gerardo drawled. "If you can."

And he was smiling as his hand flashed out, catching Louis by the back of the head, his fingers compressing until his friend's knees buckled.

"You are weak, Gino, no match for me. Spare yourself the punishment. I don't want to hurt you."

And contrarily, his grip strengthened.

"Gerardo," Bianca shrilled. "I will not allow this. You will not harm him!"

Pale eyes slashed toward the lovely vampiress. Gerardo's voice was an icy hiss. "Shut up! This has nothing to do with you. You have no power over me. This is between Gino and me, as it should have been long ago. You will not interfere. I am not your fool!"

Bianca stood stiff and still, her eyes glittering and as inanimate as Louis's black stone, but amazingly enough, she faded back and was silent.

Gerardo was grinning with malignant delight as he turned back to his friend. "Just you and me, *il mio amico, mio fratello*. And *il signora bella*. Like the old days, Gino, will you share with me? I believe I am in love. Will you let me make her *la mia ragazza?* My sweetheart? It would only be fair, after all. It would only be right. What do you say, Gino? Shall we be friends again?"

Louis grabbed his wrist and gave it a savage twist. At the same time, his other elbow came up to strike a rattling blow full in the face. Freed as Gerardo stumbled back, Louis retreated as well, warily shielding Arabella behind him.

Gerardo touched his fingertips to the split in his lower lip, examining the blood, then sucking it off with obvious relish. "Just a taste, so I can anticipate feasting upon your bride. I am going to kill you,

Gino, and then I will make her my own. That would be justice, no?"

"No."

Gerardo was circling in a jaunty stride, and Louis revolved with him, keeping himself between the other vampire and his mortal wife, keeping careful tabs upon Bianca's whereabouts. Then Gerardo stopped and opened his arms wide.

"Gino, why do you fight? You cannot win. I am faster. I am stronger. Do not make me break your bones. Settle the debt, my friend, and we can go our own ways. Let me take her, and I will forgive you. Bianca, she is nothing. She need not stand between us." But in spite of his bold words, he glanced over his shoulder to where the icy blonde stood, her features cold and strangely remote, to see if she would intrude. She made no move.

"I owe you nothing, Gerardo. What happened you brought upon yourself. I will not pay for it any longer."

"Then you will suffer for it."

And he struck with an unexpected swiftness, catching Louis by the throat and hurling him a good twenty feet, as if he'd been nothing more than a child. Louis seemed to pause in mid-air, braking his flight without ever touching ground. Then, he was charging Gerardo, fueled by a killing fury and a centuries-old frustration. And Gerardo met his head-on rush with a fierce anticipating smile.

They came together with a crash of unnatural force. Snarling, they both went down, locked in immortal combat. Any of the blows they struck would have shattered the human frame, but because they could not truly damage one another, the pain was temporary and their struggle all the more intense and ferocious.

But Gerardo was faster and stronger, and many of the blows he dealt went unseen by Louis until the brunt of them shuddered through him. His face was bleeding and his body ached from abuse, but anger and hatred and love pushed him to continue even when it grew obvious to both of them that his power would not sustain him. Gerardo had him by the collar and the trouser band and began to smash him head-first into the stone wall.

"Time to say *buona notte, il mio amico.*"

Through the mist of pain, Louis heard Arabella's shouts and fierce curses as she threw herself upon Gerardo's back in a futile attempt at distraction. He collapsed on the dirty floor, dazed and helpless, as Gerardo turned to confront his human attacker.

Arabella shrieked in alarm as cool fingers clamped down on the back of her neck, dragging her up tight to Gerardo's chest. Pinning her to him, his head bent and she felt the sudden sting of his teeth, followed by the sensation of weightlessness as he drew deeply from her. Her hands fluttered and finally clung to the folds of fabric at either of his shoulders. She heard Louis's far-off roar of rage and her own frail moan, but neither acted upon Gerardo's conscience.

But something did, because he pulled back to regard her with astonishment.

"*Mi scusi.* I did not know."

Arabella staggered when he released her, faint and stunned by his unexpected charity. His hands cupped momentarily beneath her elbows to provide support and his pale eyes held hers, delving deep.

Such a strong beat for a heart so small.

She heard his voice with a seducing clarity within the privacy of her mind. He'd taken enough of her blood to forge that mental link and to realize something she had not known herself.

It is Gino's? But of course it is. And Gerardo smiled briefly, a joyous expression that was as strangely sweet as it was beautiful. *He should take better care of his first to be born and its mother.*

Arabella gasped as she took his meaning. A child! She was carrying Louis's child!

And as Gerardo turned toward his fallen friend to remark upon his discovery, Louis surged up in his wife's defense. Gerardo easily intercepted the failing punch and with a hard twist broke his arm. His other hand forked beneath Louis's chin, crushing about his windpipe, stopping his breath, stilling his fight.

"Gino, give up. I do this out of love for you." And suddenly, his appearance softened with a poignant plea for understanding. "Let me put our struggle to a final rest, my friend."

Not sure he could trust what he saw in the other's pale eyes, that fragile offer of friendship he'd yearned for over the centuries, Louis pulled back, panting hard and uncertain.

"Gino, time to end this."

But even as he reached out to Louis, Gerardo was driven abruptly forward from the dreadful impact of a steel bar punching through his back and out his chest. His look was one of supreme surprise as his legs crumpled and he fell into Louis's arms while Bianca stood behind hm, smiling grimly.

"You are a fool, Gerardo," she claimed coldly. "I told you I would not let you harm him."

Louis went down to his knees beneath the sagging weight of his friend. Gerardo was clutching at him, his head heavy upon his shoulder, his breath rasping noisily as he struggled to speak.

"Gino . . . care for them. How I envy you. Forgive . . . forgive me as I forgive you."

Holding him, weeping over him, Louis whispered, "I forgive you, *mio fratello, mio amico.*" And closing his eyes, Louis felt Gerardo give a massive sigh and go still against him. He could hear Arabella sobbing softly close by.

After a long moment, Louis's eyes opened again and he looked up slowly, his gaze a cold, brilliant fire. "You," he said to Bianca. "You will pay for this."

Bianca's momentary alarm eased to a sneering look of contemptuous superiority. "And how do you mean to see to that miracle, Gino? You, who could not best Gerard, think you can defeat me?" She laughed, then gasped as Louis thrust out his palm and a powerful pressure struck her in the chest, flinging her back across the room when he had yet to touch her. She was gulping for air as Louis eased his fallen friend gently to the floor and stood.

"Where did you learn such a thing?" she wheezed. Then she gave a soft moan. "Eduard. *Mon Dieu!* Eduard taught you." And for a moment she looked mortally afraid. With lightning speed, she streaked across the floor, snatching up Arabella and wrapping her forearm about the other woman's neck. "Stand where you are or I will snap her spine."

"Let her go, Bianca. It's over."

"No," she snarled, controlling Arabella's struggles with a numbing squeeze. "I will not lose you, Gino. I have loved you for centuries and you have denied me the pleasure of having you. Come with me, hunt with me, live with me as my companion through the ages, or she will die right now."

Louis stood panting, pensive, rubbing at his arm as bone knit and flesh healed.

"No, Louis, you mustn't—"

But Bianca choked off any further words. "You and me, Gino. Remember? Remember how it was? So beautiful. So powerful. You and me. No worlds would go unconquered before us. Come with me." She moistened her lips. "And this time, I will be your slave."

"No."

Her features mottled with disbelief and rage. She screamed at him. "You are mine! I made you! I will have you! Forever!"

Again, the calm and final, "No."

"Then she dies!"

Arabella drew a quick breath and because her vocal cords were too compressed for speech, she sent a mental message.

I love you, Louis.

"Bianca, harm her and I will destroy you."

She laughed. "How? You may have some of Eduard's tricks, but I am more powerful."

"But I have one power you lack, one that will see you in ashes." And he looked toward the bank of cloudy windows running along one wall. "Can you smell the dawn? How far have you to go to find safety?"

Bianca tore her gaze away from the brightening sky with a look of panic. "You will burn, too!"

"Shall we wait and see? Let her go and seek your coffin, or be reduced to—fireplace soot."

She was breathing in quick snatches, the scent of daybreak quivering through her. Her fingers spasmed around Arabella's neck. "All right, Gino. I must flee. But I will not let you win all. She comes with me, and tomorrow night, she will rise up as my slave."

"The devil, you say!" Uttering that oath, Arabella scooped the mended chain of her father's gift from out of her bodice and pressed the silver cross to the back of Bianca's hand. There was a sudden pungent scorch and a shrill cry. Arabella stumbled forward as Bianca released her, shrieking with a howling fury.

Clutching her hand and seething with a demented pain, the vampiress fixed the two of them with a prophetic gaze. "Have one another, then, but my time will come. Time will always be in my favor. We will meet again. I will have you, Gino—in this lifetime or the next." Then she whirled with a preternatural speed and seemed to vanish.

As Arabella surged into her husband's arms, the first pink of dawn warmed the grimy panes of glass behind them.

"Are you all right, my love?"

"Yes. Oh, Louis, hold me."

And he did, for a long, intense moment, breathing in the mortal sweetness of her, filling up with the eternal love of her. Until distracted by her soft gasp.

"Gerardo—"

Louis turned to follow her stare and saw the steel bar where it lay on the floor. There was no trace of Gerardo Pasquale. Not even ash.

Master! Miss Arabella!

"Takeo, in here!"

The boy burst into the warehouse at a run, not pausing until his arms were wrapped tight about the both of them. Then he whisked off his cloak and flung it over Louis.

Come. I've seen to the demon's underlings. They'll trouble us no more. I've a carriage waiting. We must get you home, Master Louis.

Already feeling the discomfort of daylight heating through him, Louis nodded and let them lead him out. The distress was worse outside, and he was groaning from it as they bundled him inside the carriage and drew down the shades. He huddled beneath the cloak, held tight in Arabella's arms, as fever and chills shook through him.

They reached the house and Louis was barely able to walk as they guided him inside. There, Bessie Kampford greeted Arabella with a cry of happiness and a teary embrace. She even had a kiss to press against Louis's bloodied temple. Within the cool, familiar caverns of his home, he was able to recoup his strength and give out terse orders.

"We must leave here. Takeo, arrange for movers to pack up the house and for my solicitor to settle my affairs. I will not underestimate the danger by delay. We must be away before the authorities come with questions about the fire and Doctor Howland's—death." Suddenly, he couldn't face the anguish in

Arabella's gaze, not with his heart so filled with blame. He strode into the deeper shadows of the parlor, saying, "Takeo, bring me a change of clothes. I will not lie down in these."

Arabella watched him from the comforting circle of Bessie's embrace. And she was worried over his reaction. Gently, she slipped from the elder woman's cosseting attention.

"Mrs. Kampford, I know the events of this eve have worn upon us all, but if you are not too weary, would you see my belongings are gathered and packed away? There is much wisdom in his lordship's words. We must not tarry here."

Bessie straightened with her admirable courage. "Yes, Ma'am."

Slowly, Arabella advanced toward the remote figure in the study. Louis stood with his back to her, and she could read his tension in that stiff, straight line. She could tell the brightening hues of daylight were hurting him, yet he lingered. And her apprehension mounted.

"Louis?"

He turned, and the sadness etched upon his face alarmed her.

"I have brought ruin to your life, Bella. I have allowed my arrogance to overcome my caution and embroiled you in the curse I live. I would release you from it now."

"Release me? Louis—"

He held up a slender hand to silence her protest. "I am sorry, Bella. All those grand promises I made you, and I cannot keep a one of them. Your father is gone, and now I have no future to offer you."

Fighting down the immediate pain of loss, Arabella crossed the separating space to hug him about the shoulders. He was stiff and still within her embrace. "Shhh! That's not true, Louis. I love you. We have more future together than you know."

"What I am is what I will always be. How can you love me?"

She laughed softly. "There is no logic in love, Louis. Love is like the beauty of the heavens. It needs no reason to exist. Do not deny me the glimpse of paradise we've made between us."

"I can never be the man you deserve."

"Then perhaps I do not want that man. Don't ask me to settle for less than I have found with you, my lord. I won't."

She rode out his tremendous sigh. "You are too brave, little one. You've seen what our future holds. Think of it, Arabella."

"I am," she murmured, as her palms rubbed up and down the powerful length of his forearms. "And I am impatient for that future."

His chuckle vibrated beneath her cheek. "You are a bold piece of work, wife." His lips brushed across her brow and his voice lowered to a husky rumble. "And I love you madly. I could not go on without you beside me."

"Then I shall always be there with you." She pressed a kiss to the unnatural warmth of his throat, sketching those kisses up to his jaw, then turning his face with the touch of her hand so she could claim his mouth. He returned her kisses with an insuppressible ardor, breaking away at last with a soft curse and the wish that the sun would delay its rise long enough for him to explore the moment further.

"You must rest, my lord, and recover your strength. While you sleep, I will see everything is packed, and we shall be away before nightfall. I want to leave London and its bad memories behind. There is no reason to stay and every reason to go. I would like to begin our lives over, someplace where the threat of your past can't reach us." At least for a time.

Silence. For a moment, she feared he meant to argue, but all he said was a quiet, "You will stay with me?"

"I will always be there with you when you wake, my love. Always."

He caught the hand she'd pressed to his cheek and kissed it tenderly before pillowing his head upon it. "Vienna," he said to her. "We will go there. There is much activity, and we can lose ourselves in the crowds and color. You will like it. It has a cluster of great minds and culture."

"All right. Vienna it is. And amongst those great minds, perhaps we can find one with the knowledge to continue my father's work. I refuse to give up on that hope and I refuse to give up on you. I do not fear the future so long as I am with you. Trust in my strength as I trust in your love for me."

"I do."

Takeo arrived to interrupt further discussion. Arabella stepped back so Louis could strip off his soiled garments. With a faint smile, he withdrew the heavy black stone from the pocket of his bloodied coat. He gave it to Arabella with the words, "Keep this. It may come in handy again."

She shared in his bittersweet smile and clutched the obelisk to her as her eyes adored the sight of smooth immortal flesh moving over a powerful inhuman form. Her husband. Her love. Whatever else he was didn't matter. She wouldn't let it matter.

"Takeo, arrange for transportation to carry me to the country house within the hour. I needn't press upon you the importance of being circumspect."

Takeo bowed to him, then took up Arabella's hand to press the back of it briefly to his cheek before he left them. Louis looked on with a fond bemusement.

"It would seem you've made a conquest of my young friend."

Arabella smiled up at him. "We've found we have much in common, my lord. Come. We must go below. It's not wise to push fate by remaining."

Louis allowed her to lead him down into the cool chambers where his daylight bed awaited. When he climbed into his box, he was surprised when Arabella came in with him, stretching out in close companionable warmth, as if they were beneath their big upstairs canopy.

"Might I rest with you, my lord?"

"It's cold—"

"I have this cloak, and I am content to stay with you a while."

She nestled against his shoulder, sighing softly. She had no desire to be apart from him until all the danger of the past night was far behind them. For now, Bianca and Gerardo were vanquished, but she would feel better when they were a continent away. Where Louis could grow strong again.

"There is no place I'd rather be," she vowed with a quiet passion.

"Then I am pleased to share my accommodations."

His hand curved about her cheek, turning it so he could claim her lips in a lengthy and expressive perusal. But even the strength of his love could not best the pull of his weariness. He was smiling as his eyes closed and his hand stilled against the warm contour of her face.

"Sleep well, Louis, for when I wake you at the midnight hour with my kiss, we will be on our way to another life. And we will be a family: you, me, Takeo, and Bessie, the five of us. Sleep, and know that I love you."

Puzzlement brought his eyes open again. "Five?"

She moved his hand to her flat abdomen. "I carry our future, Louis." And she waited with breath suspended for his reaction. It was subtle at first, his eyes darkening with wonder to a deep jade green, his lips parting in amazement, then bowing slightly upward in a smile.

"Our child."

Her features warmed with pleasure at the thrilled way in which he spoke those words.

"The promise of eternity that you once gave to me. You see, my love, you have kept all your promises."

And with that, she kissed him and he returned it with all the tender passion he possessed to the limit of his waning strength. His eyes didn't reopen when she lifted away, but his smile remained. Arabella touched the contours of his face lovingly.

"If you dream while you sleep, dream of a future for the three of us; and when you wake, we will make those dreams come true."

With those words to caress and comfort him, Louis Radman sank into slumber.

Arabella sighed in her contentment, drawing the cloak closer about her shoulders for warmth as she rested alongside her husband. Within the quiet of her mind came a soft, crooning whisper, the accented tones those of Gerardo Pasquale.

Buon giorno, cara. Il piacere e stato mio. The pleasure was mine. Love him as I loved him.

Her head resting above her husband's heart, Arabella smiled and pledged, "I will."

Look for the second spellbinding installment of Nancy Gideon's enthralling vampire romance trilogy to be published by Pinnacle Books in October 1994.

Please turn the page for an exciting sneak preview of
MIDNIGHT TEMPTATION

A sleek shadow slipped between rocks strewn along the gorge bottom. Sure of foot and just as fleet, the woodland creature made no noise; at least, none discernible to the average ear. But to the figure crouched low amid the heather, the animal's passing was heralded by a definite pattern of sound. The soft panting breaths, the steady beckoning of its heartbeat; all the invitation the stalker needed.

Closer the small predator came, unaware that the hunter in search of its nightly prey was about to be the hunted. And without warning, an agility that could evade the talons of a hawk failed before a more unexpected attack.

Snatched up from the ground and all hopes of escape, the creature squirmed in desperation; then, realizing the futility of this, it merely hung limp, its heart pounding, its eyes glassy with terror. And the soothing words of its captor did nothing to lessen its fear.

"It's all right. I won't harm you."

Nicole Radouix held the trembling fox gently, stroking it with a hand both cautious and admiring. How soft its fur, how frantic its respiration. Beneath the silky coat, she could feel the frightened patter of the animal's pulse, and that beat as much as the creature's warmth charmed her into a mesmerized study.

Though she'd caught the fox on a whim, just to see if she could, now that she had it clasped close enough to experience its panic, she couldn't make herself release it. Instinct she didn't understand rose strong and sharp within her, and her restraining hand tightened about the delicate rib cage until it felt as though the animal's wild and fragile heart was fluttering in her palm. Sensation stirred, making her own breaths come in quick succession. The fox would have understood the basic urges spiking through her. So would any hunter of the weak and less nimble.

Power. Control. Satisfaction.

Hunger.

But these feelings were not normal for a girl of seventeen, and even as she recognized them, Nicole grew afraid.

Mon Dieu! What was she thinking!

Carefully, appalled that she was ready to hurt such a glorious creature, she lowered the fox to the ground and opened her hands. For a moment, the animal stood frozen in uncertainty.

"Go now. You're free."

The sound of her voice was all it took to send the fox running. There was a brief flash of dull red color before it darted between the rocks to safety. It realized, as Nicole refused to, how close it had come to dying.

Nicole stood with eyes closed, drawing in deep breaths of the twilight air. Its crispness flushed the strange darkness of her mood and eased her aroused senses into a more relaxed state. It had happened again, that loss of reason to foreign urgency, and she didn't know what to do.

She couldn't very well approach her respectable parents with news that she was helplessly drawn by the desire to kill. They would think her mad. She herself was beginning to believe it, for surely it wasn't normal for the human senses to be so razor-sharp and honed to the lure of a heartbeat.

Suddenly agitated to the point of tears, Nicole began to run. She knew there was no way to escape what lay within her, but she'd found there was safety among her own kind. When surrounded by the peasants and the pleasant visitors to their village, her acuity was muted by the confusion of many and she felt as average as any of them. Only when she was alone did isolation provoke her passions into their unnatural state. And here, in this small community where roads ran through ploughed fields and houses of gray stone with pale sea-green doors and roofs muffled by moss seemed asleep even until noon here, silence and solitude were too often her companions. And with them came the awareness of what was waking inside her.

The streets of Grez were empty of the artists who posed their easels each day behind the row of little houses to capture the serene beauty of the Loire and the brooding Fontainebleau forest that bordered the horizon. Many of the cottages had been converted into studios and during the summer months were packed with painters and musicians who came to soak up the stillness. Many of them were English, like her mother, and all were a delight to a lonely young girl who'd been no farther from home than the stands of mammoth oak, beech, and Norway pine. She'd never seen the cities they'd spoken of, and their words made enticing pictures upon an impressionable mind until she begged to be allowed to visit at least Paris, which was only some forty miles to the north. But her parents were adamantly opposed. What, they asked again and again, could she find in Paris that they didn't provide her with here? She had an enviable education via an extensive library. She had the artists to converse with and the local peasant families to care for. And she was greatly loved within the elegant walls of her father's château. What more could she wish for?

How could she explain? How would they ever understand that she needed the noise, the distraction, the crowds to hide in? Because she feared if she was left to her own devices much longer, something terrible was going to occur.

She raced along the quiet streets. Sounds of merriment wafted out from behind the closed cottage doors and from the inns that stood side-by-side with farm buildings. But those excluding sounds did nothing to lessen her sense of separation. So she hurried on toward the home she was raised in, to the family who was devoted to her, hoping that among them she could find peace. And perhaps on this night, she could find as well the courage to confront them with the truth.

The château was some distance from the village, nestled against the fringe of forest. Its plain stone walls warmed like the sand by the sea in sunlight, and its pink brick loggias up above glowed blood-red when caught by the setting sun. It was a spacious home made up of Italian-style terraces, a high French roofline, huge chimneys, and a courtyard surrounded by arcades and galleries; a study of grace and strength combined, much like the man who'd designed it to be a pleasing blend of Classic and Renaissance styles. Within, brick walls were hung with tapestries and works of art, but held no mirrors to reflect back the scene of wealthy elegance. Within, Nicole would find relief from what troubled her soul.

She was breathing hard when at last she approached the entry door. Unwilling to startle those inside with her rather wild appearance, she took a moment to smooth her skirts and to catch up the long trails of ebony hair that had escaped the coil behind her head, hoping the respite would lessen the flush in her cheeks and the panic in her eyes. Before she could move forward, that great door opened and two figures appeared there in silhouette against the light burning bright within. She recognized them immediately as her parents and their pose as one of intimate conversation. They stood close together, too involved in one of their many secrets to notice her among the shadows. She waited and she listened unashamed. How else would she ever learn of anything that went on within their secluded walls?

"Must you go out tonight?" her mother murmured, from where she'd burrowed against his shoulder. Her eyes were closed and her voice caught with an edge of strain.

Very gently, her father's hand stroked down the spill of her hair, hair once as dark as her daughter's, but now shot attractively with strands of silver. His words were as soothing as his caress. "I must, little one, not by choice, but from necessity. I needn't explain these things to you, my love. You know I would rather spend the evening with you."

"Then stay." Her fingers curled in the folds of his coat, as desperate in effect as the snag in her voice. If he was moved by either plea, he didn't show it.

Instead, he told her, "I love you, Bella. I will not be long," and he began to untangle himself from her grasp. Before he was completely freed, she reached up to clasp his face between her hands, pulling him down for a scorching kiss. The exchange didn't embarrass their daughter as she watched from the concealing shadows, for they were always candid in their displays of affection. They were a very loving couple, at least in Nicole's romantic mind. Some were puzzled by the bond they shared. Her mother was English. At one and forty, she was still a fine-looking woman. But the man she'd married was obviously of the upper classes: wealthy, cosmopolitan, and handsome enough to have any woman of rank he desired. And he'd chosen the daughter of a London physician, a woman who looked old enough to be his mother. He appeared more Nicole's contemporary, with his unlined features and easy grace. But it was ever apparent that the woman he'd married was the woman he adored. At least, Nicole had always believed that to be true, in spite of the whispers she'd heard that said just the opposite.

It was rumored that during his many absences from home, the beautiful Louis Radouix spent his time courting a string of young peasant women who fell easy prey to his cultured charm.

They were just ignorant, Nicole told herself, as she staunchly defended her family. Rural minds couldn't comprehend the kind of man her father was. They mistook the innocent captivation of his smile for calculated seduction and his acts of generosity for ones of scheming intent. Had they ever seen her father the way he was now, tenderly framing her mother's face within his palms, they would not cast doubt upon his devotion. Had they ever seen them together, playfully rolling about on the sofa while lost to laughter, or him with his auburn head pillowed upon her lap, murmuring how lucky he was to have her with him, they wouldn't be so quick to gossip that he was bored with her charms. A man as enchanting and mysterious as Louis Radouix was bound to stir up talk. His secluded way of life bred whispering. Even his own daughter was left in the dark about much of his doings and found herself inventing colorful scenarios to explain what he would not. Their lives were wreathed in secrets only man and wife were privy to, so it was no wonder curiosity flourished and blossomed into maligning murmurs and speculation.

Questions about where her father spent his daylight hours never led to any answers. Nicole learned at an early age to merely accept that he was gone and to be glad for his return. She liked to imagine that he was a spy, sometimes for her mother's native England, sometimes for Italy, the country of his birth. He was suave and furtive enough to be cast into that role. But when he was home, he was her loving father, quick to take her up for a tight embrace, always ready with a delightful story about faraway places he'd visited in his youth. He was the buffer to her mother's sheltering. Had Arabella had her way, Nicole would never set foot outside the walls surrounding the château. Such terrible panic lit her mother's eyes whenever she was a trifle late in returning home. There was a shadow of unmistakable fear that crossed her competent features whenever she heard of a stranger asking about the reclusive owners of the pink-tinged château. It had something to do with their rapid flight from England in the year before Nicole's birth. It was somehow connected to the vague responses she got whenever she asked about the past. Arabella lived like a cautious fugitive and would have kept her daughter smotheringly close had her husband not eased the girl away. It was Louis who'd gently admonished, *Let her be free, my love. You watch too close. You worry too much. Let her enjoy life.*

So naturally, it was her father she thought of when it became apparent she could no longer contain her troubles. He would listen and he would have some solution at hand, while her mother would undoubtedly lock her in her room and dispose of the key. It wasn't that her mother didn't love her; not at all. She was a most pampered child. But there had always been an edge of caution to her mother's attention, the feel that she was being carefully observed. Perhaps it was because Arabella was English and the English were notoriously prim and watchful of their children. Nicole was not about to give her cause to hold any tighter a rein than she already did.

Nicole waited in the darkness until her parents shared one long last kiss. Then Louis stepped back and her mother let him go. Nicole was intent upon following him, yet she saw the look of helpless despair etching Arabella's features as she turned back inside the house. Saw, but didn't understand, the cause of her misery. It perplexed her for only a moment, then Nicole focused upon her own problems as she scurried silently after her father.

There was only a thin slice of a moon overhead. Nicole was hard pressed not to lose the dark-garbed figured ahead amongst the shadows of the wood. As she followed, she kept a careful distance, working on what she would say to him, working up the needed bravery to speak the words. She would begin with the dreams, dreams that were both freeing and frightening. Then she would tell him of her unusual strength and perceptions. Lastly and most disturbingly, she would have to confess her developing taste for raw foods. Because he loved her so, he would not be dismayed. He would not turn from her in horror. Or at least, that was what she hoped as she goaded herself on. She was concentrating on this task when he stepped into a small leafy copse where the scent of pine was sharp and sweet and night sounds made a subtle music. He stopped there, head turning slowly, as if in search of something. Before she could approach him, she noticed his stance stiffening; then she, too, saw they were not alone.

A woman emerged from the far hedge of pine. She was cloaked for discretion, and the way she came straight toward him told Nicole that this was no chance meeting. Nicole stood, as frozen as the fox had been, paralyzed by what she was sure she was about to witness: the destruction of her secure world.

Louis waited until the woman reached him. Neither spoke. Slowly he unfurled the hood of her cloak to reveal features as youthful as her own. His fingers worked the fastenings, and the length of coarse wool fell about her feet. Then he began to undo the strings of her peasant blouse, loosening the fabric so that it fell away from the soft white glow of her skin. With a murmur of something too low to hear, he bent his head, his mouth moving in a seducing sweep along the young woman's uplifted features, trailing down to the exposed arch of her throat. The woman moaned aloud. The sound was rich in rapture.

Nicole clapped her hands over her own mouth to

contain her cry of distress and outrage. How could he? How could he leave her mother, his wife, to rendezvous with this unworthy creature? How could he so betray her who loved him? How could he so callously destroy her faith in him, her admiration for him, with this illicit moonlit tryst?

She must have made some unconscious sound of protest, for suddenly his burnished head jerked up and the woman in his arms gave a sharp cry akin to pain. Nicole tried to meld back into the shadows, but in her haste and upset, her movements were clumsy and the snap of underbrush gave her away. Her father spun in her direction, and for one brief horrifically clear moment, Nicole saw him as he really was. He was no womanizer out to chase a local skirt. He was no cold-hearted cheat ready to break the trust of the woman who wed him. What he was was something much worse.

For in that chill ribbon of moonlight, Nicole saw all too plainly the sightless glaze of the woman's eyes and the smear of crimson at her torn throat. A crimson that liberally stained her father's mouth and the sharp teeth he'd bared in a monstrous snarl.

She ran. There was no room for anything in her mind save wild thoughts of flight. She surged through the darkness, losing the path, losing her way in her heedless panic until she heard him behind her.

"Nicole!"

With a sob she raced onward, feeling the limbs of unseen trees yank at her free-flowing hair and the brambles rip at her ankles. Breath came in labored gasps as she staggered through the night, plunging ahead while her senses strained behind for sounds of pursuit. She heard nothing. Seeing the lights up ahead as beacons of salvation, she burst out of the forest in a mad scramble across the yard. Inarticulate sounds escaped her. For on this night, she must surely have gone mad to have pictured such a scene.

The familiar sight and welcome of the inside of her home went by in an unrecognizable blur as Nicole bolted for the stairway rising up majestically through the structure's center. She stumbled upon the carpeted steps and was continuing on all fours when one of her elbows was caught from below. She gave a fearful cry, afraid to look behind her.

"Nicole, wait. Don't run from me."

She risked a glance and saw her father there, his uplifted features stark with despair, his eyes steeped in tragedy, his chin wet with fresh blood.

She gave another incoherent cry and jerked free. Even as she surged upward, his voice followed, so broken, so heavy with pain.

"Nicole ... please! Let me explain!"

Weeping frantically, she reached the upper hall and darted to the safety of her chambers. She flung the door shut, shot the bolt, and leaned back against the sturdy wood, shock rattling through her in fierce, teeth-clattering spasms. Then, even before she heard him, she felt his presence on the other side of the door ... a whispering chill of something not quite human.

"Nicole, don't be afraid of me. I won't hurt you. Let me explain what you saw."

Her breath caught up in a sob as she watched the knob turn this way and that. And she waited, shaking fitfully, but he made no attempt to force his way in. Not physically, at least.

"Nicole ... I love you."

She squeezed her eyes shut and shuddered uncontrollably. "My God, what are you?" The question tore from the heart of her confusion.

There was a long beat of silence, then his quiet reply. "Your father."

"No," she moaned in denying misery.

"Let me in. Let me explain. Please."

"No! Stay away! Stay away from me! Demon! Monster! Stay away! You are not my father!"

On the other side of the barring portal, Louis Radman writhed beneath those damning words. And he couldn't deny them. For that was exactly what he was. Demon. Monster. Worse.

"Louis?"

When he turned toward his wife, she gave a soft cry. She'd never seen such devastation in his gaze.

"What's happened? Louis, tell me."

He looked at her through welling eyes and spoke in fractured syllables. "She saw ... she knows."

Wordlessly she took him in her arms, sharing his hurt, absorbing his grief and guilt, wishing there were some way to absolve him of it.

"Bella ... what are we going to do?"

Arabella held him tightly. The day she'd dreaded had come at last.

"We will tell her the truth."

Look for MIDNIGHT TEMPTATION on sale at bookstores everywhere in October 1994!

Dear Readers:

After sixteen 'Dana Ransom' historicals and contemporaries and a couple of regencies as 'Lauren Giddings', I was ready for something different. Little did I know *how* different when I met with my editor, John Scognamiglio, for the first time two years ago at a conference in Chicago. He had an idea for something ... unusual; a line of paranormal and supernatural romances, and he wanted to know if I wanted to write about vampires (all this over juice at breakfast!) I told him I'd think about it, not really convinced it was something I wanted to pursue. I went up to my room to practice my conference speech but the idea of vampires had sunk in its teeth. I started remembering all those hours spent watching *Dark Shadows* as a teen and the nights scaring myself silly with *Night Gallery* and the frustration of wishing Coppola had spent as much time with characterization as he had with costume, and within the hour, I was calling John to tell him I had plotted out a three book series—when did he want the outlines? (Too bad I didn't have a laptop handy!)

MIDNIGHT KISS was a great book to write. The genre allowed me to sneak over the boundaries of romance to create a truly to die for hero and to make up a world where normal rules don't apply. And I got to resurrect a couple of wonderful demons who will complicate matters in the books that follow in October of '94 and May '95.

Nancy Gideon

P.S. I love to hear from my readers. You can write me at P.O. Box 526, Kalamazoo, MI 49004 or in care of Zebra/Pinnacle Books. For bookmarks and my newsletter, enclose a SASE.

IF ROMANCE BE THE FRUIT OF LIFE—
READ ON—
BREATH-QUICKENING HISTORICALS FROM PINNACLE

WILDCAT (772, $4.99)
by Rochelle Wayne
No man alive could break Diana Preston's fiery spirit . . . until seductive Vince Gannon galloped onto Diana's sprawling family ranch. Vince, a man with dark secrets, would sweep her into his world of danger and desire. And Diana couldn't deny the powerful yearnings that branded her as his own, for all time!

THE HIGHWAY MAN (765, $4.50)
by Nadine Crenshaw
When a trumped-up murder charge forced beautiful Jane Fitzpatrick to flee her home, she was found and sheltered by the highwayman—a man as dark and dangerous as the secrets that haunted him. As their hiding place became a place of shared dreams—and soaring desires—Jane knew she'd found the love she'd been yearning for!

SILKEN SPURS (756, $4.99)
by Jane Archer
Beautiful Harmony Harper, leader of a notorious outlaw gang, rode the desert plains of New Mexico in search of justice and vengeance. Now she has captured powerful and privileged Thor Clarke-Jargon, who is everything Harmony has ever hated—and all she will ever want. And after Harmony has taken the handsome adventurer hostage, she herself has become a captive—of her own desires!

WYOMING ECSTASY (740, $4.50)
by Gina Robins
Feisty criminal investigator, July MacKenzie, solicits the partnership of the legendary half-breed gunslinger-detective Nacona Blue. After being turned down, July—never one to accept the meaning of the word no—finds a way to convince Nacona to be her partner . . . first in business—then in passion. Across the wilds of Wyoming, and always one step ahead of trouble, July surrenders to passion's searing demands!

Available wherever paperbacks are sold, or order direct from the Publisher. Send cover price plus 50¢ per copy for mailing and handling to Penguin USA, P.O. Box 999, c/o Dept. 17109, Bergenfield, NJ 07621. Residents of New York and Tennessee must include sales tax. DO NOT SEND CASH.

GOT AN INSATIABLE THIRST FOR VAMPIRES?
LET PINNACLE QUENCH IT!

BLOOD FEUD (705, $4.50)
by Sam Siciliano
SHE is a mistress of darkness—coldly sensual and dangerously seductive. HE is a master of manipulation with the power to take life and grant *unlife*. THEY are two ancient vampires who have sworn to eliminate each other. Now, after centuries, the time has come for a face-to-face confrontation—and neither will rest until one of them is destroyed!

DARKNESS ON THE ICE (687, $4.50)
by Lois Tilton
It was World War II, and the Nazis had found the perfect weapon. Wolff, an SS officer, with an innate talent—and thirst—for killing, was actually a vampire. His strength and stealth allowed him to drain and drink the blood of enemy sentries. Wolff stalked his prey for the Nazi cause—but killed them to satisfy his own insatiable hunger!

THIRST OF THE VAMPIRE (649, $4.50)
by T. Lucien Wright
Phillipe Brissot is no ordinary killer—he is a creature of the night—a vampire. Through the centuries he has satisfied his thirst for blood while carrying out his quest of vengeance against his ancient enemies, the Marat Family. Now journalist, Mike Marat is investigating his cousin's horrible "murder" unaware that Phillipe is watching him and preparing to strike against the Marats one final time . . .

BLIND HUNGER (714, $4.50)
by Darke Parke
Widowed and blind, pretty Patty Hunsacker doesn't feel like going on with her life . . . until the day a man arrives at her door, claiming to be the twin brother of her late husband. Patty welcomes Mark into her life but soon finds herself living in a world of terror as well as darkness! For she makes the shocking discovery that "Mark" is really Matt—and he isn't dead—he's a vampire. And he plans on showing his wife that loving a vampire can be quite a bloody affair!

Available wherever paperbacks are sold, or order direct from the Publisher. Send cover price plus 50¢ per copy for mailing and handling to Penguin USA, P.O. Box 999, c/o Dept. 17109, Bergenfield, NJ 07621. Residents of New York and Tennessee must include sales tax. DO NOT SEND CASH.

FUN AND LOVE!

THE DUMBEST DUMB BLONDE JOKE BOOK (889, $4.50)
by Joey West
They say that blondes have more fun . . . but we can all have a hoot with THE DUMBEST DUMB BLONDE JOKE BOOK. Here's a hilarious collection of hundreds of dumb blonde jokes — including dumb blonde GUY jokes — that are certain to send you over the edge!

THE I HATE MADONNA JOKE BOOK (798, $4.50)
by Joey West
She's Hollywood's most controversial star. Her raunchy reputation's brought her fame and fortune. Now here is a sensational collection of hilarious material on America's most talked about MATERIAL GIRL!

LOVE'S LITTLE INSTRUCTION BOOK (774, $4.99)
by Annie Pigeon
Filled from cover to cover with romantic hints — one for every day of the year — this delightful book will liven up your life and make you and your lover smile. Discover these amusing tips for making your lover happy . . . tips like — ask her mother to dance — have his car washed — take turns being irrational . . . and many, many more!

MOM'S LITTLE INSTRUCTION BOOK (0009, $4.99)
by Annie Pigeon
Mom needs as much help as she can get, what with chaotic schedules, wedding fiascos, Barneymania and all. Now, here comes the best mother's helper yet. Filled with funny comforting advice for moms of all ages. What better way to show mother how very much you love her by giving her a gift guaranteed to make her smile everyday of the year.

Available wherever paperbacks are sold, or order direct from the Publisher. Send cover price plus 50¢ per copy for mailing and handling to Penguin USA, P.O. Box 999, c/o Dept. 17109, Bergenfield, NJ 07621. Residents of New York and Tennessee must include sales tax. DO NOT SEND CASH.

MAKE THE CONNECTION

WITH

Z-TALK *Online*

Come talk to your favorite authors and get the inside scoop on everything that's going on in the world of publishing, from the only online service that's designed exclusively for the publishing industry.

With Z-Talk Online Information Service, the most innovative and exciting computer bulletin board around, you can:

- ♥ CHAT "LIVE" WITH AUTHORS, FELLOW READERS, AND OTHER MEMBERS OF THE PUBLISHING COMMUNITY.
- ♥ FIND OUT ABOUT UPCOMING TITLES BEFORE THEY'RE RELEASED.
- ♥ DOWNLOAD THOUSANDS OF FILES AND GAMES.
- ♥ READ REVIEWS OF ROMANCE TITLES.
- ♥ HAVE UNLIMITED USE OF E-MAIL.
- ♥ POST MESSAGES ON OUR DOZENS OF TOPIC BOARDS.

All it takes is a computer and a modem to get online with Z-Talk. Set your modem to 8/N/1, and dial 212-545-1120. If you need help, call the System Operator, at 212-889-2299, ext. 260. There's a two week free trial period. After that, annual membership is only $ 60.00.

See you online!

KENSINGTON PUBLISHING CORP.